STEPHEN LLOYD JONES studied at Royal Holloway College, University of London and is the director of a major London media agency. *The String Diaries* was his first novel. *Written in the Blood* is his second.

Praise for Stephen Lloyd Jones and *The String Diaries*:

'*The String Diaries* is a page turner, and will keep you awake late into the night' *SFX*

'I just couldn't put the book down. A definite must read' www.jonturner1974.wordpress.com

'This is very much a superior supernatural story, intelligently plotted and well written' www.curiousbookfans.co.uk

'Impossible to leave alone for too long' www.bcfreviews.wordpress.com

'Will keep you reading long into the night . . . totally unique reading experience . . . an author to watch' www.falcatatimes.blogspot.co.uk

'Intensely readable' www.drying-ink.blogspot.co.uk

'[An] enjoyable read . . . an entertaining thriller which moves at a good pace' The British Fantasy Society

'*The String Diaries* is edge-of-the-seat-turn-on-d-cancel-all-okbag.co.uk

By Stephen Lloyd Jones

The String Diaries
Written in the Blood

WRITTEN
IN THE
BLOOD

STEPHEN LLOYD JONES

headline

First published in 2014 by
HEADLINE PUBLISHING GROUP

First published in paperback in 2015 by
HEADLINE PUBLISHING GROUP

1

Cataloguing in Publication Data is available from the British Library

ISBN 978 1 4722 0472 1

Typeset in Bembo by Avon DataSet Ltd, Bidford-on-Avon, Warwickshire

Printed and bound in Great Britain by Clays Ltd, St Ives plc

Headline's policy is to use papers that are natural, renewable and recyclable
products and made from wood grown in well-managed forests and other
controlled sources. The logging and manufacturing processes are expected to
conform to the environmental regulattions of the country of origin.

HEADLINE PUBLISHING GROUP
An Hachette UK Company
338 Euston Road
London NW1 3BH

www.headline.co.uk
www.hachette.co.uk

For Mum and Ken

PART I

CHAPTER 1

Interlaken, Switzerland

The face contemplating Leah Wilde from the petrol station's restroom mirror was her own, but it wouldn't be for long. With the door locked, and the scent of disinfectant sharp on the air, she pulled a passport from her bag and studied the image of the woman it contained.

Pouched skin hanging beneath tired eyes. Cheekbones robed in fat, framing a fleshy nose. A filigree of lines branching from the lips, like the contours of a landscape glimpsed from space. A mole to the left of the chin. Earlobes like pale tears of candlewax.

Leah closed her eyes, took a breath, and heard Gabriel's words inside her head.

Create a mould, and pour yourself in. See what you want to be, and be. Don't fear the pain. Pain is good. Pain is the price.

But pain wasn't good. And now here it came: an unwelcome prickling at first, like the rash caused by a nettle's sting. Quickly it intensified, needles sinking deep into her face. She gritted her teeth, felt the skin around her mouth loosen and pucker, felt her heart thump in her chest as the blood surged into her head, her flesh swelling, stretching, slackening.

Reaching out, Leah gripped the washbasin. She held on tight, stomach slopping around inside her, waiting until the pain, finally, began to recede.

When she opened her eyes she saw beads of sweat shining

on a forehead mapped with age lines and blemishes. An older face. A stranger's.

At some point she must have dropped the passport into the sink. She fished it out, shaking off droplets of water, and opened it back to the photograph.

Again she studied the woman's image. Compared it to the face watching her from the mirror.

Good.

She was ravenous now, stomach cramping with urgency, but her hunger would have to wait. She'd pulled into the petrol station near the town of Jestetten, a few miles from the Swiss–German border; she needed to get out of here, and fast. Removing a baseball cap from her bag, Leah screwed it down onto her head, keeping her eyes on the ground as she returned to her car.

At the crossing she showed the passport to a border guard, submitting herself to a cursory inspection before being waved through. In Zurich, she abandoned the car in a side street and checked into an anonymous chain hotel.

The next morning, under a different passport and with a different face, Leah rented a motorbike from a garage in the city. After following the kinks of Lake Lucerne's shore to Altdorf, she turned west and rode through the Susten Pass, a route that wound among mountain peaks so extraordinary they drew the breath from her throat.

Perhaps it was the drama and raw beauty of the Bernese Oberland's landscape, but as Leah guided the bike along she felt the weight of her indecision begin to lift. No one knew she was here; they had forbidden her outright from coming, had forbidden her even from investigating this. But she knew it was the right thing to do, the only thing left she *could* do, however dangerous it might be.

She reached Interlaken a few hours after midday. The town perched between Lake Brienz in the east and Lake Thun in the west, twin cobalt bowls that reflected the blade-like sharpness of the Alpine sky. Looming above the town to the south, the fortress peaks of the Jungfrau, the Mönch and the Eiger, jagged brushstrokes of rock and snow.

Leah found a small hotel along the Aar, the river that connected the two great lakes and formed the town's northern border. Her first-floor room was basic but clean: table and chairs in one corner, cupboard in another. Opposite the bed, a cabinet on which sat a TV, coffee-maker and kettle. Shuttered French windows opened onto a narrow balcony. Below slid the Aar's turquoise waters.

Throwing her rucksack down on the bed, Leah returned to the door to check that it was locked. A spyhole gave her a distorted view of the deserted corridor outside.

She filled the coffee-maker with water and set it to brew. Pulling off her boots, she lay back on the mattress and waited for the room's heat to thaw her limbs. During the four-hour ride through the mountains, the chill October air had stolen through her leathers and frozen her skin.

For the first time in her life, she was truly alone. No one within shouting distance should this plan of hers lead to disaster. Few among the remaining *hosszú életek* – that hidden evolutionary branch of humanity to which she found herself bound by blood – even knew what secret the town clasped in its bosom.

She wondered how long it would take before her mother and Gabriel discovered her disappearance. She wished she could reassure them of her safety. But it was too early for that. Too early to tell whether she *was* safe.

In the corner of the room the coffee-machine began to hiss. Rising from the bed, Leah reached through the net curtains and checked that the French windows, too, were locked. She unzipped her rucksack, rifling through her gear until she found the pistol she had hidden there.

Leah turned it over in her hands. The Ruger was small enough to conceal on her person, but – loaded with hollow-point rounds – lethal enough to stop most threats with a single shot. She took out two spare magazines and stacked them on the bedside table.

Stripping off her motorcycle leathers, she carried the gun into the suite's tiny bathroom and left it on the basin while she steamed herself in the shower until her skin flushed red with heat.

Afterwards, wrapped in a bath sheet and with the pistol within easy reach, Leah poured herself a mug of coffee. Pulling a hardback book from the rucksack, she found a pen and sat at the table.

The volume, bound in black leather, was her current diary. She had lost count of how many she had filled over the years, but she had written an entry every day since that afternoon, fifteen years earlier, when her mother and Jakab had burned together at Le Moulin Bellerose.

Opening it, she reread her words from the previous day, a simple list of activities: slipping out, unnoticed, from the forest retreat in Calw; driving across the border into Switzerland; signing for the package that waited for her at the hotel reception in Zurich; unpacking the Ruger and its ammunition in her suite before folding herself between the bed sheets and finding sleep.

Leah tapped her pen against an empty page. She wondered how tonight's entry would read. Wondered whether there would be one.

After writing a summary of her trip through the mountains, she used the phone beside the bed to call down for room service. But when the food arrived twenty minutes later she couldn't eat it. Trepidation had shrunk her stomach, and the smells wafting from the tray threaded her with a nausea too acute to overcome. Moving to the French windows, she unlocked the shutters and pushed them open.

Frigid air feathered into the room, contracting her bare skin into goosebumps. Across the Aar, the mountain peaks south of the town rose like claws from a bear's upturned paw. They really were castles of stone; monuments of colossal proportions, as if a race of giants had raised them there in supplication to an angry god. She'd read about the Alps – her backpack was stuffed with guides and maps – but little of her time spent researching this place had focused on its topography. She had not expected the mountains to affect her as deeply as they did.

On her return to the table she noticed something on the room service tray she hadn't seen before, poking out from beneath the leatherette wallet containing her bill. Frowning, she nudged the wallet aside, revealing a square envelope. Her name was intricately calligraphed across the front.

Heart knocking against her ribs, Leah snatched up the Ruger from the bed. Seven rounds in the magazine. Nine-millimetre hollow-point. They would open like a flower on impact, punching fist-sized holes into whatever stood in her way.

Head cocked, ears straining, fingers greasy where they curled around the gun, Leah forced herself to be still. She knew that her hearing was sharp, knew that if anyone lurked in the corridor outside she would sense them – unless they, like her, were *hosszú élet*.

After two minutes had passed and she had heard nothing but the muttering of water in the hotel's pipes, she removed one hand from the gun and reached behind her. Locking the French windows, she pulled the net curtains back into place.

Barefoot, Leah padded across the room to the door. She paused again, listening. When only silence greeted her, she pressed her eye to the tiny spyhole. The lens warped her view, but she could see that the corridor remained deserted.

She returned to the tray and picked up the envelope. The paper was thick, luxurious. Breaking it open, she withdrew a square of cream card. At the top it bore an embossed logo in gold and black: a series of interlinking chains, like a Celtic knot.

I warned you not to come. I am delighted you chose to ignore that advice. Let's dine together, tonight. A car will collect you from outside your hotel at eight o'clock and bring you here, should you wish. Rather more convenient than a motorcycle – it grows cold in these mountains on autumn evenings.

I cannot guarantee your safety from here on in, but of course you know that.

'A Kutya Herceg'

A shiver took hold of Leah as she read the last line, born as much from fear as from the frisson of anticipation the words produced. She dropped the card onto the table beside her, spine tingling from a cold lick of distaste.

A Kutya Herceg. The Dog Prince. A theatrical affectation, but from what she had heard of the man, he enjoyed how his reputation had developed until it had gained an almost mythic status. A Kutya Herceg was, she knew, one of the more forgiving of his titles. It did not allude to his ruthlessness, his monstrousness when provoked.

How could he have learned of her arrival so quickly? She'd entered Switzerland using one fake passport, had rented the motorbike using another. From the Susten Pass she'd ridden directly to the hotel, memorising the route and the names of Interlaken's streets in advance. Since discarding the disguises she'd adopted for her journey, the only people to have seen her face were the middle-aged woman at reception who handed her the room key, and the youth who brought in her lunch.

Outside, the snow on the mountain peaks had blushed to pink as the sun dipped towards the waters of Lake Brienz. The Alps looked like they were bleeding.

At a quarter to eight, fifteen minutes before the car was due, Leah opened her rucksack and pulled out a tissue-paper parcel.

From it she unwrapped a long-sleeved embroidered lace dress in midnight blue. She changed quickly, slipping her feet into nude patent shoes with a heel far higher than she usually wore. Twisting up her hair into a pile on top of her head, she secured it with two steel chopsticks; their points had been filed to a needle sharpness.

She stared at herself in the mirror and turned her head from left to right, wondering what he expected to see. From a travel bag she removed lipstick and eyeliner and quickly applied make-up to her face. She examined herself again.

Better.

Pulling out a glass bottle of perfume, Leah considered it for a moment before replacing it, unused. She picked up the Ruger, checked that the safety was engaged and slid it into a sequinned clutch purse. Tucking her diary back into her rucksack, she packed up the rest of her belongings. If she needed to leave here quickly, she wanted everything to be ready.

Beyond the window, except where the mountain peaks blocked their light, a sprinkling of stars pricked silver holes in the sky. Shrugging on her biker leather over the dress, she left her room and walked down the stairs to the foyer. The hotel's glass doors slid apart and Leah, holding the clutch purse as nonchalantly as she could, stepped outside.

Now that the sun had set the Alpine air was brittle, teasing a mist from her breath. She tasted something on her tongue, a subtle sourness, and thought she sensed an imminent change in the weather: a premonition, perhaps, of snow. She shook her head at the thought.

Across the street a graphite Rolls-Royce Phantom, like an armoured rhinoceros, idled against the kerb.

Leah stared at the vehicle: at the enormous flat-fronted grille; the headlights like narrowed eyes; the winged Spirit of Ecstasy, poised for flight, perched on the bonnet.

Its windows were black, reflecting the night.

Don't let them see your fear.

Blowing air from her cheeks, Leah crossed the street, threw open the Phantom's rear door and slid into a world of mahogany and cream leather. She pulled the door shut behind her, a heavy-sounding clunk. Immediately, as if a switch had been flicked, the noise of the street traffic ceased.

No one occupied the seat beside her. In front, a man sat behind the steering wheel. She could see curls of black hair, a strong and tanned neck.

He turned in his seat, and when he saw her sitting there he flashed white teeth. His irises were feathered with violet, a shade she had never before seen in the eyes of a *hosszú élet*. Leah thought she caught something else lurking in that expression too: something that froze her blood a little. She recalled the line from the note:

I cannot guarantee your safety from here on in

Again, that frisson of expectation, stirring the hairs on the nape of her neck.

'Leah Wilde,' the man said.

She nodded. 'Who are you?'

He ignored her question. 'Lean forward for me. Before we go any further, I need to take a look at those pretty eyes.'

She slid to the edge of her seat, bringing her face to within a foot of his own. His eyes really were extraordinary: striations of passion fruit and lavender; unworldly, cold and, this close, unsettlingly intense. She watched as the streaks of violet intensified and began to bleed towards the edges of his irises, like dye leaching into a vat of ink. Leah gripped the leather seat with her fingertips, feeling her own eyes respond in kind. There followed a curious unspooling of fear and longing.

Her mother's rules, voiced so often in times past, echoed in her head: *Trust no one. Verify everyone. If in doubt, run.*

The seraphic beauty she saw dancing in this stranger's eyes verified that he was, at least, *hosszú élet*. Yet whether he wore his own face tonight or that of another's, she could not say.

Leah knew that her inability to discern the difference placed her at a disadvantage.

Those eyes, though. She could not remember how long it had been since she had met another of her kind for the first time. Her heart quickened in her chest; she felt its pulse in her ears. The scent of his cologne washed over her.

Flinching away, the man stared through the windscreen at the cars passing on the street. Then he twisted back around. 'How old are you, Leah?'

She held his gaze. 'Twenty-four.'

The moment seemed to lengthen, stretch out between them. His nostrils flared.

'So it's true,' he said.

'It's true.'

'And we're to believe that you came here, all on your own: a single girl, into the lion's den, without any protection what-soever.'

'You can believe anything you want,' she replied. 'But I'm here alone. Just as I promised.'

He stared at her, his expression hardening. Abruptly he turned away. Putting the Phantom into gear, he flicked on an indicator and pulled into traffic.

They drove south out of Interlaken, following a twisting road that threaded its way through dark pine forest as it rose towards the peaks. Theirs were the only lights on the road. 'We're leaving town?'

He found her eyes in the rear-view mirror. 'You wanted to meet A Kutya Herceg.'

'I thought he lived nearby.'

'He doesn't.'

Leah clutched the purse on her lap, feeling the hard angles of the Ruger through its sequinned fabric. 'Is it far?'

'A while yet.'

The Rolls-Royce accelerated, powering them up the road's gradient and around its curves towards the starlit peaks above them. As Leah settled into the seat's leather embrace, she tried to avoid glancing too frequently at her driver. Every so often she sensed him lifting his eyes from the road to study her.

Are you sure about this? Are you absolutely sure?

Yes. It was the right thing to do: the only thing. She knew she wouldn't be thanked, knew that her actions tonight would sow even more division among the few *hosszú életek* that remained. But if *someone* didn't do something soon – something radical – then all that her mother and Gabriel had worked for in the years since her father's death would be undone.

Even so, by coming here alone, with no one aware of her destination, she placed herself in extraordinary danger. Her driver had taunted her about walking into the lion's den, but Leah knew that was exactly what this involved. She had heard the stories. Some of them sickened her.

They wound up through black ranks of fir and pine, moonlight glimmering on frost-rimed needles. The air at this altitude looked sharp enough to cut her skin. All around them, the Bernese Alps presented dizzying faces.

Finally the Phantom slowed, turning onto a private single-lane road that took a sharp ascent through the trees. A minute later they left the forest behind and emerged onto a rising strip of tarmac. When it swept around to the right, Leah gasped.

An enormous chalet complex rose up ahead: four curving levels of wood and glass, topped with multiple gabled roofs. The building glowed with a golden light, an architectural bauble clinging to the face of the mountain. The windows of its middle floors reached from floor to ceiling, at least four metres in height, served by crescent-shaped balconies that curved their entire width. Somewhere inside she could see the flickering reflections cast from a swimming pool.

To the left of the building a five-car garage had been chiselled directly out of the rock. Strip lights blazed inside. Below the house, a wide lawn receded into darkness. Across the valley, in full view of the huge viewing windows, rose the rocky monolith of the Jungfrau. Snow sparkled on its summit. On its north-eastern shoulder loomed the Mönch and the Eiger.

Her driver brought the Phantom to a halt on the tarmac. He glanced at her embroidered lace dress, then up at her scuffed motorcycle jacket. 'It's minus ten outside. You're not exactly dressed for mountain weather.'

'No.'

'Wait here.' He climbed out and went to the boot. Moments later he appeared at her window, holding a calf-length fur; it shimmered silver in the moonlight. He opened her door and held out the coat to her. The air that raced inside the car made her eyes sting at its bite. 'Put this on.'

Leah swivelled her legs and stood, feeling her skin burn with cold. Slipping her arms into the fur, she wrapped it around her body and followed him across the tarmac to the ground-floor entrance. The front door was a rounded slab of oak hung within a curving transom decorated with stained-glass panels. Its fittings were brass, polished to a liquid shine. Scorched into the centre of the wood she saw the same woven motif from her dinner invite.

Her driver stepped into the entrance hall and beckoned her to follow. Feeling a flutter of nerves in her belly, knowing that whatever reservations she'd entertained about tonight's encounter it was now too late to change her mind, Leah crossed the threshold.

When the door closed behind her, she heard the clunk of several mortices engaging simultaneously, sealing her inside.

CHAPTER 2

Calw, Germany

Hannah Wilde listened to the scream echo through the building and clenched her teeth at the sound. The agony in that cry dragged claws down her spine and sank teeth into her belly. Wincing, she flicked open the hinged lid of her wristwatch and felt for the position of its hands: twenty past three in the afternoon.

It had started around six o'clock the night before. Twenty-one hours now: a long labour by anyone's standards.

Rising from her stool at the makeshift kitchen's breakfast counter, Hannah placed her coffee mug on the drainer and walked across the tiled floor of the room. When her bare feet touched carpet, she turned right and moved into the hall.

She smelled Gabriel before she heard his breathing – that familiar combination of maltiness and astringency, which, for some strange reason, always reminded her of cider. A draught touched her skin. She sensed him turn to face her. 'How's Flóra?' she asked. How's she doing?'

'I don't know how the poor mite can have any strength left.'

'Is she bleeding still?'

'They think they've stemmed it. But if this baby doesn't come soon . . .'

Hannah nodded, curling her hand around Gabriel's arm as another scream rattled along the corridor. He didn't need to finish his sentence; the consequence of sacrificing yet another life to this project of theirs was too wretched to consider. 'We can't lose her to this. We just can't.'

'They're doing everything they can.'

'It's not enough.'

'Han, they—'

'Oh, I don't mean them,' she replied. 'I mean all of this. We've been bashing our heads against a wall for fifteen years, Gabe.'

'I know. But what else would you have us do?'

'You know what else,' she said. And knew that he did. Since discovering her true ancestry years earlier, Hannah had committed herself to restoring the *hosszú életek*'s dwindling numbers; but she'd never expected her greatest obstacles to come from within the very society she sought to preserve. A miracle to some, an abomination to others, her mixed blood had provided an opportunity, however controversial, to reverse what the genocide centuries earlier had begun and nature had perpetuated since.

Through the closed door of the delivery suite she heard a moan of pain followed by a shriek. A crash as something turned over.

Someone shouted. Tanja Komáromy's voice, their senior midwife. Gabriel moved to the door, threw it open. 'What's happening? What can I do?'

Tanya's voice was elevated but controlled. 'She's having a baby, that's what. Flóra, *kedves*, you're doing great. Just great. Gabe, help me and move that trolley out of the way.'

Another scream, piercing and drawn out, as if winched from the woman's lungs by hook and line.

'Shall I give her more pethidine?' Rose Doyle, now. Their usually calm Irish nurse sounded exhausted.

'No time. This baby wants to say hello. That's it, Flóra, fantastic. Short breaths. And when the next contraction hits, I need you to push.'

Sobbing, from the bed. 'I can't.'

'Yes. Yes, you can. You're doing brilliantly. This baby's coming and you're going to fall in love the moment you see it, so I need you to gather your thoughts together and push.'

Intuiting the position of the room's occupants from the sound of their voices, Hannah navigated through darkness towards the bed. 'Flóra, take my hand.' Sweat-soaked fingers found hers.

Lowering her face to the pregnant woman's, Hannah spoke softly. 'This is it, Flóra. How amazing, eh? What you dreamed about for so long. One last push and that's it: a baby. All yours. A new life in your arms.'

'It hurts so much.'

'I know. It's not easy, this. It never has been.'

'I'm scared. It shouldn't be this bad, should it? Oh God, I can feel it *coming* . . .'

'Don't be scared, don't be. Your baby's almost here.'

'No, I can't, please. I *can't.*'

'Yes, you can. You're strong. So strong, and—'

'Oh, don't, Han. Help me, please. I want it to stop, it's . . . it's—'

The woman's words flowed into another scream, ripping loose from somewhere deep.

'That's *it*! I can see the head!' Tanja Komáromy again, shouting now. 'One more push. One more!'

Body arching upwards, Flóra bellowed. Hannah heard a slippery sucking sound and smelled the sweet, biscuity scent of birth fluids.

'You did it!' Rose shouted, jubilant.

Hannah listened for the first sounds of a baby's cries, telling herself not to tense when she heard nothing in the first few seconds. She didn't want Flóra to sense her concern.

'You have a son,' Tanya said. 'A beautiful boy.' Then: 'Rose, turn him over. Quickly.'

She could hear the two women working urgently at the foot of the bed.

'What's wrong?' Flóra whispered. 'Is he breathing?'

'We need to clear his airways,' Tanya said. 'The ventilation mask, please.'

Flóra squeezed Hannah's fingers. 'Tell me. Tell me he's going to be all right.'

'Of course. Of course he is.'

Why on earth did you just promise her that?

She heard the *shlep-shlep-shlep* of a hand pump. Counted sixty compressions. A minute's worth.

'Rose, watch for any bleeding.'

Shlep-shlep-shlep.

The pump stopped.

Silence.

'Hannah?'

She was about to answer when she heard it: a tiny mewling cry, as delicate as a dewdrop. Her heart swelled. She sensed a presence by her side, and knew that Tanja was lowering the newborn onto Flóra's chest.

'Oh,' Flóra whispered. 'Oh, *oh*. He's perfect. Just a perfect little man.'

When Hannah felt the woman's fingers slip from her own, she moved backwards, wanting to grant Flóra the space to welcome her baby into the world.

But it was not just that. Sometimes she found this part difficult. Knowing that the newborn was part of her – had been created from one of her own eggs – made these births a curiously bitter-sweet experience.

'Tanja,' Rose murmured. Far from sounding relaxed now that the baby had started to breathe, the nurse's voice radiated alarm. 'Look.'

The senior midwife hissed, and for a moment the silence held. Then: 'OK, Flóra, you're bleeding, quite a lot, and we're going to have to stop it. I want to put an oxygen mask on you, OK? Just breathe, nice and slow, that's it. Rose, what can you see?'

'I can't tell. I'm sorry, I need you to take over.'

'That's fine. Set up an IV. And get the mask on her.'

Hannah heard Tanja curse, suddenly knew it was bad. This had happened before: two months earlier, to Annaliese Mayr, and four times before that. On all five occasions the women had died, bleeding to death in the delivery suite with their newborn crying in a cot beside the bed. Even *hosszú élet* intervention had not helped. As quickly as they'd laid on hands and pumped their blood into the women it had spilled out, draining onto the delivery room floor along with all their hopes of salvation.

It's happening again. We're going to lose her.

She had known Flóra for four years. When the woman heard about their programme, and their attempt to reverse the *hosszú életek*'s decline, she came to see Hannah and Gabriel, pleading with them to become one of their volunteers. At first they were wary: Flóra was well past the age they had set as their notional upper limit. But Flóra had worn them down, methodically dismantling their objections and pointing out that their limits were just that: notional; arbitrary; based not on science – there was no science here to guide them – but on a hunch, a best guess.

As Flóra broke down their arguments and told them the story of her entire tragic past, they began to love the *hosszú élet* woman who had sought them out, and decided to abandon the limits they had set.

We can't lose her.

Hannah could smell the blood now. A hard scent; all angles and points. Sharp in her nose. Like wire.

And then she heard something, far worse than the smell. Something she had

plik

heard on five occasions before, in this very room: the steady patter of a mother's blood as it dripped off the hospital bed and hit the rubber-coated floor of the delivery suite.

plik plik plik

None of them understood what caused this, or why it happened so abnormally often in these assisted pregnancies. It was why, Hannah knew, she was reviled as a bringer of death among the *hosszú életek* almost as often as she was revered as a giver of life.

Not for anything would she be turned away from this. But it made the agony of losing someone no easier to bear.

'Rose, is the placenta intact?' Tanja asked.

'Yes, I think so.'

'I need you to be sure.'

'Wait. Yes, I'm sure.'

'Good. OK, Flóra, I'm going to need you to be brave again. We have to stop this bleeding. I want you to clear your head and focus your mind inside your body. Can you feel the source of the bleeding?'

plik plik plik plik plik plik

'I can't feel anything down there. It's just . . . numb.' Her voice sounded odd. Thick.

'Listen. I know you're tired. You've earned a rest, and as soon as we've fixed this you can sleep, I promise you. But focus for me, OK? You've a baby that needs you. We have to fix this.'

Hannah stepped towards the bed. 'Stay awake, now,' she urged. 'Listen to Tanja.'

Flóra sighed. 'I can't feel anything.'

plikplikplikplikplikplikplikplikplik

Tanja's voice again, raised now, all attempts to disguise her concern abandoned. 'Flóra, Rose is going to put your son in the crib while we do this. He'll be right next to the bed. Take him, please. Hannah, you might want to hold her hand again.'

She heard a tiny snuffle of protest as the baby was lifted away. Flóra moaned.

'Right, we need to work quickly. Gabriel, top of the bed, please. Rose, you're going to have to help me here. I need heart rate and pressure. Regular calls. Somebody sound the alarm. We need everyone in this building outside that door, ready to lay on hands and donate blood.'

'Hannah?' Flóra's voice again. Barely a whisper.

She bent closer, took the woman's fingers. 'Yes, darling?'

'I'm not going to make it.'

'Don't say that. Come on, squeeze my hand. Deep breaths. Listen to what Tanja tells you.'

Throughout the building, a gentle two-toned alarm began to sound. Hannah could hear doors opening, footsteps running. They'd installed the device after Jennifer Kedzierski had died. On hearing it, everyone knew to make their way to the delivery suite, in case their blood was required to save a life.

It hadn't helped on the two previous occasions. Frida Kun and Zsófia Vida still bled to death in here. They just did it more publicly, more agonisingly, in full view of their stunned and grieving *hosszú élet* family.

'It's all right,' Flóra whispered. 'I did it. I had a child. One more of us. Look after him, won't you?'

'You're going to look after him yourself.'

'Promise me.'

The blood no longer dripped onto the floor. It poured, like water overflowing from a bath.

Hannah squeezed her friend's hand, but she couldn't bring herself to make that promise yet. It would feel like she was passing a death sentence.

Perhaps that's exactly what this is. Exactly what you've brought about.

No. She wouldn't listen to that voice, not here. Later, when this was over, she'd allow herself to face that particular torture.

So you've already accepted it, then. Accepted that you've killed her.

Tanja's voice again, rising over the hard smell of the blood. 'OK, I want everyone to watch their step. It's slippery in here and we can't afford any accidents. Rose, help me get her legs into the stirrups. Gabe, I may need you to hold her down. We can't do this with anaesthetic. She needs to feel what I'm doing. Max, in here please. And I want three others. Form a wider circle. I don't need you yet, so keep out of the way until I do. Careful now.'

'*Hannah, promise me.*'

'Hush. Listen to what Tanja has to say.'

She heard the room beginning to fill with people and tried to map their positions around her: Gabriel to her left, ready to brace Flóra's shoulders should the need arise; Tanja at the foot of the bed; Rose on the far side, attaching Flóra to the monitoring equipment.

Behind Hannah, Max Zabek and one other, waiting to lay on hands; a further two volunteers behind Rose, ready to do the same. None of them was Leah. Hannah wondered where her daughter was, wondered whether the girl was on her way.

An electronic *bing* announced the monitor stirring to life, followed by a metronomic chime as it began to measure Flóra's heartbeat.

'BPM is two-fifteen,' Rose said. 'Two-two-five and rising.'

'Pressure?'

'Fifty-five over thirty.'

'OK, it's time. Donors, I need you to step forward. Careful where you tread. Let Rose and I work around you. Hands on Flóra, please. She's losing blood fast, and we've got to raise that pressure *right* now. I don't want anyone being a hero – we won't be able to look after you. If you feel faint, let us know and stand back. Someone will take your place. We have plenty of cover. Flóra? Flóra, listen to me. In a moment I'm going to put my fingers inside you. Understand?'

A moan of protest.

'I'm sorry, *kedves*, but I have to. We need to find out where this blood is coming from. Only you can stop this. If you can't feel where the problem is yourself, I'm going to have to guide you. Gabriel, hold her shoulders. She's going to thrash.'

Hannah smelled a sourness to the air now: fear on everyone's breath. She heard Gabriel manoeuvre himself into position. Then, the scream. The worst sound in the world. So piercingly loud it seemed to cleave the air in two, curling around Hannah's teeth and wrenching them in their sockets.

'*Hold* her!'

Another scream. Agony, pure and white. Flóra's arm thrashed and Hannah lost her grip. She reached out to catch the woman's hand and Flóra's fist struck her cheek, knocking her backwards.

'*Uh-uh-uh-uh-uh.*'

Blood cascading onto the floor like milk from a jug. The hot, sharp stench of urine.

Somehow Hannah caught the flailing hand. Pressed it down against the mattress. Bit her lip. Tried not to cry out from frustration, from the brutal, visceral horror of what she was witnessing.

The noise erupting from Flóra's throat was no longer a scream. It sounded guttural, primal, as if an animal was being eviscerated on the bed.

'That's it!' Tanja shouted. 'Feel that, Flóra. Just where I had my finger. I can't get . . . there it is!'

Flóra shrieked. Writhed, snake-like.

'Talk to me. Can you feel that? Can you?'

'. . . *yes* . . .'

Beside her Hannah heard Max hiss with exhaustion. He staggered backwards. Instantly someone took his place.

'Good. That's great. I can't do this myself. I can just about touch it. I need you to focus there. Close it up. Think scar tissue. I want a hard tight scar. Go, Flóra. Now.'

'*Oh . . . my God, my God, my God . . .*'

'Keep focusing. Scar tissue. Knot it up. Seal it off. Come *on*.'

'*I . . . I . . .*'

'You know how. You've always known. Don't you give up. Don't you stop.'

'BP's rising.' Rose's voice. 'Seventy-five over forty.'

'You're doing it! Keep going. For your son, do you hear me? For your son.'

'Ninety over fifty now. Heart's one-seventy.'

'Beautiful. I'm going to remove my fingers. You know where to focus now. Keep your mind on it. Don't let the pain distract you.'

Hannah could tell when Tanja removed her hand because Flóra jerked up in the bed, then slammed her head back against the pillows.

No one spoke for a few minutes, listening to the slowly decelerating bleep of the monitor.

Hannah felt the prick of tears on her cheeks. When spontaneous applause broke out from the mass of people in the corridor, she sobbed with relief; a cathartic expunging, saturated with emotion.

'Thank you, everyone,' Tanja said. 'You're amazing, all of you. And if I could have you out of the room now – this girl needs rest.'

Gabriel moved to Hannah's side, sliding his arm around her waist. 'We'll come back later,' he said. 'See how she's getting on.'

She nodded, allowing herself to be steered from the bed. Out in the corridor, they passed the fertility centre's kitchen, where many of the volunteers were now gathering, and arrived at the building's glass-fronted rear exit. Gabriel waited as Hannah slipped her feet into the moccasins she had left there. Together they crossed the courtyard to the nearest of the site's five private chalets.

The moment Hannah opened the door, Ibsen nosed his way through the gap and licked her hand. She bent to the dog, hugging him tightly, greedy for his closeness. 'There you are, boy. Have you been bored cooped up in here? I'm sorry, Ibsen. But guess what? Flóra had a baby. Yes, a baby, that's right. You'll get to meet him soon, don't worry. We can't have a dog in the delivery suite though, I'm afraid, not even one as soppy as you. So you'll just have to wait until Flóra's well enough to visit. Which won't be long, I'm sure.'

Ibsen was one of the last puppies Moses had fathered before the grand old Vizsla had died seven years earlier. They'd trained him as Hannah's guide dog, and he'd been her companion ever since.

She stepped into the foyer, following the dog into the kitchenette. 'Leah?' When her call went unanswered, Hannah said, 'Gabe. Have you seen her?'

'Not today.'

'Unlike her to miss a birth.' Strange, too, that the girl had ignored the alarm.

'Perhaps she went riding. I'll call Matthias.'

'No, don't bother him. She'll turn up when she's ready. I'm opening some wine. Do you want a glass?'

'Sure. Back in a sec.'

'Gabe . . .'

'It won't take long.'

Hannah pulled a bottle of Chablis from the fridge. She heard Gabriel talking on the telephone in the next room.

He came back into the kitchenette. 'They've lost contact with her. Matthias said he's been trying to call you.'

'I left my phone here last night. What did he say?'

'He thinks Leah deliberately gave his guys the slip. Hasn't checked in since.'

She felt the hairs on her forearms lift. A sudden lightness in her stomach: 'How long?'

'Over twenty-four hours since they last saw her.'

'My phone.'

He passed it to her. Hannah called up her voicemail.

Beeeep

'Hannah, this is Matt. Don't freak, but Leah upped and left this afternoon without letting any of us know. Just wanted to check in with you. Call me back.'

Beeeep

'Matt again. I still can't reach Leah on her phone. Call me straight back when you get this.'

Beeeep

'Mum, it's me.'

Hannah stiffened at her daughter's tone. The girl paused, as if she considered something difficult, trying to find the right words.

You know what's coming.

'You're not going to like this,' Leah continued. 'I know you think we still have options. But I'm not sure we do. I think time is running out. We have to explore every possibility now.' Another pause. 'I've made contact with them. Please don't worry. I love you. I'll call you soon.'

Life, turning on a pin.

Hannah had been about to pour a glass of wine, and now she felt hollow, sick, a vacuum sucking at the heart of her, in the place she usually carried Leah.

Gabriel's voice was thick with foreboding. 'She's gone to meet the *kirekesztett*.'

Since defeating the man who called himself Jakab at Le Moulin Bellerose all those years ago, Hannah had given little thought to the criminal castoffs of *hosszú élet* society who moved, largely unseen, through the world. She thought about them now. The direct translation of *kirekesztett* was *outcast*; it referred both to the sentence of banishment itself, and to the exiled individuals the rulings created. Over time, Hannah knew, the *kirekesztett* had formed a secretive network of convenience led by the most ruthless of their number. Revenge killings of *hosszú életek* had become one of the more visible elements of the group's activities.

'They'll tear her apart,' she whispered.

CHAPTER 3

Interlaken, Switzerland

When the mortices engaged, sealing the door behind her, Leah felt a spike of apprehension twisting deep inside her gut.

It was the sound of a bank vault closing, the sound of motor-driven rods slamming home, a fortress locking down. Her lungs grew tight. She wanted to open her mouth and suck in a breath, but she knew she could not allow her *kirekesztett* driver to see how the building's security features affected her. Aware she was being watched, and perhaps not solely by him, she moved further into the hall – *get out! get out! get out!* – and turned around.

At a glowing wall panel, he keyed in a code and pressed his face to a lens. The device scanned his iris, and then it chimed.

'You get many unwelcome visitors?' Leah asked, struggling to keep the fear from her voice.

'We've had a few,' he replied. 'They don't tend to come back.'

Nodding, Leah glanced about her. The entrance hall was shaped like the inverted interior of a ship's wooden hull, a cavernous yet womblike space. The floor shone golden with varnish, illuminated by spotlights recessed into the ceiling and by flickering candles nestled in wall sconces and alcoves.

Masks hung from the left-hand wall: hundreds of them.

Through the research she had conducted while investigating the history of the *végzet* – the series of masked balls that, in times past, had symbolised the entrance of the *hosszú életek* youth into adulthood, and the restricted opportunities of formalised courtship – Leah knew their names and many of the forms.

She saw blank-faced yet curiously expressive Japanese *noh* masks side by side with bulge-eyed Balinese *topengs*. Chinese *Shigong* dance masks hung next to long-faced African tribal masks carved from wood or constructed from stiffened hide. She saw a Native American collection: leather examples from the Navajo and Apache; Iroquois false faces of wood and cornhusk; Cherokee gourd masks used for storytelling.

Another section of wall held a mass of Venetian carnival masks, some fashioned from leather but most from porcelain or glass, augmented with gesso or gold leaf, hand-painted and decorated with gems and the feathers of ostrich, peacock or duck. She recognised square-jawed *Bauta*, *Columbina* half-masks, pure-white *Volto* masks and the freakishly beaked *Medico della Peste* face coverings worn by seventeenth-century physicians while treating plague victims.

Finally, towards the end of the hall, raised above the rest, she saw them. So many hanging there: the polished pewter masks worn by young *hosszú élet* men to the first *végzet* of the season; the delicate bronze-leaf designs of the second *végzet*; the jewelled magnificence of the masks used for the penultimate *végzet* and the simple lacquered sculpts of the season's finale. In total, perhaps three hundred masks gazed down from the wall. Leah felt the dead stare of six hundred eyes.

Perhaps it was inevitable that a tradition of such ritualised courtship should have evolved. The *hosszú életek* did not produce offspring easily, and even then for only a short period in their lives. The low birth count, along with the extreme nature of their longevity, meant that the entire community had an interest in the successful courtships of its youth. Inevitable, too, for a people defined by an ability to govern the contours of their flesh, that a symbol of concealment should play a part in those rituals.

The wall opposite the masks was festooned with clocks: ornate French rococo cartel clocks in gilt bronze or gold; English tavern clocks; metal pendulum clocks with exposed weights and chains. A walnut display cabinet contained row upon row of gold pocket watches. At the far end of the hall, a pair of longcase Comtoise clocks guarded two sets of carpeted stairs.

The air hissed and snickered with the movements of cogs, oscillators and gears. It sounded to Leah like the masks were conversing.

To her left, a short flight of steps descended to a narrow corridor. To her right, the polished brass door of an elevator. Above it, a rack of antlers from a red deer stag.

'Before you meet him,' said her driver, 'a few formalities.' Gesturing towards a panelled door, he shepherded her into a cloakroom. At the far end she saw a rack of skis, poles and snowboards. Beneath it, a bench piled with gloves, helmets and goggles. Coats and hats hung along one wall, opposite three steel gun cabinets.

Leah removed the fur and handed it to him.

'I'm going to need your gun,' he said, draping the coat on a hook.

She tensed. 'Gun?'

He turned to face her. 'Let's not make this awkward. I'm sure you understand I can't let you roam the house with a loaded weapon, and I'm guessing you didn't arrive without one. It's either in your purse or somewhere under that dress, although quite where you could have stashed it . . .'

He stared, waiting.

Leah's spike of apprehension had escalated, now, into a gnawing sense of dread. She did not like the way he seemed to mock her with his eyes. Knowing that she had little choice, she thrust her clutch purse at him. 'I want it back when I leave.'

He unzipped the purse and removed her Ruger. At another electronic panel he keyed in a code and two of the gun case doors rolled open. One case held a rack of hunting rifles above a shelf of handguns; the other contained boxes of ammunition. He stashed her Ruger inside the first. 'I'd better take those chopsticks too. Smart thinking to bring your own cutlery, but I don't believe sushi is on the menu.'

His eyes pinioned her. Reaching up, Leah pulled the accessories free. She handed them over and shook her hair loose. Naked now, or might as well be.

And no one knows you're here.

He turned the chopsticks over in his hands, fingering the points. 'Anything else?'

'No.'

'I might have to ask you to step out of that dress.'

Her skin prickled. 'You've exactly zero chance of that.'

They continued to stare at each other.

Finally, he tossed the chopsticks into the second cabinet and keyed the entry panel. The doors slid closed. 'Ready?'

'Let's find out.'

Back in the hall of masks, the air was alive with clock-work whispers. Raising his hand to indicate the main stairs, he told her, 'These lead to the first floor. He's waiting for you up there.'

She swallowed. 'Any tips?'

'About what?'

'Any advice on how best to handle him? I mean, looking around, he seems . . .' She indicated the masks, then the clocks. 'A little odd.'

'Perhaps,' he replied, eyes narrowing, 'you'd better keep that to yourself.'

With nausea coiling in her stomach, unsettled by his shifting demeanour, hoping it wasn't indicative of the man who awaited her, she walked up the carpeted stairs to the floor above.

★ ★ ★

It was a room like no other. Its subdued grandeur wicked the air from Leah's lungs as she stepped inside. Floor-to-ceiling windows curved the entire hundred-foot length of one wall, offering views of the floodlit lawn and the moon-frosted summits of the mountains known locally as the Monk, the Maiden and the Ogre, nesting in a spiked mass of lesser peaks. A curtain of stars glittered above them.

An open fire pit dominated the centre of the room. On it a pile of logs burned brightly, smoke rising into a flared metal flue suspended from the ceiling. To the right of the fire lay a vast living space dotted with sofas and armchairs. Antique side tables held marble busts, stained-glass lamps, bronze sculptures of the Greek gods.

By the windows, the twin halves of an enormous amethyst geode rose nearly six feet in height. Their purple crusts of quartz crystals sparkled like the insides of a dragon's egg.

The floor was scattered with animal skins. Zebra lay beside reindeer beside bear. She saw a lion skin complete with preserved and snarling head. Its canines shone in the firelight and its glass eyes raised Leah's skin into goosebumps. Next to it lay a tiger skin, the animal's jaws wide in a dead gape.

Moving her eyes away, Leah turned towards a Regency dining table of polished mahogany. Twenty seats, upholstered in maroon velvet, stood around it. Two place settings had been laid; in front of one of them sat an old man.

He waited with fingers steepled together, watching her with lifeless grey eyes that stared out of a shrunken, hairless head.

Guarding a darkened archway behind him, held upright by supporting brackets and a tall iron bar, stood the fossilised skeleton of a creature Leah could not identify, but knew must be long extinct. It reared up on hind legs, measuring perhaps nine feet to the top of its broad skull. Four huge canines curved out of its jaws. It reached out with claws like polished granite.

'*Ursus spelaeus*,' the old man said, breaking the silence. His voice was a rich baritone, lengthening to a sibilant hiss.

'Although I prefer to call him Johann, after Johann Christian Rosenmüller, the anatomist who named his species. He's a cave bear, Leah. Around sixty thousand years old. He was found in the caves at Drachenloch, not so far away from here. Magnificent, isn't he? We think the Neanderthals may have worshipped *Ursus spelaeus*. If it's true, you can certainly see why.'

His mouth widened, tightening his lips. The smile – if you could call it that – revealed two rows of pointed yellow teeth. 'They weren't exaggerating when they said you were young. I trust your journey was uneventful?'

Those flat grey eyes scraped over her skin and she shivered, speared by their intensity.

'Your driver showed me nothing but courtesy.'

The skin around his mouth crinkled like tissue paper. 'Did he? I'm pleased to hear it. Come,' he said, indicating the empty place setting. 'Sit. I have so few guests these days. And rarely any as infamous as you. I'm keen to make your acquaintance.'

Leah walked towards him, the heels of her shoes echoing like hammer strikes on the hardwood floor. She pulled out the chair he had indicated and sat. 'Infamous?'

'Well, of course. We thought we'd watched our last generation grow. We believed – fervently so – we would never see another *hosszú élet* child. Nor, for that matter, the hope of one.'

He clapped his hands, opened them. 'And then, from nowhere, your mother appeared, throwing everything we knew into disarray, closely followed by yourself. And just look at you. Baby-soft skin. Tight flesh. Innocent eyes.'

He inhaled through his nose, and Leah realised he was savouring her scent. The old man breathed out, chest rattling like birch twigs. 'Something irresistible about the smell of young blood pumped by a strong heart. I do hope we'll get along, you and I. It was unwise of you to come, but you know that. A young woman, fiery and fresh. There are those amongst us who haven't experienced such delights for far too long. I'm afraid the sight could stir up old emotions, old . . . appetites.'

'I can look after myself.'

He laughed, a dog-like bark. 'I doubt it.'

Leah glanced down at her place setting. The silver cutlery was engraved with vine leaves and grapes. Each piece bore an ivory handle carved into the shape of tulip petals.

She noticed that one of her three forks was slightly askew. Frowning, she reached out and rearranged it. As she did so, she saw that a dessert spoon was similarly out of alignment. She nudged it back into position. Realising what she was doing, she flinched and sat upright, giving the old man an apologetic smile.

'Something wrong?'

'I . . . have this thing,' she said. She laced her fingers together and thrust them into her lap. 'I like things to be in order. In their right place.'

His eyebrows rose. 'Is there anything else you'd like to adjust?'

Leah opened her mouth, hesitated. 'Actually, there is. Your sculptures of the Olympians behind me. They're all facing the window. Except for Aphrodite, that is, who, for whatever reason, is facing the door.' She paused. 'It's killing me.'

The old man blinked. He lifted a hand. 'Please.'

Leah crossed the room to the statue and rotated its base until the goddess's eyes stared out of the window.

Returning to her seat, she blew out a breath. 'Thanks. I can concentrate again now.'

'How curious. Is it a mental disorder?'

'You could call it that.'

'Indeed. Shall we dine?'

'Let's.'

He inclined his head, and a pair of doors opposite her swung open. A man and woman entered, dressed in black. Parking a metal trolley near the table, the woman removed two entrees, placing them before Leah and her host. The man opened a bottle of wine and filled their glasses. Taking a book of matches from his pocket, he lit eight white candles in a candelabra.

Leah picked up her wineglass. A Kutya Herceg picked up his.

'To unanticipated pleasures,' he announced, raising his glass towards her. It rang when it touched her own. Again Leah felt his eyes roving over her skin; an unwelcome skittering, like the dry flicker of a lizard's tongue.

'You haven't told me your name,' she said. 'I presume you don't want me to call you Kutya.'

He barked another laugh. 'You can call me Ágoston.'

'Well, Ágoston, I guess I should start by thanking you. For seeing me, I mean. I know you were sceptical.'

'I'll listen, as I agreed. Just don't give me any reason to regret my decision.'

She picked up her fork. 'I'll try to avoid that.'

The two servants wheeled the trolley out of the room, closing the doors behind them.

'You may dispense with the small talk,' he told her. 'I'd like to know why you've been trying so hard to find me.'

She looked up and met dead eyes.

Tell him.

She was no longer sure this was a good idea.

Tell him.

'Because you have something I want.'

'And that is?'

'How much do you know, Ágoston?'

'This will take far longer if you answer every question with one of your own. Tell me what you want.'

'I want an introduction.'

'To whom?'

'To whom do you think?'

'I'm at a loss.'

'Then you're losing your touch.' She cringed as the words rolled off her tongue, but knew that if she capitulated too easily she would lose his respect. And if she lost that, she would find herself in even greater danger.

'How many others know where you are tonight, Leah?'

'Enough.'

'Do you know that when you lie, your pupils dilate? Ever so slightly. And those gorgeous blue eyes grow a little darker.'

'I want you to pass on a message.'

'To whom?'

'To the rest of the *kirekesztett*,' she said. 'Specifically, the *kirekesztett* women.'

He blinked. 'And why would I do that?'

'Because I have an invitation for them. An offer.'

'I can't think of any offer you could make that would interest any of the women I know.'

'Why don't we let them decide that?'

'What is your offer?'

Leah picked up her glass. She drained it, placing it back on the table. 'A child.'

Ágoston stared. He took a long sip from his wine and leaned back in his chair. Somewhere in the room, she heard a clock ticking.

'Well?' she asked.

His face was a reptilian mask: unreadable. He blinked, eyes crawling once more over her body. 'What are you talking about?'

'You said you thought you'd watched the last generation grow. That you'd never see another *hosszú élet* child. Or the hope of one.' She took a breath. 'Well, there *was* hope, for a while, but it's trailing away from us now. Obviously you have a grasp of our history. Of the cull, back in 1880, that led us to where we are today.'

'The *Éjszakai Sikolyok* wasn't a cull, Leah. It was a massacre.'

She hadn't witnessed the genocide, ordered by the old Crown of Hungary, that the *hosszú életek* had named The Night of Screams. She suspected A Kutya Herceg probably had.

'You also know,' she continued, 'the reason *why* it decimated us. Despite our longevity, we're fertile for only a short period in our lives, and once it's passed . . .' Leah opened her fingers, as if scattering dust. 'What do you know of my mother?'

'I know she's not a true *hosszú élet*. I know that the pair of you are a bastard mix.'

Leah hesitated, then shrugged. 'Accurate, if a little vulgar.'

His eyes glittered.

'We found a way, you see. A chance to offer us hope of a future. It wasn't easy – and that's an understatement that trivialises the sacrifices made by a group of women far braver than I could ever hope to be. We asked for volunteers, *hosszú élet* women past the natural age of childbirth, and we tested them. And after years of wrong turns, red herrings, failures, we found a way – together – to help them to become mothers.'

Leah watched Ágoston's Adam's apple as it moved in his throat.

'How?' he asked, and his voice cracked, as dry as straw.

'I can't tell you that. Not yet.'

His eyes narrowed. He gripped the sides of his chair, trembling now, barely holding himself together. 'Oh, I think you will.'

Dismayed, she realised that his reaction was due neither to surprise, nor wonder, but rage. She pressed ahead, sensing that she had little time. 'The chance of a future, Ágoston. A new generation. But the tragedy is, that despite everything we've achieved, we're just not getting there fast enough. This chance; it's been reduced to the basest of calculations. Simple maths, if you like. We know the numbers we need to turn this around. We know our ratio of successful pregnancies. And we know how many volunteers we have. The maths just doesn't work. We're so damned close and yet, despite everything, we're not going to succeed. Not without help.'

Leah raised her eyes back to his and saw they had darkened to black. He was furious, and she could not tell why. She knew she stood on a precipice here, knew the stories she'd heard of A Kutya Herceg were more than mere cautionary tales.

But she had come all this way – *they* had come all this way – and if she risked his wrath, and her life, with what she needed to ask, if that was the gamble she had to take, then take it she would. Because someone had to. Someone had to ensure that the sacrifices made by her mother, Gabriel, and all the women who had given their lives back in Calw did not amount to nothing.

After all the *hosszú életek* had bequeathed to the world, someone had to prevent them from fading into oblivion. She might be the only one left who could.

A Kutya Herceg's jaw was shaking. 'What are you asking, Leah?'

'I'm asking . . .' She swallowed, clasping her hands together, growing angry at her fear, her lack of resolve. 'I'm asking you to talk to them. I'm asking you to pass on my offer. We can give them children, if that's something they want. With their help, we might just build a new generation. We might just offer ourselves hope.'

The moisture had fled from her mouth. She could feel her heart knocking against her ribs. Just glancing at the expression on this shrunken old man's face terrified her in ways she had never anticipated.

Clutching the table with whitening fingers, blood draining from his face, A Kutya Herceg, self-proclaimed leader of the *kirekesztett*, rose to his feet. 'You come into this house,' he whispered, lips curled back from his teeth, 'and you think you can sweep away a thousand years of blood with this *bastard* offering?'

Leah stared, mouth clenched tight. She knew that to interrupt him, to reply in any way, would be the worst mistake she could make.

He raised his voice. 'You walk in here, knowing nothing at all of who we are, of the outrages we have suffered, of the lives ruined – *desecrated* – and you ask us to become your guinea pigs in an *experiment*? In a laboratory trial designed to save the very society that ostracised us in the first place? Is that what you're asking? Is that the proposition you've dared to walk in here brandishing?'

The room's double doors banged open and the man who had driven her to this mountain hideaway strode in. His face was pale, and his eyes had lost the last of their violet streaks. They shone, twin black spheres.

In his hand he held her snub-nosed Ruger. '*Após! Állj!*'

The old man saw him and raised a finger, jabbing it towards her. A stream of Hungarian poured from his lips.

When Leah translated his words, she discovered just how terribly she had miscalculated.

CHAPTER 4

Budapest, Hungary

1873

The boy, crouching in a windblown corner of the Citadella, had not known that his father intended to speak before he died.

If he had, perhaps he would have stayed away. Perhaps he would have sought the shelter of Szilárd's wine cellar where he had spent most of the last four days, tucked away among the dust-caked bottles of Szekszárd Kadarka and Tokaj Muscat, throwing his *Jövendőmondás* cards at the brick wall and trying to read his fate in the light cast from a hurricane lamp. Perhaps.

For each of the last four nights he had lain beneath the covers of the canopy bed in the guest room Szilárd had donated, staring out of the window at the slices of moon bobbing on the Danube's waters, thinking about his father, his two brothers, wishing he could remember his mother.

He was told nothing of his new circumstances. On the first day, Szilárd summoned him and explained the rules that would govern his time here. He could wander freely within the confines of the house. But he must not venture outside and he must not speak to anyone who visited.

He ate his meals in the kitchen by the fire, watching the cook prepare Szilárd's favourite dishes: fiery paprika-laced *halászlé* – chunks of catfish and sturgeon floating in a soup as brown as river mud – and chimney-shaped *Kürtőskalács* she baked from a cinnamon-flavoured pastry wound around a tapered spit that hung above the grate. Occasionally one would slide into the fire and, cursing, she would tear off the ruined part and hand the rest to him. The caramelised sugar crunched in his mouth, but all the boy could taste was ashes.

The rest of the servants ignored him, or snatched glances with eyes impossible to read. On the fourth evening, his uncle summoned him to his study a second time.

The boy had always thought of Révész Oszkár Szilárd as a shambling bear of a man, a grizzled creature of the wilds forced against his nature to fold himself into the lifestyle demanded by the *hosszú életek* elite. Szilárd's enormous belly hung over his belt like a round of cheese; it made him look slovenly however fine the tailoring of his clothes. The backs of his hands were carpeted with coarse black hair and his voice, when he spoke, hummed from the depths of his chest like notes teased from a double bass.

Sometimes a yellow-toothed grin lurked inside his nicotine-stained beard. But not tonight. Tonight his mouth was closed, pinched. His eyes looked bloodshot and old, and the skin beneath them sagged, revealing two defeated crescents of wet red flesh. The sight of them made the boy's throat ache. How changed his uncle had become these last few days; how changed they'd all become.

Despite his pain, he held himself at attention and waited in silence. If his father could show strength in the face of what had befallen them, if his uncle could, then so would he.

It was summer still, so no fire crackled in the study's hearth. The room's light came from a pair of gilt girandoles, dripping with crystal, at the edges of Szilárd's desk. Beside one of them stood a bottle of pálinka and a glass. The bottle was half empty. Beads of the spirit glistened on the hairs of the man's moustache.

'How old are you, Izsák?' his uncle asked.

'Eleven, sir.'

'Eleven. Still a boy. *Kicsikém*. I'm so sorry for you.'

On the wall, the pendulum of a regulator clock rocked left, right. Izsák felt himself falling through the silence between its beats.

Szilárd lurched forward, clearing his throat. He reached into the pocket of his jacket and removed a pipe. Tamping tobacco into its bowl, he clenched the stem between his teeth, struck a match and sucked.

Brown leaf crackled and he breathed a fragrant cloud, heavy with the scent of leather and dried fruit. 'Never had a son myself. Nor a daughter.' Fingers of smoke crept through the air. The boy's uncle shook his head. 'What am I saying? As if you didn't know that.' He grunted. 'No heirs. No noses to wipe. Never in my life met the right woman for that. Met plenty of wrong ones. An army of them, I can tell you. Long time ago now. You're a boy still, Izsák. But you're going to have to become a man.'

'Sir?'

'You've heard what your brother did?'

'Yes.'

'Go on.'

'He hurt a woman.'

'You know how he hurt her?'

The boy felt his cheeks reddening. He nodded miserably.

Szilárd sighed. He sucked on his pipe. Blew out smoke. The clock ticked, lengthening the seconds between them. 'He raped her, Izsák. No point tiptoeing around the word. Doesn't soften it any if we don't speak it aloud. I went over to Buda and saw her with my own eyes. She didn't deserve that, and your father didn't deserve it either. Nor Jani. Nor you.'

'What will happen?'

'It's already decided. All eight members of the *tanács* voted in favour, and the *Főnök* – despite whatever reservations our leader may have had personally – ratified it. I don't know how much pressure those councilmen were facing, but the result was unanimous. He's been cast out. A *kirekesztett* now, and a part of us no longer. I won't speak his name. Neither will you.'

'I didn't mean him.'

His uncle nodded. 'Jani, then. They've blocked your oldest brother's courtship of the Zsinka girl until this is done, revoking his right of *végzet*. And not just his . . .' Szilárd stopped, frowned. He poured himself a shot of pálinka and threw it down his throat. 'They've sent Jani to find the *kirekesztett*. I wouldn't have believed them capable of that. But they're panicking. Desperate to find an end to this. Your brother will bring him back to Budapest and he'll face trial. It'll be swift justice. Bloody.'

'Sir, I know about Jani. You told me before. I was asking—'

Szilárd cut him off with a raised hand, and suddenly Izsák knew that his uncle had been leading up to this, had been feeling his way towards the news he needed to deliver.

When finally he began to speak, it seemed as if the man addressed himself rather than the boy. 'It would be easy to blame the *tanács* for their actions,' he said. 'And in fact I do. But the council's convinced it has no choice.'

Izsák opened his mouth to speak, but again his uncle waved his words away.

'The palace is involved now. You've been sheltered from this – tucked away in Gödöllö with your father – and rightly so. But we enjoy little goodwill in this city these days. The temperature here has plummeted.' He poured himself another drink. 'Some of us counselled that to live so openly among the populace would one day invite disaster. Too often has our presence here encouraged envy, distrust. Something like this happens and all that resentment boils over. They've demanded that an example is made.'

'Of my father?'

'You know that he saw . . . you know he saw the *kirekesztett* afterwards.'

'They had a fight.'

Szilárd nodded. 'The *Főnök* had instructed your father. A direct command. He requested that József bring the *kirekesztett* to face trial.'

'But he let him go.'

'Your father knew how serious the situation was, and despite everything, he allowed the boy to walk out of there. Jani is on the *kirekesztett*'s trail, but the damage has been done.'

'What will happen?'

'I'm sorry. I really am.' Szilárd stared into Izsák's eyes. He picked up his glass, swirled the Pálinka into a whirlpool. 'His blood will be laid to rest.'

The boy blinked. He frowned at his uncle, deciding that he hadn't understood. 'My brother's blood?'

'Your father's, Izsák. József's.'

'Surely—'

Szilárd's eyes were dark. 'I'm sorry to be the one to tell you. I've loved your father like a brother since the day your mother introduced us. He's a fine man. A fine man. Whatever you hear in the coming days, always remember that. He made a mistake, that's all. A moment of weakness, yes, but still one brought about by love. At any other time, perhaps the *Főnök* could have shown leniency. But with the Crown involved, with the attention that's been focused on this, with our own *tanács* clamouring for a show of steel, his hand's been forced. The *Főnök* has no choice, Izsák. No choice.'

The boy's throat was so tight he could barely give breath to his question. 'When?'

'Tomorrow.'

He nodded, a stiff jerk of the head. 'Where will it happen?'

'It's best you don't know that.'

'Are you going?'

'I must. For József, I must.'

'Can't I come with you? Stand by you?'

'Oh, lad.' Szilárd rested his elbows on the desk and planted his face in his palms. He stayed in that position for a full minute. The boy saw his shoulders shake once, twice. Finally the old bear smeared tears into his hair and scratched at his beard, blowing out his cheeks. 'It's a brave thing you ask. József would be proud. *Is* proud. But it's no place for a boy; no place for a son. Something bad happens to a crowd when its blood is up. You would not be safe.'

'Can I see him? Before?'

'I'm afraid not, *kicsikém*.'

The boy dropped his eyes to the floor. His throat felt like a fist clenched it, choking off his words.

He hated himself for the question that clawed to the front of his mind just then, disgusted that he should think it even as he digested the horror of his uncle's news.

What will happen to me?

After their meeting, Izsák wandered the house alone, touring its floors, searching for something – anything – to block out that monstrously selfish thought. In Szilárd's library he pulled books from the shelves and stacked them in the middle of the floor, creating a tower that reached far above his head before it finally toppled. In another room he discovered, hidden in a drawer and wrapped in rags, a bundle of oiled *déjnin* knives, testing their sharpness by drawing the blades across his skin. In the wine cellar, he trailed his fingers over the necks of bottles at random until he found one with a pleasing shape and smashed it against the wall. Staring at the broken glass and the scarlet splashes on the brickwork, his stomach twisted with shame; he picked up all the pieces and hid them in an empty sack.

Izsák encountered the servant on the staircase as he was seeking his room at the top of the house.

The man was running a cloth over the dark wood of the banisters. 'Orphan in the morning,' he muttered.

Breath catching in his throat, Izsák stopped on the stair and turned. He saw the servant bend closer to the wood, as if examining it for blemishes. The question spilled out of him before he had a chance to think. 'What did you say?'

When the servant lifted his head, Izsák saw that no *hosszú élet* eyes confronted him; these were unremarkable, a dusty blue.

The man's face was hard and bitter – sharp angles, thin lips, pocked skin. His body seemed twisted somehow, as if his spine had warped as it had grown. One of his legs bowed out at the knee, longer than its twin.

'*Some* people sayin' this is how the end starts,' he said. The words were thick in his mouth, as if forced past a swollen tongue. '*Some* people sayin' you goin' a be rounded up, driven out. All of you. *Some* people sayin' they've had enough of Long Lives and their ways. That you can't be trusted no more.'

'Who's saying that?'

Wary, the servant's eyes flicked up and down the stairs. 'Not me, of course. *I* wouldn't say nothin' like that. *I* seen how dangerous you are. That girl, the one your brother took, *she* seen it, too. Not much help to her, though, was it?'

'What do you want?'

The man straightened as best he could. 'What do *I* want? I don't want nothin' much. But some people do. *Some* people want to know that what they're looking at is what it is. That it won't do them no harm. *Some* people sayin' your time has come.' The servant glanced over his shoulder again, before drawing closer. '*Some* people sayin' you're all goin' to *burn*.'

His face cracked into a grin, flashing brown teeth.

Izsák flinched, tripped against a step. Scrambling up the last few stairs on hands and knees, he ran along the hall, hearing the man's wheezing laugh bounce off the walls. Wrenching open his guestroom door, he dived inside and slammed it behind him. He glanced around: canopy bed; wardrobe; writing desk. A single high-backed chair. Two leaded windows, looking down on to the Danube's waters. On the floor, an empty bedpan.

Why had he trapped himself? He was alone here, marooned

at the top of the house, far away from Szilárd and the servants two floors below. From this room there was no escape should his tormentor decide to follow. No key sat in the door's lock. If only he had kept one of the *déjnin* knives. If only he had pocketed one of the glass shards from the cellar.

And what would you have done with them?

From the hallway came a creak as the servant arrived at the top of the staircase.

Izsák hiccupped. The back of his throat burned with bile. He pressed his spine against the door, braced the tips of his boots against the floorboards.

He looked across the room at the cupboard. Far too heavy to move. Even if he had the strength, he had no time to heave it into position.

Rap-scuff.

The sound of the servant limping along the hall, dragging his game leg.

Rap-scuff. Rap-scuff.

Izsák opened his mouth to cry out, but his voice had left him. He breathed in half-sobs.

Rap-scuff.

Other side of the door now. Right outside.

The doorknob jangled. An experimental nudge of the wood against his spine. Izsák opened his arms and flattened his palms against the wall.

He heard a breathy whistling, and it took him a moment to realise that it was the sound of air rushing in and out of the man's nostrils. So close.

Izsák shifted his position, pressing his shoulder into the door. He splayed his feet. Perhaps, locked in position that way, he might keep the door closed a fraction longer should the man attempt to burst inside.

The keyhole was just to the right of his head, a lozenge of empty space. Swallowing the bile in his throat, Izsák moved his head towards it. He placed his eye over the hole.

And saw another eye staring in at him.

A rasping voice floated through the crack between door and jamb. '*Some* people sayin' they goin' a take your papa up to the Citadella in the morning. That the palace wants it done right, with witnesses. Not hidden, the way you usually does things. *Some* people sayin' they goin' a bleed him out, right there. And let the woman who got raped watch it happen. *Some* people sayin' there's goin' a be celebratin' after. Drinking and dancing. This is just the first, *them* people say. The first one, what starts everything that follows. A sign to the rest of us faithful. Of the *burnin'* to come.'

'Please,' Izsák whispered. 'Please stop.' He couldn't wrench his head away, couldn't tear himself from the sight of that terrible blue eye. He knew that if this ghoul tried to force the door open, he would collapse to the floor, would curl himself into a ball and screw up his eyes and wait for whatever followed. He was too terrified to do anything else.

'Orphan in the morning,' gloated the voice. 'You got your uncle a while longer. But they won't let you stay with him. Oh, no. And once you're on your own . . .'

The eye disappeared. The crippled servant slammed his weight against the wood. Izsák screamed, scrambling across the room to the window.

The door rolled open, a toothless maw, revealing nothing but an empty hallway and the *rap-scuff rap-scuff rap-scuff* of the servant's feet as he slouched back towards the stairs.

Later, much later, lying in darkness in the canopy bed with the covers pulled up around his throat, Izsák thought of his father. And, even though he knew he shouldn't, he thought of Lukács . . . or Jakab, as he'd now been renamed.

It didn't seem possible that his brother could have done what everyone was saying. It had always been Jani who had frightened Izsák the most: Jani with his quick temper and quick fists.

Jakab had been a little strange, a little distant, but he had been mocked ruthlessly for most of his life: first by his older brother, later by those who came to visit the house in Gödöllö, and later still by the *hosszú életek* ladies he met at the *végzet*. Such unending abuse, Izsák thought, must leave its mark.

Jakab was out there, tonight, somewhere in the world. Like Izsák, he was alone too. And, locked up in an even darker place, their father. The Balázs family, scattered and broken. Izsák could not think on that for long. He knew his old life was over and that this – the press of his palms against the walls of his room, the taste of bile in his throat, the itch of the servant's eye on his skin – was all that was left, but he ached for his life back at home nonetheless, ached for the return of his brothers, his father.

At some point, exhausted, while considering all that he had lost, Izsák found sleep. He woke once in the night, ripped from a dream where he was tied to a plank in a rotting cellar and teeth were biting him, gnawing on the flesh of his arms, his cheeks, his calves.

He snapped his eyes open, mouth parched, feeling the room slide around him. Just as Izsák remembered where he was, and what he was, and what they had all become, he heard the excited rasp of breathing close by his ear, the whistling of air through swollen sinuses, and smelled the sweet-sour stench of rotten gums. A pressure lay on his chest. Someone holding him against the mattress.

He clenched his eyes shut. Balled his fists.

'*Not long now,*' whispered the stiff and twisted creature who had intercepted him on the stairs. The servant's face was so close that his lips wetted the boy's ear when they moved. '*Your father in the morning. Then your rapist brother. Then your older brother. Then your uncle. Who does that leave, Izsák? Who?*'

The pressure on his chest slackened. Now he felt a cold finger touch his neck. It moved, drawing a line across his throat. '*All dead soon, little one. All the Long Lives burned in a pile. Bones and ashes. Bones and ashes. Then we take back our city.*'

'*Miksa!*' A woman's voice, from the doorway. 'Come away from there.'

Izsák opened his eyes and squinted across the room. Szilárd's cook stood by the door, her red face and hanging chins illuminated by the lamp she held before her. When her eyes met his, he saw no warmth there; she appraised him like a mortician examining a cadaver.

The cook switched her attention to the crippled servant bent over the bed. 'There'll be a time,' she said. 'It isn't now. Come away.'

Dropping his head, hissing with frustration, the ghoul bared his teeth. He scraped across the floor to join the cook. Together, they stared at him in the smoky light, then moved away along the hall.

Izsák lay rigid, tears sliding down his cheeks, listening to the *rap-scuff* of the servant's feet as the man dragged himself to the staircase.

Heart juddering so violently he feared it might tear itself loose, he climbed out of the bed, padded across the floorboards and eased the door shut. He dressed quickly in the darkness, only daring to light a candle once he had pulled on his boots. Opening the cupboard, he looked down at the collection of belongings he had brought from Gödöllö: a few clothes, a small suitcase, a box of metal soldiers, a silver hairbrush that had belonged to his mother.

Izsák slipped the hairbrush into the pocket of his coat. He added a single metal soldier. From under his pillow he retrieved a leather purse of coins. He blew out the candle, shook off the molten wax and tucked the stub into another pocket. Tiptoeing back to the door, he paused there, listening for any clue that would indicate his visitors had returned. He wanted to bend to the keyhole and check that the passageway was clear, but it was too dark to see, and he was too frightened by the idea of that pale blue eye blinking at him from the other side.

Hand on the knob, Izsák eased the door open. Cool air

pressed at him. He stepped into the hall, finding with his boot the narrow rug that would smother the sound of his footfalls. Keeping inside its border, he moved towards the stairs, shoulders bunched, arms stretched out before him.

At the top of the staircase his hand found the smooth wood of the banister. Izsák remembered the ghoul polishing it, thought he could feel the residue the creature had left, greasy beneath his fingers. He knew it was his imagination, but he couldn't dismiss it.

The second stair creaked under his weight. The fifth. The ninth.

Down to the first-floor landing. A stained-glass window rippled with the moon-cast reflections of the Danube, ghostly greens and blues. Below the window, a side table displayed a model of a river schooner. He skirted it, wary of tangling himself in its rigging and dragging it to the floor. Down the next flight. Another step groaned, an empty stomach sound in the stillness. Creeping down the final set of stairs, Izsák halted in the ground-floor hall.

Somewhere, a clock ticked: Szilárd's study. A pop of collapsing embers from the cook's fire at the back of the house. He should take some food. But the possibility of meeting the woman again, now that she had revealed her intentions, was too dreadful to contemplate. Instead he turned right and slipped into the room where he had discovered the *déjnin* knives. Navigating by touch, he found the drawer and slid it open, wincing at the squeak of its wooden runners. He felt inside for the bundle of rags, removed one of the blades and returned to the entrance hall, tucking the knife into his belt.

Szilárd's study lay to his right, its door hanging wide. Someone had extinguished the candles of the gilt girandoles on the desk; the room was draped in shadow. He knew he would find writing paper and one of Szilárd's fountain pens in the desk's drawers. Perhaps he should write his uncle an explanation of what he'd seen: the house wasn't safe; the staff were on the brink of revolt.

His uncle had always treated his servants well, with far more affection than Izsák's father had shown his own household. What had changed?

Everything's changed. Everything. It's not just this house that isn't safe. Nowhere is.

He should leave a note. But what could he say? He wasn't thinking clearly enough to pen more than a hysterical sentence or two. Anything he wrote would read like the paranoid scribbling of a child, yet could he abandon the one man who had offered him sanctuary, without leaving a warning of what was coming?

Somewhere above, a floorboard squealed. Izsák stiffened. He felt his bowels flutter. When he heard someone stirring deeper inside the house, he lost his grip on the last tattered edges of his self-control. He lunged for the front door and snatched at the handle.

The door rattled against its deadbolts, monstrously loud. Crying out, feeling for the cold metal runners, he snapped the bolts free, yanked the door open and fled outside.

Down the steps. Across the moonlit courtyard. Towards the arched entrance gates.

They were locked.

Izsák gripped the bars. He shook them in frustration, sick with fear. Glancing over his shoulder, he peered up at the house. Its blank windows stared back at him.

The gates rose a full twelve feet, topped by spikes like sharpened arrowheads. Izsák hauled himself up, finding footholds in the latticework. They swayed back and forth, hinges screaming. He lost his footing, nearly fell. Wrapped his limbs around the bars.

Over the top. You have to go over the top.

How many people must he have woken by now? The servants would be pulling on clothes, grabbing cudgels. They'd assume he was a thief. Perhaps they would recognise him before they attacked. Perhaps they would split his skull regardless.

He heard a shout from inside the house, a window being raised. Wanted to close his eyes and freeze. Moaned and pulled himself higher instead. Rolled over the arrowheads at the top of the gate. Sliced his hand. Gashed his stomach.

And then he was on the other side, swinging free in the moonlight. A shape appeared in the doorway. It clutched something, long and slim. Izsák knew what it was. He opened his fingers and let go of the bars. Felt himself falling. The road rushed up and slapped him. His elbow cracked on stone.

He clambered upright. Felt a looseness to his right ankle. Held in a shriek of agony.

The night opened its arms. And Izsák staggered into them.

CHAPTER 5

Calw, Germany

Phone held to her ear, Hannah Wilde turned in circles, untethered, furious at the darkness in which she was trapped. A memory rushed at her, and for a moment she was back in the upstairs bedroom of Le Moulin Bellerose fifteen years earlier, twirling around in that cathedral of light, seeing its French windows hanging open and knowing that Jakab had been there, and had escaped with her daughter.

This was worse.

Back then she still had her sight. She had been capable of action, of pursuit. Now she was adrift in an ocean of midnight. It pressed on all sides. Mocked her.

When the call connected, Leah's phone switched to voicemail and Hannah wanted to scream with despair. 'Leah, please call me,' she begged. 'As soon as you get this. Please.'

Next she placed a call to Matthias Schachner, the Austrian who ran their security operation.

He answered on the first ring. 'Hannah, I'm so sorry. We've never had any trouble before.'

'Tell me what you know.'

'Mostly what I said in my message. Last time I saw her was yesterday afternoon. She went into town, came back. We had a chat and she seemed fine. No hint there was anything wrong. Her passport's still here.'

Hannah shook her head. 'She has others, Matt. We all do. What about her car?'

'Gone. We're searching for it. Nothing yet.'

'Phone?'

'It's off. And we can't trace it till she switches it back on.'

'She probably won't. She knows you'll find her that way.'

'Have you heard from her?'

'Yes.'

'Do you know where she's gone?'

She hesitated. 'I can't say. Not over the phone.'

'I'll be with you in ten minutes.'

Hannah terminated the call. She reached out for the counter-top, needing something to anchor her. 'A Kutya Herceg,' she said. 'What do we know about him?'

'We know plenty,' Gabriel replied. 'But not much that's recent, or really of any use. Not where he lives. Not even which part of the world to start looking.'

'So how can Leah know, Gabe? How can *she* have figured it out?'

'Because she's smart, that's why. She's like her mother – she doesn't play by the rules, and she doesn't give up.'

'What will he do to her?'

'A Herceg's a pretty savage character. But he's not insane. He won't act without reason. It's not in his interest to harm Leah.'

'It's not just him, though, is it? It's the rest of the *kirekesztett*. I've only ever met one of them. He slaughtered seven members of my family.'

Silent, Gabriel snaked his arms around her.

Who did she have to blame for this? Only herself. When she had learned, all those years ago, the truth of what she was – of what Leah was – the knowledge had almost crushed her. Up until then she had spent her life trying to discover more about the *hosszú életek*, with the sole purpose of using that knowledge to kill the one, Balázs Jakab, who hunted her.

Through the research she'd carried out during those years of terror, she'd traced the origins of the *hosszú életek* back to earliest records of the Hungarian people. She'd learned of their extreme longevity, their low fertility, their ability to manipulate the very contours of their flesh, and heal themselves and others. The discovery that she was *one* of them felt too huge, too wrenching, to throw a leash around and tame.

As a young mother, Hannah would have been happy to see every last one of the Long Lives burned in a pile. Then, of course, she met Gabriel, son of the *hosszú életek* leader, the *Örökös Főnök*, and her life grew more complicated still. She reined in her hatred of the *hosszú életek* people and focused it instead on Balázs Jakab alone, until it burned with a white heat. And then she burned *him*, inside the mill at Le Moulin Bellerose.

Hannah had expected to die that afternoon in France; had expected the stench of her melting flesh to be the last thing she smelled, the flames and the horror of that scene the last thing she felt. She had wanted to survive so her daughter wouldn't be alone. But she had been willing to give up her life to defeat Jakab; and, in a way, she had welcomed the prospect of death. Her journey had been too long, too brutal, and she yearned for the peace that death might bring.

Blinded, scarred by the memory of that day, tortured by the loss of her husband, she had survived, nevertheless, due to Gabriel and his mother. They had brought her, by degrees, back into this world. But what they recovered was a wretched creature, a broken thing.

So many times, in the months that followed, Hannah asked herself whether she would have served Leah better by succumbing to the flames. She didn't adapt easily to her loss of sight. Her role, for as long as she could remember, had been as protector to her family. Now she found herself dependent on its support. In some ways she felt she'd been left with the very worst of outcomes: a survivor, yes, but not as she would have wished.

She remained as a burden, a shackle. At nine years old Leah found herself, within a matter of days, robbed of her father and left with a blind and emotionally fractured mother. How the girl had coped, Hannah would never know.

And then, in the midst of all that, they found out the truth of what they were, discovered the awful reality – that they were actually a part of all this: not just part of the greater *hosszú életek* family either, but part of *him*, part of Jakab. Even now, it sickened her to consider it.

Balázs Jakab. Balázs Lukács, as once he had been called. The murderer of her husband, her parents. So many others.

Somewhere during his journey of blood, Hannah had learned, Jakab had supplanted one of her ancestors long enough to father a child. And on the heels of that revelation came the knowledge of its terrible consequence.

Until her heritage was revealed, the *hosszú életek* had believed Gabriel was the last of their race. Even though the Irishman concealed it well, Hannah had glimpsed the awful bleakness he carried with him: no one with whom to share his life; no possibility of children; a lifespan that offered him nothing except the prolonged horror of watching his friends and loved ones dwindle away.

And then all of that changed. Gabriel passed to Leah the distinction of being the world's youngest, and for a time, in the months that followed, there arose a strange jubilation among those who heard of her existence.

Hannah tried to keep secret the exact details of their heritage, but of course it eventually slipped out. And when it did, that jubilation – which had always been a fragile thing at best, a curious reaction to a stay of execution virtually meaningless in the greater scheme of things – fractured.

Hannah and Leah were *hosszú életek* . . . and yet they were not. One half of their lineage was irrefutable: Jakab's blood seethed in their veins. They were Balázs bastards, descendants of the very *kirekesztett* son who had triggered, with his crimes in

Budapest, the outpouring of venom that, in part, led to the great *hosszú életek* cull.

One half *kirekesztett* monster, and the other half? Peasant stock, in the eyes of many. To some, below even that. Balázs Jakab had mated with a *simavér*, a flat-blood commoner with no history, no claim on the world. It wasn't even meant to be possible: their very existence challenged the veracity of some passages within the *Könyve Vének*, oldest and most revered of *hosszú eletek* texts, and source of all their laws.

As the truth grew more widespread, it split the community in two: those who welcomed Hannah and her daughter, and those who sought to distance themselves.

Hannah could not have cared less. Debating the quality and validity of a single family's heritage while their numbers dwindled further each year struck her as insane. Proof, if any were needed, that the societal fractures preceding the *hosszú életek*'s last days had already begun to appear.

Although adaptability, in the purely physical sense, was one of their greatest assets, for many it appeared, in the intellectual sense, to be a trait tragically lacking. While they could adapt the colour of their eyes and the contours of their flesh, they found it impossible to evolve their definition of what it meant to be *hosszú élet*.

Again, Hannah could not have cared less: until, of course, she began to understand the implications for Leah. Without intervention, her daughter would cement her position as the last of them, destined for an old age of solitude and misery, an unthinkable final act to the tragedy that had haunted them for so long.

Blinded by the fire in the mill, Hannah could no longer guard Leah's physical safety. But there was something else she could offer the girl – something only she could provide – and it was a task to which she committed herself with all the conviction and single-mindedness of her former life.

In her body, she knew, lay the possibility of redemption.

Perhaps they would never learn the reason why Balázs Jakab's *kirekesztett* blood had combined with *simavér* and borne fruit. Perhaps they did not need to know. But the chance of regeneration it offered them, however small, was undeniable.

The move would bring her into conflict, once again, with some of the *Könyve Vének's* strictures. To Hannah's supporters those passages were virtually indecipherable, and contextually irrelevant besides. To her opponents they provided a banner of protest to rally behind: irrefutable proof that what she attempted was heresy. While so many busied themselves with the debate of its rights or wrongs, Hannah busied herself with the work itself.

In the months that followed, she gathered around her a group of like-minded souls. Gabriel, naturally, was the first. Others soon followed. Their single intention: to use the miracle of Hannah's blood to end the entropy and repopulate, bring new life.

They had started here, in this very building deep inside Germany's Black Forest. Together, they rejoiced at each new life they created, wept as Death snatched so many away. And slowly, over time, they realised that even with everything they had achieved, it would not be enough. They'd granted themselves, at best, a reprieve; a little light to banish for a time the shadows gathering in their future. It was a stuttering light, a smoky stump of a thing, and in her darker moments Hannah questioned whether what they had done had been any use at all. They had created new life, yes. But not enough. Tragically, perhaps all Hannah had helped to create was a new generation of grieving mothers.

She had tried to withhold the awful truth of her failure from Leah, excusing her deceit as a desire to check and double-check what basic maths could have told her with a moment's effort. Until now, she thought she had succeeded.

In hindsight, Leah was far too intelligent, far too intrinsic a part of this, not to have grasped the stark reality. Perhaps, in compassion for her mother's guilt, she had kept that knowledge to herself. But through her actions today she had revealed herself. She had lost patience with their lack of success, their slow decline, and she had gone to do something about it. Where that decision would now lead, Hannah could not begin to imagine.

Wherever you are, Leah, please God be safe. I can't lose you. Not you.

She heard, from beyond the kitchenette's windows, a sputtering and a popping of gravel: the wheels of heavy vehicles crunching over stones.

Gabriel drew in a breath.

'What is it?'

'We've got visitors,' he replied. 'Looks like it's the *tanács*.'

Hannah felt herself quail at his words.

CHAPTER 6

Interlaken, Switzerland

Leah was still staring at A Kutya Herceg across the dining table, heart thumping in her ears, when the man who had ferried her to this mountain hideaway strode in through the room's double doors, clutching her snub-nosed Ruger. '*Após! Állj!*' he barked, gesturing at her host.

The old man spun around to face him. He raised a hand and jabbed it towards Leah. '*Ki kell dobnunk a boszorkányt a folyóba. Hátha lebeg!*'

Horrified, Leah glanced from one to the other. She pushed the chair back from the table and rose to her feet. Her grasp of Hungarian had improved over the years; now, her scalp prickled at his words.

We should throw this witch in the river and see if she floats.

For a moment, confused by the rush of events, Leah had thought her driver intended to rescue her from the old man's wrath. Then the word he had used when he'd first appeared came back to her: *Após.*

Father.

It wasn't her he had come to rescue at all. 'He's your father?' she blurted, and instantly regretted it.

After a moment's pause, the younger man turned to her. She could see the anger burning on his face. 'You catch on fast.'

Leah's host spat out another stream of Hungarian invective, his finger still hooked towards her.

'*Elég, Após,*' the younger man replied. '*Elég.*'

'*Fiú*—'

'No,' he insisted. 'I will *deal* with this. I have questions of my own. If she doesn't co-operate, you can have your turn.'

The two *kirekesztett* stared at each other, father and son. After what seemed like an eon of frozen time, the father relaxed his grip on the table. When he cast his eyes back at Leah, she saw murder lurking there – cold violence. With a swiftness that surprised her, he marched out of the room.

A Kutya Herceg's son shut the door. 'Sit down,' he said. And, because of the way he looked at her, she complied without a word.

He pulled out the chair opposite and sat, placing her pistol on the table with a clatter. He spun it, trapped it with his hand, spun it again. The barrel ended up facing her. 'Either you're incredibly stupid, unbelievably arrogant, or monumentally naive. I'm trying to work out which.' His eyes were dark, the last tints of colour fleeing to the outer edges of his irises.

'Perhaps I'm all three.'

'Lonely, too, I imagine. Am I right?'

The question jolted her. All of a sudden she felt horribly exposed by his gaze, as if with a single question he had peeled away her layers of armour and shone a light into the parts she tried to keep concealed.

'You must be,' he added. 'Growing up in fear, the way you did. Never able to put your trust in people. Moving from place to place.' He paused. 'Watching your father die.'

She stiffened, and again his expression shifted, as if, having probed her with a barb, he now backed away to examine its effect.

Nodding thoughtfully, he continued. 'Then you find out the truth of what you are. And what *is* that exactly, Leah? Some would say a monstrosity. A bastard half-breed. Neither fully one thing nor another. The *hosszú életek* may have welcomed you into their fold, but they don't fully trust you, do they? You must sit awkwardly with them.'

'What can you possibly know of that?'

'You'd be surprised. But what I want to know now – what I insist upon knowing – is why you're here tonight.'

'I'm sure you heard what I told your father.'

'I'd like to hear it directly, all the same.' He spun the gun through another revolution, and even through her fear Leah cringed at the sound of the metal scratching a groove into the flawless mahogany slab.

He stared at her a moment longer, and she saw the violet striations once more begin to feather his eyes. Silent, he pushed the weapon with his fingertips. It slid across the table towards her. Leah caught it under her hand.

'Come with me,' he said, standing.

'Where are we going?'

Ignoring her question, he disappeared through the arch beside the skeleton of *Ursus spelaeus* and into the unlit chamber beyond. The darkness gloved him in an instant.

The gun doesn't make you safe. It's a test. Nothing more.

Leah picked up the Ruger. On her feet now, dismayed by a trembling in her limbs that made the floor feel as if it undulated beneath her, she followed.

It took a moment for her eyes to adjust, and then dark shapes began to coalesce from the shadows. The chamber resembled one section of a quartered pie. Its curved wall, like the larger living space at her back, was constructed from floor-to-ceiling glass. Through it, across a dark canyon like a crack in the earth, she saw the three towering megaliths of the Bernese Alps, their snow-frosted summits suffused with a spectral glow. Studding the sky above those peaks, instead of the miser's dusting of stars Leah might have witnessed from town, she saw a galaxy of twinkling lights, so many that it seemed as if a magician's purse had been spilled across the heavens. Even as fearful as she was, their beauty awed her.

Her chaperon stood to her left, the floor beneath his feet like a slab of polished black glass. 'They say there're as many as four hundred billion stars in our galaxy,' he murmured. 'And our galaxy's just one in perhaps five hundred billion others. That's about seventy each for you, me and every other human who walks the earth.'

Unable to decide how to respond to an observation like that, Leah risked a question instead. 'Will you tell me your name?'

Keeping his eyes on the night sky, he replied, 'You can call me Luca. Luca Sultés.'

'Is that your real name?'

'It's as good as any other.'

'I seem to have upset your father.'

'He has a long memory. And he's not as trusting as I.'

'You trust me, then?'

'No. I don't.' Sultés turned towards her. 'Why did you come, Leah? Why are you here?'

'I told you. I want your help. Your father's help.'

'You want us to divulge the details of every *kirekesztett* woman alive who's managed to scrape out an existence while avoiding the attentions of your *Merénylő*.'

At his mention of *Merénylő*, a word that referred to the *hosszú életek* leader's assassin, a role that had existed for centuries, she shook her head. 'He's not my *Merénylő*. I'm a monstrosity, remember? A bastard half-breed.'

Sultés was silent for a while, considering her. 'You know, the original building plans for this house refer to where we're standing as the sun room. But I've always called it something else – the fainting chamber. Because so many of our visitors, when we reveal its secret, do exactly that.'

He smiled, but little humour resided in his expression. His eyes were predatory.

Such a dangerously compelling face, she thought. One moment his features communicated warmth, and the next they seemed as grave-cold and passionless as those of a corpse.

She became aware of her chest rising and falling, and was

certain he noticed it too: noticed, also, the flush rising on her cheeks.

He was testing her; playing some kind of game.

Her skin shivered.

Sultés removed a small plastic remote from his pocket. He pressed a button and the floor beneath her feet switched from polished black to blazing white.

It took her a moment to work out what had happened. Then, stomach abseiling away from her, lungs trapping a scream in her throat, Leah realised that the white light came not *from* the floor but *beyond* it, and that she stood on a glass divide suspended above hundreds of feet of empty space. A descending series of powerful spotlights shone up at her, set into the mountainside's vertical face all the way down to the distant rocks below.

The fainting chamber.

She couldn't move. Couldn't breathe.

All her life she'd been terrified of heights. Hers was not the usual, healthy fear present in most people; she had an almost fanatical aversion.

The anchored safety of the living room waited only a few yards behind her, but it might as well have been located on a different continent. Her muscles had frozen. She felt a bead of sweat roll down the inside of her dress. 'Please,' she whispered, squeezing her eyes shut. 'Turn it off. Get me out.'

'It's funny,' he said. 'Most people, when they see this for the first time, are a little shaken. But there's a small minority who have a much stronger reaction. Strange, but I can always tell in advance how someone will react.'

An inch of glass beneath her feet, and then . . . *nothing*. Leah heard Sultés's heels click against the floor as he moved to her side. She cringed, wondering how much pressure it would take for the glass to crack, and for how long they would plummet if it shattered.

'Are you insane,' he asked, 'to walk in here, into this last refuge of *hosszú élet* innocents, and ask for our help to repopulate the very society that spurned us, then tried to slaughter us?'

She clenched her teeth, insisted to herself that she stood on a floor of granite, thousands of reassuring tonnes of it. 'I don't wish to be disrespectful,' she hissed, 'but you can hardly describe your father's followers as innocents and expect much credibility.'

'So you think the *tanács*—'

Her eyelids were squeezed so tight she thought her eyeballs might burst. 'I'm not here to make moral judgements on sentences passed down by the council. I'm not one of you, remember? Not one of them. Not one of anything, really.'

'So why do you care?'

'Please. Turn off the—'

'Answer me. Why would you put yourself in danger like this? You've just admitted you're not one of them. Not in their eyes, at least. You lost half your family to a *hosszú élet* madman. So why? Why do you care?'

Leah ran her tongue around a mouth as dry as the pages of old books. 'How could I not care?' she whispered. 'How could I stand aside – how could *anyone* stand aside – and watch an entire people disappear into oblivion? Balázs Jakab was a monster, but he never defined the *hosszú életek* race. I've heard the stories about your father. I'm sure half of them are falsehoods, and maybe you both have good reason to hate the people who cast you out. But when I was nine years old and I lost my father, and nearly my mother, some of those very people you despise took me in and looked after me, and they're good people. Wonderful people.

'As I grew older I learned about our history, of the contributions the *hosszú életek* have made. I can't turn my back on that. No one with any shred of conscience could.'

She stopped. Silence followed her words.

Then: 'Open your eyes.'

'I can't.'

'Open them.'

Shaking with dread, but knowing that if she failed, now, to do as he asked, she placed everything for which they'd worked in jeopardy, Leah managed to prise them open, and tried to block out the sight of that yawning white chasm beneath her feet.

Luca Sultés watched her with eyes laced with violet. Unblinking.

Like a snake, she thought. Beautiful, yet cold-blooded.

'Who knows about this?' he asked. 'Who knows you were coming to see us?'

She forced herself to maintain eye contact. 'No one.'

'The *tanács*—'

'The *tanács* would have a fit if they knew.'

'More than that, I suspect.'

He began to laugh. A hearty, warming sound, as rich with humanity as any she had heard. Luca Sultés laughed until the tears ran down his cheeks.

Later, after he had led her out of the chamber and poured her a glass of wine that she drained in almost one swallow, Leah returned to her place at the table. She had imagined she wouldn't be hungry after his test, but when the serving staff reappeared and served the main course, she discovered she was ravenous.

She studied Luca Sultés surreptitiously as she ate, and although she knew he was aware of her attention, she found herself unable to abandon her examination. Taking another sip from her wine, Leah asked, 'So where do we go from here?'

'Tomorrow I'm taking you on a trip.'

'Where are we going?'

'To meet someone.'

'Who?'

'You'll find out. Someone better qualified than me to decide if what you ask is possible.'

'And tonight?'

'Tonight you stay here. As my guest.'

She stared at him across the table. 'If I refuse?'

He returned her gaze. 'That wouldn't be safe.'

'It wouldn't be safe to refuse, or it wouldn't be safe to leave?'

'Take your pick.'

'You want me to stay in the same house as your father? Someone who was threatening to kill me an hour ago? And that's safe?'

'You surprised him. He doesn't like surprises. I'll talk to him.'

'I don't have any of my things.'

'They've already been collected from your hotel.'

'A little presumptuous.'

'You like to fence, don't you?' he replied, brow creasing with irritation.

'I like to make my own decisions.'

'Make one, then.'

'OK.' She took a breath, blew it out through her cheeks. 'I'm going to have some more wine.'

After dessert, after two sweet glasses of Tokaji, Leah, exhausted by the evening's events, blood still singing in her veins from her experience in the sun room, was ready to retire.

The woman who had helped to serve dinner appeared to convey her to her room. Luca Sultés wished her a restful sleep, before turning away to the window at his back. She glanced at her host once as she passed through the double doors into the hallway beyond. Eyes narrowed, he was staring out at the night-swathed mountains, as if searching the darkness. She wondered what he saw.

Leah followed the maid up two winding staircases to the top of the house, arriving in another long hall. The walls here were hung with paintings. Those closest to her were watercolours, their subjects elusive and light, ethereal brushstrokes that seemed to celebrate all that was beautiful and pure. But as she progressed further along the hall the paintings, and their subjects, grew darker. Watery pastels evolved into savagely vivid oils. Scenes that appeared transcendental regressed into baroque depictions of violence and war: dramatic contrasts of darkness and light as practised by Giovanni Baglione, Caravaggio and others.

At the far end of the hall, isolated from the other works and lit by a single wall spot, hung a painting that reminded Leah of something she had once seen in a Toronto art gallery: *Massacre of the Innocents*, by Rubens.

It made her stomach tighten to look at what it depicted. Against a background of classical columns, a group of soldiers tore into a crowd of semi-clothed civilians. Swords were plunged into breasts; throats were slashed open; babies were dashed against stone steps. The eyes of the soldiers shone as they carried out their slaughter. The wounded and the dying slipped in blood, pulling others down on top of them. Leah could almost hear their screams.

Was this how the *hosszú életek* remembered the genocide of the late nineteenth century? She shuddered to imagine what it must have been like. And also she wondered: had Luca Sultés – or his father – started this collection of art with the piece that hung before her now, beginning in horror and crawling steadily towards the light? Or had he begun where she had entered the hall, in celebration of beauty and hope, gradually descending into depravity, wading through years of blood to this final scene of butchery? She suspected the answer would not be the one she sought.

The maid opened the door to Leah's suite and encouraged her inside. The room was huge. A bed crowned with six white pillows stood against the near wall, beneath a stunning vaulted ceiling. The wide windows offered a view of the moon-touched mountains beyond. A door opened onto a sweeping balcony.

Along one wall, a fireplace and a basket of logs. In a corner, a chair, table and reading lamp. On the chair rested her rucksack and motorcycle helmet. An alcove led to a marble-tiled en suite. A second door, in the opposite wall, appeared to grant access to the adjacent room. No key sat in its lock.

The maid moved to the windows and began to pull the drapes.

'That's OK,' Leah said. 'I can manage.'

The woman smiled her acquiescence, and when she raised her head Leah noticed her eyes for the first time: midnight blue, flecked with chocolate and almond. *Hosszú élet* eyes.

She wondered what might compel a *kirekesztett* – when the opportunities of a blinkered world were so obviously ripe for harvest – to become subservient to another.

Fear, she wondered? Isolation? The need to belong?

'What's your name?' Leah asked, and immediately saw those arresting blue eyes dip to the floor.

'Ede.'

'How long have you been here, Ede?'

The woman smiled again, eyes still lowered, and Leah recognised an uneasiness in her expression that pained her.

What does she see when she looks at you? She sees Leah Wilde, bastard descendant of Balázs Jakab. Half hosszú élet *and half not.* Kirekesztett, *by virtue of her birth. Twice damned, in truth, and yet by quirk of timing and fate accepted into that society denied to so many others.*

'Do you know why I'm here?'

Ede pulled at her fingers, nodded.

'Do you think I'll succeed? Do you think he'll let me talk to them?'

A pause. 'I would.'

Leah watched her a moment longer. Then she stepped back, not wishing to prolong the woman's discomfort. 'Thank you for showing me up.'

After Ede had bade her goodnight and closed the door, Leah moved to the windows. She stared out at the night – at the sky now obscured by cloud, at the glistening teeth of the Jungfrau, the Mönch and the Eiger.

Snowflakes had begun to fall. Already the steeply receding lawn, flanked by dark forest to the west and by a sheer drop to the east, had turned white.

Leah was about to move away from the window when she thought she saw a hint of movement at the edge of the trees. She stepped closer to the glass, feeling a prickle of something – some underdeveloped *élet* sense, perhaps – across her skin.

There it was again. A black shape moving in deep shadow.

Now she saw it move out of cover and on to the snow-covered lawn. This far away, she couldn't tell what it was. It moved fluidly, but whether on two legs or four she did not know. On the opposite side of the lawn, from the lip of the precipice that fell away into darkness, another appeared.

The two silhouettes converged, lining up in front of the house perhaps a hundred yards from the windows. Leah glanced around at the lights blazing in her room; she would be clearly illuminated to whoever or whatever lurked outside. Alarmed, she shielded herself behind a section of window frame. She reached out a hand and tested the balcony door. Locked.

The mysterious shapes on the lawn were motionless now. While she couldn't discern a particular outline to them, or even individual limbs, she sensed that they stared up at the house.

Something seemed to spook them. As one, they bounded across the lawn into the cover of the trees, and Leah acknowledged that they couldn't be human, couldn't be human at all. But what kind of animals they were – what kind of *thing* – she could not begin to guess.

She tested the door again, tried to shake it in its frame. It denied her attempts.

Leah closed the curtains and undressed. After brushing her teeth, switching out the lights and slipping beneath the bed's covers, she lay in the darkness, thinking. She recalled the strange collection of masks and clocks that had greeted her arrival; the increasingly macabre artworks hanging in the hallway outside. And then she began to consider the man in whose house she stayed.

A Kutya Herceg.

We should throw this witch in the river and see if she floats.

He was rumoured to have killed scores of Eleni over the years, the Crown-appointed organisation responsible for the genocide of 1880. But if the stories she'd heard were to be believed, he had turned on his fellow *hosszú életek* far earlier than that. Could she reconcile those tales with the man she had met tonight? It disturbed her to admit it, but yes, she could.

And what of his son, Luca Sultés?

Sultés defied any attempt at definition. Could she possibly begin to trust *him* in light of what she knew about his father? At the very least, could she try to forge a partnership with him, in pursuit of the goal to which she had devoted herself? She might have to.

Leah turned onto her side and saw, through the shadows, the door that linked this room to the next. Light from the other side picked out its shape. She remembered she had not tested it to ensure it was locked. Too late now. She could feel sleep reaching for her. It had been a long day. Exhausting. Perhaps the start of a journey that would lead her to the place she needed to go. Perhaps one that would lead her somewhere immeasurably more dark.

Time would tell. Time, always, would tell.

Once, in the night, climbing up from a dream in which silhouettes of muscle and teeth pursued her through a forest as dark as the far side of the moon, she thought she heard something moving on the other side of the windows. A snuffling against the glass.

She opened her eyes, still not fully awake, and in the moment before sleep claimed her once more, pulling her back to the tangled undergrowth of the forest and the chase, she thought she glimpsed, through a gap in the curtains, a blast of condensation against the window, the vapour of an expelled breath, and an eye, glimmering like an oily reflection, roving over her body as she lay prone beneath the sheets.

CHAPTER 7

Calw, Germany

Hannah led the *Örökös Főnök* Catharina Maria-Magdalena Szöllösi and her entourage into the communal garden that lay behind the cluster of single-storey chalets. Wind stirred the fallen leaves, carrying autumnal scents of cyclamen and witch-hazel.

The flower garden had been Gabriel's idea. They had planted it within months of buying the land on which the centre now stood, choosing the plants together, deliberately selecting species known for their scent. At any time of year, Hannah could come out here and enjoy the fragrance of the blossoms: narcissus and lily of the valley in spring; jasmine, honeysuckle and lavender during the hot months of summer; in winter, through a pall of rich wood smoke, the dizzying scent of Daphne odora.

She remembered how, when she'd been a child, her father had visited the university physic garden in Oxford when he needed solace and some space for his thoughts. Usually this fragrant garden in Calw, with its myriad of fragrances and the soft music of its wind chimes, worked the same magic on Hannah. Not today.

The lawn needed mowing. Blades of grass, like tangled hair, snatched at her feet as she walked her guests to the picnic table. Somewhere overhead, the distant drone of a light aircraft cut through the forest quiet. She heard her guests pulling seats away from the wooden table, slats creaking as they sat. The *Főnök*, she thought, faced her, flanked on either side by two *tanács* councilmen, Anton Golias and Oliver Lebeau. To her left, she heard Gabriel set down a tray of coffee.

It was a myth, Hannah knew, that a person's sense of smell grew any more acute once they lost their sight. But she had learned that *hosszú életek* senses were far more sensitive than those of *simavér* stock. Since the discovery of her heritage, and her subsequent education from Gabriel, Hannah had begun to develop those remaining senses beyond anything she could previously have imagined. Her hearing, to Gabriel's amusement and delight, now surpassed his own. Her sense of smell had developed such that she could predict changes in the weather, often hours in advance. And, although she had not shared this last revelation with anyone, she thought she could sometimes detect the shifting emotions of the people around her. Whether that was due to smell alone – some subtle combination of hormones and sweat – or something she intuited, in part, from the cadence of their breathing, Hannah did not know. What she did know was this: along with the scent of cyclamen and witch-hazel drifting out of the forest, and the rich aroma of brewed coffee, she could clearly detect the *Főnök* and her councilmen, and the curiously conflicting emotions of love, distrust, fear and tension that seeped from their pores in an aromatic brew, sharp and bitter, malty and soft, too tightly embroidered to unpick and assign.

It troubled Hannah, that blend. She could sense them watching her, and it made her skin itch. She felt the cold scratching of fear in her stomach, and it angered her; she had spent too many years afraid. Each new spike was like a drop of mercury in her veins.

She didn't want to be sitting here, feigning an air of calm, while somewhere out there her daughter faced dangers unknown. Matthias had reassured her that Leah would be found soon enough, but how could he promise her that? How could any of them? For fifteen years she'd dedicated herself to the task of arresting the *hosszú életek's* decline, always with the hope of securing her daughter's future. Right now she was seeing the unintended consequence: the girl she lived to protect offering herself as a pawn in that very battle.

To combat her anxiety she stood, feeling for the pot and cups on the tray, and served coffee. Sitting back down, Hannah held her own cup close to her nose, trying to lose herself in the aroma of roasted beans.

'I believe it's a day for celebration,' the *Főnök* said.

Do not reveal your emotions.

Hannah forced a smile. 'It's a day for catching up on sleep,' she replied, rolling her neck.

'It was a long labour?'

'Nothing extreme. But . . .' She decided she might as well be frank. 'It wasn't without its complications.'

A click of bone china as the *Főnök* placed down her coffee cup. 'Did she need intervention?'

'Yes.'

The woman paused. 'You nearly lost her.'

'But we didn't,' Gabriel said. 'Flóra appreciated the risks. And now she has a son, another—'

'Gabe, please. We understand all that. Truly we do. I ask only out of concern for the mother. None of us feels anything but delight at this news.'

Across the table, Anton Golias grunted.

'Something to say?' Gabriel asked. Hannah heard the ice in his tone.

'You know my feelings on it. Flóra was too old. It was a risk.'

'There have always been risks.'

'Some more extreme than others.'

Hannah stiffened at that. 'What else would you have us do, Anton? Look at the alternative. Would you prefer that?'

'Of course not. But some would say you should take greater care when choosing the women you recruit.'

'And who should make that choice? You? The rest of the *tanács*? Flóra came to us willingly. You know that as well as I. Is it for us to deny her?'

'Five women have died on these premises in the last six months.'

'And fifteen babies have been born.'

'So we've reduced ourselves to statistics, is that it?'

'Can you suggest a different approach?' Hannah asked. 'Should we pack it all in, go home quietly and light a candle to commemorate the last of us? We're fighting a war here, in that building behind me. Fighting a grim, backs-to-the-wall last stand: against nature, against the consequences of the Eleni outrages all those years ago. Like any war, we're going to have casualties. It's messy and it's horrific, and believe me that if you stayed here a week and watched what we do you'd see how we suffer – and how we rejoice – with every inch of ground we advance or retreat. Do you think we don't grieve for each volunteer we lose? Do you think we don't live with their loss every day? Tell me a better way and I'll listen.'

The sound of wind chimes filled the silence.

Anton sighed. 'I don't wish to attack you, Hannah. I know your intentions are pure. We all know. And I don't have a better solution for you. But I have to consider the greater good.'

'This *is* the greater good.'

'Only if you have a chance of succeeding. If not, all you're doing is accelerating the very outcome you're trying to reverse. From what I hear, you're fast running out of options.'

Hannah felt Gabriel's hand on her arm. She knew, immediately, what he feared she might say: that there *was* another option, but the *tanács* was too entrenched to consider it. She wouldn't speak of that, of course, especially not now; especially considering where Leah had gone.

Instead she swallowed, calmed herself. 'I appreciate the need for debate. Of course I do.'

'I'm sure,' Anton replied. 'You know this project split the *tanács* in two. I don't agree with the more literal interpretations of the *Vének Könyve*, and neither do I see their relevance to what we face today, but you should know that the voices of orthodoxy are becoming increasingly loud. I'm here to ensure that the risks you're taking don't grow so excessive that you lose what support you still enjoy. Even some of your strongest supporters are starting to say the pair of you have too much personal interest in this to be objective.'

Gabriel laughed. 'How can any of us *not* have a personal interest in this?'

'Some are also saying,' Anton continued, 'that considering Hannah's heritage, she's hardly the most obvious person to be leading this programme.'

Oliver Lebeau's chair creaked as it shifted under his weight. Now he interjected: 'Yet we all know how ridiculous those objections are. Without Hannah, there *is* no programme. It wouldn't exist.'

The *Főnök* said, 'Please don't think we came here to attack you, Hannah. It's not the reason for our visit.'

'It isn't?'

'We've learned something. It may be nothing. But if what we're hearing is true, then it affects us all, and it affects your situation directly.' Addressing her councilmen, she added, 'I'd like to speak to Hannah and Gabriel alone. Oliver, you wanted to see the facilities. I believe someone is available to show you around.'

The two men stood, and Hannah heard them walk back across the garden to the complex. Wind sighed in the trees. For a while, no one spoke.

'I'm sorry you had to listen to that,' the *Főnök* said. 'Anton can be blunt, but his intentions are good.'

'Are they?' Gabriel asked.

'He takes his responsibilities seriously.'

'And we don't?'

'Of course. That's not what I meant.' She sighed. 'Look at us: you and me. Prickly like this. If our mother could see us now . . . I never realised how wise you were to turn down this role.'

'Not much wisdom needed for that, sis. I've never been good with rules. Hardly the best choice of candidate to enforce them. If our mother could still see us, she'd say you were the obvious choice to succeed her and you know it. I work better from the side-lines. Always have.'

'Things have changed so much. The *tanács* plot and scheme, bicker like school children. These days the role of *Főnök* seems mainly one of mediation.'

'Another skill you inherited from mother, and one that I lack. You were always the best choice. The only choice.' He paused. 'I still don't understand how the *tanács* can be so backward about what we're trying to achieve.'

'Those passages in the *Vének Könyve* are problematic.'

'And while your councillors argue about their interpretation, we're trying to ensure our very survival.'

'We were never going to reverse a thousand years of ingrained doctrine overnight. If you could take a more visible role—'

'My place is here, Cat.'

She sighed. 'I know.'

'So let's not skirt around the reason for your visit. The *tanács* situation is hardly new. Although if Oliver can impose his will on you, it's worse than I thought.'

'I could hardly deny his request to see this place.'

'We agreed to keep it secret.'

'But not from the *tanács*.'

'The location, we did.'

Catharina remained silent.

'So tell us. What is it? What's happened that's brought you all the way out here to Calw? I take it you haven't dug us up any new volunteers.'

'Is Leah here?' the *Főnök* asked. 'She should listen to this. It affects her, too. More than anyone, perhaps.'

Hannah felt her stomach plummet at the mention of her daughter's name. 'Leah's not around right now. Whatever this is, we'll pass it on.'

'Can you contact her? Ask her to come back?'

'She'll be gone a few days. Please, Catharina, just share your news. I'll make sure Leah knows as soon as possible.'

'Very well. But once we've spoken, we'll need to brief Matthias. You're going to have to step up security. Perhaps even relocate. And we're going to have to talk to the parents. Check every one of the children.'

That cold scratch of fear from earlier had begun to bore out a furrow. 'The way you're talking, this doesn't sound like something that could be nothing.'

'No.' The *Főnök* paused. 'Hannah, have you ever heard us talk of the *lélek tolvajok*?'

Beside her, Gabriel's chair creaked. 'There hasn't been an abduction in years. You told me the *tolvajok* were dead.'

'Maybe not,' his sister replied.

CHAPTER 8

Yosemite National Park, California, USA

Angel River sat beside her sister as her mom's boyfriend Ty steered their rental RV through the rock-hewn tube of the Wawona Tunnel. The yellow lights hanging from the granite ceiling threw carnival shadows around the vehicle, twisting the faces of her family into goblin-like leers.

In her lap Angel held her phone. Glancing down, she activated its countdown timer and stared at the numerals on the screen.

16 days 19 hours 14 minutes 21 seconds

Over two weeks until this trip was over. Two weeks of living and eating and sleeping together inside this huge space-age bus.

It'll be good for us, her mom had promised back in Oregon, eyes crinkling at the edges as she smoothed Angel's hair and kissed her forehead. *Good for all you guys. You want to spend some time getting to know Regan and Luke, don't you?*

Yes, she replied. She did. And she said it partly because she knew her mom needed to hear it; and her mom needed a break. But Angel also said it because it was true – in a way. Admittedly, she found Luke a little creepy. But he was fourteen. And most fourteen-year-old boys *were* a little creepy. He didn't say much, just stared at his phone a lot and listened to his music. A few times she'd caught him looking at her, although not really in a sex way: more with a kind of sad longing. Now that *was* weird. Especially since he was about to become her stepbrother.

Luke's older sister Regan, conversely, had turned out be funny, confident and effortlessly glamorous in a way Angel could only dream about. She'd expected the girl to be distant – what sixteen-year-old wanted to be friends with a thirteen-year-old kid? – but Regan included her in every joke, every conversation. Angel's two siblings, Elliot and Hope, had become equally enchanted with their future stepsister.

From the throne-like driving seat up front, Ty raised his eyes to the rear-view mirror, a big dumb grin on his face. 'OK, Brady Bunch, get ready for Yosemite!'

In the centre of the tunnel a white eye had appeared, rushing towards them. Angel was reminded of the books she had read about out-of-body experiences, reincarnation.

Perhaps this is my reincarnation, she thought. And then, just as quickly: *Stop being so damn melodramatic.*

Moments earlier the white eye had been the size of a coin. Now it had swollen to the size of a grapefruit. Every yard eaten by the RV's tyres drew them a yard closer to their final destination in Vegas . . . and a yard further from Angel's old home in Oregon; her old friends; her dad. It felt, in a way, like a betrayal.

Bad shit happened. Let's get the fuck out.

But it wasn't like that. Not really. Ty was an OK guy, just about. He annoyed the hell out of her sometimes, and his Brady Bunch gag had tired pretty quickly. He did seem to love her mom, though. Angel knew it was selfish, but she just wasn't ready for a new dad.

The white eye at the tunnel's end kept growing, flaring around its edges like a corona. They shot under an illuminated sign hanging from the tunnel's roof.

PREPARE

Angel felt a rash of goosebumps breaking out on her skin. It chilled her, that sign. Somehow prophetic.

Come on, Ty, make a gag.

But it was her mom, riding shotgun in her cut-off shorts, with flip-flopped feet resting on the dash, who referenced the sign. She swivelled in her chair, eyes shining like jack-o'-lanterns. 'Ready, gang? *THREE . . . TWO . . . ONE!*'

And suddenly they were through, barrelling into daylight, into blue sky and granite Sierra Nevada peaks and forested valley, and a view Angel had seen on a hundred different postcards and travel guides. She felt her lungs filling, a grin forming. Exactly the reaction she hadn't expected.

'Wow!' her brother Elliot yelled, twisting off the bench seat in the RV's living space and planting his palms against the window.

There was something prehistoric about the scenery beyond that glass. Something that reminded her of those old movies she'd watched: *One Million Years BC* starring Raquel Welch, and *The Lost World* – not the *Jurassic Park* sequel, but the sixties adaptation of a novel by one of her favourite writers, Sir Arthur Conan Doyle.

On the north side of the valley rose the granite block of El Capitan, its vertical cliff face climbing thousands of feet. On the south side, Angel saw a waterfall cascading over a crevice high up in the rocks, wind blowing the water out in a spray as it tumbled towards the valley below.

'Bridalveil Fall,' Ty said, pointing as if he heard her thoughts. 'Twice as tall as the Statue of Liberty.'

That was another thing about him. When Ty wasn't making gags, he was relaying facts. Hundreds and hundreds of them, and always to Angel, as if he believed he'd found in her a fellow trivia addict. Where he got them from, she didn't know. He didn't appear particularly cerebral. Certainly not today, in safari shorts that revealed skinny white knees, and the T-shirt hanging from his frame with its depiction of a wizard and the words *THAT'S WHAT I'M TOLKIEN ABOUT* emblazoned across the front.

Thanks to Ty she knew that the Wawona Tunnel was 4,233 feet long, and that it had held the record for the longest road tunnel in California since 1933. She wondered what possible use she would ever find for that information.

'You heard of the Ahwahneechee tribe, Angel?' Ty asked.

She shook her head.

'Original inhabitants of Yosemite. They thought that breathing the mists of Bridalveil would give you better marriage prospects.'

'Pity Mom didn't come here earlier, in that case,' Angel replied. She grinned at his reflection, to show that she was joking.

Ty grinned back, to show her that it was OK. Then his eyes narrowed. 'They also believed an evil spirit lives by the falls, and you should never look directly into its waters when you leave the valley.'

'Or what?'

'Or you'll be cursed,' he told her.

'Fascinating.'

'Yeee–up.'

They followed the road east, alongside the inky waters of what Ty explained was the Merced River, behind a steady procession of cars, RVs and motorcycles.

It seemed to Angel that half of California had descended upon Yosemite today. She turned in her seat as they passed the waterfall, anxious for one last look.

They reached the campground a short while later. Ty slowed the RV to a crawl before hauling on the wheel and swinging the vehicle in through the entrance. Lining the road, the cinnamon–red trunks of huge ponderosa pines soared a hundred feet and higher, their ancient bark split into thick crusted plates.

The forest floor was a field of dead needles, cones and smooth grey boulders.

After jumping out at the ranger station to pick up their camp pass, Ty steered their vehicle around the looping campground road, searching for their site. They found it easily – the only vacant slot – and parked up, swapping the steady rumble of the RV's diesel for the muted hiss of the Merced. She could see it there, glinting between the trees.

Marked by a half-circle of five giant ponderosas, their site consisted of a flat patch of swept ground for their motorhome, two picnic tables, a fire ring and a food locker. Up front, Ty rotated his driving seat so that he faced the RV's living space. 'OK, Bradies. Quick safety briefing. Need you all to be careful about food while we're here. Why's that?'

Angel's brother shot up his hand.

'Elliot?'

''Cuz of bears will eat you,' he said, puffing out his chest.

On the couch opposite, Angel's sister Hope picked up her magazine. 'Just great,' she muttered.

Ty clapped his hands. 'Well, *bears* is correct, Elliot. But there's no need to worry. We treat 'em right and they won't bother us. There hasn't been a fatal bear attack in Yosemite, ever.'

'What about non-fatal?' Hope asked, eyes never lifting from her magazine.

Ty paused at that, and then he brightened. 'Well, like I said – we treat 'em right, and they won't bother us. Most people who get tangled up, it's because they didn't follow precautions.'

'Which are?'

'It's our food they want. Smell drives them crazy. They'll do anything to get their paws on it. And I mean anything.'

'Ty . . .' Angel's mom warned, laying a hand on her fiancé's arm.

He twitched. 'You're right, you're right. Sorry, got carried away again. OK, simple rules. We keep all the food in the RV, and we keep the door and all the windows shut. You put your uneaten food back in the RV. Don't drop anything outside or throw anything out. Simple. Let's hope we're lucky enough to spot a few.'

'Did you bring any pepper spray?' Hope asked.

'It's not allowed in Yosemite. If you see a bear too close, you just shout at it to back the hell up. Now, who wants to come outside and barbecue a couple of steaks?'

Later, after Ty had coaxed them out of the motorhome and suffused the forest with the kind of roasting meat smells which, had Angel been a bear, would have driven her into the midst of their camp ready to tear the head off anyone prepared to get in her way, they dragged the two picnic tables together and ate.

It was then that Angel decided she'd discovered another thing about Ty. Yes, the lame jokes and useless facts could get old pretty quick. But the guy could cook. It wasn't sophisticated and it certainly wasn't healthy, but it was the some of the best food she'd ever tasted: rump steaks marinated in a homemade chilli sauce and barbecued until they were charred on the outside but so soft you could cut them with a spoon; chicken wings sticky with honey; shrimp in lime; corn dripping in butter; potato salad and coleslaw. They tucked their heads down, all seven of them, and bashed elbows until they were fit to burst. Angel even managed to fill her plastic tumbler with Blue Moon when her mom was looking the other way.

Afterwards, sitting on logs around the campfire, with the evening sun blushing the clouds to pink and setting a flame to the granite peaks, and with the sound of the river like soft applause, Angel looked at the gathered faces and wondered if they might just all work out. Her mom and Ty; her sister Hope and her brother Elliot; her new siblings, Regan and Luke. She'd been sceptical of this trip. Even now, she was unsure of how Vegas would suit her, and she grew tearful when she thought of what she'd left behind. But when she saw Ty put his arm around her mom and saw her mom rest her head against his shoulder, Angel decided that she might be able to do this, would at least *try* to do this. For her mom's sake if no other's.

When the stars came out, she asked if she could go down to the river and watch the moon floating on the water. Her mom sat up straight, and Angel just knew she was going to tell her it was too late. But then Regan stood up and said she wanted to see it too.

They walked to the river's edge in companionable silence. Angel found a flat boulder and they sat, staring across the water at the silhouettes of California black oaks and incense cedar. She felt something pressing against her thigh, and when she put her hand into her pocket her fingers closed on the amber locket the stranger had given her earlier that day.

'What is it?' Regan asked, leaning over.

Angel frowned. She hadn't really thought about the woman since their encounter, which was odd, considering how much she had affected her at the time.

'Just a locket.'

'Where'd you get it?'

'Someone gave it to me. A gift.'

'It's beautiful. Kind of spooky, though.'

'I like it.'

'Yeah. It's cool. Looks really old.'

Angel swung the locket like a pendulum between her fingers. Its chain resembled a series of interlinked silver beetles. They'd stopped for lunch at a roadside diner on Route 41, somewhere north of Fresno. And that's where she had met the stranger.

The diner had a picnic area. Just a few scarred benches and a climbing frame for kids. While Ty and her mom took a table inside and figured out what everyone wanted to eat, Angel came out to check her emails and escape the diner's piped R 'n' B. The locket's owner appeared a few moments later, sitting at the second bench with a coffee and a pastry.

Angel couldn't help but stare. The woman was, without doubt, the most beautiful creature she had ever seen. Her features were so startlingly perfect, in fact – so *proportioned* – she didn't seem real: seaweed-green eyes striated with shards of emerald and pearl; pale wheat-blond hair falling over her shoulders in tresses that shimmered with captured sunlight; cheekbones that looked like they had been cut by a jeweller. She wore a white cotton summer dress under a black cardigan, and python-skin cowboy boots. Her bag looked like it was made from snakeskin, too. The amber locket hung at her throat.

The woman took a sip of her coffee and bit into her pastry. Not in an attractive way. She opened her mouth wide and tore off a huge piece, chewing it quickly, as if she hadn't eaten in days. In another two bites the pastry was gone, leaving nothing but a few flakes dusting the woman's dress. She opened a paper bag and removed a second, devouring that one in the same fashion. Crumbs clung to her lips or fell into her lap. She swigged down coffee and wiped her mouth with the back of her hand. Seeming to notice Angel for the first time, she smiled.

Angel flinched, impaled by all that human beauty concentrated purely on her. It felt like staring into a supernova. She felt compelled to say something. 'I like your necklace,' was all she managed.

'Thanks,' the woman replied. Her voice was deep, far richer than Angel had expected. Stupid, but those green eyes seemed to reach inside her head, reading every thought she'd ever spun.

'How are the pastries?' she asked, and winced. Such a dumb question.

The woman laughed. 'I need to brush up on my table manners, huh?' She inclined her head towards the front of the building. 'Did you arrive in the RV?'

Angel nodded.

'Big family. Are they really all your brothers and sisters?'

'Two of them. The others . . . they're my mom's boyfriend's kids.'

'Where are you headed?'

'Yosemite first. For some *bonding* time.' She heard the childish derision in her voice, and instantly regretted it. 'Then on to Vegas.'

'You don't want to go?'

'I . . .' Angel shrugged. 'I don't know what I want.'

'Feels like a big change.'

'Yeah, I guess.'

'Well, big changes are coming.'

'What do you mean?'

The woman stood, brushing crumbs from her clothes. 'Exactly that.' She reached up to the back of her neck and removed the necklace. 'Here. I think you should keep it.'

To have this flawless creature suddenly so close was strangely disconcerting. Her perfume was spicy and floral. Overpowering. Angel felt a prickling along her spine, as if a locust had been tipped inside her shirt and was crawling around on her skin. 'No, I couldn't. It's—'

'Oh, hush.' The woman draped the necklace around Angel's shoulders. 'You can do anything you like. Life's for living, and you never know how much longer you've got.' Turning, she walked to the picnic area's gate and let herself out.

Angel watched her disappear past the side of the diner. A few seconds later an engine roared and a black Chevrolet Chevelle, with two white stripes painted on the hood, accelerated hard down the road, leaving a cloud of tyre smoke.

Now, sitting on the rock beside Regan, watching the moonlight rippling on the water, listening to the sounds of a radio playing inside someone's RV, Angel found herself wondering who the blond-haired woman had been, and where she had been going.

Big changes are coming.

'You know, my dad can be kind of a geek,' Regan said. 'But he's OK. If you give him a chance.'

'I know.'

'For what it's worth, he loves your mom.'

'I can see that. I can see he's good for her.'

'But?'

Angel shrugged. 'I'm not sure there is one.'

Regan reached out and squeezed her hand. 'That's good. Because I—' The girl stopped.

'Because you what?'

'Keep your voice down. *Look*.'

Angel raised her head, and that was when she saw the bear. The animal was on their side of the river, following the curve of the bank directly towards their boulder. It swung its muzzle from left to right as it approached, its head like a bullet between its shoulders.

Fear slid into her, squeezing her lungs.

'Stand up,' Regan whispered, and Angel could tell she was scared too. 'Remember what Dad said. Let's back up a bit. I don't think it's seen us.'

Angel pushed herself to her feet, willing her sneakers not to slip on the wet rock. Their RV was only fifty yards away. But the bear was closer. She heard it grunting now – a sound like a saw cutting timber.

It paused. Raised its snout to the moon. Lowered its head and stared at them.

'OK, we're leaving,' Regan said.

'Should we shout at it?'

'Do you want to?'

'No. I don't think that's a good idea. Definitely not.'

They backed away, covering the fifty yards to their site in silence, eyes straining towards the bank. The bear didn't move. But it followed their progress until, eventually, it lost them behind the trees.

Perhaps it was the adrenalin still running through her from that encounter, or perhaps it was the altitude of the Sierra Nevada, or perhaps it was none of those things; but for whatever reason,

Angel found she couldn't sleep. Long after they had rolled out their beds and switched off the RV's interior lights, she lay in the darkness next to Hope, listening to her sister's steady breathing.

When she heard the motorhome's side door open, and the subtle shifting of the vehicle's springs that suggested someone had stepped out, Angel rolled onto her side. Their bed was situated in the elevated section above the driving compartment, what Regan's family called the attic. Beside her head was a tiny curtain drawn across a twelve-inch-high window stretching the length of their mattress. Reaching out a hand, Angel pulled the curtain aside and pressed her face to the glass.

Below, she saw Ty appear from under the awning above the RV's door and stroll over to the embers glowing in the fire pit. In one hand he held a bottle of Blue Moon. He took a swig from it, then he reached into the breast pocket of his shirt, pulled out a joint and screwed it into his lips. After spending a few moments lighting it, he took a long pull.

Oh, Ty. I'm learning something new about you every day, aren't I? Does Mom know about this, you sly old hippie, you?

Angel grinned in the darkness, watching as her future stepdad took another hit, breathing marijuana smoke up at the leaf canopy. She was about to drop the curtain back in place and give Ty some privacy when she spotted something else, lurking just beyond the circle of light thrown by the dying camp fire. A movement, in the shadows of the trees.

Angel frowned, pressing her face closer to the glass. What she saw next made her mouth fall open in surprise. It made no sense, but there could be no doubt. She recognised the cobra-skin boots and the shock of pale hair, luminous in the moonlight. The stranger from the diner was as beautiful out here beneath the stars as she'd been back in the picnic area outside Fresno.

Ty continued to smoke. The tip of his joint burned a bright orange. He arched his back and rolled his head, like a cat unwinding from a dream. The woman emerged fully from the cover of the trees. She took two steps towards him. Her shadow fell behind her. Away from Ty.

Angel had begun to breathe faster. She tilted her head to avoid fogging up the glass.

What's she doing here? Did she follow us?

Idiot. Of course she followed us.

But why? Is Ty screwing her?

Of course not, you freak. Look at her!

The woman took another step, closing the gap to only a few yards. Her snakeskin bag hung over her shoulder, the scales shimmering as if the bag were alive and coiling against her torso.

She was right behind him now. He took another drag, swigged from his beer. And then he turned and faced her.

The woman's eyes widened. Even from where she lay, Angel could see the green fire in them.

Ty exhaled a plume of smoke, like a steam train venting. He frowned, but the corners of his mouth curled upwards, as if both surprised and pleased at the arrival of his guest. He licked his lips.

The woman in the snakeskin boots reached out a hand to Ty's face. He flinched away, just a fraction, just for a moment. And then he stopped himself, staring into her eyes. His jaw dropped open.

Her fingers were long-boned and graceful, the nails painted with a clear gloss. They hovered beside Ty's cheek, tantalisingly close. Finally, she touched him.

Angel could not explain what happened next. The instant the woman's fingertips made contact with his flesh, her legs gave out beneath her and she collapsed into a heap, head smacking against the forest floor.

Ty stared down at her body. He took another hit on his joint, blew out smoke and flicked the butt into the fire. Then he looked straight at Angel.

She dropped the curtain back into place and rolled onto her back, gasping. Her heart slammed in her chest.

Christ, what the hell? What was that? What WAS that? What did you just see, Angel? What the hell did you just see him do?

She strained her ears, mouth parched of moisture. Now she heard a dragging sound outside, a scuffling. Terrified, but compelled nonetheless to take a second look, she bent her head back to the glass and lifted a tiny corner of curtain, just in time to see the woman's legs slide around the side of the RV, her snakeskin boots ploughing two black furrows through the pine needles.

A clunk from the back of the motorhome. The rear baggage storage opening. A thud. The sound of something sliding. The almost imperceptible sagging of their vehicle as it adjusted to a new weight. Angel caught sight of Ty returning.

She dropped the curtain back in place before he saw her. Lay down on the bed. Gripped the amber necklace in her fist. Prayed. Not for anything particular. Just prayed.

Oh Lord. Oh Lord. Please. Oh Lord.

The side door opened. The motorhome dipped as Ty stepped inside.

Angel heard the door swing shut behind him. Heard the sound of her blood pumping in the darkness.

CHAPTER 9

Interlaken, Switzerland

When Leah pulled back the curtains in her room the next morning she revealed a different world from the one she had relinquished for sleep. Clouds had rolled through overnight, but they were gone now; the sky was the fragile blue of a robin's egg. In their wake a covering of snow had unfurled across the landscape, bringing with it a startling silence. The air seemed poised, expectant.

And on Leah's tongue that sensation was back, a subtle sourness, somewhere between the taste of lemon and olive.

I *was* right, she thought. I *can* sense it. And how wonderful is that?

The sun was a pinwheel of fire in the east, hanging low in the sky. It infused the morning snow with a copper hue, violet in the shadows. To the south, the three giants of the Bernese Alps appeared unreal – jagged expressions of a Cubist's art.

Leah was about to turn from the window when she saw them in the snow, on the balcony outside her room: a double row of individual depressions, each one sinking four inches to the wooden deck beneath.

Prints.

They were circular in shape, as if someone had stilt-walked along the balcony wearing tin cans on their feet. But whatever had left these tracks had walked upon four feet rather than two.

Leah groped backwards through her memory for the image

she had glimpsed the night before as she broke the surface of a dream and caught a shape moving beyond the glass. At the time she had barely considered it; a fleeting dream shadow, something that had lingered a while and then faded. Now, staring at the prints, she tried harder to remember. She recalled a dark mass; a blast of condensation against the glass; a jewel-like flickering of deep-set eyes.

Something else remained of whatever had visited. It clung to the glass at about chest-height: a curving slick of mucus, like a question mark shaped from ghee. Frowning, Leah unlocked the French window and slid the panel of glass sideways along its runners. A frozen slab of air pressed inside, pinching her skin.

She stepped onto the balcony and gasped as her bare feet plunged into snow. Turning back to the window's outer pane, she bent closer to the glass and examined the yellowish smear. It was streaked with a darker pigment. Leah reached out, hesitated, then slid a finger through it, grimacing at its cold, gelatinous texture. She raised her hand. Sunlight glimmered on the secretion attached to her finger.

The stench of it hit her then: a foulness in her airways, lodged deep and clinging. Alive, like a curling slug in her throat. Spluttering, repulsed, Leah shook her head to repel it. Crouching down, she pressed her hand into snow and wiped the residue away.

She saw something else, then: a hair. It stood straight, trapped against the wall of one of the depressions. After her experience with the mucus she didn't want to touch it, but she forced herself, plucking it from the snow and holding it up to the light. Close up, it looked more like a bristle than a hair, a serrated shaft of stacked arrowheads, with a pale bulb and a sharp, hard tip. Leah stepped to the balcony's railing and dropped it over the edge, watching it spiral away.

She suddenly needed a shower. Needed to scrub her hands, inhale good hot steam and rid the last clutches of that corporeal stink from her nose.

Afterwards, skin red from its water blasting, she dressed in jeans, checked shirt, jumper and boots.

Someone knocked at the door. 'It's open,' she called.

The maid, Ede, slipped into the room. 'If you're ready for breakfast, I'll take you down.'

Something different about her this morning, Leah thought. A distance. She watched the woman for a moment and then shrugged, following her out of the room.

She found her hosts in the first-floor living room, where she had dined the previous evening. A Kutya Herceg sat at the head of the table; his son to his left. The remains of an enormous breakfast lay before them. Silver tureens contained steak, sausages, bacon, black pudding and scrambled eggs. She saw fried tomatoes, hash browns; a bowl of steaming mushrooms; triangles of toast; smoked mackerel and salmon. Splayed out in a fan among the jars of jam, marmalade and pepper sauce lay the morning editions of papers from around the world.

Ágoston, sitting erect in his chair, was reading the front-page story from *Le Monde*. Luca Sultés, in contrast, slouched in his seat. He smoked a panatela, the cream smoke snaking up to the ceiling where it hung above his head like a raincloud. Beside him stood a silver coffee pot and a half-drunk glass of grapefruit juice.

He watched her approach the table. 'Leah. I trust you slept well?'

'I've had better nights.'

Frowning, he turned to the maid. 'Thank you, Ede. That'll be all.'

A Kutya Herceg folded up his newspaper and laid it down. He examined Leah with lukewarm detachment. 'My son,' he said, 'believes I owe you an apology.'

She met his eyes, relieved to see that the violence they'd contained the previous night had all but disappeared. 'What do you believe?'

He grunted. 'I believe that on occasion, as men begin to age, a certain irascibility can creep into their nature.'

She nodded. 'I've had a few experiences of that.'

Ágoston stood up, and Leah realised that his admission was as close to an apology as she was going to get.

'I have a shoot this morning, and I must get ready,' he announced. 'So I'll leave you in the hands of my far less irascible son. Please try not to corrupt him.'

Once the old man had gone, Leah picked up a bowl and scooped muesli into it from a tub. She added milk to her cereal, poured herself a glass of juice, and sat down. The sight of the cooked meat, cooling in its juices, reminded her of what she'd seen clinging to the glass of her bedroom window. She paused over her breakfast, a worm of nausea curling in her stomach.

'Something wrong?' Luca asked, crushing out his panatela.

'You had visitors last night,' she replied. '*We* had visitors.'

'Oh?'

'Don't pretend you didn't know.'

He poured himself a cup of coffee, stirred in sugar. 'You saw?'

'I saw.'

He nodded.

'What were they?'

'I thought you were *hosszú élet*.'

'So?'

'So perhaps it's time you started to educate yourself.'

'Are you going to tell me?'

'Not over breakfast.'

'Are they dangerous?'

'To some.'

'To you?'

'Not as much.'

'Then who?'

He stared. 'My father advised you not to come What might you infer from that?'

Leah took a sip of her juice. 'Something was outside my window last night. I don't know if it was one of them, or something else. But it was on the balcony.'

Luca opened a silver cigar box and removed a fresh panatela. He lit it with a slim gold lighter. Puffed out smoke. 'Impossible.'

'I saw it.'

'The security sys—'

'Go upstairs if you don't believe me. Whatever it was, it left tracks. Smeared something godawful on the window.'

His eyes still hadn't left hers. Did she see a trace of unease in them?

Luca went to a bureau and opened a drawer. He removed her Ruger and placed it down on the table. Last night she'd returned it to his care. 'Keep it with you from now on,' he said, and strode out of the room.

After finishing her breakfast, Leah poured herself a coffee and took it to the viewing window, staring out at the mountains beyond.

Luca returned a few minutes later, his eyes troubled.

He checked. And now he knows it's true.

'Come on,' he said, throwing her a coat. Not a fur, this time. A mountaineering jacket.

'Where are we going?'

'You wanted to speak to one of the *kirekesztett* women.'

'I want to speak to all of them.'

'You can speak to one, and I want to be there. Depending on her reaction, maybe more.'

'Who is she?'

'Are you coming or not?'

Pulling on the jacket, Leah pocketed her pistol and raced to catch up.

Outside, the morning air was frigid, but the sunlight, where it touched Leah's neck, conveyed a delicate warmth. Luca tossed her a pair of gloves. 'It'll be colder where we're going.'

'Which is?'

'You'll see.'

The doors to the five-car garage were rolled up into their recesses. Overnight, someone had cleaned the Phantom and parked it back in its bay.

Now, an enormous Ford pick-up waited on the tarmac. Luca pulled a set of keys from his pocket. The truck's door locks jumped, and its indicator lights flashed. A few moments later they were heading down the hill, the vehicle's oversized tyres crunching over snow.

Interlaken's snowploughs had been busy overnight. The main road had been scraped clean, revealing a smooth grey strip split by a single white line.

Luca headed south, following the route's curves in silence. To their left a mountain stream tumbled and hissed, swollen with the morning's snow melt. To their right, a high wall of flat-edged bracing stones kept the mountainside from spilling onto the roadway.

The sun climbed higher, its light scattered by the branches of trees. All around, the slopes were dense with scrubby mountain pine laden with powder.

When their road broke out into a grassy plateau, Luca ducked his head and peered up at the sky. He seemed to concentrate for a moment, and then he slammed on the brakes, swerving into a rest area where five snow-dusted picnic tables stood in a row.

'What's wrong?' Leah asked, hand braced against the dash. Luca threw open his door and climbed out. 'OK,' she said, addressing the empty seat. 'Best not tell me.' In turn she jumped down and walked to the back of the vehicle.

Luca was staring up at the sky. He raised a finger. 'Look.'

She cast her eyes upwards and saw it wheeling above them, wings outstretched, a wide brown shape against the morning: the unmistakable silhouette of a raptor.

'Golden eagle,' he said, smiling. Luca put the fingers of his right hand to his mouth and whistled, high and mournful, two individual notes.

Above, the bird adjusted its wings and arced away from them. Then it looped back and dived. For a moment Leah thought it intended to strike, but it levelled out just in time and skimmed over their heads, close enough for her to feel the turbulence of its wake. The eagle banked, swooped back towards them. Legs thrust forward, with a mighty beat of wings, it landed on the truck's tailgate.

Leah gasped. She watched it tuck away its wings, talons clicking and scraping on metal. It turned its head to study her with flat amber eyes.

'Stunning,' she said. 'Beautiful.' Neither word really did it justice.

'Deadly, too,' Luca told her. 'And intelligent. They've been known to drag goats off cliff tops. Easier to kill them that way.'

'Right up your street,' she said. 'Is it male or female?'

The bird opened its beak and cried, a hooting high-pitched call.

'This one's a girl.'

'How do you know?'

'She just told me.'

Leah's mouth dropped open. 'That can't be true.'

He paused, and then he was laughing. 'Your face,' he said. 'No, it isn't true.'

'Funny,' she snapped, feeling her cheeks beginning to burn. 'Hilarious, actually.'

His laughter abating, Luca considered her. 'You still have a lot to learn, don't you?'

'About what?'

'About you. About us. The *hosszú életek*, I mean. About what's possible, and what isn't.'

She prickled with irritation. 'An ignorant little girl, you mean.'

'Not at all.' He nodded back towards the bird. 'The females are always larger. That's how you can tell.'

'I'm surprised you haven't tried to stuff her and take her home for your father's collection.'

'I think he has one, actually.'

'Will you teach me that call you used?'

'Perhaps. Watch this.' He extended his arm and clicked his tongue. The eagle flapped its wings once, then hopped on. Luca's arm dipped as it took the bird's full weight. The creature's talons closed around his woollen jacket, cutting into the fibres.

He's showing off, she thought, with a jolt. *Luca Sultés is trying to impress me.*

As if receiving from him some silent signal, the bird launched itself into the air and flapped into the sky.

A single feather had fallen into the truck's bed; a shaft of white, the vanes a mixture of coffee and cream. Luca picked it up. 'Here,' he said, handing it to her. 'For you.'

Leah rolled her eyes. 'So chivalrous.'

Be careful. And don't be stupid. You don't want to get into this.

She was still holding the feather as she climbed back into the passenger seat.

They followed the road further south, winding through scenery that looked like it had been carved open with a knife. The river beside them boiled with white water. Already the morning sun had melted most of the overnight snow, revealing lush meadows and delicate Alpine plants.

They passed a sign to Stechelberg, the road straightening as it led them along the wide floor of the Lauterbrunnen valley. She saw cows grazing its pastures. Higher up, black and white long-horned goats.

The town itself was tiny: a bed and breakfast, a hotel and a scattered collection of homes. Luca steered the truck into a car park beside a huge concrete building. One side was a gaping hole from which four heavy cables rose up and out, climbing at a steep angle. A large sign read:

Stechelberg
867m 2844 ft

'You've got to be kidding.

Luca switched off the engine. 'It's the only way up.'

'She doesn't live in Stechelberg?'

'Nope.'

'I can't do it.'

'You've heard of exposure therapy?'

'Yeah. And you can keep it.'

'Shall I drive us back?'

'What?'

He pointed through the windscreen. 'If you want this badly enough, you'll do it.'

'Why all these tests?'

'View it as therapy.'

'I'm not sure I'm the one who needs it.' She opened her mouth, hesitated. 'Give me something in return.'

'I'm not sure you're in a position to bargain right now.'

'Your visitors. Outside on the lawn last night. Tell me what they were.'

'You really don't know?'

'I have no idea.'

'Then you were even more foolish coming here than I thought. If you're not careful, your ignorance is going to kill you.'

'So help me out. Educate me.'

'They were *lélek tolvajok*.'

She frowned. 'What?'

'Exactly. You have no clue what I'm talking about, do you?'

Leah shook her head.

'You grew up with *hosszú életek*, yet they've prepared you hardly at all.' He stared through the windscreen at the mountains beyond. 'Perhaps they thought the *tolvajok* had all died out. Or perhaps it's only *kirekesztett* they prey upon now. Whatever the reason, it's still inexcusable. They should have told you.'

'Prey upon?' She watched his eyes, unease clawing at her.

'The *tolvajok* have preyed upon *hosszú életek* for as long as we've both existed.'

'You said earlier they're only a danger to some.'

'They're a danger to all. But yes, some more than others. You, especially so.'

Those claws sank deeper now. 'Why me?'

'Because of your age. Because of what they'll want from you.'

'Which is?'

He pointed through the window at one of the cable cars sliding into the building.

'We need to go. Now. Or we're going to miss our ride.'

She shook her head. 'I can't, Luca.'

'If you want this enough, you will.'

'It's not as simple as that.'

'Yes. It is.'

Inside the building, Luca purchased their tickets and they boarded the next car to dock. Leah's heart was a hummingbird in her chest. The car was wider than a bus and virtually all glass. It swung gently as it began to rise – bizarrely quiet – and she heard herself moan as her stomach slipped away from her.

Quickly the valley floor receded, the building from which they'd emerged dwindling first to the size of a shoebox, then a matchbox. Leah clenched her teeth so hard she expected, at any moment, to feel them shatter. She wanted to close her eyes but, morbidly fascinated, found that she couldn't.

They rose higher. This was no cable car route that skimmed the surface of its mountain slope. Soon they were impossibly high above the earth. She could see the whole of the Lauterbrunnen now, opening up like a vast canyon below her.

Waterfalls plunged over cliffs, misting as they plummeted hundreds of feet past rock.

The cable car trembled and Leah tasted bile.

This is not happening. I am not this high up.

Mercifully, through the front-facing windows, she saw the winching station above them begin to grow larger, its brown steel ribs sharpening into view. Its huge sign read:

Gimmelwald
1367m 4485 ft

A village of traditional log cabins clinging to the mountainside, Gimmelwald was an even smaller community than Stechelberg. Laundry fluttered from washing lines. A few blond-haired children ran through its only street.

Leah breathed out explosively as they lurched to a halt inside the station, but Luca shook his head. 'Not quite.'

'Another?'

'Another.'

'We couldn't drive up?'

'No roads.'

The second cable car took them up to Mürren. According to the sign she saw as they arrived, they'd reached an altitude of 5,413 feet. The doors opened and they filed out, the air greeting them so bitter it drew tears from her eyes. Leah paused to recover her breath, heartbeat beginning to slow as she felt solid ground beneath her feet once more.

Mürren, despite its greater altitude, was a much larger village than the farming community of Gimmelwald. Clearly a tourist destination, it was startlingly beautiful nonetheless. Houses opened onto back gardens that dropped away at surprising angles, hemmed by low wooden fences. There were no cars.

At this altitude, snow still clung to the branches of trees and sat heavy on the rooftops. A wisp of cloud passed overhead, so low that it skimmed the tops of the buildings. Overshadowing everything, the grey stone peaks of the Alps.

Off the main street, Leah followed Luca to a black-painted chalet with bottle-green shutters. He bounded up the concrete steps and yanked on a bell pull.

'What's her name?' she asked, squinting up at the windows. The ground-floor shutters were all closed.

'Patience,' he said.

'That's her name?'

'No. That's some advice.'

'Unbelievable,' she replied. Then, 'Have you told her?'

'I thought I'd leave that to you.'

'What's she like?'

He scratched his chin. 'Let's just say she doesn't get out much.'

The door opened, revealing a dark, wood-panelled hall. A woman's face appeared around the edge of the jamb and Leah's stomach twisted into knots.

CHAPTER 10

Budapest, Hungary

1873

Few of the city's inhabitants walked the streets at this hour, and Izsák wished to avoid the ones that did. The moon was waxing, daubing Pest's architecture with a spectral luminescence. He kept to the shadows, ducking out of sight when he heard footsteps or the snort and clatter of a horse. The hilt of the *déjnin* blade chafed his side.

He had but one intention: find his father; find the only person left in this city who could make everything right.

All dead soon, little one. All the Long Lives burned in a pile. Bones and ashes. Bones and ashes.

He would not believe it. His uncle had told him that the *tanács*, at the Crown's request, intended to sacrifice his father. The crippled servant had implied the rest of the *hosszú életek* would soon follow.

It couldn't happen. It couldn't.

If he could get to the Citadella, he could uncover the truth. He could prove to himself that the last two days had been a nightmare and nothing more. He accepted that his father was to be punished, but the man's blood would not be spilled.

If Izsák could find him, if he could stand beside József as he was judged, perhaps the *tanács* would be shamed into showing even greater leniency. Perhaps they could both be back in Gödöllö by tomorrow night.

Stand next to your father? You couldn't even summon the courage to warn Szilárd!

But this was different.

This was all he had.

The Citadella stood at the top of Gellért Hill on the Danube's west bank, the highest elevation for miles around. The stone fortress had been built by the Habsburgs twenty years earlier, a strategic position from which its cannon could target both Pest and Buda should the cities choose to revolt.

Izsák could reach the foot of the hill via the Széchenyi chain bridge, but he dared not risk crossing it at night. Someone was sure to challenge him.

Instead he walked the streets of Pest, waiting for sunrise. He passed the huge Academy of Sciences building, and sat for a while tucked behind a pillar at the top of the steps to St Stephen's Basilica. Wind stirred the leaves of a newspaper beside him. It was a mournful sound. He wrapped his arms around his knees and closed his eyes. If only Jakab were here; his brother would know exactly what to do. Izsák accepted that Jakab had done a bad thing over in Buda, but perhaps that had been a mistake, too. A dreadful misunderstanding.

No. He's a rapist. You know that.

When Izsák opened his eyes hours later, the sun had risen and he could hear birdsong. His backside ached where it pressed against stone. Pain thumped behind his eyes. He climbed to his feet and dusted himself down. Pulling the knife from his belt, he slipped it into an inside pocket; with the arrival of dawn, he'd be unwise to display a weapon so openly.

By the time he crossed the chain bridge over the Danube's wide brown ribbon, the morning's river traffic was already moving. He saw tugboats, full-sailed schooners, a paddle steamer churning the water to foam. Gulls hovered and cried.

Even this early, the sun was warm on his back. The notion,

now, that his father would die this day had shrunk to the status of an infant's night terror. The crippled servant had frightened him, yes. But Izsák's reaction, fleeing from the man and the house, had been foolish, panicked. Once he heard the *Főnök* speak, once he saw his father and proved to himself that József was safe, he would talk to his uncle. The servant would be disciplined. There would be an end to it.

He arrived on the Buda side of the river and began the climb up Gellért Hill to the Citadella. The building squatted on the summit, a graceless fortification of pale stone, punched with square holes for its battery of cannon. Some walls curved, others zigzagged. A group of soldiers, in blue tunics and peaked caps, lounged around outside the entrance. Most had rifles slung over their shoulders; one, holding a sheaf of papers, wore a sword at his belt. Relieved, Izsák saw they were making casual conversation, cracking jokes. It felt far from the atmosphere of an execution.

A procession of carriages had accompanied him up the hill. Beside the fort's entrance they began to deposit their passengers. All were *hosszú életek*, and their faces were set: tight mouths, downcast eyes. Individually or in small groups, they consulted with the soldiers before passing through the gatehouse. Izsák followed the next party. He was nearing the arch when one of the bluecoats called out to him.

'You, boy! Where do you think you're going?'

He spun around, skin prickling as the soldier approached.

'I *asked* you where you're going.'

'I . . .' He hesitated. 'I have a message for our *Főnök*, sir.'

'Your *Főnök* isn't here.'

'I know that. But the *tanács*, sir. I need to find one of them. They'll pass on the message when he arrives.'

'What's your name?'

'Áron, sir. I've come all the way from Pest.'

'Well, Áron, you can piss off all the way back to Pest. No one goes inside unless their name is on that list.'

'But—'

'Go on, else I put my boot in your arse.'

The officer wearing the sword had been watching the exchange, and now he strode over. He frowned at his subordinate, thrusting his chin towards the entrance. 'Let him in.'

'We—'

'Look at his eyes, Smid. Are you blind? He's one of them.' The officer turned to Izsák. 'You know who you're seeing?'

He nodded.

'Quick, then. Find him, pass on your message, and get out. I don't want to have to send my men to look for you. Understand?'

'Yes, sir. Thank you.'

Balázs József sat at the writing desk in the *tanács* town house and gazed down at the street outside. The room was well appointed, painted canary yellow and furnished with good quality furniture. A Persian rug covered most of the oak floor; gilt-framed oils of hunting scenes hung on the walls. Behind him stood a four-poster bed, and in one corner a walnut bureau contained the few belongings he had brought here. On the bureau's surface, a silver tray held a collection of spirit bottles and a pair of crystal tumblers.

He heard the clatter of a key and the sound of the door swinging open. Then, the unmistakable rattling breath of the *Főnök*.

'József, it's time,' the old leader said.

He nodded, placing the graver he had been using down on the desk before him. Holding up a pocket watch to the light, he turned it over in his hands. Sunlight bounced off its gold hunter case; a circle of white, like a darting fish, flickered across the wall.

József looked down at the inscription he had made.

Balázs Izsák
Végzet

He was no master engraver, but the job would have to do.

'József?'

He stood, turned, surprised at what he saw. The *Főnök* appeared sunken, as if the man had aged a thousand years in the past week. His flesh hung slack around his face. Only his eyes remained sharp: chips of jade and azure.

József held out the watch. 'Here. It's for my son. Will you give it to him?'

The *Főnök* took the watch, running his thumb over the inscription. 'It's a handsome piece. I'll ensure the boy receives it.'

'Not yet. For his *végzet*.'

'József—'

'Yes. For his *végzet*. I've left the year blank. I won't be here for him. Somebody will have to complete the engraving.'

The old man breathed deep and the flecks of jade in his eyes faded. He wound the watch's chain around his fingers. 'My old friend—'

'Please,' Josef said, holding up his hands. 'No more words. I'm ready.'

Perhaps one hundred *hosszú életek* had gathered on the grassy quad inside the Citadella's walls. They formed a loose and silent semi-circle before the wooden stage. From his hiding place among a stack of barrels on a half-loaded cart, Izsák wished he could join them. Despite their grim expressions, the uniform solemnity of their dress, they felt like a lost family, a safe haven denied him by more than mere physical distance. But now that he had positioned himself among the barrels, he dared not reveal his presence. Along one wall, a line of bluecoats stood at attention. Additional soldiers patrolled the battlements.

Wind snapped the pennants flying from the quad's flagpoles. Among them he recognised the Hungarian national flag – a crown between two angels on a tricolour of red, white and green – and the dual-crown flag of Austria–Hungary.

The stage was empty except for two plinths constructed from delicate ironwork, standing waist-height to a man. Each was topped by a shallow metal bowl filled with burning coals. Grey smoke fluttered on the breeze.

Izsák saw a party of dignitaries appear on the far side of the archway. Not *hosszú életek*, this group, although their faces were just as stony. They took up a position to the left of the stage. Although he did not recognise them, he suspected from their deportment who these men must be: representatives of Crown and State.

Following the dignitaries, a second group entered. Walking inside a protective circle of bluecoats, they comprised perhaps twenty citizens of the city. Their faces displayed a curious mix of emotion: unease, loathing, triumph. They shot cautious glances at the gathered statesmen, poisonous stares at the *hosszú életek*.

At their very midst, supported by an older couple, walked a straight-backed young woman, tanned from the sun. She wore a grimy dress gathered in at the waist. Her hair was tucked beneath a cap and her mouth was a tight line. Izsák noticed that she was trembling; a moment later, he realised who she must be.

With the arrival of the newcomers, the atmosphere in the quad changed. The soldiers on the walls ceased their circuits and stood motionless, staring down at the crowd. Somewhere, a bell began to toll. A flock of pigeons rose into the air, wings slapping. Now a third group filed through the arch, and Izsák felt his heart thump against his ribs.

Two tall *hosszú életek* led the procession. Eyes black, they scanned the crowd as they approached the stage. Both wore dark tunics, with a pair of sheathed *déjnin* knives hanging from their belts. Behind them, aided by a white-suited youth carrying a parasol, walked the *Főnök*. Behind him, flanked by two more dark-eyed *hosszú életek*, and followed by the eight members of the *tanács*, walked Izsák's father.

Balázs József, in a navy frock coat over a white shirt, stared straight ahead as he walked, lips moving softly.

The crowd murmured, watching as the front half of the group walked up the steps to the stage while the *tanács* peeled off to join the State dignitaries. On the wooden platform, still flanked by the two *hosszú élet* guards, József halted behind the *Főnök*.

The old leader, grey periwig perched on his head, raised his hands and the whispers in the crowd faded. Except for the snapping of the pennants on the flagpoles, the Citadella was silent.

The *Főnök* swept the quad with his gaze, and Izsák realised that he was purposely meeting the eyes of every individual who stood before him. Once he was finished with the crowd inside the quad, he raised his head and gazed at each of the soldiers on the wall in turn. Finally, he lowered his hands.

'Friends,' the *Főnök* said. He paused, and then he nodded. 'For that is what we are. Friends united by a shared history. A history that has often been turbulent, a history that has often been bloody. We have suffered hardships together, have suffered wars together, have experienced the cautious joy of reunification together. I address not my fellow *hosszú életek* with these words. I make no such distinction. I address everyone who has gathered here today, brought either by duty or the desire to see justice.'

He took a breath. 'While we, as *hosszú életek*, have lived among you as friends, we have not always chosen to show our faces. We've been too secretive, perhaps. For long periods in our shared history, that was a necessity born from conflict. But it is not, I am prepared to accept, a style of living compatible with the modern age. It is difficult to maintain trust that way. Even among friends.

'Events of the past week have pained many of you. I share that pain. Those events have sparked anger, resentment, further division. I empathise with your anger. I understand your resentment. More than anything, I seek to heal that division. And, as *Örökös Főnök*, I tell you I must bear some responsibility. I promised a swift resolution to this outrage, and so far I have failed.

'What must come . . .' The *Főnök* hesitated, and Izsák saw his Adam's apple bobbing in his throat. 'What must come today – what we do here – will, I hope, demonstrate the seriousness with which we take our responsibilities as citizens of this great city. When a crime is committed in the modern age, the people are entitled to seek justice. Today, you will witness the first part of that justice. Soon, I promise you, we will find the *kirekesztett* who has brought this shame upon us. We will gather here again, and you will witness the conclusion.

'All friendships experience challenges, periods of difficulty. But true friendships also endure. True friendships heal. Ask yourself if this is a true friendship and I hope you'll agree that this is what we have.

'The *kirekesztett* known as Jakab faced challenges of his own, of that there is no doubt. But they were not insurmountable. With courage, they could have been overcome. Instead, Jakab chose a darker path. He chose to distance himself from his family, and he chose the path of violence, of deceit.

'He will be found. The responsibility for finding him was given first to this man you see before you – his father, Balázs József. Despite the seriousness of the *kirekesztett*'s crimes, Balázs József chose to ignore that responsibility. He defied a direct order from the ruling *tanács*. And from his *Örökös Főnök*.

'We cannot, as our long tradition dictates, allow bad blood to thrive. The right of *végzet* has been stripped from the Balázs family until the *kirekesztett* son has been returned. And for his complicity in the *kirekesztett*'s escape, Balázs József is today brought here before you all, to face a judgement of his own.'

The *Főnök* turned and inclined his head to the guards standing beside Izsák's father. They stepped forward and József moved with them, until he was directly between the two coal-fired braziers.

Izsák gazed at his father standing tall in his beautiful clothes. He wanted to call out, but he knew to interfere now would be the worst thing he could do. That József was to be punished, here in front of this crowd, was now undeniable. But the *Főnök* had not yet spoken of that punishment. There was still time to show leniency.

A second pair of guards approached the stage, carrying between them a long bundle swaddled in cloth. They laid it at József's feet and began to unwrap it. The crowd edged closer, blocking Izsák's view. He saw a gleam of polished metal. Leather straps. A murmur rippled through the gathered *hosszú életek.*

The guards finished their task and filed off the stage. Izsák craned his neck and what he saw paralysed him. His stomach flopped like a fish.

The *Főnök* stared at the faces of the *hosszú életek* nearest the stage, at the soldiers in their uniforms, at the representatives of Crown and State. Such expressions he saw reflected back at him; such conflicting emotion. He found it difficult to meet their eyes with anything resembling the detachment he knew, he must display.

He had spent the past week debating options of leniency. In the end, it had all been for nought. He knew what his people demanded. The *tanács* had feigned a willingness to debate the options, but they had swiftly moved to parrot those views.

Can I blame them? They're sick with fear. We've grown too entrenched here, too entwined. Too immersed in the beating heart of this city, this country, this region. We've grown heavy and fat on our wealth, our collective power. We've become addicted to our influence, our mystique. And it's all a myth. An illusion. A crystal tower, standing on sand.

The Crown wished to see a strong response, and the *tanács*

wished to oblige. *The greater good.* It was a phrase he had heard too often these last days. He had campaigned as hard as he dared, but he stood in a crystal tower of his own, just as delicate, and he knew there were some in the *tanács* eager for its fall.

For every isolated *kirekesztett* incident, a thousand stories swept through the city and its provinces. Those incidents, while rare, had begun to create a tale – a myth – as dangerous and compelling as that of deliberately seeded propaganda. He wished there were someone more suited to steering them through this mess of their own making. But who else could he trust with their future?

Balázs József had damned himself by his actions, and not only by his failure to bring his son to justice. Since the death of his wife the man had turned his back on society, had shunned the endless carousel of politics and intrigue. Through his lack of engagement he had lost both his friends and the last vestiges of the community's warmth. Now, when the *hosszú életek* needed a sacrifice, the man found himself stranded and alone.

Above the Citadella, gulls wheeled and cried.

'Balázs József,' the *Főnök* said, forcing himself to meet the eyes of their collective sacrifice. 'You've repeatedly acknowledged your complicity in the escape of the *kirekesztett* son responsible for the defilement of Krisztina Dorfmeister. Do you, at this final time of asking, wish to change that plea?'

The horologist shook his head, and the *Főnök* felt ice forming in the pit of his stomach.

'Think carefully now, and speak for all to hear.'

Balázs József filled his lungs. 'If what I did was a crime, I am guilty, Lord.'

The crowd murmured.

'Do you have anything else to say?'

The man stared, eyes a swirling mix of magenta and shadow. Flecks of orange glinted there, like sparks cast from hammered steel. He turned to face the crowd, raising his voice so it carried across the Citadella.

'So many anxious faces I see here today. So much anger.' József nodded. 'I'm sorry for the pain my son has caused. I'm sorry for his deeds. And I'm more sorry than you'll ever know for my part in this. I know what I did was wrong. Yet if I had my time again I would do exactly the same thing. I don't profess to be a perfect man. I don't profess to be a good man. When my wife Bernadett died I wallowed in self-pity. I neglected my sons. One, as we now know, went on to rape a girl in Buda. Would he have done that had I raised him better? Possibly not. Am I to blame for his crimes? In part, certainly. Could I ever, if given the opportunity again, take Jakab's life? No. I could not. And I won't deliver him up for someone else to do the same. For that, I am to be punished, and rightly so. Clearly I am flawed. But perhaps that flaw is what *makes* me a father. I won't wet my hands with my son's blood. I don't ask for your forgiveness today, nor your mercy. I ask, simply, that you put yourself in my shoes and consider: What, really, would I have done?

'I ask you this for one reason. My eldest son has agreed to bring the *kirekesztett* back to Budapest to face justice. As I speak to you, Jani is already on that road. His right of *végzet* has been revoked until he succeeds at his task. I won't comment on the burden that responsibility has placed on him. I only note that he has agreed to shoulder it.

'I have one son left. A child. Some of you know him. Those that do, know him to be a gentle soul. I beg only this. Let this end with Jakab – and let this end with me. Izsák is not yet twelve years old. An innocent, a victim of this situation as surely as anyone. Please: watch over him. Allow him to grow. And help him to heal.

'I am to be judged today. But tomorrow, in the way you treat an innocent, you will all be judged. Tell my boy I love him. Tell him his mother loved him. And show him that he is loved, still.'

The *Főnök* watched his old friend, wondering what impact, if any, the man's words had made. The crowd was growing restless. He could delay this no longer. Reaching up, he removed the horsehair wig from his head. 'Balázs József, the judgement of the *tanács* stands.' His voice cracked. 'Your blood must be laid to rest.'

He sought among the gathered faces until he found his *Merénylő*. Even in the day's heat, the assassin wore a long leather coat and wide-brimmed hat. His eyes, the colour of rotten teeth, glimmered as he approached the stage. In one hand he held a metal *capsich*, wickedly sharp, and in the other a short-bladed knife.

József's shoulders slumped. Already, the guards had removed his frock coat and rolled up the sleeves of his white shirt all the way to his biceps. Each forearm had been lashed to a polished pewter gutter. Three feet in length, the end of each pipe rested on the curved bowl of a brazier.

The *Merénylő* bent to József's right forearm, examining it closely. He balanced the tip of his blade against József's skin. Then, with a practised movement, and a curious snuffling exhalation, he slashed lengthways with the knife, opening a four-inch furrow. Quickly he slid the razored cone of the *capsich* into the man's ulnar artery, and folded the thin metal paddles of the *capsich's* cuff around József's wrist.

The horologist winced, lifting his face to the sun. Blood began to course down his arm. It dripped into the polished gutter, rolled and gathered speed. The first splashes hit the brazier's coals with a hiss and a puff of grey smoke. Along the pewter pipe, a narrow river began to form. It pulsed with the beat of József's heart. As the flow increased, the hiss of the coals intensified. Bubbles swelled and popped on their surfaces, collapsing into ash. Smoke boiled up, whipped away on the breeze, ferrying a smell like roasted meat.

Licking his lips, the *Merénylő* pressed his fingers into the crook of József's left elbow. With a second downwards slash, he opened the artery in that arm too. He attached the second *capsich* and retreated.

From the crowd, a man barked, 'Stand firm, József! God's speed!'

The *Főnök* searched the front row and found the bearded face of Révész Oszkár Szilárd. Blotches of red had appeared on The Bear's cheeks, and from his eyes glowed scratches of vermilion and jade. He crushed his fists together, chest heaving.

On the stage, József found his brother-in-law's face. Clenching his teeth, the horologist straightened his spine. Briefly, he smiled his thanks.

Blood slopped in the guttering. József's right leg began to shake. A spasm passed through him.

Incredulous, the *Főnök* saw a globe of phlegm arc towards the stage from the group of the city's citizens. It spattered against József's cheek.

'You deserve to rot, Balázs!' shouted a voice. 'You and your bastard sons.'

Some in the crowd gasped. Others surged forward, a hunger burning in their faces. Another missile looped through the air, this one striking József in the chest and leaving a bloody smear. Only when it fell to the floor did the *Főnök* recognise what it was: a purpled chicken liver. A handful now struck the man, one finding his neck, the others leaving dark stains on his shirt.

Szilárd roared, twisting left and right. 'What is this! Who *does* this?'

On the stage, József's legs buckled. The guards either side of him took his arms and held him upright, frowning as they scanned the crowd.

A few feet away, a man hawked and spat a thick lump at József's face. Szilárd roared again. He waded through the press of bodies, slamming his fist into the stranger's skull. The man went down and the crowd cried out.

'Enough!' the *Főnök* shouted. 'Allow him some dignity!'

A coin bounced off the back of Szilárd's head. The Bear

ignored it. 'József, *look* at me,' he growled. 'Only at me.'

The horologist's wrists shone red. His mouth hung slack but he raised his eyes and found his brother-in-law's face.

'It'll be over soon,' Szilárd told him. 'You'll be with Bernadett.'

'She's in a better place than I'll see,' József whispered. He began to gasp.

'No. *No*, József. You did well. You *did well*. I'll watch the boy, I promise. I'll look after him.'

József closed his eyes. Chicken livers hit his chest, his face.

'Let go,' Szilárd said. 'You've done everything you can. Go on, József. Let go.'

Izsák opened his mouth to scream as the *Merénylő* sliced into József's flesh, but no cry formed in his throat. His fingers gripped the rough wood of the barrel top, and he could not tear them loose.

Go out there! You can stop this! This is why you came!

But he couldn't move. And he couldn't speak.

His father's blood hissed and spat as it boiled away on the coals. Izsák choked at the sight, gagged. Yet still he did nothing.

They're killing him. Right there. Your father, *Izsák. They're bleeding him out, just like the cripple told you they would. And you're doing nothing about it. Nothing!*

He struggled for breath. Heard his uncle's voice, coaching József to stand firm. At least someone was with him. At least someone in this crowd of ghouls showed some compassion, some bravery.

The scene blurred, and for a moment it was a relief. Somehow Izsák loosened his grip on the barrel. He wiped his eyes, saw something strike his father's cheek. A moment later a cluster of missiles curved through the air, hitting József's chest, his face.

Szilárd roared.

And there, behind the barrels, Izsák found his voice.

'Leave him alone!' he screamed. As the words tore loose from him, his paralysis lifted. He slithered over the barrel and jumped down to the grass. 'Stop! Stop it, all of you!'

As the onlookers surged towards the stage, Izsák dove through spaces in the crowd, screaming his lungs hoarse. Close by, a man reached for him, but Izsák had pulled the *déjnin* knife from his coat and he slashed at the stranger's fingers, severing one and opening deep cuts in the rest.

'Grab him!' a soldier yelled. 'Get him out of here!'

He whirled, holding the knife in both hands, slashing at anyone who came close. He opened a wide circle, and when he looked back to the stage, he saw his father staring at him, an awful look of grief on his face.

'Oh, Izsák, no,' he moaned. 'Somebody, please. Somebody.' His face crumpled. 'Don't let my boy see this.'

The tramp of boots. Soldiers converging. 'Let him go!' Izsák cried. 'It's not his fault!'

On the stage, the guards holding József's arms released him, jumping down onto the grass.

'You should not be here, Izsák,' the *Főnök* said, eyes stricken.

He brandished his knife. 'Set him free.'

Someone in the crowd laughed. A man grabbed him. Izsák struggled loose, turning and slashing. The man cried out.

Now the *Merénylő* drew his sword and stepped onto the grass.

'Don't you dare!' József shouted. He turned towards the *Főnök*. Don't let this happen! Don't let him hurt my boy!' Eyelids flickering, his legs gave out beneath him. As he fell, his strapped arms dragged the guttering with him, and his right foot hit one of the braziers.

It toppled. Burning coals tumbled onto József's chest, scorching his shirt. They bounced between the folds of his trousers, into the creases of his armpits. Had he remained conscious, he would surely have rolled away.

Instead, he began to burn.

The *Merénylő* strode towards Izsák, black coat flowing behind him.

The boy slashed with the knife.

Effortlessly, the assassin sidestepped.

One of the dignitaries turned to a nearby soldier and pointed at Izsák's father. Face livid, jaw clenched, he hissed, 'End this farce. *Right* now.'

'No!' Izsák screamed.

The soldier unshouldered his rifle. Lifted the sight to his cheek.

Szilárd bellowed.

A single shot rang out.

József's head knocked against the wooden platform as the bullet smashed through his skull. His left leg kicked and then he lay still.

On the stage, the *Főnök* lifted a hand to his mouth.

Izsák dropped the knife.

Stared.

His father alive. His father dead.

A boy with a family. A boy without.

A future.

A future lost.

The *Merénylő* swung his fist into Izsák's nose.

The boy spun, thoughts loosening in his head. He saw the fluttering pennants on the flagpoles, vivid slashes of colour. Birds wheeling in the sky. Gaping mouths in the crowd. Dark eyes. He saw Szilárd, down on his knees. Soldiers surrounding him, weapons raised.

He saw his father's corpse, and then – *even* then – as his face punched the grass and he felt the cold press of earth against his cheek, Izsák heard that treacherous question ringing in the head, singing in his ears despite the horror he had witnessed, and it clove him, destroyed him, proved to him beyond doubt that he was a failed son, a disgrace, a creature utterly incapable of empathy or love.

The question: *What will happen to me?*

The last things he saw, before the darkness gathered him up, was the predatory grin of the *Merénylő*, and, on the stage behind, the dust-speckled soles of his father's boots.

CHAPTER 11

Mürren, Switzerland

The woman peering out from behind the chalet's front door possessed a face of waif-like delicacy. At first, Leah thought they might be similar in age. But this woman's eyes – liquid brown, fringed with gold and as deep as mine shafts – betrayed a wisdom and a wariness that could have come only from decades of experience far outweighing Leah's own.

On her feet she wore Chinese silk slippers embroidered with pink roses. She'd wrapped a long angora cardigan around her frame.

The woman gazed down at Leah, and then she turned to Luca. 'So, who are you today?' Despite her fragility, her voice was hard. Strong.

'Luca,' he told her.

'Very well. And your friend?'

'I'm Leah Wilde,' Leah said, wanting to make this introduction on her own terms. 'Thank you for seeing me.'

The woman nodded. She trailed back inside the house, silk-bound feet whispering across the floor.

Leah turned to Luca, eyes questioning. When he gestured at her to go inside, she stepped into the chalet's hallway and followed the woman to the front room.

It was a restful space, spartan and cool. A low table stood on the varnished floor, its legs supporting a single slab of glass. Four maroon cushions had been arranged around it, and on its surface three Chinese tea bowls rested on bamboo mats, beside a steaming pot.

On the far wall someone had painted a mural of a woodland glade, rendered in pale green inks. A lacquered rosewood screen separated this part of the room from a dining area beyond.

When her host gestured to a cushion, Leah removed her boots and sat. 'I've never been to China.'

'I was happy there,' the woman replied. She shot Luca a dark look. 'A long time ago now.' Her eyes returned to Leah and she sank down opposite. 'You can call me Soraya. Would you like tea?'

'Please.'

Soraya poured three cups of green tea and placed one before Leah. 'Well. Now that we've made our introductions, you might tell me why you're here.'

Leah nodded, anxious now of how this woman might react to her, fearful of the consequences if this meeting did not go well. 'I don't mean to be blunt,' she said. 'But you're *kirekesztett*. Aren't you?'

Soraya's eyes narrowed, although seemingly more from pain than anger. 'It's a leash as good as any other.'

'I'm sorry. I had to ask. And . . .' Leah wondered how to phrase what she must ask next. 'Is it just you here? Did you ever have children? A family?'

The woman cringed. Hot tea splashed from her bowl onto her fingers. She laughed, and Leah could tell she had been stung by the question. 'Does this look to you like a place where children might live?'

'It doesn't, no. Did you want them?'

Another laugh, as brittle as matchsticks. 'What, so that they, too, could experience the unique delights of a *kirekesztett* life?'

'Soraya . . .' Luca warned.

Her eyes flashed. 'You'd have me lie to her? Would that make you feel better? Would that ease your guilt?' She turned back to Leah. 'It's an impertinent question from a stranger, I think, but since you seem to have come such a long way to ask it I'll indulge you, why not? Yes, I wanted a child. Of course I did. The reality, as I'm sure you're aware, is that it takes two to make a baby. I would have needed a partner. A lover. After the *tanács* made their pronouncement on me, how was I ever going to do that?'

Luca bristled at her words. 'We could have found someone,'

'Oh yes? One of Father's friends, perhaps. A murderer. Or maybe a rapist. That would have shortened the odds, I suppose.' Soraya shook her head. 'No. I wanted a child once, but it wouldn't have been right. And now . . .' She shrugged. 'Now, it's too late. And probably a blessing, in truth.'

So that was what connected these two, Leah thought. They were siblings.

Crouching forward on his cushion, Luca said, 'Tell her.' His eyes had darkened, the violet streaks escaping to the edges of his pupils. 'Tell her why you're here.'

Leah put down her tea. She swallowed; laced her fingers together. 'Soraya, what if I told you it might not be too late?'

The woman stared, her eyes unreadable. For a long while she said nothing. Then: 'You came here to talk. So talk.'

Leah did.

She explained, in the vaguest terms she could, the discovery, fifteen years earlier, that she and her mother were proof of something no one thought possible. She talked of how Hannah had assembled the group whose goal had been to unlock the mystery of the Wilde bloodline, in the hope that they could reverse the *hosszú életek*'s decline.

She recounted the years of failure and heartache, and how, just when it seemed like no solution would ever be found, a child was born.

Vita, they called her; the Latin word for *life*. Born as the result of an egg donated by Hannah Wilde, fertilised in vitro and carried to term by one of the programme's surrogate *hosszú élet* volunteers. It shouldn't have worked, and yet it had.

It gave them hope. More births followed. For a while the future looked bright. But for every miracle like Vita, they experienced a multitude of failures. Slowly it became clear that despite everything they had achieved, it wasn't going to be enough. While her mother had never admitted defeat, Leah could see the reality for herself. They simply did not have enough volunteers.

'And that's why I came to see you. If you want to be part of this, if you'd still like to have a child of your own, then I wanted you to know that it's perhaps not too late. I can't guarantee anything, and I haven't even begun to tell you of the dangers, but a year from now . . .' She shrugged. 'A year from now you could be a mother. The child might not share your genes, but it would be yours in every other way. Yours to love, yours to raise. I just wanted to come here and offer you the chance of that.'

She stopped, suddenly breathless, unprepared for the emotion that clenched her throat. They had done so much back in Calw, had come so far. And now everything they had accomplished, everything they could *still* accomplish, might rest on the reaction of a solitary *kirekesztett* woman, kneeling on a cushion, in this Mürren chalet at the top of the world.

Soraya's face had drained of colour. She placed her tea bowl down on a bamboo mat. 'Get out,' she whispered.

Defeated, Leah bowed her head. She'd known the chance of a positive outcome had been slim. But to hear it confirmed still pierced her with sorrow.

Grim-faced, Luca got up. 'Leah, come on. Let's go.'

'Not her. You,' Soraya said. 'Leave us, Luca. Go find a coffee house or something. Entertain yourself. I want to talk to Leah alone.'

Leah glanced up at him. She saw a tenderness in his expression, as he considered his sister, that melted her.

'You're sure?' he asked.

'Do as I say.'

Luca kept his eyes on Soraya a moment longer, then put down his tea and walked out of the house.

Leah sat staring at the table. When Luca had returned his bowl to its resting place he had knocked one of the bamboo mats out of alignment. She itched to nudge it back into position, but she kept her hands tight in her lap.

Mouth closed, she waited for Soraya to speak, knowing that anything she added now would be superfluous, that she had made her plea as best she could, and all she could do was hope.

Soraya said, 'It's a lot to take in.'

'Yes.'

'You've kept this well hidden, I must say. You've managed to ambush even Luca with these revelations of yours, and that's not something that happens often.'

'The *tanács* wished it to remain secret. They didn't want to give anyone false hope.'

Soraya tilted her head and stared, unblinking. 'How old are you, Leah?'

'Twenty-four.'

She nodded. 'How old were you when you found out you were *hosszú élet*?'

'Nine.'

'And when did you find out you were the last? That there were no more *hosszú életek* your own age?'

'When I was fifteen.'

'Not an easy thing for a fifteen-year-old girl to accept.'

Leah laughed. It caught in her throat, perilously close to a sob. She felt a flush rising on her cheeks.

'And yet,' Soraya continued, 'you *had* to accept it, didn't you? Until years later you find yourself here, among *kirekesztett*, among a second hidden society of *hosszú életek*, of whom you know so little. The question must burn in you.'

She could not trust herself to speak. Her hands, she noticed, had begun to shake. She plunged them deeper into her lap, feeling the strange woman's eyes upon her, feeling as each second passed the layers of armour with which she protected herself – like the hard coating of a pearl – melting away until they exposed the single gritty truth at the heart of her: her fear, her utter terror, of ending this journey alone.

She remembered the unutterable sense of loss she had felt the day she grasped the reality of her future: that if she were indeed the last *hosszú élet*, that if she had inherited that dreadful honour from Gabriel, then she was staring out into a world which, uniquely for her, contained no possibility of a soulmate, no one searching for her until their paths, knitted by fate, interwove. No one to confide in, to wrap herself around. No one with whom she could share her life.

At first she had refused to accept the brutal truth of it. Before his death, her mother had found with Nate the kind of closeness for which Leah yearned. Her grandmother Nicole, too, had created a relationship with Charles Meredith as fulfilled as any Leah had witnessed, unencumbered by the mismatch of their blood.

Both relationships had ended prematurely, of course, before their bonds could be tested. What would have happened once it became clear that while Charles and Nate aged, Nicole and Hannah did not? What heartache might that have brought? What pain?

Leah had seen one example of the anguish such an improperly balanced relationship could bring. She'd witnessed with wincing clarity the grief and the horror on Sebastien's face the day he walked into the kitchen at Le Moulin Bellerose and came face to face with the woman he had loved all those years ago. Éva must have looked, to Sebastien's tired old eyes, as beautiful as the last day he had seen her. How much must it have cost him to see his own face reflected in her eyes? How much must it have cost *her* to see Sebastien gnarled and beaten down by age, the ravages of time as visible as the actions of the ocean on a storm-tossed piece of driftwood?

Then, when Leah turned twenty-one, she met Thibaut.

He was a medical student, a surgeon's son, and their paths collided while he was on vacation from his studies in Frankfurt. At first she found herself incredibly awkward in his company; Thibaut exuded an effortless confidence, a mastery of everything he touched or considered. But he quickly put her at ease.

It took them two weeks to realise they were in love. Within a month, they had become like two heavenly bodies, orbiting each other in mutual fascination and worship.

She dated Thibaut for six months – keeping his existence a secret from her mother and Gabriel – before he invited her to stay at his parents' summer house in Moustiers-Sainte-Marie, southern France. There, Leah met his father for the first time, and experienced her first jolt of unease. The man was Thibaut's blood in every way: same grey eyes, same jawline, same wide shoulders and slim waist.

Although Raymond Aguillon's hair was the same black as his son's, it was feathered with grey, and beginning to recede at the temples. The skin around his eyes and throat had sagged a little, and the veins on the backs of his hands stood out a little more prominently. His forearms were grizzled with a thatch of coarse hair, and a few tufts grew on his earlobes.

Leah realised she was looking at a version of Thibaut in thirty years, a period during which Leah would have aged physically perhaps a handful of seasons. She pushed aside her unease with a burst of irritation, telling herself she could deal with that. She loved Thibaut: loved the man he was now; loved the man he would become.

Raymond Aguillon, she saw, possessed the same thirst for life as his son, the same love of conversation and laughter. He shared the same values. Could she imagine sharing her life with someone that much older, physically, than herself? Could she imagine being intimate? Yes, she could. Especially if they had already made a life together. Older couples continued to find each other attractive as they aged. Why shouldn't she?

Then, a month later in Paris, she met Thibaut's grandfather, and her unease blossomed into something darker, unfurling rotten flowers in the pit of her stomach, dripping a poison into her blood that she could feel swimming towards her heart.

In the kitchen of a tiny apartment within a few minutes' walk of the basilica on the hill of Montmartre, Leah stared across the table at a vision of Thibaut crippled by time.

Romain Aguillon, Thibaut's grandfather, shared the same eyes as his son and grandson, but they had grown milky with age. His body had shrivelled. His hair had fallen out, along with all of his teeth. His ears had continued to grow; two enormous gristle cups on each side of his head. He hawked dark phlegm and spat continuously into a handkerchief. When he stood to make coffee, he pulled himself along the counter with fingers stiffened into claws. His hands shook. He asked Leah her name four times before he remembered it.

She sat there, watching him, unable to stop the tears forming. That rotten flower unfurled new leaves and rolled creeping shoots through her veins, seeding her with dismay. Her emotions must have sat plainly on her face, because when Thibaut turned to her, his smile disappeared and he asked her what was wrong. Unable to speak, Leah fled outside.

Later that night, she castigated herself for the despair that had gripped her. Again, she asked herself the question: could she, in what might feel like the passage of only a few short years, imagine waking up each morning beside someone so cruelly emaciated by time as Romain Aguillon?

She would not need to think about the practical considerations of intimacy. There would be none at that stage of his life. She would have to content herself with caring for him, helping him to bathe and dress as he shambled inexorably towards his death.

Could she?

Alone with Thibaut that evening in Paris, Leah stared into his strong grey eyes and told herself that she could. She loved him, loved the essence of him, his soul and not his shell.

Would she be happy? Towards the end, perhaps not. Every day would be filled with mourning for the man who had once been her equal, both physically and mentally. Balling her hands into fists, she told herself that their years of happiness would pay for the pain at the end and the empty years that would follow. And she almost convinced herself.

They went to bed and Leah lay awake, and there in the darkness she realised how selfish her line of thought had been. She had considered all of this from her side alone, as if her own happiness were all that mattered.

Ashamed, she forced herself to view the situation through Thibaut's eyes. She remembered again the day, in the kitchen at Le Moulin Bellerose, that Sebastien had walked in to find Éva: how, in horror, he had hidden the cracks of his face and staggered outside, not wishing her to see the effects time and gravity had wrought on him.

Finally, late into the night, Leah knew what she must do. The idea of leaving Thibaut cramped her stomach so badly she could hardly stand. But if she stayed, if she allowed herself the luxury of more time, she would be indulging herself and failing him.

Weeping silent tears, bending over him in the darkness to kiss his forehead and smooth his brow, she mouthed a goodbye, packed her things and walked out into the night.

Despite their seven months together, he had never visited her home. The address she had given him was a fabrication. As she walked to the train station, she switched off her phone and threw it into a bin. It was the last she ever saw of Thibaut Aguillon.

Looking up, Leah found Soraya staring across the table at her, and knew that the woman read her thoughts as easily as if they had been etched onto her brow in ink.

Soraya was right: the question did burn in her. Through

disappointment and heartbreak, Leah had discovered why the *hosszú életek* did not look for partners among the *simavér*. And with the exception of the newborns who had arrived over the last few years, she remained the youngest among them.

The *kirekesztett*, however – disgraced and severed branch of that wider family – were an unknown. Leah was realistic enough to accept that most had deserved their exile, had committed crimes so repugnant that they likely deserved an even worse fate. But she also suspected that, on occasion, past *tanács* rulings of *kirekesztett* had been as harsh, or even more so, as whatever crime had sparked the judgement.

The possibility she dared not voice still existed. And even though she remained too frightened to unwrap the thought in case it disintegrated to dust, it spoke to her in dreams, rising up through her subconscious to haunt her.

'I'm sorry,' Soraya said. 'I know it's not the main reason for your visit. But if you came here, also, in the hope of finding love, you'll leave empty-handed. There are plenty of *kirekesztett* men who would spread your legs as soon as look at you. But none your own age. And even the ones you might look favourably upon have a history that would doubtless revolt you.

'We've been as barren in this nest of thieves and murderers as the *hosszú életek* we left behind. And by the grace of God, some might say . . . if any of them believed in Him any more.'

The words were like a vice, a plunge into iced water, but Leah forced herself to keep her chin raised, forced herself to breathe as if the wind had not been crushed from her lungs.

She felt a pressure building in her throat, a bolus of sadness and grief. And then, appalled, she found she was crying. Not racking graceless sobs; the tears came silently, and when Soraya saw them she moved around the table and took Leah into her arms.

They sat clutching each other that way for some time and, as Leah finally began to recover, she realised that Soraya trembled in her arms too. They laughed, wiping their faces and apologising.

'I think I might want this,' Soraya said eventually. 'I can't believe it, but I think I might.'

'I'm not here today to get an answer. I just wanted to offer you the choice. There are other things you should know before you make your decision. I haven't told you about the physical dangers yet, or what might happen if this leaks out too soon. There are some among the *tanács* who'd consider my presence here an outrage. But I don't believe they have the right to sit as gods and pass judgement upon who's worthy enough to bear children.'

'The *tanács* really don't know about this?'

Leah shook her head. 'It's complicated. I won't go into details now. Does that make a difference?'

'Not at all. In fact, I kind of like it.' Soraya hesitated. 'If I decided to do this . . . I really would be accepted?'

'You'd be accepted by everyone who's worked on this project. But the *tanács* can't know. We'd have to keep it a secret. It's the only way.'

'I'm guessing this isn't going to be as easy as just saying yes and coming back with you to this place of yours.'

'No. Being blunt, I've only just met you, and the centre's location is a secret. Its work – if lost – would mean the end for us all. But we can discuss all that later.'

'So what happens next? You need more than just one of us, I imagine.'

'Luca promised me that if you reacted favourably, he'd speak to others, ask them if they wanted to meet me, and draw up a list of any who said yes.'

'It won't be easy.'

'I know that.'

'Then let him make his calls, and draw up that list.' She paused. 'You're attracted to him, aren't you?'

Leah shook her head.

'Come on. I'm not stupid. You need to squash that. For your own sake.'

'I will.'

'I hope so. My brother is a lot of things. A suitable partner, he isn't.'

'I'm sure you're right.'

'Would I really have a baby?'

'You'd have a chance. A good chance. That's all I can offer you.'

The woman stood and for the first time since Leah had met her, her eyes seemed to sparkle.

CHAPTER 12

Budapest, Hungary

1873

The debate chamber of the *tanács* town house was located on the building's first floor. Its rear windows looked down into the formal square garden of the quad; its front windows faced the street.

The chamber's floor was laid with Italian Carrara marble polished to a high white shine – the same type of marble, the *Főnök* knew, used by the Emperor Hadrian to construct the Pantheon in Rome. It was a comparison that gave the old man little comfort.

The walls here were intricately stuccoed, and the domed ceiling bore a fresco designed to give the illusion that the space was open to a sky populated by ephemeral, benevolent gods.

Perhaps that's what we thought we were. Benevolent gods.

Now look at us.

He had picked the room not for its grandness or its symbolism, but for its light. The days following the events at the Citadella had contained far too much darkness, had bred shadows like a plague. The ruling *tanács* had become dependent on light, *addicted* to it; throwing back curtains, brightening rooms with candles, lamps and the hot sharp glow of electricity.

But light alone, the *Főnök* knew, could not end this crisis.

He sat at the oval table in the centre of the room, fingers steepled, staring at a vase of fresh-cut roses, red and white. Beside the flowers, its gilt-edged pages bound in vellum, rested an early copy of the *Vének Könyve*, most ancient of *hosszú életek* texts.

A pair of double doors in the chamber's long wall opened and a servant appeared. 'He's outside, Lord.'

The *Főnök* lifted his eyes from the roses. 'Has he eaten this morning?'

'We offered him breakfast, Lord. He refused.'

'Thank you. Please show him in.'

When Balázs Izsák walked through the doorway, the *Főnök* hoped to encourage him with a smile. But the boy's eyes were downcast. The servant pulled back a chair and Izsák sat, holding his hands together in his lap. While his face had healed physically from the blow he'd been dealt by the *Merénylő* days earlier, the trauma of witnessing his father's execution was etched into every inch of his flesh.

Pale skin. Shadowed eyes. Bloodless lips.

'Izsák?'

The boy lifted his head.

'You must try to eat. You need your strength right now. Food will help.'

He nodded. Listless.

'I had enormous respect for your father.'

'You killed him.'

'I—'

'Didn't you?'

The question jolted him; he wasn't used to interruptions. He took a breath.

Carefully now. Put yourself in the boy's place.

'What's befallen you, Izsák . . . what you saw. We all wished to protect you from that. This is a terrible, terrible thing that's happened. A monstrous thing. I don't, for one moment, expect you to forgive me for the choice I had to make. Perhaps one day you'll understand why, but forgiveness . . .' He let the sentence hang. 'I can't bring your father back. I can't erase the crimes of your *kirekesztett* brother. And neither can I return to you your old life. You're an innocent in all this, and I'm sure you feel like you're alone right now – that you've lost everything, everyone. But you're *not* alone. Far from it. Although you're grieving, Izsák, I'm sure you must have asked yourself, over these last days: What will happen to me?'

The boy stiffened. A flush of colour spread out across his cheeks.

Ah. So that's it.

'It's a survivor's question, Izsák. Not ignoble. Don't torture yourself over it. I can't change the past but I can, hopefully, ease your fears for the future. You heard your father's words before he died; we all heard them. I wish to honour his request. We've found a place for you. A safe place.'

'My uncle,' the boy began.

'Is incapacitated at present. And there are difficulties there.' The *Főnök* smiled. 'I would like you to meet someone.'

This time, when the doors opened, they admitted Dr András Benedek.

He knows, Izsák thought, reeling from a dagger-twist of shame as the old *hosszú életek* leader stood to greet the arriving stranger. *Somehow he's looked inside me and he's seen what lurks there: that even in my grief, all I worry about is myself.*

The newcomer was a short and portly man with wavy white hair, eyebrows like tufts of stiff cotton, and fern-green eyes striated with hazelnut. He was impeccably dressed: black trousers and highly polished shoes; a white shirt under a scarlet silk waistcoat fastened with buttons of pearl. His fingernails were immaculate. His skin looked soft and clean.

'Izsák,' the *Főnök* said, 'I would like you to meet Dr András Benedek.'

The doctor cleared his throat and smiled, displaying teeth

that were white and straight. 'I'm very pleased to meet you, Izsák. And I'm deeply sorry for your loss.'

'Thank you, sir.'

The *Fönök* placed his hand on the man's shoulder. 'Not only is our Dr András the most distinguished physician in Budapest, he is also – if you'll allow me, Benedek – one of our most celebrated philanthropists. He has taken into his care, over the years, countless *hosszú életek* youngsters like yourself, who, for one reason or another, have become separated from their families.'

The doctor blustered at the term *philanthropist*, but he nodded enthusiastically nevertheless. 'I have a place for you at my home, Izsák. A little ways along the river. Not far. Fine views, and very clean. You'll make friends, I'm sure. Others your own age.'

Izsák stared at his shoes.

An orphanage. That's what he means. I'm going to live in an orphanage.

The doctor's enclosed carriage was waiting on the street outside. With its shining black woodwork, polished brass coach lamps and spotless windows, it was as flawlessly presented as the man himself. The carriage door displayed the András coat of arms – a black lion and a harp against a shield quartered in white and green.

The horses, dappled greys in gleaming tack, shifted restlessly. A driver jumped down from the box and opened the door for them. András Benedek climbed inside, followed by Izsák.

They sat facing each other on seats of green leather, the same shade as the shield painted on the door. The interior walls were upholstered in green velvet. A polished wooden box was strapped to a shelf above the doctor's head. Again, the lion and a harp, on a quartered shield. Folded travel blankets displayed the same embroidered badge.

'Have you washed today?' András asked, studying Izsák's face.

'Yes, sir.'

'Hmm. Let me see your fingernails.'

He held them out. The carriage lurched, and with nothing to brace him he almost fell into the man's lap.

'Microorganisms,' the doctor said, as the carriage clattered along the street. 'You must guard against them.'

He nodded. 'I will.'

'Do you know what they are?'

'No, sir.'

'Ah. Well, for now, just be careful to keep your hands clean. It's how they spread, you see. Microorganisms lurk everywhere, Izsák. On food, in faeces, in the *very air*. I don't want you to worry, though. Tansik House is very clean. We're scrupulously hygienic.'

Izsák did not know what to say to that, so he thanked the man and stared out of the window at the sliding expanse of the Danube beside the road.

As their carriage rolled through the front gates into a huge rectangular courtyard, Izsák discovered that Tansik House was a *house* in the very loosest sense; it was virtually a palace. Reaching four storeys in height, the building was far wider than it was tall, with a massive central portico supported by six Corinthian columns. The front façade boasted more windows than Izsák could count, and the roof bristled with chimneys. In the centre of the courtyard, a fountain flung water thirty feet into the air. Their carriage curved a path around it, windows misting with spray, and pulled up beside the front steps.

'Based on a design by Palladio,' András told him. 'I've lived here sixty years. Starting to feel like home, actually. I hope you'll be happy.'

Izsák followed the doctor up the steps and found himself, moments later, in a grand entrance hall, itself the size of a church, on a chequerboard floor of black and white marble. Twin staircases, curving up from each side of the hall, served a grand gallery above them. On one wall hung an enormous oil painting of a man whose face shared many of the doctor's features. From the opposite wall hung a war banner, its fibres bleached and mouse-frayed, but still faintly displaying the same heraldic badge Izsák had seen on the coach. András Benedek, he realised, came from a *very* old family.

Now a set of doors opened in the left-hand wall and three maids came through, the first carrying a liquid-filled bowl and the others following with squares of linen.

'Ah, here we go,' the doctor said, pleased. 'We must wash off the germs from the road.' He dipped his hands in the bowl and stirred them around, drying them on a towel he took from a maid. 'Chlorinated lime water,' he said. 'Kills the micro-organisms. Very important for modern hygiene. I've made an extensive study. Follow me, I'll show you to where the others stay. '

András had established the children's quarters along the first floor of the south wing of Tansik House. Another man met them there. Dark hair, pale eyes, sombre suit.

'This is Trusov, Izsák, without whom we would all be cast adrift. I'll leave you in his care. We dine at seven. I join you when my work allows. Trusov, did Master Balázs's belongings arrive?'

'In his room, Doctor.'

'Splendid. Well, Izsák, I'll leave you now. Welcome to Tansik House.' Smiling, he walked away, footsteps echoing along the hall.

Trusov appraised him. 'Balázs, is it?'

He nodded.

'Follow me.'

Trusov led him down the hall and opened a door on the left. They entered a large, bright room. Its walls were painted a lemon yellow, the floorboards varnished a rich brown. The fireplace was stacked with kindling.

In one corner stood a single metal-framed bed. A wardrobe,

a washstand with jug and bowl, a writing desk and an empty bookshelf completed the room's furniture.

Moving to the window, Izsák looked out on formal gardens culminating in a circular pool, at the centre of which rose a limestone statue of a figure on horseback. Beyond that, he saw the dark windows of the north wing.

'There's a bathroom at the end of the hall, plumbed for hot water,' Trusov said. 'Your bath day is Wednesday. The maid brings hot water to your room every morning at six. Let her know if you run out of soap.'

'The doctor,' Izsák said. 'He's very keen on cleanliness.'

Trusov frowned. 'He's a little eccentric. But he's an outstanding man.'

'Oh, I didn't mean—'

'You'll get used to him.' The man strode to the wardrobe and threw open the doors. Izsák's clothes hung inside. Arranged on the bottom shelf was his paltry collection of belongings from Szilárd's house: the small suitcase, the box of metal soldiers, the silver hand mirror.

Trusov picked up the mirror, turning it over in his hands. 'You realise this is very valuable.'

'It was my mother's.'

The man glanced down at him. 'Then I'd hate for you to lose it. The children here are generally honest, but sometimes things go missing. I'll look after it for you. Just in case.' He nodded, the decision made. 'You can see it whenever you want.'

'Thank you. Do you live here too?'

'I have an apartment at the end of the hall. Very satisfactory. Well, I'll leave you to settle in.' Tucking the mirror into his pocket, Trusov left the room.

Izsák moved to the bed and sat down. He stared at the empty bookshelf, at the cupboard with its single box of soldiers and its suitcase, and told himself not to cry. The tears came anyway.

Two days since he'd watched his father die. Two months

since Jakab had raped the girl in Buda and disappeared. Two months since he'd seen Jani. Now one of his brothers hunted the other, and Izsák knew that only one would ever return from that encounter. Perhaps neither. Nothing waited for them in Budapest except their spineless younger brother, and who would want to return for that?

All those days he had asked himself the question: *What will happen to me?* And now he was looking at the answer. A silent room in a stranger's house; an empty bookshelf; a place to wash and be clean.

A tear rolled off his nose and struck the back of his hand.

Perhaps if you'd focused on something other than your own selfish needs, this wouldn't have happened. Perhaps if you'd been braver, more decisive, perhaps if you hadn't cowered in the Citadella, quaking with fear until it was too late to save—

'Hello.'

With a cry, Izsák shot up off the bed. A scrubbed face was peering around the door frame, and he saw that it belonged to a girl perhaps a year or so older than himself. She was, at once, both intimidatingly beautiful and hopelessly frail, her limbs like birch sticks connected by lumpen elbows and knees. Her face, framed by tresses of hair as dark and glossy as licorice, looked older than it should, forced somehow, as if she had decided to make herself a woman despite her lack of years.

She smiled, a hesitant experiment, and when he wiped his face of tears she slid into the room and climbed onto the bed.

'I'm Etienne,' the girl said. 'You're new.'

Nodding, he sat back down.

'What's your name?'

'Izsák.'

'Family?'

He shook his head, sensing it was wiser to keep his history to himself for now.

'You were crying.'

'I . . . it's just a bit new, that's all.'

'Lonely.'

He took a long, shuddering breath. Shrugged. Then he raised his head. She returned his gaze with large, round eyes. Despite her sparsity of flesh, her skin was rosy. Chlorinated lime water, Izsák thought.

'I know a cure for loneliness,' Etienne said. And then, as casually as if she were plucking a book from a shelf, she reached between his legs and gripped him.

Shocked, Izsák scrabbled away from her. 'What are you *doing*?'

'It'll make you feel better.'

'I don't want that.'

Etienne looked confused. 'Do you want to touch me instead?' she asked, taking the bottom of her dress and rolling it up past her knees.

'No!'

She tilted her head at him. 'You prefer boys.'

'*Ets!*'

Izsák twisted towards the door. This time he saw three boys hovering there. As one, they slouched into the room.

The tallest frowned at the girl on the bed. 'Put it away, Ets. No one wants to see that this close to breakfast.' He turned to Izsák. 'I'm Béni.' He pointed to the scrawnier of his two companions. 'That's János.' Indicating the third boy, a fat youngster with a spool of dribble clinging to his chin, he added, 'And that's Pig.'

Pig spied the box of toy soldiers in Izsák's wardrobe and let out a squeal. 'Bang men!' he cried. 'Bang men! Can I, Béni? Can I?'

Béni raised an eyebrow. 'Can he?'

'Well, I suppose. As long as he's careful.'

Pig clapped his hands in delight and snatched up the box. Sitting cross-legged on the floor, he tried to ease off the lid with stubby, clumsy fingers. When he couldn't manage it, he raised his head to Béni, crestfallen.

Sighing, Béni crouched down and opened it, sprinkling the metal soldiers into a heap. Pig clapped again, the string of drool now so long it connected him to the floor.

Béni looked up. 'So, new boy. What's your name?'

'His name's Izsák,' Etienne said. 'And he's my friend.'

'Everyone's your friend, Ets,' Béni said. He turned back to Izsák. 'What happened to you?'

'Nothing.'

'Something must have. You're not here as a treat. Parents dead?'

Izsák hesitated. Then he nodded.

'You'll get used to it. And you'll either survive here or you won't. First thing's to learn the rules.'

'Rules?'

'Keep yourself clean. The doctor's funny about that. Microorganisms. His favourite thing.'

'He told me about them.'

'Course he did. Lessons on weekdays, mostly in the mornings. Stay out of the north wing, that's where the doctor lives. Don't let him catch you stealing from his library. He's funny about his books, too. Oh, this is really important. If you see his daughter, don't talk to her.'

'He has a daughter?'

Béni nodded. 'Same age as us, about. You'll see her in the garden sometimes. Just stay away.'

'Why?'

The boy stared for a moment, and his eyes seemed to lose their focus. Then he glanced back down at Pig. 'Food's the best thing. As much as you want, as long as you brush your teeth afterwards. Stay away from Trusov if you can.'

'He's nice,' Etienne protested.

Béni rolled his eyes. 'Yeah. If you like being fucked. Has he stolen anything off you yet?'

'He offered to look after my mirror.'

'You give it to him?'

'Yes, I—'

'Last time you'll see that.' He pointed to the soldiers. 'We should divide those up. Easier to hide them that way.'

Izsák wasn't about to be made foolish twice. 'I'll keep them safe.'

'Fair enough. Want to see the rest of the house?'

He did. Anything, in fact, to get out of this room, so suddenly full of people. He climbed to his feet. 'Is it just you four? Here, I mean?'

'Two others at the moment. Magdolna and Rózsika. Six of us in all. There were more. But . . .' He shrugged. Again, that strange look in his eyes. 'Now there's just us.'

On the floor, Pig had lined up the toy soldiers in a row. Now he dragged his finger through their ranks, knocking them all back down. 'Bang!' he said. 'Bang! Bang!'

They ate dinner that evening in the formal dining room - steaming bowls of *paprikás krumpli* with sweated greens and fresh bread. Lunch, Béni explained to him, was the big culinary event of the day, but they ate well at breakfast and dinner too. Izsák saw Magdolna and Rózsika, two sisters who bowed their heads and ate in silence. When the doctor failed to join them, Béni explained that András Benedek's presence at table was a rarity.

That night, alone in bed, Izsák stared up at the high ceiling in his room, yearning for sleep but with a mind too disorientated to find it. He owned no watch, no clock to tell the time, but he knew he lay there for hours. As the moon rolled out of sight, arcing over the roof of Tansik House, his thoughts turned again to Jakab and Jani. He could not understand, even now, how the *tanács* had seen fit to set brother upon brother. Jakab had sinned, yes, but Jani had done nothing wrong. As if the execution of their father had not wreaked enough destruction on their family.

When he heard movement in the hall, Izsák slipped out of bed and tiptoed across the room. Bending to the keyhole, he recognised the bone-thin shape of Etienne as she passed. The girl wore a long nightdress, hanging like a shroud from her sharp shoulder blades.

Izsák eased open his door and poked out his head. He watched her advance to the end of the corridor, where she knocked at a door. When it opened he saw Trusov's face, ghoulish in the candlelight spilling from the room beyond. Etienne entered, and the door closed behind her.

Izsák went back to his bed. A few minutes later, he heard, floating down the hallway outside, the steady creak of bedsprings, a metronomic nightmare in the darkness.

That first week at Tansik House rolled by in a welter of new experiences. Izsák spent his days with Béni and János, exploring the mansion and sitting through lessons with Ludwig Heidegger, the bespectacled Belgian academic who visited five days a week, taught them Latin and mathematics, and every lunchtime filled his leather case with as many bread rolls, pastries and slices of ham as he could comfortably spirit away.

He fell quickly into the daily routine. Up at six to wash his hands and face, breakfast at seven, lessons at eight. Lunch was served in the dining room, or on a blanket outside if the weather was clement. Each night he lay rigid in his bed, unable to find sleep until the wheezing gasps of Trusov's bedsprings ceased their exertions. He didn't know what he should think about that, or what he should do about it, conscious he hadn't even raised the subject with his three friends. Some nights, when he spied Etienne returning to her room, he noticed that her nightdress was stained with blood. He saw no wounds on her face or elsewhere on those evenings, and wondered whether the girl healed herself of her injuries before she left Trusov's apartment.

On his eighth day at Tansik House, Izsák met the doctor's daughter.

He was sitting on a bench in the formal gardens opposite the

pool, *Gesta Hungarorum* open on his lap, reading a passage he
had been set by the Belgian tutor.

The girl, a fresh wisp of white cotton and blue ribbon,
appeared at his side, tucked her skirts under her legs and sat
down next to him. 'Hello,' she said. 'I'm Katalin. I've read that.'

Izsák stared. 'Are you new?'

She laughed. 'No. I'm not new.'

'What are you doing here, then?'

Katalin nodded towards the plinth rising from the middle of
the pool, and the statue of the man riding horseback atop it. 'I'll
give you a clue. That's my grandfather.'

His mouth dropped open. 'You're the doctor's daughter.'

'Finally the boy catches up.'

'I'm not supposed to talk to you.'

'Who said that?'

'They all said.'

Katalin frowned. 'Why not?'

'I don't know.'

'Do you obey rules you don't understand?'

'I—'

'You're him, aren't you? I mean, *he's* your brother. The one
that's caused all the trouble.'

Izsák dropped his head. 'Lukács.'

'You shouldn't say his old name. He's a *kirekesztett* now.
Jakab, they're calling him. In fact, better that you say nothing at
all, to anyone. Your other brother's gone after him, hasn't he?'

'Yes.'

'I heard about your father.'

Tears sprang into his eyes. An automatic reaction, every time
someone reminded him of what he'd seen at the Citadella.

'Don't cry, I'm sorry. I shouldn't have said anything. I'm not
really very good at making conversation. Here.' She proffered
a delicate square of silk. He scrunched it into his eyes, handed
it back.

'Keep it,' she said. 'I have a drawerful. Looks like you need it more than me. I'm really sorry. I didn't think. Sometimes my mouth just runs away.'

'It's OK.'

She nodded. 'What do you want to be?'

The girl's thoughts seemed to dance randomly. He struggled to keep up.

'What do you want to be?' she repeated. 'When you're older?'

'I'm not sure.'

'Well, you should think. Everyone should have a plan.'

'I don't.'

'Maybe it would help if you thought about it a bit. About the future, I mean.'

'I suppose. I suppose I just—'

'*Balázs!*'

Izsák saw Trusov bounding down the steps from the house. The man marched towards them, his face scarlet.

'I have to go,' Katalin said. She jumped off the bench, brushed down her skirts and hurried back to the house, averting her eyes from Trusov as he passed.

By the time he reached Izsák the man was panting, face wet with sweat. The cords of his neck were swollen and throbbing. 'What were you doing with her?' he hissed.

Izsák shot to his feet. 'We were just talking. She—'

He never finished the sentence. With brutal force, Trusov slapped him across the face. Izsák reeled backwards, blood flying from his mouth.

He crashed to the paving stones, too stunned to feel any pain. Shaking his head to clear it, he saw the man bearing down on him and tried to scrabble backwards. Trusov was too fast. He caught a fistful of Izsák's clothes and dragged him towards the pool, eyes like black holes.

Izsák tried to twist loose, but Trusov brought up his knee. He heard one of his ribs crack. Grabbed by the back of the neck, he found himself staring over the lip of the pool.

'You do *not!*' the man screamed, and dunked Izsák's head

beneath the surface. The cold water was a shock, the sudden darkness more so. He thrashed, desperate to break loose, but another knee connected with his ribcage, emptying his lungs in a stream of bubbles. Now the pain hit. He clamped his mouth shut against it and went loose, terrified that the last of his breath would escape.

Trusov jerked him back over the lip in a slopping tide. '*Talk!*'

Again, Izsák plunged beneath the water. He hadn't taken his chance to breathe. His diaphragm convulsed. He fought against the compulsion to open his mouth.

Now he felt himself dragged out of the pool once more. This time he gasped a huge lungful of air.

'To the *girl!*' Trusov screamed. Trembling with rage, he flung Izsák to the ground and stalked back towards the house.

Lying on his side, Izsák curled up his limbs, a crippled insect. Water dripped from his hair, staining the paving stones black. He took short breaths, each one slicing a blade into his torso where his attacker had split his ribs.

Pig found him.

'Hurt you,' the boy said, crouching down and stroking Izsák's head. 'Not good man. Hurt you.'

Izsák found just enough strength to nod. They stayed like that for a while, until Pig waddled off and returned with Béni and János. Together, they helped him back to the house.

An hour later he sat on a chair in the doctor's study, watching as the man felt his ribs.

'Trusov tells me you hurt yourself while trying to escape from him. Is that correct?'

'I . . .' He hesitated, certain that to tell the truth of what had occurred would not serve him well. 'Yes, sir.'

András Benedek frowned. 'He says he found you talking to Katalin. That when he approached, you attacked him and ran. He chased you and you fell.'

Izsák bowed his head. Too late to change his mind now; he would have to concur with whatever script the doctor's madman had written. Miserable, he nodded.

'You're most welcome in this house, Izsák. But you must obey our rules, and one of those rules is that you must not have any contact with Katalin. Do you understand?'

'Yes, sir. I'm sorry. I didn't know.'

'That's right. Nobody told you, and that's not your fault. But I'm telling you now. You must respect my daughter's privacy.'

'I will. May I ask a question?'

'Certainly.'

'Why? I mean, why the rule?'

The doctor jerked, eyes widening. Then his expression softened. 'We keep a very clean house, Izsák. The most hygienic in Budapest, I'd like to think. But I can't clean your blood and yours, I'm afraid, is tainted. We'll educate you, feed and clothe you, send you out into the world. But I can't do anything to purify your blood. So until modern medicine catches up, I'm afraid we'll have to keep you apart from girls like Katalin.' He patted Izsák's leg. 'Now, stand up. Let me show you how to heal your ribs.'

Later, as he lay in darkness on his bed, his repaired bones itching, someone knocked at his door. He was too lethargic to move. Too shocked, perhaps, by Trusov's attack; even more so by András Benedek's words.

He wondered who it was. He had not yet heard the swish of fabric that announced Etienne's nightly pilgrimage to Trusov's apartment. If Béni or János stood outside, they would likely go away if he refused to answer.

The knock came again, louder this time. Again Izsák ignored it, willing his visitor to leave. And then the door opened and Katalin slipped inside.

He shot up in bed, panicked. 'You can't be here,' he hissed.

'Well, I am,' she replied, crossing the floor and perching on his bed. 'I couldn't sleep. Not after what happened.'

'If they find you—'

'I know. They'll take it out on you, not me. I'm sorry. This is really selfish. I don't want to get you into any more trouble. But I had make sure you were all right. Are you? All right, I mean?'

'I've felt better. Trusov – he's crazy.'

'They all are, a little.'

'What kind of place is this? Where the hell have I ended up?'

There was little humour in Katalin's smile. 'Purgatory,' she said.

'That's not funny.' Izsák hesitated. 'Do you know about Etienne?

'About her and Trusov? They're not exactly discreet. He feels guilty about it, I'm sure. I think that's why he gets so angry. I think that's why he went crazy when he saw you talking to me.'

'I don't understand.'

'Trusov's not the predatory type, whatever you might think. What he is, is weak. He didn't pursue Ets. She pursued him.'

'Come on.'

'It sounds unlikely, I know. But it's true. The sort of attention she gets from Trusov is all she's ever known. It's why she tries to make herself look older. Why do you think she's here, Izsák? What's happening to her now, it was happening before. She had a father, uncles. They did that, treated her that way. After a while I think it became the only way she could seek affection. Has she tried it with you?'

'The first day.'

'See? It doesn't make Trusov any less of a monster for taking what she offers. But now he's done it, I think he worries he'll do it to someone else, too.'

'Like you.'

'Exactly like me. And that scares him. When he saw you talking to me, all that anger came out.'

'Aren't you frightened?'

'Of course. But I always carry a knife. If he tries it, I'm going to stab him.' Katalin reached out and touched Izsák's chest. Her fingers were cold. 'Just here,' she said. 'Right through his heart.'

Outside, they heard a creak of floorboards as Etienne made her way along the hall, seeking her comfort.

Izsák shivered. 'What kind of place is this?' he asked again.

'A bad place,' she said. 'You should lock your door at night.'

He stared at her, at the haunted eyes that stared back at him. He wondered if she referred to Trusov, but somehow he knew she was talking about something far worse.

CHAPTER 13

Mürren, Switzerland

Sitting at a window table in the wood-panelled restaurant of the Hotel Berchtold after her meeting with Soraya, Leah found that her stomach was cramping with hunger. She scanned the restaurant's menu and called over a waiter, ordering a plate of cured meats and a basket of fries. Luca Sultés, sitting opposite, requested sparkling water and a bowl of fruit. On the street outside, a trio of snowboarders walked past, gear slung over their shoulders.

'So,' Leah said, after the waiter had returned with their order. 'Soraya didn't throw me out.'

'She didn't.'

'You weren't expecting that.'

'Wasn't I?'

'You tell me.'

Luca stared at his bowl of fruit. Then he reached forward and plucked up one of her fries. 'I didn't know how she would react. But I thought the chances were slim.'

'You underestimated her.'

'Perhaps I underestimated you.'

'Perhaps you did.'

'I know what you're going to ask next.'

'We had a deal,' she replied. 'If Soraya said yes, you'd speak to the others. You'd give me a list of those prepared to talk.'

'She hasn't said yes. Not yet.'

'I think she will.'

He nodded. 'Perhaps.'

'So you'll talk to the others.'

'I said *maybe* I would talk to the others.'

'What does that mean?'

'Patience isn't really a virtue with you, is it?'

'I don't have time for patience. You know how precarious this is. You'll either help me or you won't. I know you've already made your decision. Whatever I say won't sway you. So let's just hear it.'

Luca glanced outside at the mountains, and then his gaze returned to her face. The violet patterns in his eyes glowed so vividly they seemed to drain the colour from everything around them. 'I'm not quite the games player you think.'

'Meaning?'

'If Soraya wants to take this chance, I'll support her. If others wish to join her, that's a decision for them, not me.'

'So you'll agree to do it?'

He shrugged. 'I thought I just did.'

At his words, Leah felt the breath go out of her in a wave of exhaustion and relief. She felt so tired, all of a sudden, that it was an effort not rest her head against the window pane. 'What happens now?'

Luca finished his water. 'We go back to the house. Later, I'll make some calls. You'll stay with us tonight, and in the morning—'

'I have a hotel.'

'No.' His expression hardened. 'You'll stay with us tonight, and you'll listen when people offer you their protection. I don't know what you're used to back home, but don't tell me you come and go as you please, because I won't believe it. I hear a lot. I know the *tanács* is in a state of turmoil. The new *Fönök* has failed to bring unity, and I wouldn't be surprised if it all boils over soon. When what you're doing over here gets out, you're going to throw a live grenade into the middle of it, and that's when you'll need to keep your eyes open and know who your friends are.'

'It won't get out.'

'You don't think? Listen to me. If I have one skill, it's how to read people. I can tell you're doing this for the right reasons, and I can also tell that you have no idea how much danger you're putting yourself in. Out here,' he said, motioning towards the mountains, 'it's even worse. You're in the Wild West now. There are no rules beyond that glass. No safety net.'

'What's out there, Luca, that makes you so concerned for my safety? You talked of the *tanács*, but don't ask me to believe you're worried about them. This is more immediate. This . . .' She frowned. 'It has something to do with your visitors last night, doesn't it? Those . . . *tolvajok*.'

Luca stared at her, tight-lipped. Was that *fear* she saw in his eyes? Surely not.

He leaned across the table, keeping his voice low. 'We'll go back together, like I said. You'll stay another night. We'll talk, and later this evening I'll make some calls. In the morning you'll have your list. How many names it'll contain, I can't say. But one thing I can tell you. You'll not find many of the women you seek in Switzerland. We're going to rack up some air miles getting this done. The—'

'Hold on. We?'

'We'll visit those women together, Leah.'

'No. No way.' She saw his expression darken further, and ignored it. 'I go alone, Luca. I'm grateful for your help, but this is something I need to do by myself. No debate. Afterwards, when it's done . . .' She let her words hang.

His frown held a moment longer, and then began to fade, as if he sensed that any attempt to change her mind would fail.

'Is the cable car really the only way down from here?' she asked.

'There's a train. We can take that.'

'You're a bastard.'

'Are you cured?'

'Of bastards? I guess not.'

He grinned, and then his eyes drifted over to the window and his expression froze.

Leah switched her attention to the street outside, and the warmth fled from her limbs.

The figure crossing the road towards the hotel was tall – easily over six feet – and impeccably dressed. He wore a jacket of herringbone tweed over a pale doeskin waistcoat. A scarlet cravat was tied at his throat. His corduroy trousers were mustard yellow, over lace-up shoes as glossy as black treacle. A fedora sat on his head, a jay feather tucked into the band, and he carried a walking cane, swinging it to and fro. Beneath the hat, a great bunch of dirty blond hair was gathered in a loose ponytail.

As the stranger stepped onto the pavement, Leah realised that although he carried himself like a man of middle years, his face looked wrong. Mismatched, somehow. Fleshy and jowled and unquestionably aristocratic, it was nevertheless lined with cracks and folds, like sun-baked earth. His eyes were lost in the sunken concavities of his skull.

The creature – for that, she suddenly intuited, was what it really was – came to a halt on the other side of the window. When it swung its head towards Leah a thrill of fear rushed through her, as if she'd been plunged into iced water. There was something awful about its face. Something apelike behind its countenance; doglike.

Luca rose to his feet. His coat caught the empty water glass and knocked it on to its side. It rolled across the table and came to a rest against a tray of condiments. 'Get up,' he hissed. 'Now.'

Outside, the stranger lifted its cane. A flared silver python's head topped the slim black shaft, its fangs picked out in gold. The sharp end, capped in metal, struck the window with a click: the sound of a toenail, or claw, or talon.

'*Leah.*'

She shook herself. Tore her eyes away.

Luca's face was pale. 'We need to go. *Now.*'

Nodding, she stumbled to her feet. The bell above the restaurant's entrance jangled and she turned in time to see the stranger appear in the doorway. Almost at once, Leah noticed the odour. It seeped towards her, fleeting and elusive, but she shuddered with its foulness nonetheless. It was the scent of decay, of corrupted flesh; a greasy, eye-watering *meat* smell.

This close, even in her fear, she registered something strange: the creature's clothes were flawless, not a speck of dirt or a scuff or a trailing thread. The black shaft of its walking stick shone like a rod of purest midnight. In fact, the only article out of place was its hair. Dark blond and thick, matted and foul with grease, tangled almost to dreadlocks, it was gathered in a bunch that trailed halfway down its spine; a strangle of worms.

Nostrils pulsing, it sniffed, a long inhalation. When it exhaled, Leah caught that odour again. This time there was nothing subtle about it; it was the smell of an opened coffin, a blast of putrefaction, the stench of a corpse pile.

The stranger lifted the cane and tapped the end of it three times on the floor. It seems lost in thought, puzzled. And then it turned its face to her and she saw its eyes clearly for the first time – two black chasms of emptiness. It grinned, lips skinned back from its teeth, and Leah felt as though someone had pressed a finger through her eye and scraped a nail down the inside of her skull.

She felt a hand grasp her shoulder. Nearly screamed. But it was Luca, pulling her from the table.

'Come on,' he urged, dragging her away. She struggled to make her legs move, found herself being towed backwards, past empty tables and startled waiters, into a kitchen of stainless-steel work surfaces and bubbling pots, and outside to a storage area of stacked wooden pallets and bins.

'What was it?' she gasped, eyes swimming with the sudden cold. 'What *was* that?'

But she knew the answer without being told. And suddenly she was very frightened indeed.

'We're not safe yet,' Luca said. 'Run.'

Inside the restaurant, the *tolvaj* remained still, head cocked to one side. Something looped away from it, buzzing, and landed on the nearest table: a bluebottle, fat and bloated. Its metallic body shimmered as it crawled around in a circle, vibrating its wings with a sound like a burst of static.

A second bluebottle landed beside it. It skittered around the first, as if unsure of what exactly it was doing there. After a moment's hesitation, it climbed onto the other insect's back. There, on the restaurant table, the two bluebottles began to mate.

CHAPTER 14

London, England

On the third floor of the Georgian town house where she lived, Etienne stood at the bedroom window and watched storm clouds, like a pack of grey wolves, race eastwards towards Mayfair from the direction of Hyde Park.

In the distance, a flicker of light singed the monochrome day and moments later she heard a grumble of thunder, and felt it in her chest. Down on the street, black cabs scurried like sparrows beneath the eye of a hawk. It was ten minutes to one in the afternoon. Her guest would be arriving soon.

Etienne felt a brush of emotion; a shallow wave breaking against her. She examined it with curious detachment – so rare for her to feel anything these days – and discovered that what she felt was unease.

Strange.

Yet out of all the visitors she entertained within these walls, the one whose arrival she now anticipated possessed the singular ability to dredge feelings in her, stirring up the silt-laden graveyard at her core like the dragged nets of an ocean trawler. Pity, distaste, revulsion even; she'd felt all those, to a greater or lesser extent, during her times with him. But unease? That one was new, and she rolled it around in her head, savouring the stomach-gnawing bitterness of it.

She could, of course, refuse him. Jackson and Bartoli, on

duty in the building's fortified ground floor, could fight off an armed assault team if she wished.

Usually she tolerated only one of her security personnel in the house at a time; their presence was a disagreeable impingement on her privacy. This morning, however, she had phoned Jackson – of all her guards the most trusted – and suggested that he spend the day with Bartoli. The coming storm, she lied, had left her feeling vulnerable.

Etienne knew that Jackson heard the deception in her voice – how long since she'd ever felt *vulnerable*? – but he did not question her, and now he toured the ground floor with Yoko, his four-year-old Vizsla, checking rooms and windows.

Yes, she could refuse her visitor. But she would not. She had not purchased this sprawling Mayfair residence – the art that hung from its walls, the clothes that hung in its dressing rooms, the beautiful, luxurious *silence* of this building standing in the elegant heart of London's most desirable district – by recoiling in the face of danger. She had lived here near seventy years, had ceased to want for money or luxuries far longer. Yet still she continued at this task.

This vocation of yours, she added, mocking herself.

She knew that a hunger dwelled in her, in that place where happier emotions should reside, a hunger she could neither sate nor deny. While her compulsion to scratch that itch never faded, she knew that she performed a service to the world in these cool West London rooms. While it was work for which she would receive not a single word of thanks, its value, Etienne believed, could not be denied.

Outside, another peal of thunder rolled over London from the park. When the sound receded, Etienne heard a *snick* as the hands of a gilded rococo clock on the mantelpiece found their one o'clock groove and chimed the hour. A moment later, the phone beside her bed buzzed. Barefoot, Etienne padded across the carpet and picked it up.

'He's here. Outside.' Jackson's voice. 'Bartoli's watching him now.'

'Then let him through. All the usual checks. Don't lower your guard with this one.'

'Of course not.'

'Send him up as soon as you're satisfied.'

'The Aviary?'

'If you would.'

Etienne replaced the phone's receiver and walked to the corner of the room, where three floor-length mirrors waited. She discarded her kimono, the silk fluttering like butterfly wings as it shimmered to the floor.

Lifting her head, she began to examine every inch of her body, critiquing the muscular curves of her calves and thighs, the pleasing concavity of her stomach, the swell of her breasts. She glanced over her shoulder at the subtle bumps and shallows that formed her spine. She held out her arms and stared at her skin, at the honey-golden colour of it, at its tiny pale hairs. Turning her hands palms down, she searched for age lines, for a broken nail or a spot of dirt or a dry cuticle. She found none.

Etienne raised her eyes to the reflected face that looked back at her and saw a mask of living flesh. Flawless. Emotionless. Exactly what she expected to see. Her eyes betrayed nothing of her thoughts. Even so, she could not meet them for long. While her body, in its sculpted perfection, often enthralled her, she could never hold her own gaze for more than a moment. Instead she examined lips, nose, teeth. She had not styled her hair today but she had combed it; it hung either side of her face, a glossy curtain of blue-black.

Turning full circle, watching her body through all the angles the mirrors provided, Etienne decided she was ready. Her visitor would not wish to see any of this, but she needed to. This had become a ceremony she performed before the arrival of every one of her guests.

Naked, she opened the bedroom door and walked out into the hall, the cool air raising on her skin a rash of goosebumps that faded as quickly as it had appeared.

The Aviary waited on the second floor at the back of the house, accessed via a landing off the building's central staircase or through an adjoining antechamber. Etienne had no desire to meet her visitor on the stairs. Instead, she walked along the third-floor hall from her bedroom, bare feet sinking into the carpet, and let herself through the last door on this side of the landing. Unlike the other rooms in the house, all of which had been renovated, *this* room and the one immediately below it remained as they had been found.

Paper curled from its walls. Flaking paint peeled from woodwork. At its centre waited a spiral staircase of cast iron, corkscrewing down into the antechamber below. Etienne descended, the metal rungs cold against her feet.

The walls and ceiling of the antechamber were stained, decrepit. Cobwebs shivered in corners. The single window was grey with dust; beneath it stood a neglected dressing table and stool. Five wooden wardrobes lined one wall. Along another, three more angled mirrors, and the door that led to the Aviary.

Etienne placed her fingers on its handle and paused, listening. The room beyond was silent, but she would struggle to hear him even if he stood right on the other side.

Contemplating that, she found herself jolted by another emotion, one that had not visited her in years: fear.

She closed her eyes.

Ridiculous. What's happened to you today?

Outside, thunder rumbled, as if somewhere in the city skyscrapers were toppling.

Perhaps it's the storm, she thought. Perhaps it's just that.

Etienne opened the door. A moment later, her spiking heartbeat already beginning to slow, she stepped across the threshold.

* * *

Strange, in a way, that she still called this room the Aviary. No birds sang in its cages; no wings beat a draught upon the air. When she had purchased the house all those years ago, this part had been uninhabitable, untouched since its Victorian resident had expired following a prolonged dive into insanity. Down in the cellar she'd found, wrapped in bandages, a portrait of the man. His pale face loomed from the canvas, hair pasted to his scalp, eyes bulging in paranoia. Several times Etienne had thrown the painting away. On each occasion, unable to explain why, she had rescued it.

Elsewhere, she discovered evidence of the man's dark obsessions. The Aviary was boarded up when she arrived. She tore down the planks herself, using a claw hammer to prise them away from the jamb. When she found the door locked, and its key absent from the bunch she'd inherited, Etienne hacked through the wood with an axe, bursting into a room as resistant to reason as the mind of a lunatic.

Against the far wall stood a row of ebonised display cases, similar to those she'd seen in the Natural History Museum over on Exhibition Road. Dust caked the glass like a skin, and when she wiped it away she saw the eyes of perhaps twenty birds staring out at her.

They had been preserved, but badly: bodies overstuffed, beaks broken, glass eyes imprecisely attached. As Etienne smeared her hand further along the dust-felted windows, she revealed a taxidermy project more peculiar and twisted than anything she could have imagined. The animals lurking inside those cases had never walked naturally upon the earth. *Parts* of them had; that much was obvious. But the woeful specimens that greeted her possessed a carnival-show horror. They were hybrids, abominations: creations sewn together by a misfiring mind. Here, the head of a cat attached to the body of a chimp. Beside it, the shrivelled head of a new-born lamb fused to the body of a snake; crude bat wings had been stitched all the way along the snake's torso.

In one corner of the room Etienne saw a heap of animal bones, reaching as high as her waist. And, hanging from the ceiling, the birdcages. They reminded her of lobster pots, although these had been fashioned from iron or brass. In some perched the skeletons of parrots, their bones held together with wire. Other cages contained heaps of tiny, air-dried carcasses – vaguely feathered husks that had presumably lain there since they'd fallen from their perches a century earlier. The floor was spattered with old droppings. On shelves, collections of bird skulls.

Etienne threw open the windows, letting in air and light. She took out the museum cases and their residents, burning them in the garden. The bone pile and the shelves with their papery skulls disappeared. She instructed her workmen to paint the walls, floorboards and ceiling a brilliant white, but she didn't remove the birdcages. She emptied them of their dead, cleaned and painted them, and snapped off each of their doors. After that she hung them back up, perhaps a hundred of them. With the Aviary's windows open, their metal chains and bars clinked as they swung against each other in the breeze.

Today, however, the windows remained closed, and the birdcages were still: silent and empty prison cells from which the dead had taken flight.

A rattan screen zigzagged the width of the room, dividing it in two. Waiting nearby, a single chaise longue, upholstered in gold fabric. The only additional colour on this side of the screen came from the hundreds of tiny birds delicately hand-painted on to the walls: scarlet macaws, iridescent toucans, flashing kingfishers; no more than a single example of any individual species, each one rendered in a size no longer than her finger.

Etienne moved to the chaise longue and sat. She pressed her knees together. Through the gaps in the rattan screen, she saw that the room's partitioned side was unoccupied. At its centre stood a single Louis XV armchair. Unlike the chaise longue, it was upholstered in blood-red silk.

A door opened. A draught set the bird cages jangling. The door closed and she heard footsteps. A creak from the springs of the blood-red chair.

Etienne sensed him, now. Sensed his darkness; his rage; his white-knuckle self-discipline. She knew that the face he wore in her presence was not his own; other than his name, it was *all* she knew of him, despite the length of their acquaintance. Masking one's features like that among fellow *hosszú életek* was a gross breach of etiquette, but his deceit seemed to trouble him not at all.

'*Salut*,' she murmured, listening intently for any tension in her voice. She found none.

'*Salut*.'

'It's been a while.'

'It's been four and a half months.' There was a playfulness to his tone. The vaguest hint of mockery, too.

Etienne knew exactly how long it had been. Before their last meeting, she hadn't seen him in six months. Before that, a year. The frequency of his visits was increasing, and she wondered what that meant – if not for her, for him. 'You've been well?'

She could hear the smirk in his voice. 'You care about that?'

'I prefer you to be happy.'

'Of course you do.'

From the way his tone changed, she knew that the smirk had soured into a sneer.

'You still have the photographs?' he asked.

'It's one of them you want?'

'Yes.'

'The mother or the daughter?'

A pause as he considered. She thought she heard him lick his lips. A dry rustle, like leaves in a drain. 'The daughter.'

She nodded. 'You know how much that will cost?'

The smirk was back. 'Oh, I know *exactly* how much it will cost, Etienne.'

Her forehead puckered into a frown. Rarely had he demonstrated such animosity so early in his visit, but she dismissed it. 'You remember the *Bellicoso*?'

'One of my favourites.'

'Wait for me there. I'll be along shortly.'

Chair legs scraped on wood. A door opened. The birdcages clashed like distant cymbals.

Back in the antechamber, Etienne sat at the warped dressing table. Outside, wind flung a fistful of raindrops against the window, the sound like pebbles dropped on a snare. Lightning flickered. Once, twice.

She opened the table's slim drawer and reached inside to pull out the photographs – a stack of mismatched images as fat as two playing-card decks slapped together. Most of the photographs were in colour, but some were black and white or sepia, brittle and faded.

A rubber band held them together. Etienne slipped it off and began to sort through the images: a blurry shot, sun-faded and cracked, of a bikini-clad woman on a beach; a monochrome image of a serious-looking woman standing outside a terraced house, the photograph torn in half to remove the face and torso of the man whose arm snaked around her; a line of Parisian dancing girls in feathers and heels, one of them circled in black ink; a daguerreotype of two young sisters in profile, black hair scraped into tight buns.

Etienne sorted through them. Every image bore a name and a date on the back. Many of these women were long dead. Some had escaped the men who sought them. Some had simply disappeared. But each picture told a story of violence or tragedy or obsession. In many ways these women were Etienne's caged birds, and she wondered whether in some way she helped to set them free.

Towards the centre of the pile she found what she was looking for – a cluster of five glossy photographs fastened together with a paperclip. She returned the rest to the drawer and laid out those she had selected in a line across the scarred wood. Five faces stared up at her. Four belonged to the same woman, and three of those – larger and better preserved than the rest, suggesting that they had been displayed at one time in a frame – showed her at an earlier stage in her life: dressed as an angel in a school play; posing on a sports field with hockey stick and ball; splashing around in the sea with an older man, his face so similar that he must have been her father.

Beside these photographs, two smaller images, scuffed and stained, as though they had been kept for years in someone's wallet. The first showed the same girl, older now, perhaps in her late twenties. She sat on the grassy slope of a hill. She was smiling, but she looked weary. Behind her, sunlight glimmered on the surface of a glacial lake.

Etienne turned the photograph over and stared at the name written there: the mother, this woman. She placed the image down and picked up the last photograph. This one showed a girl, perhaps eight or nine years old. She sat astride a bicycle, smiling for the camera.

The daughter.

Etienne turned the image over. On the back she found two dates scribbled in ink. The first was the girl's birth date. The second, written by a different hand, recorded her age when the photograph had been taken.

She worked the numbers in her head. If the girl still lived, she would be twenty-four by now. Bending closer, Etienne studied her face, examining her bone structure, the gap between her eyes, the curve of her jaw, the rounded protrusions of her cheekbones. And then she held the image away from her and imagined how that face would change as it aged: from eight-year-old girl through to twenty-four-year-old woman.

Returning the photograph to the table, Etienne rested her hands on her thighs, palms up. She closed her eyes. Emptied her lungs. When next she took a breath she felt a prickling sensation upon her lips, as if someone had begun to tattoo her.

The needle pricks spread out, leaving a smaller, narrower mouth in their wake. Like a moving rash of bee stings, the points of pain crept across her face and she felt her muscles pulling, tightening, stretching. They quested upwards, towards her eyes, and when they encircled them Etienne felt her fingers curl and twitch as twin spikes of agony lanced her.

Gritting her teeth, she felt her spine shift and arch. She hissed as her breasts contracted, a stranger's lips curling back over her teeth. Her shoulders cracked, two loud crocodile-jaw snaps in the silence. She felt the tattooist's needles reach the end of her nose, the tips of her earlobes. The strange electric pain hesitated there, and then she felt her nostrils narrow and lift, the lobes of her ears fatten.

She opened her eyes, stared at what she found. Tilted her head to one side. Licked her teeth. Pouted. Smiled.

Rising, she went to one of the wardrobes and opened it. Inside, she allowed her hand to trail over the garments that hung there. She selected a simple cotton shift dress. In its fabric and its styling it resembled something a young woman from a working family might have worn a century earlier. She stepped into the dress, not bothering with any underwear, and then into leather sandals.

Back at the dressing table, she selected a bottle of Guerlain's Jicky and touched the scent to her throat and wrists. After a final examination in the three full-length mirrors, she climbed the spiral staircase back to the room above and let herself onto the landing. On the far side of the stairwell waited the doors to six rooms, all individually named: *Feroce*, *Chiuso*, *Bellicoso*, *Sostenuto*, *Duolo*, *Capriccioso*. Each one was decorated to accommodate the varied appetites of her guests.

The *Bellicoso* lay at the end of the hall. She followed the balcony railing around to the right and walked down the thick carpet to the last door. It was in this place and others, doing this work, that Etienne had made her fortune. She did it, she told herself, not just for the riches her exploits brought her, not just to satisfy that itch lurking at the heart of her. Some of her visitors were good souls driven half-mad with grief for deceased wives. She helped to ease their loss. The rest of her clients were driven by darker compulsions, and the decor in some of the rooms she passed reflected their tastes. In those cases, she helped the women – far less qualified than she – who would quench those desires, willingly or unwillingly, should she choose not to make this her task.

Etienne paused at the final door. Glanced at the wooden plaque with its scorched black lettering.

Bellicoso.

From the skylight two storeys above her head, lightning flickered out a serpent tongue. Thunder rolled.

Heart accelerating once more in her chest, no longer from fear but a sudden thrill of anticipation, she opened the door and entered the room.

Darkness waited inside. Heavy drapes were drawn against the day. On either side of a four-poster bed candles sputtered in wall brackets: two yellow circles of smoky light. She noticed the bitter aroma of an extinguished cigar, the citrus scent of cologne. And underneath those, an electric odour of excitement, of barely controlled fury.

In one corner was a wingback chair, and sitting in it, a long shadow. It gripped the chair's arms with spider-dark fingers.

When Etienne ventured closer, clutching her hands together in a parody of womanly surrender, she saw a face stretched wide, and caught a glimmer of teeth.

'*Leah*,' the shadow said, rising.

She moved towards him. Glancing away to the bed, she saw what he had placed there, and realised that today was going to be one of *those* visits, and that the soundproofed walls of the *Bellicoso* would do well to keep its secrets and smother her screams.

Her stomach twitched and fluttered, a butterfly net filled with captives yearning to be free.

Because she knew it would please him, she allowed a single tear to roll down her cheek. 'Jakab,' she replied, bowing her head.

CHAPTER 15

Budapest, Hungary

1876

Izsák woke to screams. His eyes snapped wide in the darkness, breath frozen in his throat. Curling his fingers around the bed sheets, he gripped them for anchorage, his entire body tense.

Was he alone in here? Yes. He thought so. A lumpen shadow in one corner was simply his coat hanging from its peg.

On the floorboards, the moon had painted four oblongs of pale light. Izsák slipped from his bed and stepped into one of them. After a moment's pause, he moved to his desk. It stood piled with papers, writing instruments and the tiny metal parts of a dismantled model steam engine: washers, pipework, fly-wheel, a badly oxidised firebox, all in a neat row; the accumulated clutter of his three years at Tansik House.

Beside the engine parts stood an oil lamp and matches. Fingers shaking, Izsák struck a match, eyes closed against the flare. He lit the lamp, lowered its glass chimney and dialled up the wick. He was about to pick it up when he heard a moan float down the corridor outside. Such misery bled from it, such pitiful horror, that Izsák found himself cowering from the sound.

He did not want to go out of the room.

Then don't. Stay here. What do you think you're doing, anyway? You're a coward; always have been. Cowards don't investigate danger.

They make sure their door is locked, and they wait until the danger has passed.

But his door was already locked; he was sure of that. He'd been fastidious about securing it every night since Katalin's warning to him all those years ago. From here he could see the sharp shadow of the key's iron circle, twisted to the ten o'clock position that had become his habit.

The same night he'd received that advice from Katalin, he'd asked the doctor's daughter a question: *What kind of place is this?*

Even now, he remembered her response: *A bad place.* During the years he had been resident at Tansik House, Izsák had found no reason to dispute Katalin's words.

He picked up the lamp, angered by that mocking voice inside his head. He *was* a coward. But the rooms adjacent to his own contained the only friends he had. They might need him.

And what of Katalin? She would likely be asleep in the north wing. Izsák doubted that the screams, even as sharp as they'd been, would have carried so far. Whoever was out there, whoever was behind this, could be searching the building for her even now.

Forcing himself to act, shaking a carnival of shadows from his oil lamp that danced like demons on the lemon-yellow walls, he crept to the door. Reached for the key.

Outside, he heard another key turning. The sound came from Béni's room, to the left of his own. Spurred on by it, Izsák let himself out into the hall.

A second bobbing light swelled towards him, and he nearly shrieked. Abruptly he saw whose face rode above the lantern glow. '*What's happening?*' he hissed.

Béni's lamp, lighting him from below, had robbed his face of its usual humanity. The boy grimaced, magnifying the effect. 'Sounded like Pig. Let's go.' Without waiting for consensus, he turned away and moved down the hall.

Cringing at the worm of fear curling in his gut, Izsák

followed. Pig's room was two doors down from Béni's. As they approached, banishing the shadows with the swinging lights of their lamps, Izsák saw that the boy's door was ajar, presenting a perfect rectangle of darkness.

Pig never slept with his door open. And he never suffered from the kind of night terrors that would lead to a scream like the one they'd heard. Something awful had happened – might still be happening.

Izsák heard more doors unlocking. The creak of hinges. Frightened eyes blinking in the gloom.

From out of the slab of darkness marking the threshold to Pig's room looped a tiny winged missile. It banked towards them, buzzing, and *tinked* off the glass of Béni's lamp. Waving it away, the boy glanced over his shoulder to check that Izsák still followed. He found his friend's eyes, nodded. Then he crept closer to Pig's door.

'What are you doing?' Izsák whispered. A fist-like pressure gripped his throat. He could barely force out his words.

'We have to check on Pig,' Béni shot back. 'He's only . . . *szar*, what's that stink?'

Izsák noticed it the same moment he heard his friend's words. A death smell, rich and thick, bloomed from the darkness, as if the bloated corpse of some Danube suicide had been fished from the river and dragged inside the boy's room.

He felt his stomach lurch in revulsion. His mouth flooded with saliva. He shuddered, desperate to rid his nose of that stink. 'Béni,' he hissed. '*Béni*.'

Ignoring Izsák's plea, Béni lifted his lantern and stepped into Pig's room, leaving nothing but a diminishing half-circle of light to mark his passage.

Heart slamming in his chest, Izsák edged closer. He did not want to see this. He wanted to run, lock himself away. Squeeze his eyes shut until this was over. But Béni was inside, now. He could not abandon him.

Pausing beside Pig's doorway, Izsák took a shallow breath,

almost gagging from the foulness it carried into his lungs. Then he craned his neck for a look.

Inside, the drapes pulled across the window had banished the moon's weak glow. Béni sat on the floor. Beside him, his oil lamp provided a shimmering halo of light. In his lap, he cradled Pig's head.

The larger boy was shivering, weeping. Mucus ran from his nose. 'Not want,' he said, tongue thick in his mouth. His face contorted. 'Not want, not want, not want.'

Izsák crept closer. Even though the stench was at its strongest here, it was already beginning to recede, the last traces burned in the flames of their lamps. 'What happened, Pig?'

'Not want! *Not want!*' the boy screamed, lurching upright. His eyes had lost all their colour, leaving two black orbs feathered with crimson. 'Toll Man come. *Toll Man! TOLL MAN NOT WANT!*'

Movement in the doorway at Izsák's back. He whipped around and saw the twins, Magdolna and Rózsika, their disembodied faces floating like hunter's moons. Neither girl spoke, staring past him at the figures clustered on the floor.

Now he heard approaching footsteps, someone running down the hall. Trusov appeared, red-faced and breathless. When the man saw Béni on the floor, holding Pig in his arms, his eyes widened and he stiffened, glancing back into the hall behind him. It took him only a moment to recover. 'Out,' he snarled. 'All of you. Back to your rooms.'

Béni frowned. 'Something scared him, sir. He's terrified. I don't—'

Trusov burst between the twins and surged into Pig's room. Grabbing Béni by the hair, he yanked the boy to his feet and kicked him into the hall. 'I *said* back to your rooms!' he shouted. Turning on Pig, he pointed at the bed. 'Get in. Get *in*, you fat, useless *balfácán*.'

Pig stared, eyes teary and uncomprehending. Trusov grabbed a fistful of his nightshirt and dragged him on to the bed.

'*NOT WANT!*' Pig screamed. '*NOT WANT! NOT WANT!*'

Spittle shining on his chin, Trusov slapped the boy's face. Pig thrashed and Trusov slapped him again, so hard he left a scarlet handprint. This time the blow had its desired effect. Pig lay rigid.

Another moan rolled down the hall. Earlier, Izsák had thought it shared the same source as the scream but now he realised he'd been wrong. It came from behind him, this sound – back along the hall past his own room.

Béni climbed to his feet. 'Give me your lamp.'

Izsák did not want to relinquish it. From where his errant spark of bravery came he could not say, but instead of handing over the light he raised it higher and padded back the way they'd come, towards the source of that dreadful lament.

He heard his breath rushing in and out of his lungs, a sound like forge bellows, and smelled that graveyard stink, growing stronger once more, so cloying he could taste it on his tongue: maggot-bitter, an invisible cloud of putrefaction and decay.

A bluebottle buzzed him. Moments later, another one swung out of the darkness and landed on his wrist. Prickly and fat, it threw off a grotesque shadow as it skittered across his skin.

Repulsed, Izsák shook it off. And then, up ahead, he saw a ghost materialise from the gloom, a funeral shroud hanging from its skeletal frame – although, he acknowledged, it wasn't really a ghost at all. Something just as wretched, even so: the resident ghoul of Tansik House.

Etienne.

The moment she recognised him, the girl pointed across the hall to another empty doorway.

'János,' she said, voice husky. Her hair was mussed, and there were bruises around her throat. Trusov's brutish work, no doubt. 'It's in his room.'

'What's in there, Ets?' he whispered. 'What have you seen?'

'It *took* him.'

Béni gripped his shoulder. 'Either go and see, or I will. But let's not wait.'

Izsák stared at the open doorway of János's room, at the shadows that lapped at its edges, recoiling from the rotten dead-man smell wafting out of it. Something waited for him there, inside that room; something that would prove the world was infinitely more hostile than his experiences of it so far.

It would change him, if he investigated that darkness. He wasn't sure he could cope with its revelations.

Let Béni do it, then. He offered, didn't he? Give him the damned lamp, let him risk his own neck. Get back to your room and lock the door. Pull the bedclothes over your head and maybe you'll wake up from this. Maybe you'll—

No.

He would not. János was his friend, one of only three or four people in his life he could trust.

Going to the door, moving fast to outrun the cowardice that threatened to overtake him, Izsák thrust the lamp inside, watching the shadows flit to the far corners.

A solitary pillow lay twisted on the bed. Its covers had been dragged halfway across the room. The back of János's chair, where the boy usually draped his clothes, was bare.

On the floor, cowering away from the lamplight, curled a wretched shape. It shivered and twitched, fingers clutched to its face.

Not János. Someone else.

Izsák didn't want to get any closer, didn't trust that *thing*, whatever it was. He was already within its reach, should it dart out a limb and snatch at him.

He raised the lamp higher and the room's occupant moaned. Kicking its legs like a grossly overgrown spider, it managed to scissor backwards into a corner. Izsák's light found a gap between its fingers and revealed a glimmer of white eye.

'*Careful*,' Béni hissed.

Ignoring his friend, Izsák edged closer, seized by the sudden, inexplicable conviction that this tormented soul, cringing away from his lamp, presented little immediate threat. 'I won't hurt you,' he murmured, taking another step. 'I won't.'

Scrabbling to its haunches, the figure snapped out a hand. Béni cried out in alarm, but Izsák saw that it held its palm outwards; a simple gesture, intended to shield itself from their eyes. He took another step into the room, and when the light cast from his lamp banished the last of the shadows he saw for the first time what sheltered there, and gasped, appalled.

An old man crouched in the corner, squinting up at them with blood-tinged eyes. His skin was grey-white, the pallor of woodland fungus. In places the flesh on his face seemed to have parted from his skull. It hung in loose folds. One cheek had slid so low it had exposed a crescent of moist red bone below his eye. Two flies were glued to its surface, their proboscises lowered.

'Where's János?' Béni shouted from the doorway. 'What have you done with him?'

The old man spasmed. One of the bluebottles riding below his eye vibrated its wings, a sound like meat ripping. '*Nnnn . . .*' he tried to say, and then he vomited, a biscuit-coloured stream of foul-smelling liquid. He retracted his hand, crossing his arms across his chest.

He spasmed again, more violently this time. The back of his skull cracked against the wall. '*G . . . Gone,*' he stammered. '*N . . . N . . . Not long. Not . . . long.*'

Izsák was shaking now, too. Not from fear, but from a despair so deep it gnawed at his heart. He felt tears spring into his eyes.

The merciful course of action would be to find a weapon and club this wretched creature until it lay dead at his feet. But while Izsák's uncharacteristic injection of bravery had led him so far, it would not, he knew, allow him to obey that thought.

'What's your name?' he asked, wanting to reach out a hand, yet nauseous at the very contemplation of it.

The old man shuddered, collapsing onto his side. He gasped once and let out a rattling breath, like air rushing from a punctured coffin. He did not move again.

Rigid with dismay, the two boys watched his fingers uncurl, as if in death he offered each of them some parting gift.

Behind him, Izsák heard quiet sobbing. He turned, and found Etienne standing in the doorway. The fact that the sobs came from her, a girl he'd never seen display an ounce of emotion despite the years of abuse inflicted on her, made them infinitely more piercing: the most harrowing sound he had heard since the rifle shot that had split his father's skull apart and changed his life forever. Stumbling over to her, Izsák put an arm around Etienne's neck and drew her close.

For two days afterwards, clouds massing over the Danube emptied sheets of rain onto the city's streets. Water boiled in Budapest's gutters and carried debris in a sloshing torrent to the great river.

Katalin visited him at midnight on the third evening after János's taking, as a crisp wind blew the rainclouds away towards the west. He heard her coded tap in the darkness, and sat up in bed as she slipped into his room, a heady cloud of lavender.

The moon picked out the crease in her brow. 'Your door was unlocked,' she said, padding across his floor in bare feet.

'Trusov took our keys.'

'He did what?'

'The morning after János disappeared. We went down for breakfast, and when we came back after lessons they were gone.'

Her mouth dropped open. 'I have to tell my father. If—'

'*No.* You can't, Katalin. He mustn't hear anything from you about this. You'll bring trouble on us all.'

'You can't sleep behind an unlocked door.'

'What choice do I have?'

'Izsák, please. You saw what happened.'

'I saw something. I don't understand it.'

'All the more reason to take precautions. You have to find a way to block your door at night.' She cast around the room, taking in the wardrobe, the washstand, the bed. 'Budge up.'

'What?'

'Are you deaf? I'm not going to molest you.'

She stripped back the covers, revealing his pale legs. Flushing with embarrassment, Izsák pulled down his nightshirt and slid closer to the wall. Katalin climbed in beside him, the bedsprings creaking, and he felt the heat of her body against his own. The girl's scent, so close, was dizzying.

'It's happened before. Hasn't it?' he asked, needing to break the silence that had formed between them.

'How did you know that?'

'Just a guess. Something Béni said once. That there'd been others here, and that they'd gone. He didn't want to talk about it.'

'It's *végzet* in a few days, Izsák. I don't know why, but when they come, it's always at this time of year.'

'They?'

'Sometimes it's just one, like a few nights ago. Other times, more of them.'

'Who comes?'

'You really don't know?'

'Are you going to tell me or not?'

She bit her lip. 'Father calls them the *gyermekrablók*. But you might have heard them called something else. *Lélek tolvajok*.'

Izsák's skin prickled. He *had* heard the term before, somewhere in his past. He didn't know what it signified, exactly, but he remembered it was synonymous with loss. 'Tell me,' he whispered.

She told him.

Afterwards, they sat in silence, watching the moon trace a path across the sky. At some point during her story, Katalin's hand had moved beneath the covers and taken his own. Now, she moved her thumb back and forth along his index finger, seemingly unaware of the effect her touch had upon him.

While he felt sickened at what she had revealed, a small part of him rejoiced at the intimacy the incident had sparked. And then he thought of Pig, rocking himself back and forth – *TOLL MAN NOT WANT!* – and that small measure of happiness decayed into guilt.

Beside him, Katalin snuggled down under the covers, her hair trailing across his pillow.

'You can't stay here,' he said. 'If we get caught—'

'I won't,' she whispered. She let go of his hand, closing her eyes. 'But just for a little while. Please, Izsák.'

How could he refuse her? Upright in the bed, he studied her face, listening as her breathing began to lengthen, thinking about all she had told him.

In later years he would never be able to explain why he did what followed. After what felt like hours, yet was perhaps only an interval of minutes, he leaned over her sleeping form and kissed her mouth.

The moment their lips touched, Katalin blinked. 'I'd been wondering how long it would take you to do that,' she said. Snaking out an arm, she slid her fingers around the back of his head. 'I never thought I'd have to wait this long.'

Izsák stared into her eyes, at the reflections of moonlight that glimmered there. His chest rose and fell against her own.

Outside, in the hall, he heard a rustle of movement as Etienne passed his door. But whether she was coming or going from her nightly appointment with Trusov, Izsák could not say.

CHAPTER 16

London, England

The sky was darkening to wet ashes as Leah steered her Mercedes hire car out of Heathrow, and by the time she arrived in Central London the beams of her headlights were sparkling in the puddles.

A week had passed since she'd said goodbye to Luca Sultés in Interlaken, and she cursed herself daily for the number of times he'd appeared in her thoughts since. She'd visited several European cities, and had met six *hosszú életek* women that the *tanács*, in their wisdom, had condemned as *kirekesztett*.

At the women's request, she'd agreed to meet each in a public place. Five of them arrived alone; one brought along a partner. Of the six, two rose to their feet and walked away the instant Leah explained the reason for her visit. A third became so instantly abusive that on that occasion Leah was the one to retreat, alarmed at the attention they were drawing.

Of the remaining three *kirekesztett*, the woman who had brought her partner along agreed to Leah's proposal on the spot, tears shining on her cheeks as she reflected on the possibilities she'd imagined had disappeared forever. The other two requested more time to consider, which Leah was happy to grant.

In a single week, she might have found more volunteers than their programme back in Calw had managed in eight months. And Luca's list contained yet more names.

One of those she was on her way to meet now. Unlike the others, this woman had asked that Leah visit her at home; unfazed, it appeared, by the possibility that the contact was part of some *tanács* plot.

Half an hour after leaving the airport, Leah turned onto the stratospherically affluent Mayfair street programmed into the satnav and slowed down until she found the address. She parked in a reserved space and switched off the engine, listening to the rain finger-tap a rhythm against the sunroof.

The house was huge, a whitewashed Georgian terrace that rose a neck-craning five storeys in height. Its imposing front door, up a flight of stone steps and shielded behind cast-iron railings, was an impenetrable slab of wood – reinforced, Leah guessed, with a steel core that would deflect the attempts of all but the fiercest of assaults.

The black bubble of a security camera bolted to the building's façade monitored her as she climbed out of the Mercedes. She tried the gate set into the railings and found it locked. Before she had a chance to press the button on its intercom, she heard a buzz of magnets as the enclosure unlocked.

Leah swung the gate open and walked up the steps. By the time she reached the top, the front door had opened, revealing a heavy-set man with a jaw that looked powerful enough to shatter bricks. He did not bother to conceal the fact that he was armed. Jerking his head to one side, he motioned for her to enter.

Breath catching in her throat, palms suddenly damp, Leah entered the marble-floored foyer and heard the door swing shut behind her. 'I'm Leah Wilde,' she said.

'You'd better be,' the man replied. 'Are you carrying?'

'No.'

'I need to check.'

'Go ahead.'

She lifted her arms and he patted her down, moving his hands along her arms, around her torso and down her legs with a briskness that demonstrated he cared only about discovering a hidden weapon.

He found none. The pat-down complete, he searched through her hair and when, finally, he satisfied himself that she carried no firearm, no knife, nor anything else she might use to endanger his employer, he pointed her towards a staircase that rose in a jagged square around each of the building's five storeys.

'Which floor?' she asked.

'Second.'

Leah counted a further four CCTV units on the way up. Their lenses, powered by silent motors, rotated as she passed.

When she reached the second floor, the man halted behind her. The lighting was softer here, illuminating pale-green walls. An enormous bay window, looking down into the street, curved around a collection of Chinese porcelain so ancient it might have dated back to the Han dynasty. Some of the pieces had been smashed and subsequently repaired.

'First door on the left,' he told her.

She nodded, feeling his eyes on her neck as she moved down the hall, sinking into carpet as dense and cushioned as the wool of a lamb's fleece. Leah knocked on the door, then went inside.

The room she discovered could have been used to entertain royalty. Its walls were decorated with leaf-patterned silk, but no artworks hung from them, only mirrors. One was so enormous it stretched the entire width of the room. Marble-topped plinths bore bronze statues of fornicating couples. A huge Persian rug covered most of the parquet floor.

In one of two wingback chairs beside a fireplace bright with flames, sat the most formidably sensual creature Leah had ever seen.

The woman's skin glowed as if lit from within. Her hair was as dark and rich as polished ebony, rolled into a simple twist fastened by a jewel-encrusted clasp. Her dress, a fluid black shimmer accentuated with sparse bursts of pink flowers, clung to her torso and trailed past her knees. She sat barefoot, one leg crossed over the other, toenails manicured but free of any adornment. Her face was as blank of expression as it was flawless, eyes a pale, frosty blue.

Leah, in jeans, boots and her old motorcycle jacket, felt her stomach sinking. She had wanted this woman to see her as an ally – perhaps even as an equal – but already a gulf seemed to stretch between them. She'd felt nervous enough meeting the six previous *kirekesztett* women, but standing here now she felt a trickle of sweat roll down her spine.

The woman continued to study her. She opened her mouth, revealing perfect white teeth and a small, crimson tongue. 'Leah Wilde.' Her voice was chocolate steeped in wine, the words a statement, not a question. Not an invitation.

Tread carefully.

'Yes. You're Etienne?'

'Indeed.'

Leah nodded. A feeling began to descend on her that she had entered not a home, here, but a lair. 'Thank you for seeing me.'

The woman indicated the empty chair with a flick of her wrist. 'No need to thank me. Anyone who can soften the heart of Luca Sultés as quickly as you appear to have managed is a woman worth meeting. Knowing how often that man can have a change of heart, I thought it prudent to meet you sooner rather than later.' For the first time Etienne smiled, although it was an expression entirely lacking in warmth. 'You're not *hosszú élet,*' she added, folding her hands in her lap.

Leah moved to the wingback chair and sat. The room was hot, but she did not remove her jacket. She sensed that without an invitation it would be deemed a breach of etiquette; she also sensed, with just as much conviction, that to flaunt any unwritten rule of conduct in front of this woman would bring their interview to an immediate close.

She found herself contemplating how far away she was from

the people who loved her. And for the first time since leaving Calw, she felt dreadfully alone. She recalled the man downstairs searching her for weapons, and the cameras that zoomed in on her progress during her passage up to the second floor.

Although it had doubtless been the right decision to leave her Ruger under the Mercedes' passenger seat, right now it felt a dangerous one. She did not know why her host had been branded a *kirekesztett*. But she did know, simply from reading the woman's face, that she was outshone, outclassed, outgunned here, in every respect. Etienne's eyes gleamed with the intensity of a wolf pup's, but they measured Leah with the feigned indifference of a far more experienced predator.

How much to tell this woman, waiting for her to speak? Every decision she made in this room felt like a step taken along a precipice. 'I am,' she replied. 'Of a sort.'

Etienne tilted her head. 'You either are, or you aren't.'

'I have *hosszú élet* blood in my veins,' she said. 'But *simavér*, too.'

'Impossible.'

Leah took a breath. It was pointless to argue. Instead, she focused her eyes and felt the familiar stirring – *tightening* – as she bade them to do her talking for her.

Etienne's lips parted, ever so slightly, in the merest feather of a reaction, and then they closed. She blinked. 'I think you'd better tell me the rest.'

Careful of every single word she uttered for the next twenty minutes, Leah did exactly that.

Halfway through her story, the *kirekesztett* woman went to a rosewood cabinet and opened its doors. She selected two crystal tumblers and from a decanter poured a measure of spirit into each. Her hands were shaking, Leah noticed. An artery flickered in her throat.

Returning to the fireplace, Etienne held out one of the glasses. This close, Leah recognised her perfume: Guerlain's Jicky.

'You're perspiring,' Etienne said. 'Are you afraid of me?'

'I'm hot.'

The woman raised a quill-like eyebrow. 'Then why are you sitting there draped in leather like that?'

Feeling foolish, Leah shrugged out of her jacket and accepted the proffered glass. She raised it to her lips, took a sip. Calvados, warming her throat.

She continued her story, and when she finished it Etienne began to question her. Leah answered as best she could, but she did not reveal the location of the centre in Calw, nor the exact nature of her and her mother's heritage.

Finally the questions ended and they sat, considering each other, in silence. The fire popped. Wind flung raindrops against the room's huge bay windows. Somewhere, out in the night, the muted blare of a car horn carried through London's streets.

'I hope I haven't wasted your time,' Leah said, after neither of them had spoken for five minutes.

'Time is not as precious to me as to some,' Etienne replied. Her eyes were on the fire, watching the flames bob and dance.

'I must ask. Now that you've heard what I have to say—'

The woman's eyes hardened; two sharp gemstones, a fraction paler than topaz. 'You require an answer? Tonight?'

'No, I wouldn't expect to receive—'

'Nor shall you.'

Leah closed her mouth, refusing to let the woman's manner antagonise her.

You're not here to judge. You know nothing of her. Nothing of what she's faced. Nothing of what she's endured.

Before leaving her home in Calw for this undertaking, Leah had set herself two rules. One: she would not ask the women she met the details of their crimes unless they volunteered them. Two: she wouldn't allow herself to become moral arbiter. No one in this world, she believed, possessed the right to judge whether a woman was worthy of carrying a child. Certainly not her. Etienne might have walked the earth a hundred years or more. The very notion that Leah, with her twenty-four years of life, was a worthy magister of the woman's suitability for motherhood was laughable.

She offered a choice, that was all; a choice that would be available to every woman she was able to find.

Rousing herself from her thoughts, she discovered that Etienne's eyes had moved from the flames to study her face. Leah shifted under their intensity.

'You're in London long?'

'A few days,' she replied. 'I have others to see.'

'You've set yourself an unenviable task.'

'I don't view it like that.'

'I admire your devotion.'

'I can't sit back and watch us fade away, Etienne.'

'No. I see that in you. But it doesn't explain why you haven't offered yourself more fully to this undertaking.'

'Meaning?'

'You're of an appropriate age. If this means so much to you, why aren't you a mother yourself by now?'

'I think I'm more suited to this. To finding—'

'That's not an answer, nor the beginnings of one.'

'No.' Leah dropped her head. When next she spoke, her voice was faint. 'I can't.'

'You can't?'

'I can't conceive. And I can't be a surrogate. My body . . .' She shrugged, raising her eyes to Etienne's face. 'Who knows why these things come about?'

'You've known it long?'

'Long enough.'

'It pains you still, doesn't it?'

'More than you could imagine.'

Etienne laughed. 'Don't be so sure of that.' She stood, dress shimmering in the firelight. 'Come back in two days. You'll have your answer then.'

Out on the street, Leah clutched her jacket around her as she unlocked the Mercedes. Frost stubbled the windscreen. Night had fallen, and with it London was beginning to freeze.

Inside the house, the beautiful *kirekesztett* woman with the wolf pup eyes stood at the window and watched Leah's car pull away from the kerb.

Despite the room's heat, she shivered. How long since she had experienced emotions such as these? She examined her hands, watched the way her fingers trembled. Turning away, she took the stairs to the third floor, walked along the corridor to the unadorned room and descended the spiral staircase to the antechamber adjoining her Aviary.

At the dressing table, she retrieved the bundle of photographs. Then she retreated to her bedroom.

Closing the door, she caught sight of herself in the three floor-length mirrors. Her face was pale, the skin of her throat flushed red. But she was still beautiful. And that was what mattered. Beauty had mattered all her life. It defined her.

Her chest rose and fell. She climbed onto the bed and sat cross-legged, pulling the rubber band off the sheaf of photographs. Soon she had laid a row of five before her.

She stared at those images, unblinking. After a while, she picked up the fifth and final photograph: a girl, eight years old, sitting on a bicycle. A smile for the camera, from a child not used to smiling.

She examined the girl's face, turned the photograph over in her hands.

Leah Wilde.

Eight years old in this photograph.

Twenty-four years old when she sat downstairs tonight.

Etienne tapped the photograph against her chin, thinking. The girl offered something incredible. Something too life-changing to *be* credible.

Decided on her course, she reached out to the telephone beside the bed. Keyed in a number long committed to memory.

The phone rang four times before a man answered.

She closed her eyes. Opened them. Turned the photograph of the smiling girl on the bicycle face-down on the bed.

'I believe,' she said, 'I've found someone you may wish to meet.'

CHAPTER 17

Yosemite National Park, California, USA

Angel River stood in the RV's doorway and peered out at a fresh Sierra Nevada morning rich with the scent of pinesap and wood smoke. Already the sun filtering through the tree canopy carried a sharp heat, warming the forest floor and adding a note of damp mulch.

Having spent most of the night too frightened to sleep, Angel had succumbed to exhaustion just before dawn. She was, as a result, the last to rise.

At the twin benches still dragged together from last night's feast, her family – Mom, Elliot and Hope – and her new *depths-of-a-nightmare* family – Ty, Regan and Luke – were hunkered down and enjoying a late camp breakfast.

Sitting beside Ty on one of the benches, her mom spotted Angel hovering in the doorway and waved her outside. 'Ah, the sleeper awakes. Come and check out this breakfast. I think our woodsman surpassed himself.'

Ty raised his head and grinned. 'Grab a plate, Angel. Plenty for everyone. You know what they say about breakfast.'

'Most important meal of the day!' the others chanted in unison.

As if this was normal.

As if nothing had happened in the night.

As if they were two happy families, growing into one.

Angel stepped out of the motor home and crossed the patch of ground to the picnic tables, limbs stiff. She stared down at the food.

Boxes of cereal and cartons of milk. Orange juice, cranberry and pomegranate. A skillet full of crisp bacon. Sausages, tomatoes and hash browns. A serving plate piled with pancakes. Loaves of bread, cut into slices, a few of them toasted. Jars of preserves. Peanut butter and chocolate spread.

'I can do you an egg,' Ty said. 'Or even a waffle, if you like. How about a couple of waffles? Butter, cream, strawberries and syrup. The works.'

He was wearing the same wizard T-shirt as the day before: *THAT'S WHAT I'M TOLKIEN ABOUT*. It looked a little greasier this morning. Ty looked a little older this morning, too. And, weirdly, a little fleshier, as if the cholesterol from last night's feast was riding high in his cheeks.

His jaw was streaked with soot. Toast crumbs and jam clung to his stubble. His eyes didn't blink as he watched her.

He knows, Angel thought.

It was real. And I saw. And he knows.

She smiled back at him; had to, to keep up the act. Mouth drawn wide, lips curled back over teeth. That was how you did it, wasn't it?

Picking up a plastic plate, she dumped bacon onto it from the skillet, added a hash brown and two slices of bread. The nearest empty space was opposite Ty. She wasn't going to sit there. No way. She walked to the far end and squeezed in between two large plastic coolers.

'You OK, hon?' her mom asked.

Angel nodded. She made a crude sandwich from the bacon and hash brown, added a squirt of ketchup, mashed the other piece of bread down on top.

'Gonna have some fun today,' Ty said.

Shaking, Angel raised her sandwich to her lips and bit into

it. The food was a dense slug inside her mouth. She worked it with her tongue. At the far end of the table, her mom poured a glass of pomegranate juice and told the others to pass it down. Angel received it gratefully, nearly choking as she knocked it back.

She heard a buzzing by her ear, and saw a large bluebottle land on top of her sandwich. It skated around in a figure of eight, a metallic-looking bead with red compound eyes.

Disgusted, she waved it off.

'Careful, Angel,' Ty said. '*Calliphora vomitoria*. They lay their eggs in dead animals. Hundreds at a time.' He grinned again. 'Someone hasn't taken a shower this morning.'

'Ty,' Angel's mom warned, digging him with an elbow.

'Sorry, sorry. I just . . . it's educational.'

'Not while we're eating, it isn't.'

Angel placed the sandwich back down on her plate. She wiped her mouth. Saw the fly loop around the table and settle on a loaf of bread.

'So,' Ty said, addressing the group. 'Are you guys all set to see the giant sequoias today? Think you'd like that?'

'Yeah!' Elliot shouted.

'You want to hear a fact? They're named after a Native American fella. Guy called Sequoyah. He invented some system of writing for the Cherokee. Fascinating stuff. We'll head over to Mariposa Grove after we pack up breakfast. Some of those trees are a couple thousand years old. Hey, Angel. You looking forward to that?'

Angel stared at her plate. She forced herself to nod.

It took them half an hour to pack up. Angel took a shower in the space-age cubicle at the vehicle's rear, scrubbing her body and her hair and her face. When she switched off the water and stepped, steaming, onto the bath mat, she thought she heard a thump – or a bang – from under her feet, directly over the RV's luggage bay.

For most of the night, she had lain in bed too terrified to sleep, thinking they shared the motorhome with a corpse. Now she knew that wasn't true. Locked away in the darkness of the vehicle's underbelly, the beautiful woman with the seaweed eyes and the sunlight hair was alive. Angel felt bile rising in her throat. In a way, this was even worse. She had been locked inside a nightmare of her own, but this new revelation brought an urgency with it. It meant she had to do something. And soon.

Dressing quickly, she brushed her teeth and pulled a comb through her hair. Back in the main living space, she glanced out of the window and saw that everyone was outside.

Not everyone. Not the woman. She's underneath you, Angel. Alive, but perhaps only barely. Stuffed into that vault like a sack of meat.

Inside the RV's kitchen, she slid open a drawer and rummaged through a heap of cooking utensils and cutlery. She found a short filleting knife, and managed to slip it into her bag just as her mom opened the door.

'OK, hon?'

'Yeah.'

'Sure?'

'Of course.'

'You OK with Ty?'

Angel grinned. 'Yeah, Mom. I'm fine.'

'Great. I really want you guys to be happy.'

'I know.'

Her mom reached out a hand. Squeezed her arm.

They arrived at Mariposa Grove twenty minutes later and parked up. Ty and her mom swivelled around in their front seats. He flashed them all a grin. 'OK, Bradies, Mariposa Grove. Some of the oldest trees in the world. And some of the largest, too.' He began to list them, reeling off names as if from a football roster. 'We've got Grizzly Giant, we've got the Fallen

Monarch, we've got the Clothespin tree and the Telescope tree.'

Reaching over, Ty massaged the top of Angel's mom's bare leg. 'Then we've got the Faithful Couple. Two trees that grew so close their trunks fused together.' He slid his hand around the inside of her thigh – high up, *really* high up – as if no one was watching, as if it was OK to touch her there while her kids sat opposite and stared.

'Oh, Ty,' her mom said. She picked off his hand, cheeks colouring.

He grinned as if nothing had happened. 'Right, gang. Let's go bag us some trees.'

On any other day, Angel would have found herself struck mute with awe at the grove's inhabitants. The flared bases of the giant sequoia trunks reminded her, in a curious way, of elephants' feet; as if she walked beneath a herd of enormous beasts whose bodies were lost in the clouds. Angel recalled a Dali painting she had once seen: *Dream Caused by the Flight of a Bee Around a Pomegranate a Second Before Awakening*.

Funny name for a painting. Even funnier that she should remember it.

The giant sequoias laid an additional texture over the dream-like nature of her day – one filled with tree-legged creatures stalking ancient groves, of smiling monstrosities disguised as middle-aged geeks, of beautiful women sealed in motorhome coffins.

Although, occasionally, she felt Ty's eyes upon her, he didn't seem to pay her that much attention. He joked with her mom, pointed out the various trees to Elliot, grinned and goofed and wandered about.

There's a woman locked inside our RV. She's alive, although who knows for how long. You have to do something.

Angel studied Regan and Luke, wondered whether it was possible that they knew. But of course it wasn't. She knew enough about serial killers to know that generally they didn't have kids. And even if they did, they didn't *collaborate* with them, forming some kind of Addams Family-style hunting party. It just didn't happen.

That woman might be dying. And you're walking through Mariposa Grove thinking about Dali's elephants and psychotic stepfamilies.

Up ahead, Ty peeled off to chase Elliot around the base of a particularly huge sequoia. Taking her opportunity, Angel went to her mother's side. 'Mom, can I grab the RV keys a minute?'

'What's up?'

'Nothing. Just need to use the bathroom.'

'They have bathrooms here.'

Ty was still on the other side of the sequoia.

'Mom, please.'

'OK. OK, honey.' She pulled open her bag, rifling through its contents. 'I wish I knew what's up with you today.'

Ty was still out of sight. He wouldn't remain hidden for long. Finally her mom pulled out the bunch of keys. 'Here you go. Make sure you lock it.'

'Sure.' Angel stuffed them into her bag. Turning away as Ty emerged on the path ahead, she tried to look casual. She took a circuitous route back to the RV, glancing over her shoulder every few yards to make sure he wasn't following.

Up ahead, the motorhome waited in a line of dusty vehicles. Ty had reversed their RV into its bay so that the rear faced into the trees. Its windows were dark mirrors, reflecting the sun. For a moment Angel thought she saw it shift on its springs, a subtle tilting. But she knew she imagined it. Thought she did . . . perhaps.

Moving quickly, she ducked along the side of the motorhome to the back. She stared up at its curving metal body, at the chrome ladder reaching all the way to the roof, its racks of running lights. The vehicle seemed to exude a cool malevolence. An awareness.

Angel shivered. Reaching out, she placed a hand against the

metal. She thought she could feel a vibration, a humming; a heartbeat. But of course it was probably the refrigeration unit, or the plumbing, or something simple like that. Even when stationary, she knew these beasts only slumbered; they never truly died.

Then Angel heard the scratching. Faint. Oh-so-faint. It stopped, and she took her hand away. Stepped closer. Inclined her head.

There. It was back. A ticking, or a scraping.

She glanced around. The RV was parked further into the undergrowth than its neighbouring vehicles; it screened her from curious eyes. No one lurked nearby.

The luggage bay lay behind a flip-down hatch low to the right, beside the licence plate. She had seen Ty opening it when they'd picked up the vehicle from the rental depot, revealing a crawlspace deep enough to stow a couple of king-size mattresses. They'd left it empty. Even with the seven of them on board, the RV was simply so huge they hadn't needed the extra space.

Angel forced herself to move. She fumbled in her bag and pulled out the keys. The smaller one opened the luggage bay. She slid it into the lock, twisted it, paused. Took a breath, held it.

Removing the key, she flipped down the hatch.

Darkness inside. Shadows.

A smell that was a mixture of sweat, urine and fear. And there, towards the very back of the crawlspace, two spots of seaweed-green light. Angel stooped, resting her hands on her knees, tilting her head to give herself a better view.

Eyes. That's what those two green spots were. The woman's beautiful green eyes, blinking out at her from deep within the motorhome's belly. Angel heard her own breath echoing inside the chamber. Felt her heart beating in her chest.

It's true. It's all true. He put her here. He put her here last night and then he lay down beside Mom and went to sleep. And then he got up this morning, as fresh and carefree as a choirboy, made us all breakfast and drove us down here to see the giant sequoias, like it was the most natural thing in the world. Like we were all a big happy fucking family and there wasn't some stranger locked up in the trunk.

THAT'S WHAT I'M TOLKIEN ABOUT.

Jesus Christ. Jesus Christ.

'Are you hurt?' Angel whispered, straining to see the woman's features. 'Can you hear me?'

'*Yuhhh . . .*' the RV's prisoner stammered.

Something scraped inside the chamber. The eyes flickered. Grew larger. Now Angel saw an arm, clad in a black cardigan sleeve. A hand, slim and graceful, fingers caked in mud.

Cracked nails. And blood.

'You're OK,' Angel told her. 'I'm going to get help. What's your name? Tell me your name.'

'*Geor . . .*' the woman rasped. '*Georgia.*'

'OK, Georgia. You hold on, all right? You hold on.'

Angel's hands were shaking. Her knees, too. Her whole body. She fumbled with her bag, nearly dropped it, yanked it open. Searched around inside. Found her phone. Activated the screen. Brought up the keypad. Typed *9 . . . 1 . . . 1.*

The voice came from behind her. 'Curious little pooch, aren't you? I knew you'd seen me last night.'

Angel screamed. She spun around. Saw at once the lettering on the T-shirt right in front of her: *THAT'S WHAT I'M TOLKIEN ABOUT.*

Ty reached out and plucked the phone from her fingers. He stared at the screen, shook his head, and tucked it into his shirt pocket.

The woman inside the luggage bay moaned and scrabbled backwards, seeking the sanctuary of darkness.

Ty grinned and, even in her terror, Angel thought: *You're older. You've aged. Since this morning. How can that be?*

'What,' he asked her, 'are we going to do about the unfailingly curious Miss Angel River?'

'You won't get away with—'

But already his hand was reaching for her, and when he touched her *OH GOD WHAT?* forehead she felt something *NO THAT'S* clutching at her brain *HE'S NOT EVEN* and curling around it, and suddenly she was screaming in agony, but it was a silent scream, and black wings were enfolding her, and then, and *then* . . . Angel felt her thoughts fracture into a million jagged pieces.

It was night when she woke. The world bumped and swayed. She opened her eyes to a malignant yellow light, swirling and flickering. Abruptly she closed them again, nausea rising.

Somewhere a radio was playing. Her brain felt as if it had been sawn in two, her thoughts incomplete, unravelling as they attempted to bridge the gap between the halves. She tried to touch her face, and realised she was bound. With the shock of that discovery, her thoughts began to knit back together.

The woman imprisoned in the RV's hold. The fingernails, once beautifully manicured, now split and caked with mud and grime.

And him. Ty. Reaching out and touching her forehead, shattering her mind into sharp glass shards.

Narrowing her eyes into slits, Angel tried to make sense of what she saw.

She was in the RV, that much was obvious. And they were moving; she could feel the highway flying by beneath her, rocking and bumping the vehicle on its springs. Yellow light bent the shadows. Black shapes slid through the RV's living space. She heard the roar and hiss of cars passing and the occasional truck, flooding the cabin with light before fading away.

On the bench seat opposite sat her brother and sister. Elliot and Hope were awake, staring, eyes like poached eggs, faces sickly in the shadows. Like her, their arms were bound to their sides.

When Angel opened her mouth to speak, Hope shook her head. A single, urgent movement: *No. Don't. Don't say anything.*

To her right, a new nightmare greeted her: Regan and Luke, slumped beside each other on the floor, both of them tied.

Luke's cheek bore a dark bruise. His forehead was gashed, the wound crusted with dried blood. Eyes closed, he snored softly, head resting against his sister's shoulder. Regan stared back at Angel. She wore the sort of look a girl might adopt after discovering that her dad was psychotic.

They didn't know. We're dead. If he tied his own children too, we're all dead.

Unable to meet the hollow whites of Regan's eyes for long, Angel squinted around at the RV's front seats. Ty was hunched over the wheel, one side of his face lit by the greenish light glowing from the dash. He was muttering something, a constant stream of words. She heard only snatches, but it terrified her. *'Enough, five is enough, not long now, back we go, yes back we go, five, five is what we need . . .'*

Crazy talk. Insane. Angel felt her vision blurring from the horror of it.

Beside Ty sat Angel's mom. She wasn't tied like the others, but something was wrong there too. Shannon River stared straight ahead, no seatbelt to restrain her, head rocking gently with the motorhome's movement. She looked so tiny, so fragile next to the green-lit monster they'd all expected to become her husband.

How long Angel sat in the back of the RV she couldn't say. Once in a while she found her sister's eyes or her brother's, but it was too hard to look at them for long, too awful to see the terror in Elliot's face, or in Hope's. Too awful to consider what might happen to them. To all of them.

Perhaps ten minutes passed. Perhaps an hour. They travelled on quieter roads now, or maybe it had simply grown late and most Californians – the free people, at least – had retired to their beds.

Now, the engine sound changed and Angel realised the motorhome was slowing. The right-side indicator pulsed orange shapes inside the cab, drenching one side of Ty's face in colour and giving him the appearance of a Halloween pumpkin.

They pulled off the highway into a rest area, gravel popping and sputtering beneath the RV's tyres. Ty killed the engine.

Silence.

Followed by the tentative chirrups of cicadas; as if even they knew that something was amiss, and that evil had rolled to a stop nearby. The motorhome settled on its springs. It ticked and creaked.

Ty threw open his door and jumped down onto the gravel, slamming it shut behind him. Angel heard his feet crunching on stones as he walked around the vehicle.

This is where it happens. This is where he kills us. I wonder who'll be first. Please not Elliot. I couldn't bear to see that.

The side door opened and suddenly Ty was moving among them, a carrion-stench clinging to his silhouette, his breath urgent and rancid. He brushed past Angel's legs and she recoiled, thinking she might gag from the stink of him.

Is this what madness does? Is this what it smells like? How quickly he's falling apart. Mind first. Then body.

She heard the sound of a cabinet door opening and shutting, its magnets snicking together. A drawer rolled out on its runners. Cutlery and cooking implements jangled and crashed.

Ty plucked something from the drawer and held it up. Moonlight glinted off a wedge of sharp steel. As if sensing that Angel watched him, he turned to face her. There was just enough light inside the motorhome to see his eyes.

She felt her skin contract on her flesh, her heart thump against her ribs.

Don't look at Elliot. Don't jinx him.

Ty grunted, an animal sound of hunger or excitement. Then he turned in the tiny space and vanished, the vehicle's side door banging shut in his wake.

Angel realised she'd been holding her breath. She blew it

out, finally allowing herself to look at Elliot, at his pale, terrified face. *It's OK*, she mouthed. *Don't cry. It'll be OK.*

Ty threw open the RV's passenger door. He grabbed a handful of Shannon River's hair and Angel acknowledged that her silent words to her brother had been lies. It wasn't going to be OK. Far from it.

Her mom didn't scream as Ty yanked her out of the seat. When her body hit the ground she made a *Nuh* sound as the breath was knocked from her lungs. Ty pulled her to her feet. Still clutching the knife, he slipped one hand around Shannon's arm and led her into the woods. She accompanied him without complaint, as if half asleep.

'Ty, no!' Angel screamed. 'Don't do this! Don't!'

Within moments, she lost sight of them. All that remained was a slip of moon, the chirrups of the cicadas and four haunted faces that reflected her own terror and magnified it.

Ty returned a few minutes later, and he came alone. No knife. Angel felt her chin thunk against her chest, no strength left to keep her head aloft.

Gone. Just like that. Her mom was gone.

Ty climbed up into the driver's seat and started the engine, the green lights of the dash once more washing over him. He hauled the RV back onto the road and accelerated.

Through the window, Angel watched the patch of forest where they had left her mom recede, dwindle and finally disappear.

They ate up road. It flashed beneath them, ferried them along in darkness. She could still hear Ty's muttering, a monotone drawl of half-formed words, sometimes in English and some-times in a language she could not understand. Perhaps it was no language at all.

Hours passed until finally, many miles from whatever remained of Shannon River, they pulled onto a narrower road, this one a simple dirt track among stunted trees and parched grass.

They bumped over potholes and through weed-choked ditches. A cupboard door banged open and a ceramic mug fell out, rolling along the isle. Ty turned his head and Angel saw him in profile, a silhouette face she barely recognised.

The road twisted and began to rise, and now they were curving around the front of a big old clapboard house, its steep gables black against the night sky. No light seeped from its mullioned windows; no hint of life within. A veranda ran along the front of the building, bowed in the centre like a toothless grin. On one side hung an ancient porch swing, and when Ty killed the RV's engine Angel heard the creak of its chains as it shifted in the breeze.

She shivered. Wanted to throw up. This was not the kind of place that promised a happy ending for any of them.

Ty threw open his door and jumped out onto the driveway. Again, he disappeared around the side of the vehicle and she heard the sound of a key, followed by a metallic groan as the luggage bay hatch popped open.

The woman. Locked in the hold.

Angel strained her ears. She heard a slipping, a sliding. The motorhome rocked beneath her. Outside, something thumped.

A moan. And then a cry.

'What's happening?' Elliot whispered.

'I don't know. I don't know.'

Now a scraping. A second thump, this one louder than the first. A female voice. Breathless, jubilant.

The RV's side door shot open and the woman with the seaweed eyes and sunlight hair leaped inside, gasping huge lungfuls of air.

Georgia, Angel remembered. Her name was Georgia.

Georgia flicked a switch and light flooded the interior. Her face was scratched and torn. Blood seeped from one side of her mouth. But she'd lost the confused vulnerability Angel had seen clinging to her inside the vehicle's cargo hold.

She glanced at each of them in turn. 'Rope, anything,' she panted, the words merging together in her urgency. 'Something to tie him with. Quick. We don't have long.'

So huge was Angel's relief that it burst from her pores like steam. She thrust her chin towards the bedroom. 'Top drawer. Use his belts.'

Georgia's eyes locked with Angel's.

Survivors.

The woman nodded. Still beautiful, even with all her injuries. 'Good girl.'

'Untie us.'

'Soon.'

Georgia disappeared into the bedroom and Angel heard her pulling out drawers. A moment later she dashed through the main living area, clutching a handful of Ty's belts. She darted back outside.

From the rear of the motorhome, a scuffling. Angel heard a crash as something of meat and bone hit a metal body panel. She tensed. Had Georgia been overcome? Was that the sound of her head being mashed against the motorhome's bumper? She wanted to cry out. But what help would that be?

Footsteps pounded around the side of the RV. Someone jumped back in amongst them.

It was Georgia.

Angel sagged. Felt tears hot against her cheeks. 'Please,' she said. 'Untie us.'

Her rescuer nodded. Examined the ropes that bound them.

'My bag,' Angel said. 'Down there on the floor. There's a knife inside.'

Seconds later Georgia was sawing through their bonds, forehead creased with concentration. She freed Elliot first. Hope was next, then Regan and Luke. The boy slumped to the floor, still unconscious.

'Outside,' the woman said. 'All of you. *Go*.'

Unsteadily, Regan climbed to her feet. She shepherded Hope and Elliot in front of her. 'My brother . . .' she began.

'I'll carry him.'

They didn't need further encouragement. Faces paper-white, they shuffled to the door and dropped down onto the driveway.

Georgia bent to Angel, attacking the rope that bound her.

'Is he still out there?'

'He can't get you,' the woman replied. 'You're safe. But we have to hurry.'

'Our phones. We should call the police.'

Georgia shook her head. 'He smashed them. We're on our own for now. Do exactly as I say and we can survive this. But we don't have long.'

When the rope fell away, Angel dragged herself to her feet. Blood rushed into her legs and she nearly stumbled. Reaching out her hand to steady herself, she hobbled to the RV's door.

Behind her Georgia crouched in front of Luke. She threw his arms over her shoulders and heaved him up.

Outside, the moon hid behind racing clouds. The cicadas were back, cheering them on. *Hurry*, their voices chorused.

Hurry hurry hurry hurry.

'Go,' Georgia urged. 'Don't look back. Don't look at what's behind you.'

Regan ran up the veranda's front steps. The others followed. She opened the screen door. Tested the handle of the door behind it. It swung wide, revealing a wedge of darkness.

'Inside,' Georgia told her.

Behind them, back on the drive, Angel heard something. A stirring. A muttering.

Regan heard it too. She flinched, as if expecting someone to grab her, and threw herself forward into the house. Elliot crashed after her, then Hope.

Angel was next. She hesitated on the threshold. Something felt wrong.

Of course it feels wrong. You're in a nightmare. Move!

She stumbled through the doorway, hearing Georgia bringing up the rear. The woman used her elbow to flick on a wall switch. Above them, in a cobweb-infested chandelier, a single bulb winked on, painting the hall with a dirty yellow light.

Dust everywhere. On the floor, a tattered rug, its colour faded to grey. A steep wooden staircase ascending into gloom. A grandfather clock against one wall, the hands of its face frozen at twenty minutes to midnight. A cracked mirror on another, liver-spotted with age. In one corner, a rotting heap of clothing. The floorboards groaned as they crossed them.

'Try through there,' Georgia whispered to Regan, nodding towards a closed door. 'Search for a phone.'

Regan, her eyes huge, looked like she was going to refuse, and then she saw her brother in the woman's arms. The sight seemed to rally her. She hurried to the door. Threw it open. Stepped inside.

Angel followed, mouth so dry she could barely take a breath without gagging.

Only then, as she moved into darkness so heavy it seemed to drag her towards the floor, did she catch the smell – that same meat stench – of something dying, and she flung herself around, knowing that she had to get out, that all of them had to get out of this house right now.

But the woman from the RV was blocking the door. She let go of Luke, allowing his body slip through her arms to the floor, and when she flicked a switch beside her two wall lamps along one side of the room bled out a sordid light. Angel saw what greeted them and opened her mouth to scream, to deny what she saw, but her throat was silent, the words refusing to come.

All she could do, all any of them could do, was stare.

Velvet curtains screened the windows at the far end of the room. Moths had feasted on them, puckering the material to rags. A fireplace held white ashes and the black stumps of logs. Newspapers lay strewn across the floor.

Arranged in a half-circle, at the very centre of the room, stood five mouldering armchairs. And in every chair sat a corpse, hunched and dry. Each face was a blister of cracked skin and sunken cheeks, so old it was impossible to tell whether it had belonged to a man or woman. Skeletal fingers gripped chair arms, and just then Angel realised that she had been wrong, that the shrunken corpses weren't corpses at all, because one by one they began to open their eyes, and when they saw the five children gathered before them their jaws cracked open and their mouths snapped into grins.

Angel turned to the woman with the seaweed eyes and the sunlight hair, and saw her smile.

'Welcome,' she said, eyes shining, and when the word slipped from her lips, Angel smelled corruption on her breath. It reminded her of the corporeal stink rolling off Ty. But as potent as her step-dad had been, he seemed positively fresh compared to this. Georgia's corruption seemed older, deeper: more foul than anything Angel had experienced before. Or would ever experience again.

The door swung closed. The five creatures in the armchairs began to rise. And the lights, as if to show mercy, flickered out.

CHAPTER 18

Calw, Germany

Hannah Wilde was walking in the woods with Gabriel and Ibsen when her phone started trilling in her pocket. The late autumn sun was low in the sky, and she could feel the faint heat of its rays struggling through the bare branches of the trees above her head. Gabriel's fingers were interlaced with her own. So precious she found these snatched moments of togetherness. So rare.

It was the handset's standard ring, which was unusual: she had assigned the few people who knew this number individual tones. 'Let me get this,' she murmured, disentangling herself from Gabriel and digging into her pocket. She answered the phone and thought, for a moment, that she heard the woods grow still in expectation.

A pause, then a voice. 'I'm so sorry,' Leah said. 'I couldn't let anyone know.'

When Hannah caught the distress in her daughter's tone, it closed her throat. She struggled to get her words out. 'I know, darling. It's OK. Are you safe?'

'I'm fine. Really.'

Trying to calm her heart enough to think, Hannah said, 'Listen to me. I know what you intend to do. I know you've decided to make contact and I understand why, but if you go near—'

'I already have.'

The girl's admission shocked Hannah into silence. Down by her feet, Ibsen woofed. She heard Gabriel take a breath, felt his hand press lightly against her back, supporting her. Instinctively, she leaned into him.

'We talked about this once, you and I,' Leah said. 'You remember, don't you? We pretty much agreed that one day the *kirekesztett* might be our only hope.'

'You've really met them?' Hannah asked, once she'd recovered her breath enough to speak.

'Yes. They . . . they haven't been at all like I imagined.'

'Don't romanticise them, Leah.'

'I won't.'

'If the *tanács* find out where you've gone, what you're trying to do—'

'That's why I need your help. Gabriel's too. Because I've already made some headway. Four women willing to take a chance with us. Perhaps a fifth, if I'm lucky. But I can't bring them back to Calw.'

'No. The *tanács* have been all over us here.'

'So if this is going to work, we'll need another location, somewhere we can gather without it being broadcast far and wide. I promised the *kirekesztett* women that they could meet some of the children before they start the process.'

Hannah felt the energy going out of her limbs. She wanted to sit down but she wouldn't give in to her fatigue. 'This is so risky, Leah.'

'I know. But I think the mothers will understand. I think they'll want to help. We just need a venue.'

Hannah thought for a moment. 'The place at Lake Como.'

'Can you arrange it? It means involving Catharina. But I think she'll agree.'

'If the *tanács* find out about this, that without consulting them we've gone to the *kirekesztett* and offered—'

'I don't care. I don't think you do either. Half of them probably agree it's the only option left. And the others – well,

their ideas are so medieval . . . someone needs to explain that
we're not living in the goddamned Middle Ages any more.'

Hannah laughed at that, buoyed by the spirit and conviction
she heard in her daughter's voice. She knew Leah was right: it
was the only option left. Even so, by acting unilaterally, the girl
exposed herself to more danger than she'd faced in her entire
adult life, and not just from the fanatical voices inside the *tanács*.
Hannah had spent the last fifteen years living in this community
of *hosszú életek*, but with the exception of Jakab she had never
met one of the *kirekesztett*. Other than her daughter's assurances,
she had nothing by which she could judge them.

*Isn't that the point? It's neither your right, nor your privilege, to sit
in judgement of anyone. Certainly not a people about whom you know
so little.*

'Are you there?' Leah asked.

'I'm here.'

Listening to the crack and hiss of the connection, feeling
every inch of the physical distance that separated her from the
daughter she had striven so long to protect, Hannah conceded
that her years as Leah's guardian had come to an end. She could
advise, and she knew that her daughter would listen, but she
recognised the steel in Leah's voice, recognised it as a trait that
linked her to the girl just as it had linked her to her own mother,
Nicole. 'You can rely on me for what you need,' she said.
'Gabe too. I'll speak to Catharina. We'll be there, waiting. How
long before you arrive?'

'Four days, maybe? I haven't been in England for years.
There are a few places I need to visit before I fly home.'

'Don't hang up,' Hannah said. 'Not yet. There's something
else I need to tell you. Something the *tanács* mentioned when
they were here.' She paused. 'Leah, has anyone told you of the
lélek tolvajok?'

The girl hesitated. 'Odd you should ask, but yes.'

'You need to listen very carefully. If what I've heard is true,
the *tanács* might be the least of our worries.'

CHAPTER 19

Budapest, Hungary

1880

Two days before the season's *kezdet végzet* – first of the four social engagements that would decide the futures of so many young *hosszú életek* – Dr András Benedek summoned Izsák to his study in the north wing of Tansik House. It was only the second time Izsák had visited the doctor's consulting chamber since Trusov's assault on him, all those years distant.

On the more recent occasion, András had brought him there to tell him of his oldest brother's killing at the hands of the *kirekesztett* known as Jakab. Izsák had cried for a day and a night at the news, and at the knowledge – so unutterably bleak – that the number of living souls with whom he shared a connection had, once again, contracted.

A year had passed since that day, and seven years had rolled by since the doctor had brought Izsák to Tansik House. So much had happened in those intervening years. He'd discovered the awful secrets the doctor's home hid from the world, and had fallen in love with one of its treasures.

Now, sitting in a leather armchair beside a window looking into the gardens, he watched the doctor pour two glasses of pálinka and took the one that was offered.

András sat in a chair opposite. As usual, the man looked scrubbed and fresh, his fingernails like perfect white crescent moons. An occasional table beside him displayed a collection of framed photographs – mementos of his travels around Europe. Izsák recognised the Arc de Triomphe de l'Étoile and the Notre Dame de Paris, but his eyes were drawn to a more unusual image: the bust of a woman wearing a seven-pointed crown. Her face was arresting in itself, but it was the scale that shocked him. Located in parkland, she dwarfed the surrounding trees.

András followed Izsák's eyes and he smiled. 'Taken at the *Exposition Universelle*. Two years ago now. And what a sight she was.'

'Who is she?'

'Libertas, the Roman goddess of freedom. They're sending her to New York once she's finished. With her torch, she'll stand a hundred and fifty feet. Astonishing accomplishment, if they manage it.'

The doctor sipped his pálinka, and his smile faded. 'If circumstances had been kinder,' he said, 'we'd be celebrating your *végzet* year. But life deals its blows, and we must make the best of what remains. Your father disgraced himself before the *tanács* and he paid the price. Your brother chose the path of murder rather than atonement, and one day, willing or not, I'm sure he'll face his accusers.

'Your blood is tainted, Izsák, and there is nothing we can do about that. But you've been an obedient house guest for most of your time here, and a willing student. I'm pleased with the progress we've been able to make with you.'

András paused, and Izsák knew he waited for some expression of gratitude. He could not bring himself to voice it.

Unfazed, the doctor sipped from his glass. 'You're a man now, as much as you'll ever be, which means it's time for you to leave us.'

Izsák stared. 'Where should I go?'

'That's up to you. It's a large world out there. Filled with possibilities. Honestly? I'd travel, if I were you. Far from here. See something of the world. Try to work out how you can leave it a better place. You're the last of the Balázs line. Your father enjoyed a good reputation before your brother destroyed it. Perhaps you can find some small way of rebuilding it.'

'My father's reputation remains intact.'

'I know we'll never agree on that, so let's not dwell on it. You'll be leaving us next week. Come and see me before you go – you'll have travelling expenses and a small amount of money, as is your right. In the meantime . . .'

The doctor rose and went to his desk, where he searched through a drawer. Finally he found what he was looking for. When he turned back to Izsák, he held a gold watch on a chain. 'Although you won't attend the *végzet*, I see no reason to withhold this from you. After Balázs József was executed, the *Főnök* passed this to me for safekeeping. I understand it was the last your father ever made.'

Open-mouthed, Izsák took the watch from the doctor. It was his father's work, no doubt of it. Even all these years later, he could pick a single Balázs József piece from a hundred lesser imitations. This was a particularly fine example.

Opening its hunter case, he gazed down at the enamelled face hand-painted with black numerals, and was instantly transported back to his father's workshop in Gödöllö, smelling the dried apple aroma of József's pipe, seeing the thatch of the man's eyebrows knitting together as he concentrated at some task.

Turning the watch over, Izsák saw the inscription on the back plate.

Balázs Izsák
Végzet

Where perhaps his father had hoped, one day, to engrave a date, a blank space waited. That day, and that date, would now never fall. Izsák slid his thumb over the indentations, realising that József might have chiselled those letters only hours before his execution at the Citadella.

Izsák still remembered the horologist's last words as he stood with lifted chin on the rickety wooden stage inside Budapest's oldest fort.

'*Izsák is not yet twelve years old. He is an innocent. A victim of this situation as surely as anyone else. Please: watch over him. Allow him to grow. And help him to heal.*

'*I am to be judged today. But tomorrow, in the way you treat an innocent, you will all be judged. Tell him I loved him. Tell him his mother loved him. And show him that he is loved still.*'

Even in his last moments, József had thought not of himself but of his youngest son. If only Izsák could have learned from that example, and lived his own life as selflessly. Now, sitting in the doctor's study, looking down at this priceless piece his father had created for him, that treacherous old thought rang in his head.

What will happen to me?

The *tanács* had not heeded József's plea. But at least his father had tried, using what powers of oratory he still possessed, to make them listen.

A tear dripped on to the watch case. Izsák wiped it off, dismayed that András might see his feelings laid bare, furious at this demonstration of his own weakness even as he recollected his father's greatest act of strength.

Stiffly, he begged the doctor's leave, pocketed the watch and hurried out of the study. Upstairs, back in the south wing that had been his home these past seven years, he sought out Béni.

The young man was sitting beside the window in his room, smoking tobacco from the ribbed clay pipe that had become his recent habit. At the desk, Pig moved the pieces of a jigsaw around on its surface. The crumbs of his last meal clung to the downy hairs around his mouth.

'You've heard the news,' Béni said, exhaling a streamer of tobacco smoke.

'We're being turned out,' Izsák replied, envious of his friend's display of indifference.

'Nonsense. We're graduating. That's how I see it. We – the three of us, I mean – survived Tansik House, against all the odds. That's something worth celebrating, don't you think?' He held out a bottle of spirit, eyebrows lifting mischievously.

Izsák declined. 'But where will we go?'

'That's up to us.'

'What will we do?'

'We'll rule the bloody world, Izsák. That's what we'll do.'

'What about Pig?'

'Pig's one of us. Aren't you, Pig?'

Their companion snorted his agreement.

'Is everyone leaving?' Izsák asked.

'No, just those of age. Us three. Etienne. That's it.'

'Trusov'll be heartbroken.'

'He'll find himself another whore. Save your sympathy for the river men spending their wages in Tabán next week. They won't know what hit them.'

'Don't, Béni. It's not funny. None of it.'

The older boy sucked on his pipe and shrugged.

Katalin came to him the night before the *kezdet végzet*, while the rest of Tansik House slept. She arrived bundled up in a shapeless brown robe, face hidden in the shadows beneath its hood. Izsák lit his oil lamp and turned up the wick, bathing the room in light. When Katalin let her robe fall to the floor, he gasped in awe.

She wore her *végzet* outfit. The dress, a shimmering king-fisher blue, was of crinoline but it hugged her hips closely, retaining her silhouette while bunching out behind. Although the recent fashion in Budapest favoured a high collar, Katalin's dress was of a more classic design, with a low square décolletage that revealed her throat and the firm slopes of her breasts.

Her arms were bare. Her hair was piled into ringlets on top of her head. A delicate strip of blue silk masked her face just below her eyes; the fabric moved against her lips as she breathed.

Strange, but despite her radiance, Izsák saw that she was nervous.

Katalin took his hands. 'I wanted you to see.'

His lungs filled with her perfume, a scent of everything that could not be. 'You're beautiful,' he told her. 'Truly.'

'If there was any way, Izsák,' she began. 'Any way at all that tomorrow night we could . . .'

He shushed her. 'There isn't. It's the way things are.'

'It's not fair.'

'What is?' He closed his mouth, forbidding himself from continuing that thought aloud: What *is* fair about Katalin going to the *végzet* alone? What *is* fair, that all I have to mark my entrance into adulthood is a pocket watch, the engraving of which will never be completed? What was fair about my father's execution? My brother's murder? The treatment of my friends in Tansik House? The treatment of Etienne?

Katalin led him to the bed and perched on it, careful not to crush her dress. 'Look at me, Izsák. I want to share something with you.'

He found her eyes in the lamplight: two mesmerising windows, which, even as he watched, began to change. He clutched Katalin's fingers, conscious of what she meant to do and knowing that he should look away, that she should not waste this gift and make *him* her first, when nothing further could ever grow between them.

He began to pull back from her.

She clutched him. '*Please.*'

Those eyes were unavoidable, stripping away his defences and unlacing the very heart of him. He saw threads of emerald weaving at the edges of her irises like twisting snakes of ivy; winking pinpricks of gold; swirling gemstones.

Izsák felt his heart race in his chest, his skin shiver and contract. His own eyes began to respond, and when they did Katalin gasped, dropping his hands and sliding her fingers around his waist.

The world receded, and for a time they were like two statues in the lamplight, staring into each other's faces, sharing the magic that twined there, surrendering to an act of intimacy older than the city itself.

When, finally, the rose blush of their skin began to fade, Izsák felt the cold weight of sorrow press down on him. To experience this, to experience Katalin in all her unattainable perfection . . . it seemed like the most despicable cruelty.

But he had a duty not to pursue her. He knew they would never find peace until they gave this up. And while his own future looked uncertain, Katalin's undoubtedly contained much light. He loved her too much to see her suffer.

Izsák closed his eyes. He allowed himself to retain a single image of hers as she shared with him the *lélekfeltárás*, that most intimate act of *hosszú élet* lovers, and locked it away somewhere deep.

He breathed out. Let go of her. Blinked. 'Thank you.'

The last traces of the display in Katalin's eyes died. Her chest swelled. 'Izsák, I—'

'No. Don't say anything.' He grinned, and now that he'd persuaded himself that this was the right thing to do, the only thing, he found it easier than he'd expected. 'You should go back.'

The first *végzet* of the season arrived, and Tansik House lit up like a Christmas bauble. While Katalin was the only resident who would attend the festivities, every great *hosszú élet* family in Budapest was hosting a celebration party. Dr András Benedek had decided to hold the city's most extravagant.

Recently installed gaslights blazed outside, illuminating the courtyard and the building's huge façade. Inside, serving staff lit chandeliers, polished woodwork and uncorked champagne bottles by the hundred. A string quartet played in the entrance hall as entertainment for the arriving guests. Izsák had heard there was to be a full performance of *László Hunyadi* later, although Béni had ventured downstairs to witness the doctor in a panic at the discovery that none of the singers, nor the orchestra he'd booked at great expense, had yet turned up. They'd laughed a great deal about that.

Sitting on the bed in Béni's room, Izsák watched his best friend open another bottle of Perrier-Jouët and refill their mugs. 'You're still going into Pest?'

Béni smirked. 'Every right-born *hosszú élet* in Budapest is misbehaving tonight. I don't see why we should be any different.'

Izsák nodded towards Pig. 'You're taking him with you?'

'Of course. Tonight the Pig becomes a man.'

'Are you sure that's a good idea?'

'I think it's a fine idea. What other chance might he get?'

'You have money?'

'The doctor advanced me some of my purse. It'll be enough.' He slapped Pig on the back. 'You're looking forward to it, aren't you?'

Already, Pig's face was flushed from champagne. His smile had a child's innocence to it. 'Good fun,' he said. 'Want.'

Béni glanced up at Izsák. 'And what about you? Are you coming?'

He shook his head.

'You're going to torture yourself instead.'

'I just want to watch her arrive. I think it'll help.'

'You're an idiot, Izsák.'

'I know. You're taking Pig to a riverside brothel and I'm the idiot.' He sighed. 'Take care of him.'

'Count on it.'

Two hours later, Izsák found himself five miles further downstream on the Pest side of the Danube, concealed in undergrowth twenty yards from the boarding ramp to the *Örök Hercegnő*, a specially commissioned pleasure barge on which Katalin's *kezdet végzet* would take place. It was one of two venues procured for tonight's opening festivities, the second located in the heart of the Buda district.

The *Örök Hercegnő* was a long flat-bottomed vessel, timber-hulled. Its graceless lines were softened by the light that glowed from the portholes of its main saloon, and from the cheery hand-blown glass lamps strung along its gunwales. Delicate music drifted from within.

Izsák watched the carriages of the *hosszú életek* arrive, depositing their young men and women onto the cobbles. Not for the first time that evening he found himself thinking of his father, and of how different things might have been but for the occurrence of a few tragic events.

Katalin's carriage was the last to arrive. The doctor had remained at Tansik House, leaving Trusov the task of chaperon. The man jumped down and took Katalin's hand as she emerged – a sudden blossoming of blue. She let go of Trusov as soon as she was able, and walked alone up the boarding ramp, disappearing into the saloon without looking back.

Izsák rested on his haunches. That was it, then. He had wanted to come here and see this; had wanted, however painful, to witness Katalin's transformation from the girl he had loved into the beautiful young woman tonight's event celebrated. Now that he had seen her go aboard, there was nothing to do except leave.

He watched the boat's crew slide back the ramp and cast off the mooring ropes. Two of them remained ashore, while the three still on board crossed the deck to the entrance doors of the main saloon, which they closed.

Izsák was just about to start his walk back to Tansik House when he saw one of the men throw a bolt across the doors. The sailor reached into his pocket and pulled out a padlock, which he used to secure the bolt in place.

The vessel nosed out into the current and Izsák's stomach flipped. Why would anyone lock the doors – the *only* doors, by the look of it – to the saloon? He studied the sailors, following their movements as they retreated to the wheelhouse at the stern, and stood up in the darkness. Now he thought about it, the men hardly looked like sailors at all. He didn't know what he meant by that – what, after all, was a sailor *meant* to look like? – but the more he watched them, the more convinced he became that his intuition was correct.

Something's wrong.

Breaking into a run, he kept pace with the *Örök Hercegnő* as it began to build speed, maintaining enough distance from the bank to avoid being seen by those on board. His blood was pumping now, heart kicked into action by a bite of adrenalin.

Two men emerged from the wheelhouse, carrying buckets. They walked along the deck to the bow, turned and retraced their steps, sloshing the contents of their pails over the saloon's timber frame.

Inside the wheelhouse, a light flared.

The deckhands finished their task and moved to the stern rail, where they began to reel in a rowing boat the vessel towed behind her. As soon as it was close enough, the first man jumped in, followed by the second.

The remaining sailor emerged from the wheelhouse. In one hand he carried a flaming baton – a slim length of wood dipped in pitch and set alight. Black smoke fluttered up from the flames. Izsák stopped on the bank, unsure of exactly what he was seeing.

The sailor flung his torch. Without waiting for it to land, he jumped into the waiting rowing boat.

Izsák watched the baton arc through the air. Tumbling end over end, it hit the barred saloon entrance and its light vanished. An instant later, fire bloomed with serpentine fury. Yellow snakes of flame raced up the walls and leaped into the night. Within seconds they had engulfed the deck, surging the length of the boat. From inside, the sound of violins.

The men in the rowing boat cast off from the stricken vessel.

Izsák shouted but they ignored him, rowing fast for Buda on the opposite side of the river.

In disbelief, he watched the *Örök Hercegnő* – pilotless now, a growing inferno – slide into the main current. Tearing off his jacket, he sprinted after it.

Already, the fire had transformed the river into a ribbon of glittering rubies. He overtook the boat, eyes searching the bank for another moored vessel – anything he could use to get out into the water.

A hundred yards further downstream a pontoon thrust a crooked finger into the Danube. If only he could reach it before the *Örök Hercegnő* swept past, he could launch himself off and land, if not on the boat itself, then close to it.

Onboard, the first screams clove the night. He saw faces crowding at the portholes. Panicked eyes, peering out.

Izsák accelerated, his stride lengthening, focusing all his will on reaching the pontoon before the boat sailed by. He tripped over stones and rubble, dodged the spindly roots of trees. This far downstream from Budapest's centre, the riverbank was less developed: vast tracts of scrub were broken by isolated haulage yards and patches of cleared wasteland. The pontoon was a hundred yards away. Eighty. Sixty.

An explosion of gravel behind him.

Izsák wheeled, and saw he was being chased. A masked shadow, legs scything.

Forty yards to the pontoon. Twenty.

Something crashed out of the darkness to his left. Another figure, this one wielding a knife. Whoever had masterminded the burning of the *Örök Hercegnő* had placed sentinels along the bank, and now he'd attracted their attention.

Izsák jinked right, coming within an arm's length of a flashing blade. He heard his assailant curse, wrong-footed. Saw another figure racing towards him. Three of them now.

The pontoon waited directly ahead, a floating walkway of greasy planks nailed to a row of barrels lashed together. Izsák hit the first boards, nearly slipped, righted himself. He sprinted down the pontoon, out across the water, the casks reverberating like timpani, dipping and bobbing.

The burning vessel, its flames now reaching thirty feet into the sky, trailed a dirty black chimney of smoke. Inside, the screaming intensified. As the bow neared the end of the pontoon, Izsák leaped.

Airborne, he heard shouts from behind, knew that his body was silhouetted. He did not know who his pursuers were, but they had committed an act of such depravity that he knew they would not hesitate to kill him too.

He hit the water, plunging into a world that was cold and silent and dark. A second later he exploded out of it. The boat slid towards him, a jewel of bright fire and brighter screams. Its bow had not yet caught, nor the front of the saloon, but the rest sloughed off flames and smoke like a gliding phoenix. Resin boiled. Planking hissed and spat.

Izsák reached for the hull as it wallowed past. The smooth wood offered no hold. Above, a balloon of fire rolled towards him. He ducked his head below the water. When he re-emerged he felt the boat's tow sucking at his legs. It was going to pass him and there was nothing he could do. He was too far beneath the deck to pull himself onto it.

No! You don't give up! Katalin's inside! You watched your father die and did nothing. You won't do the same thing again.

He cried out in frustration. Felt something brush his neck. A loose mooring line, trailing through the water. Izsák caught it. Felt it rip through his fingers, tearing skin.

He tightened his grip and the rope wrenched him, towing him along beside the boat. A wave broke over his head. He fought through it, spluttering.

One hand over the other, Izsák began to haul himself along the rope. His biceps felt like glass was piercing them. He lost his grip. Found it again.

Something cracked, incredibly loud. A part of the hull above his head erupted into splinters.

They're shooting at you. Move!

From where his strength came, he did not know. But somehow he managed to pull himself forward another few feet. The rope was leading him out of the river now. He hauled himself up.

A pistol fired, its report shockingly close. Half out of the water, still dangling a few feet below the deck, Izsák hesitated, too scared to move. The higher he pulled himself up, the clearer target he presented to those gathered on the bank.

Another pistol shot. He saw the muzzle flash. Not the bullet's impact.

Onboard the *Örök Hercegnő*, the screaming changed in pitch. Panic replaced by pain, as the air inside the saloon began to roast, and skin began to burn.

Katalin's in there. You have to DO something. NOW!

Calling on the last dregs of his strength, Izsák surged up the rope and pulled himself onto the deck, lungs seared from the exertion. Rising to a crouch, he crabbed around to the opposite side of the saloon, using it to shield himself from the marksmen. The bow section had not yet begun to burn. A row of five portholes gave him his first glance inside the *Örök Hercegnő*.

It was a scene he would never forget.

Smoke billowed across the ceiling. On the floor lay broken chairs and smashed champagne flutes, discarded pewter masks and lace veils. A stage was a graveyard of abandoned instruments and toppled music stands.

Among the debris young men and women, driven to their knees by lack of air, gagged on smoke. Those who could still stand gathered on the starboard side. Even over the roar of the flames, he could hear their screams as they tried to attract the attention of those on the bank. At the rear of the cabin, three young men were trying to smash their way through the locked doors, using a table as their battering ram. Their white shirts were smouldering, eyes betraying their understanding that the doors would not yield. Still they tried, shouting in despair when flames engulfed one of them. The man flailed in his agony, setting others alight.

Izsák saw a flash of blue in the swirling smoke, and then he was yelling Katalin's name. She stood at the bow, a handkerchief pressed to her mouth.

Hearing her name, she raced to the porthole. 'Izsák! We're trapped!'

'I'm going to get you out.'

'We're locked in!'

'Stay up this end. You're safer here.'

'There's no air.'

'Get down low.'

She pressed her hand to the glass and when he mirrored her action he cringed at the porthole's heat.

Turning away, he looked aft. Half the saloon was an inferno now. The deck, too, had begun to burn. But his clothes were soaked through with river water. They should keep him cool enough to press through the flames to the stern.

Closing his eyes and his mouth, Izsák stepped through fire, suppressing a cry as it lashed him. By the time he fought his way through, he was shaking from the pain.

He'd planned to search the wheelhouse for something he could use to force the saloon doors open. But the wind was carrying the fire's heat directly towards it, concealing the structure in rolling black smoke. No matter. It was his only option.

Izsák took a breath, held it. Screwing his eyes shut, he moved inside that choking darkness. Hand outstretched, he touched the side of the wheelhouse. Felt his skin blister at the contact.

He found the door, kicked it open, dived inside. Wanted to take a breath. Couldn't. Pawed around in the blinding smoke.

Too long. You're taking too long.

He found the wheel. Found the raised edge of a seat. Nothing else.

Out of air, he sucked in poison. Coughed. Choked. Nothing in the wheelhouse to help him. Nothing at all. Howling, he staggered out as a lick of flame touched its side and burst over it. The heat sent him sprawling. He pressed himself to the deck, eyes stinging, face turned away from the fire. Sounds all around him now. Dreadful sounds: of burning, of screaming, of dying.

He had seconds before he began to burn too. With no weapon to break down the doors, with no more ideas, he raised himself to his knees and crawled back along the deck towards the bow. A gap appeared in the flames and he scrambled through. Above, he spotted the porthole where he'd last seen Katalin.

Izsák raised himself to his feet. The glass was too hot to touch, and Katalin was nowhere in sight. He bellowed her name. Flames were spreading *inside* the saloon now. Young women writhed on the floor, dresses on fire, crackling as they burned. Behind the porthole, a face appeared.

Katalin's.

Cheeks streaked with soot and blood, eyes reflecting the scarlet heart of the inferno within, she opened her mouth and begged him to help her.

Izsák punched the side of the cabin. 'I can't get in, Katalin! I can't get in!'

'Yes, you can. Please, Izsák. Please!'

The planking beside his face burst into flames, frying the skin of his cheek. 'What can I do?' he shouted. 'What can I do?'

'Izsák, don't you dare let me burn!'

He beat his fists on the burning wood. Slammed his elbow against the porthole glass.

'*Izsák, don't you let me BURN!*'

He couldn't get in. And, because of that, Katalin would die. He watched the reality of her fate dawn on her, and saw her face grow slack. The fire was all around him now. If he didn't go soon, didn't fall backwards into the Danube and let it quench his flesh, he'd be dead too.

But still he couldn't leave her. He'd failed Katalin, but he wouldn't abandon her. An eruption of smoke concealed her. When it passed she was watching him still, with those unforgettable *hosszú élet* eyes.

He had known that this evening he would lose her, but not like this. Not like this.

Katalin closed her eyes. Her hair, piled on top of her head in dark ringlets, burst into flames. Face haloed by that furious light, she burned like a torch.

Izsák screamed as the fire consumed her. Still screaming, he lost his footing on the deck, pitching into the waiting river. Its cold embrace, extinguishing at once the heat in his flesh, was so shocking after the ferocity of the flames that he believed his heart would seize in his chest. It was a welcome thought. Perhaps if his heart didn't fail he would drown instead. He opened his mouth, tried to suck water into his lungs. But his body refused. Izsák felt his legs kicking, betraying him, pushing him up to the surface.

An hour later he was walking the streets, feet carrying him without the need for conscious thought. At first he wandered without purpose, but after a while he noticed that some vague homing instinct was drawing him steadily towards Tansik House.

Izsák saw other fires sprouting in the city, but it was only when he arrived at the doctor's mansion that he realised the burning of the *Örök Hercegnő* had not been an isolated act.

A ring of strangers surrounded the gates outside Tansik House. They carried rifles, all of them, and he saw they had dragged two carts in front of the entrance to stop anyone from entering or leaving.

The gas lamps, which earlier that evening had illuminated the building's palatial façade, were dark. No music drifted from the house. But screaming did. Half the building was on fire.

In future years, the events of the State-sponsored *hosszú életek* cull would be remembered by those who survived it as the *Éjszakai Sikolyok*: the Night of Screams. To Izsák, looking on, it represented a window into hell, and the end of everything he had known

People were dying inside Tansik House, and dying noisily. *These* voices, raised in futile supplication, belonged not to the *hosszú életek* youth, but to its patriarchs and matriarchs. They died just the same; Izsák could not have helped them if he had tried.

He turned away, mind numb, slouching back in the direction he had come. Only when the screams began to fade did he realise where he was heading.

The home of Révész Oszkár Szilárd. His uncle.

Izsák had seen the man once in the seven years since his father's death. The *tanács* had denied Szilárd the chance to bring Izsák into his home, and they had been unyielding in their decision to keep the two apart, rulings for which the boy would never forgive them.

After ten minutes of walking he found the house, mercifully untouched by fire. But something was wrong here, too. At this time of night usually at least a few windows glowed with light, but the front of the building was dark.

Hurrying across the courtyard, Izsák discovered the front door swinging free. He went inside, heart hammering anew. He had seen so much death over the last hour. He wondered whether the night held yet more horror.

Pausing in the entrance hall, Izsák waited as his eyes adjusted to the gloom. To his right, the main staircase, rising into darkness. Immediately in front of him, the passage leading to the kitchen where, all those years ago, he had sat on a stool and eaten the chimney-shaped *Kürtőskalács* that Szilárd's cook heated over the fire. He had not thought of the woman in years, yet now an old memory confronted him.

★ ★ ★

Night, and a crippled servant hovers beside his bed. A cold finger mimics a knife, drawing a line across his throat.

A voice, so close that its tongue wets his ear as it whispers in the darkness: 'All dead soon, little one. All the Long Lives burned in a pile. Bones and ashes. Bones and ashes. Then we take back our city.'

The whispering stops and he hears a second voice, echoing through time. It belongs to the cook, to the woman who feeds him scraps of pastry when she's feeling generous. 'Miksa, come away,' she hisses. 'There'll be a time. It isn't now.'

He remembered something else, too. The evening he escaped, he had tried to leave his uncle a note. But something had frightened him and he'd fled into the night. How costly might that moment of cowardice, so dismayingly characteristic, turn out to be?

The cook and the cripple had been forced to wait seven years, but their time – and the time of all in the city who resented the *hosszú életek* – had come tonight; of that Izsák had no doubt.

He found Szilárd in the study. His uncle had been nailed to the floor, wrought-iron spikes hammered through his wrists, his arms, his shoulders and his ankles. He lay in an ocean of blood, cheekbones shattered, ruined eyes sunken in their sockets like soufflés that had failed to rise.

Izsák gagged at the sight, at the cruelties the man had suffered. He was about to leave when his uncle's chest heaved and his lungs filled with air.

'*Is someone there?*' the old bear asked. Too frightened to speak – too traumatised by Katalin's death, by the sounds and the smells of all the burning and killing he had witnessed – Izsák took a step back towards the door.

You're going to leave him like that? Your own flesh? You'll creep away and leave him to die alone?

You failed Katalin. Now you'll fail your uncle, too?

He closed his eyes.

'Please,' Szilárd whispered. 'Whoever's there. Help me die, will you?'

Izsák hesitated in the doorway. He did not want to look at the ruined thing nailed to the floor. He did not want to acknowledge the awful, broken voice that addressed him.

'Uncle,' he moaned. And now that he'd broken his paralysis, he found he was able to walk through the blood and crouch at the man's side.

Szilárd's chest swelled, its thatch of hair matted with blood. 'Izsák?'

'Yes, sir.'

'You're alive.'

His words came in a rush. 'They killed everyone at the *végzet*, sir. I don't know what's going on. I don't know who they are, but they're burning all the people, murdering them.' He surrendered to a sob that shook his entire body. 'Katalin's dead. She's gone.'

Szilárd coughed, a gravy spray of something dark and thick. 'I'm sorry, boy.'

Reaching out, Izsák laid his hand on his uncle's chest, trying to calm his mind. He'd never healed anyone before, and Szilárd had lost a lot of blood, but if he . . .

'Stop that.'

'But if we don't do something you'll—'

'Die. Yes, Izsák.' His uncle took a rattling breath. Blood leaked down the side of his face. 'That's what I'm trying to do. Don't interfere. It's far too late for that. Listen. You don't have much time. Check the fireplace. You'll find a purse halfway up, on the right-hand side. Now, go. Godspeed. Get out of here before they come back.'

Ignoring the man's words, Izsák left his hand where it was, feeling the coldness of his uncle's flesh beneath his fingers. He closed his eyes, began to push, thought he felt a—

'*I said get out!*' Szilárd roared.

Ripping his hand away, Izsák scrabbled backwards until his head cracked against the side of his uncle's desk. He hugged himself, face contorted in grief.

On the floor of the study, nailed to the wood as if he commanded no greater respect than a common moth in a lepidopterist's archive, Révész Oszkár Szilárd uttered a curse at the ceiling, spasmed once and died.

CHAPTER 20

Oxford, England

An hour after speaking to her mother in Calw, Leah Wilde arrived in Oxford, squeezing her hired Mercedes into a tight parking space outside a terraced row of town houses a few minutes' walk from Balliol College.

It had been raining back in London, but the clouds had receded as she drove west, and now a red sun set fires blazing across the limestone façades of the buildings.

Just being here was enough to resurrect a welter of memories and emotions. She had heard her mother's stories of growing up in Oxford, had listened to Hannah recount how happy she had been until the day her father phoned her at school and asked her to walk out of the gates as fast as she could; Jakab had found them, her mother was dead, and their lives had changed forever.

Tragic that a place famed for its enlightenment and human endeavour could have become the stage for such savagery. Even so, as soon as Leah had seen that Luca's list would take her to England she had known she would end up visiting the city. After what her mother had told her on the telephone, the diversion here seemed even more important.

Professor Emeritus Patrick Beckett lived in a converted first-floor apartment in one of the Victorian houses along the terrace. Leah found his name beneath a bell and rang it. Moments later a device on the door clacked and its lock released. She let herself into a hallway that probably hadn't seen a fresh coat of paint in thirty years.

An uneven floor of red and white tile was home to a collection of strangled umbrellas and a console table overflowing with curling telephone directories. To the left a staircase, covered by a frayed grey carpet, rose at a steep angle. Bolted to the wall beside it hung a newly installed stairlift, its red vinyl seat and smooth metal track a jarring counterpoint to the rest of the decor. Leah followed the stairs up and to the right, where she encountered a yellowing front door.

'It's open!' The voice – high-pitched and wavering, hallmark of the very old – was the most cheerful Leah had heard in weeks. 'I'm in the snug! Second door on the right! If you see a sheepish-looking cat out there you can throttle him for me. Wretched thing just peed on my foot.'

Leah pushed open the door into a hallway so piled with books that she had to shuffle through it sideways to avoid knocking over any of the stacks. It felt both incredibly claustrophobic and wonderfully homely all at once, although the smell, a cocktail of moth balls, cooked porridge oats, rancid cat litter and old books, made her nose wrinkle. A ginger cat stalked towards her, tail held high and eyes averted, as if offended by the accusation it had just endured.

She found the door to the snug, opened it, and from within heard a stack of papers collapse and fan out across the floor.

'Don't worry about that!' cried the voice. 'Come in, come in!'

Leah slid around the door, which had wedged itself rigid over the toppled pile, and entered the strangest little room she had ever seen.

Precariously balanced stacks of reading material rose like papery stalagmites from the carpet. Old maps hung from the walls, along with a collection of what looked like English Civil War weaponry. A rusting unicycle leaned in one corner, next to a set of dust-caked juggling balls and skittles. A black and white television perched on a table, an old VHS player balanced on top. The mantelpiece held a Gurkha knife, a Newton's cradle, a sepia photograph of a fierce-looking woman and a row of Japanese puzzle boxes.

Patrick Beckett sat in an easy chair by the window, his feet propped up on a cowhide pouffe. Despite the ramshackle state of his apartment, the old professor was dressed smartly, in tweed blazer and open-necked shirt. In fact, Leah noted, the only element of his attire that seemed incongruous was the pair of bright pink leg warmers covering his trousers from ankle to knee.

Beckett looked painfully thin, but she did not believe age had done that to him. From what her grandfather had told her of the man, the professor had always displayed a bird-like intensity, mind flitting from subject to subject, body as restless as his thoughts. On the way here, she had calculated that he must be in his late eighties by now; she wouldn't have guessed it by looking at him.

Beckett followed the direction of her gaze, appearing to notice his woollen accoutrements for the first time. His mouth fell open. 'Ah. Aha! Probably looks a bit daft, come to think of it. But they're just the ticket. Better than throwing away money on gas, wouldn't you say? These old buildings, the heat just escapes through the walls. Sorry about the mess. If I'd known you were coming, I would have tidied up a bit.'

He raised eyebrows like two glorious white hamsters clinging to his forehead. 'Actually, I did know you were coming. It's Leah, isn't it? Leah Wilde, that's right. My word, I can see Charles in your face as clear as Jupiter.' Beckett frowned, scratched his head. 'You're a good deal prettier, I should add – nothing masculine about you at all, that's not what I meant. I'm very pleased to meet you. Can I ask, did you happen to bring along . . .'

Grinning, Leah unzipped her bag, pulling out the supplies he had requested over the phone. 'One pork pie,' she said. 'Yes, I checked, and the pastry's crisp, not soft, just as you specified. One bottle of HP sauce. Four cans of Courage bitter.'

Beckett's eyes shone. 'Fine work, Leah. Tremendous. Look, I'd get up, but if you wouldn't mind.'

'Where's your kitchen?'

'Right, yes. Back through there on the left, you'll see it. And I hate to ask, but when you pop the pie on a plate, could you quarter it? Help yourself to anything you find in the fridge. I think there's some milk somewhere. Check the date on it first.'

By the time Leah had cut up Beckett's pie, poured a beer and made herself a cup of tea using the milk she had brought rather than the carton of what resembled cottage cheese lurking inside his fridge, dusk had surrendered to night.

Beckett wasn't exaggerating about the house. When the wind blew, a draught whispered through his apartment, lifting the curtains she had closed against the darkness. At his urging, she lit a single plate on the gas fire and switched on a lamp in one corner. Sinking into a sofa thick with cat hair, Leah warmed her hands around her mug of tea as Beckett busied himself with pie and beer.

'So,' he said, spraying crumbs into his lap, 'Now that you're here, maybe you can help solve a mystery that's been puzzling me for the better part of thirty years.'

'If I can.'

'All those years Charles and I were friends, good friends at that, and then one day . . . just gone. Completely disappeared. His wife, too. And his daughter – your mother, I mean. I always thought, for years and years, that he'd get in touch. But I never saw him again, never heard from him. Police couldn't work out what happened. Or if they did, they certainly never told me.' The old academic looked up. 'Is he dead?'

'Patrick, I'm afraid my grandfather passed away fifteen years ago.'

Beckett put his pie down on his plate and bowed his head.

When, after perhaps a minute, he raised it once more, she saw that his eyes were wet with tears.

That he could display such grief at the news of her grandfather's passing – someone he had not seen in decades – moved her so unexpectedly that she felt a fierce wash of love for him.

'I suppose I should have expected it,' Beckett said. 'But how dreadfully sad, all the same. Your grandfather was an extraordinary man; cantankerous at times, but extraordinary nevertheless. The world's lost a rare intellect in Charles Meredith. Still, fifteen years ago, you say? It doesn't explain why he left, or where he lived out his remaining years.'

'No, it doesn't. But I doubt you'd believe the answer if I told you.'

'Ha! You'd be surprised what a man of eighty-seven will believe, given half the chance.'

'Maybe that's true. I'm afraid I still can't tell you, though. Not yet.'

He stared at her, his filmy eyes almost as colourless as rainwater. 'But you do want something from me, don't you? That's why you're here.'

'I wanted to meet you, Patrick. My grandfather always talked about you, and there are very few people left who have memories of him. But you're right – there was something else. You and Charles, you shared a passion for mythology. Folk tales.'

Beckett raised a cautioning finger. 'The terms aren't interchangeable.'

'But you know what I mean.'

He peered at her. 'Go on.'

'Years ago, you shared a particular passion, an enthusiasm for an obscure piece of Hungarian mythology, centred around a race of people called the—'

'*Hosszú életek*,' the old man breathed, and when his eyes drifted from her face and stared into the fire, a smile tugged at his lips.

Leah shivered. 'You remember.'

'How could I forget? Your grandfather came to me about them, well, it must have been almost fifty years ago. Ha! I don't remember what got him started, but he asked my advice and I pointed him in the direction of a few sources – stories and the like – that I'd collected during my travels. Then, of course, all those years later, he published that paper on them. By gods, it was the most incredible thing. It read more like a history than anything else.' He brushed crumbs from the sleeve of his blazer. 'Still gives me goosebumps to think of it.'

'Once something snared his interest, it consumed him until he mastered it.'

'Indeed it did.' Beckett took a long draught from his beer, and settled lower in his chair. 'I suppose, deep down, I always knew that he'd passed on, but I'm so sorry to hear you confirm it.'

For a while, neither of them spoke, listening to the wind as it twisted through Oxford's streets.

'I'm interested in another story,' Leah said. 'This one perhaps even older.'

'My mind isn't what it was. But if I can help, I most assuredly will.'

'It's a related story, I think, which is why I thought of you. Another myth; or folktale, perhaps. The name I've heard used is *lélek tolvajok.*'

'Ah . . .' Beckett's eyes closed and his breath spooled out. He was silent for so long that Leah began to think he had drifted off, but then he sat up straight in his chair. 'The *tolvajok*. You're quite right, of course. An even older race, judging from the sources that remain.'

'But originating from the same part of the world?'

'Indeed.' His eyes were bright again, alert. 'You can trace the roots of both back to that area of Central Europe we call the Carpathian Basin – or sometimes the Pannonian Basin. Of course, the *Pannonian* really only refers to the area of lowland that remained after the old Pannonian Sea drained out of the Iron Gates. But for our purposes, there's no need to retreat five million years to the Pliocene period.'

'Let's not.'

The professor nodded, carrying on as if he hadn't heard her. 'The *tolvajok* may be ancient, but they're not millions of years old. No modern complex life-form can claim a residency that long. By complex, I don't mean in structure. Yes, certain species of jellyfish have been with us for half a billion years or more. And just look at the coelacanth, thought to have been extinct since the end of the Cretaceous. That is, until a fisherman caught one in his nets off the coast of South Africa. I'm talking about complex in terms of brain structure, although again that's a misnomer, considering what we're discussing. But I'm getting distracted. Where was I?'

'The *tolvajok*. And their origins.'

Beckett lurched forward, licking his lips. 'Of course I was. Damned mind is going. I've been trying those Sudoku puzzles, you know. Waste of time. Anyway, we should start, as always, with the etymology. *Lélek tolvajok* is a Hungarian term. It translates, I believe, into something along the lines of *spirit thief,* or perhaps *thieves,* in the plural. But it's not the most common name for them, I must say. I'm pretty sure the Slavic alternatives are more prevalent. The Czechs called them the *zloděj těl.* The Ukrainian term is *xmapi.* In the older languages, the direct translations often describe a virus, an infection of the mind.'

'An infection?'

'Yes, although that's not a very helpful description. An infection doesn't suggest sentience.'

Leah felt the skin on her scalp contracting. 'A sentient infection?'

'Of the mind, indeed,' Beckett continued. 'Or so the stories go. You might be surprised to learn that the *tolvajok* are the precursor to many of the world's darker folktales and superstitions. Vampirism, lycanthropy . . . you name it; before the birth of those relatively modern-day creations – throughout the Pannonian Basin at least – you had the *tolvajok*. A living entity, which, exactly like any other parasite, required a physical host in which to live.'

'But you're saying . . .' She frowned. 'In contrast to other parasites, this one had no body of its own?'

'Correct. We're talking about an awareness; pure consciousness, if you like. If it helps, think of our interpretation of the soul. Do you believe you have a soul? Whether you do or you don't, it's a device that features regularly in mythology. The only difference, here, is that whereas we generally consider our souls tethered to a single body during our physical existence, the *tolvajok* have no such restrictions. They simply need a host. And when one host starts to die, they go on to take another.'

'But how could something like that exist?'

Beckett shrugged. 'You're talking to a retired philologist, not a scientist. It's the creation and distribution of the myth that interests me. But since you ask, let me ask you. What, after all, do we really know of consciousness? Historically, it's been more the preserve of philosophy than science.'

'What else can you tell me?'

'Lots, probably. If I could remember any of it. I think I wrote a paper on them once. Should be around here, some-where. You're welcome to take it if you wish.' Beckett broke off, and seemed to see the chaos of his snug clearly for the first time. He scratched his head. 'Well, maybe not. Let me see what else I recall. Ah, yes. There's a quite detailed passage about the *tolvajok* in *Gesta Hungarorum*. And there's also a Latin text – can't think of its name – held by the Charles University in Prague. It describes them quite extensively. Other than that, the references are fairly obscure.' Beckett's eyes flicked over to her and he grinned. 'One thing I can tell you is that you have a blessedly slim chance of ever encountering one. Supposedly the *lélek tolvajok* died out some time after the *hosszú életek* cull.'

'Why was that?'

'Because the *tolvajok* were dependent on them.'

'How so?'

'Well, the texts diversify somewhat on the exact reasoning but, generally speaking, when the *tolvaj* seized a host, the effect on the victim's physical body – as well as mind – was enormous. The longer the union, the more exacting the toll. Imagine an engine constantly running above its limit. The body uses up all its reserves, ages incredibly fast, and when the *tolvaj* moves on, what it leaves behind is effectively waste material.'

'I don't see the link to the *hosszú életek*.'

'All parasites harm their hosts in some way or other,' he told her. 'But the ideal relationship, if you can call any of this ideal, occurs when the parasite avoids killing its host, or at least avoids it for as long as possible. A body that ages incredibly fast is of limited use to anyone, so for the *tolvajok*, a person blessed with greater longevity—'

'Such as a *hosszú élet* . . .'

Beckett nodded. 'Exactly. They represent a far more compelling solution. Even so, as far as I remember it, a *tolvaj* needed to seize a *hosszú élet* at an early enough age if it were to take full advantage of the longevity on offer. Take one too late, and their body aged just as quickly as a *simavér* host. Perhaps it's something to do with the way the brain matures. Anyway, when the *hosszú életek* went into decline, it's said the *tolvajok* died out.'

Leah frowned. 'Or they were forced to become less fastidious in their choice of host.'

'Possibly, although according to the literature, the seizing of a new host was thought to cost the *tolvajok* dearly, too. Ultimately, if they switched too often they'd simply . . .' He opened his fingers, scattering imaginary dust. 'Drift away.'

The old academic paused, and then he glanced down at the veins mapping the backs of his hands, as if his words had led him, suddenly, to consider his own mortality. Outside, another gust of wind sent a tremor through the curtains. Leah thought of the dark landscape beyond the glass; of all those lives being lived unaware of the threats that walked among them.

'There was a fragment I came across once,' Beckett said, rousing himself. 'A very old text, late fourteenth century. Forty years or so after the Black Death swept through Europe. The original had been lost – this was a fifteenth-century copy, transcribed by a monk living in some monastery in northern Italy.

'For most of its length it narrates the day-to-day investigations of a party of witch-hunters linked to the Dominican Order, which is of interest, anyway, considering this was a few hundred years before the publication of the *Malleus Maleficarum*. According to the fragment, one day the group's inquisitor led them to an old ruin where, unwittingly, they stumbled across a nest of incredibly old *lélek tolvajok*. Roused from sleep, the *tolvajok* fell upon them, seizing new hosts from the party's members. The inquisitor was the only one who managed to get away.'

Leah felt her stomach tighten as she listened to Beckett's voice.

'The explanation,' he continued, 'was that when times were tough – after an epidemic of plague and so forth – the *tolvajok* went into hibernation, drastically reducing the toll inflicted on their hosts, until new donors could be found.'

Beckett raised his eyebrows. 'When I said earlier they probably all died out around the time of the cull, maybe I was being premature. Perhaps a few are out there still. Hibernating. Waiting for the right time to wake up and claim their inheritance.'

Leah stared at him, at his watery blue eyes, at the way his chin trembled, ever so softly, when he spoke. She remembered her grandfather telling her how Jakab had once impersonated the man during a meeting in Oxford's physic garden, shortly before her grandmother's death.

She wasn't ready for this tale. Fifteen years might have passed since the horrors of Le Moulin Bellerose, but that episode had nearly broken Leah and her mother. What Beckett was telling her now, if true, presented a threat even greater than the one they'd faced all those years ago.

'How do you kill them?' she asked.

'I have no idea.'

Her tea had begun to cool. She took a sip. 'Thank you, Patrick. You've been incredibly helpful.'

'I've enjoyed it immensely. You really do look a lot like Charles, you know. There is one other thing.'

'Yes?'

He hesitated, a faint pinkish tinge appearing on his cheeks. His eyes fell to his lap before they found her face once more. 'It'll sound like a question from a senile old man.'

'Try me.'

'OK, but don't say I didn't warn you.'

She smiled encouragingly.

Beckett licked his lips. 'Did he find them? Charles, I mean?'

'I'm sorry?'

'I can't believe I'm asking you this. But . . . the *hosszú életek*. Is that why he disappeared? Did he find them?'

Rocked by what Beckett had asked, Leah considered him. There was no way she should reveal the truth. It was dangerous not just for her. She heard the clock ticking on the mantelpiece, and wondered how many years the academic had left, sitting here alone surrounded by his old texts, his myths and his cats.

Abandoning her usual caution, she said, 'He did better than that, Professor. He married one.'

Beckett's chest swelled. A moment later his mouth dropped open. 'But that means . . . if you're his granddaughter, that means . . .'

'Yes.' She nodded. 'It means you're talking to one.'

He jerked in his chair, eyes wide, and immediately Leah regretted her words. What if she caused his heart to fail? How could she ever forgive herself?

But already Beckett was recovering. He gazed at her and she

saw, suddenly, not the eyes of an old man, but those of a boy, full of intelligence and curiosity and life.

'What's it like?' he whispered. 'Please, Leah, will you tell me?'

She slid off the chair and knelt beside him, among the piles of books. Her grandfather had told her many stories of his time at Balliol, but the best ones always involved Beckett. She remembered how the pair had spent their evenings in the Eagle and Child, how Beckett's enthusiasm for so many different subjects had inspired Charles into areas of research he would never otherwise have contemplated. She remembered how helpful Beckett had been when her grandfather began researching the *hosszú életek*. The knowledge Charles had gained from their discussions had possibly helped her mother defeat Jakab in France. 'I'll show you,' she told him.

Afterwards, once she had shared with him the gifts bestowed by her blood, the old man sat back in his chair, face so full of joy that it made her heart ache to think she would never see him again.

His smile grew mischievous. 'I feel like Samwise Gamgees when he saw the elves at Rivendell.'

She laughed and he joined her, and soon they were laughing so hard they couldn't stop, clutching their stomachs in pain and delight.

When, finally, Leah recovered, the room felt like a different place, a sanctuary where two strangers had come together and forged a bond as strange as it was tight.

She reached out and covered his hand with her own. 'I have to go.'

Beckett's eyes remained on her face. 'I've always said the world is filled with as much wonder as sorrow. You tip the scales heavily towards wonder, Leah Wilde. Thank you.'

'I'm so glad I came.'

Gripping the arms of his chair, the old man swung his pink-swaddled legs off the pouffe and pulled himself to his feet. When he offered his hand she declined, embracing him and kissing his cheek instead.

'The *tolvajok*,' he said. 'They haven't disappeared, have they?'

She shook her head. 'I don't think so. Not yet.'

'Then, please, Leah. Remember what I told you. You *must* be careful. If they discover your existence, you're going to become the most hunted young woman on the planet.'

CHAPTER 21

London, England

The sky above West London was piercingly bright by the time Leah arrived outside Etienne's Mayfair residence. Overnight, a chill wind had carried the rainclouds away, leaving streets that dripped and glimmered in the morning sun.

She switched off the Mercedes' engine and stared up at the town-house windows. For a moment an unusual feeling gripped her, as if something scratched the surface of a memory and tried to work it loose. It reminded her of the sense she'd had, that evening in Interlaken, that the weather would change overnight, and that snow was coming.

That experience had manifested almost as a taste: olives or lemons, something bitter and sour, but not unpleasant. This feeling was different: a tingle, or an itch, behind her eyes.

It's nerves. Nothing more. Etienne unnerves you, that's all. Come on. Get this done.

Climbing out of the car, she passed through the security gate and went up the front steps. The same man opened the door to her. He wore no firearm today. Was that progress, she wondered? And did he offer her the vaguest of smiles this morning, in contrast to his previous distance?

He told her to take the stairs to the second floor and then he disappeared through a door at the end of the hall. Alone, Leah ventured up the staircase, glancing at the cameras that monitored her route. Unlike before, their lenses remained still.

Something's different.

That feeling was back, too; stronger now, almost as if a tiny insect had flown into her eye, beating its wings as it died. She shook her head, blinking the image away.

Nothing had changed on the second floor. The same priceless collection of porcelain greeted her. The carpet was just as deep; the silence just as expectant.

The door to the drawing room was closed. Hesitating, Leah stared at it. She wondered, not only what Etienne's answer would be, but how she would feel about her decision. For the first time since starting this, she could not honestly say she hoped one hundred per cent that the woman she'd come to see would give her a positive answer.

Admit it. 'Unnerve' is not the word you mean.

No. But she was here, and she would do this. And she would obey the rules she had set herself at the beginning.

She knew nothing of Etienne's history, her character, how she had come to possess such enormous wealth – but she knew little, either, of the other women she had met. Steeling herself, Leah knocked on the door. When she heard a voice call out in reply, she went inside.

No flames danced in the hearth today. The ashes in the grate had been swept, and the metalwork was immaculate. Etienne sat upon the same chair by the fireplace. She smiled, and then she raised one hand from her lap and gestured towards the window.

Leah saw a man standing there. The bright sunlight streaming in from outside had transformed him almost to a silhouette, but she saw enough. His eyes, flat and pale but doubtless *hosszú élet,* were the pallor of wood smoke. Leah could not tell how old he was by looking at his face; had she not glimpsed his eyes she would have imagined him perhaps thirty years her senior. But she guessed he was far, far older than that; far older, too, than Luca Sultés, the man she'd left behind in Interlaken.

He was dressed in a sombre woollen peacoat, so dark it

seemed to gather shadows to it, and held himself stiffly, as if uncomfortable in his shape.

'I'd like you to meet someone,' Etienne said. 'This is Tuomas. We've been friends for a while.'

Leah switched her attention to Etienne, then back to the stranger standing by the window.

'After we met,' the woman continued, 'I called Tuomas and told him of your proposal. I realise that might concern you. And I do understand the importance of keeping your venture concealed from the eyes of the *tanács*. But considering what you're asking of me, I believe I'm entitled to seek advice.'

'I'm not asking anything of you, Etienne. I'm only here to offer—'

'I know,' she interrupted. 'Semantics, though, really. What I'm trying to say is that your secret is as safe with Tuomas as it is with me. He has no connection to the *tanács*. Nor anyone else.'

'Does he speak?' Leah asked, trying to lighten the mood but worried, the moment the words left her lips, that she'd crossed that invisible line of etiquette she'd sensed during her first visit. The stranger's presence distressed her in a way she couldn't quite grasp.

'On occasion,' Tuomas said. His voice was scratchy, odd.

'Sorry. My mouth runs away sometimes.'

'Not at all. I can understand why you'd be concerned. Frightened, even. But you can forgive Etienne, I hope, for wanting a second opinion before deciding on her course.'

Leah nodded. 'I can.'

'I have few talents, but you might say I'm a reasonable reader of people. Or at least I used to be. It's why Etienne asked me here, to look you in the eye and tell her what I see.'

'Which is what?'

He came towards her. This close, she could smell his cologne, spicy and dark. He studied her with those flat grey eyes and she felt as if she were being opened and sifted, her thoughts as clear as if they had been written down on paper.

'I see a young woman who doesn't grasp the danger she's in.'

Despite how uncomfortable it made her, Leah forced herself to maintain eye contact, feeling almost as if she sensed something in his expression. She thought of the cameras along the staircase – how two days earlier they had tracked her progress through the house. How this morning they'd remained still.

'I see fear and I see hope,' he continued. 'I see someone trying to do something remarkable, with little concern for her safety.' Tuomas glanced at Etienne. 'You have no concerns from me. Only my blessing.'

Confused, Leah turned away. What she saw shocked her. Tears stood on Etienne's cheeks, glittering diamonds. Flustered, the woman brushed them away, and in that single action Leah thought she glimpsed, finally, the humanity in her, concealed so masterfully until now.

Perhaps it was Tuomas's presence, or the intensity with which he had studied her, but now she found herself noticing more in Etienne's expression: an aching loneliness, and a self-control so rigid it threatened to shatter her should she allow it to fail.

'I want to come with you, Leah,' she said. 'I don't know what will happen, and I know you can't promise me anything. But the thought of a child. It's . . .' Her words seemed to fail her, and she flapped her arm. 'I've made my decision. I hope your offer still stands.'

'It still stands. Of course it still stands.'

Etienne rose to her feet and enfolded Leah in a fragile embrace. Standing back, she laughed, the sound like a dam being breached.

'Where exactly is this place you'll take her to?' Tuomas asked.

'I can't tell you that. Not yet.' To Etienne, she added: 'But I'll be in touch soon. You'll be available to fly out to us? At short notice?'

'Of course.'

Tuomas was still watching her. 'Are you going straight back?'

'Why do you ask?'

'As I said, I don't think you realise how much danger you're facing.'

'I'm aware of it. Believe me.'

'I don't. I don't mean to insult you, but I don't think you've grasped the repercussions of what you're doing. How many are there of you?'

'Enough.'

He nodded. 'I'd be happy to accompany you back'

'There's no need. Really.'

'I'd—'

'Really, Tuomas. Thank you. But there's no need.' Time for a lie, she thought, although it made her uncomfortable to speak it. 'I'm not in London alone. It's kind of you to offer, but this isn't the first time I've done this and it won't be the last.'

Tuomas studied her a moment longer, and then he moved away, hands clasped behind his back. 'In that case, allow me to wish you well.' For the first time, he smiled. 'Who knows? Perhaps our paths will cross again.'

CHAPTER 22

Budapest, Hungary

At ten o'clock in the morning, as the sun crept higher behind the clouds, the frost on the grass of Budapest's Memento Park was finally beginning to recede.

Anton Golias, coat buttoned against the cold, walked the figure-of-eight path, looking for his *tanács* colleague, Oliver Lebeau, and nursing the Styrofoam cup of coffee he had bought on his way here. The coffee was dreadful, the beans burned and bitter, and it did nothing to improve Anton's mood. He had always found the park an oddly melancholic place, but he could think of nowhere better suited to this meeting.

Built on an area of scrubland on the edge of a spartan residential district, Memento Park's skyline was dominated by the stark metal skeletons of electricity pylons linked by endless loops of cable. It was not a place of landscaped gardens, exotic plants and flowers. The air was softened neither with the delicate scent of blossom, nor by the music of water spouting into fountains.

When Hungary's Communist rule collapsed in 'eighty-nine, its Budapest populace, free for the first time in over forty years, woke to a city still dominated by the statues and monuments of its servitude. Almost immediately they were taken down, but for a while, nobody knew where to put them. Most of them ended up here, where Anton now stood. Memento Park existed not as a tribute to the old totalitarian state, but as a celebration of its demise.

He found his friend standing in front of an enormous bronze depicting a flag-waving Red Army soldier raising a clenched fist.

Oliver turned as Anton approached, greeting him with a tired smile. 'Remember this one?'

'Of course. It used to stand on top of Gellért Hill. The Soviets stuck him up there to celebrate our liberation from the Nazis.' Anton laughed sourly. 'By Stalin and his dogs.'

'Perhaps they should have melted it down.'

'No. Better that it ended up here. People should remember.'

Oliver shrugged. 'Are you ready?'

'I suppose. Have they arrived?'

'Waiting over there.'

He saw the *tanács* adversaries they'd come to meet – Ivan Tóth and Krištof Joó – standing at the steps to Stalin's Grandstand. 'Come on, then,' he muttered. 'Let's find out what this is about.'

Tóth thrust out a hand in greeting and Anton shook it with a grimace. He had come to dislike the man intensely over the past few years, but at least Tóth's smile – wide, welcoming and utterly false – seemed appropriate for their surroundings.

'Morning, Anton, morning!' he cried. 'Good of you to come. Interesting choice of venue. The point isn't lost on me, I assure you.'

Anton grunted, then greeted Tóth's sidekick with a nod. If Tóth was the natural diplomat – eloquent, loquacious and seemingly eager to find common ground – then Joó was his firebrand counterpart. The man was hardline, and habitually distrustful. Anton had not decided which of the two represented the greater threat.

A gust of wind snatched at the leaves at the side of the path, and for a moment he thought he smelled something rancid on the air, as if some creature had crawled into the undergrowth and died. 'Well,' he said, feigning a smile of his own. 'We may have our disagreements, but I'm always willing to talk.'

'That's good, that's good.' Tóth placed a hand on his shoulder, and Anton allowed himself to be pivoted and steered back along the path. 'So how are things going? Generally?'

He frowned. 'What exactly are you asking?'

'Well, I suppose I'm asking you, first, for an update on this fertility programme our *Főnök* has established. Is it continuing to bear fruit?'

'It's not the *Főnök*'s programme, as you well know. It belongs to everyone. We voted it through.'

'Not all of us.'

Fifteen years earlier, after hearing Hannah and Gabriel's proposal to arrest the *hosszú életek*'s decline, the eight member *tanács* found themselves split. Anton and Oliver supported the plan, along with two other modernisers. Tóth and Joó, strict observers of traditional *Vének Könyve* doctrine, were its most outspoken opponents. With the *tanács* at an impasse, the *Főnök* cast the deciding vote, and the project was born.

'Is that why you asked me here?' he asked. 'To debate a decision reached over a decade ago?'

'Of course not. *Te jó ég*, you're prickly this morning. It must be these old relics. Oppressive, aren't they?'

'Relics of an oppressive regime usually are.'

The flecks of silver in Tóth's eyes betrayed his irritation. This time, when he smiled, his lips were tight against his teeth.

Gotcha, Anton thought.

'But is it going well?' the man pressed. 'Surely that's a reasonable question?'

'I understand they've had a number of recent successes.'

'I've heard differently.'

He shrugged. Perhaps the *Főnök*'s greatest coup, all those years earlier, had been not the creation of the centre, but her insistence on its secrecy. The location would not be revealed to the eight members of the *tanács*. Nor would any detailed news be communicated of the programme's performance, nor the names of its volunteers or associates. The political situation was tense enough, but there were darker threats to guard against.

Tóth appeared to realise he would receive no answers to his probing. His arm fell away from Anton's shoulder. 'I've heard that some of the women are dying.'

Now he felt a coldness in his stomach, radiating outwards. If Tóth had learned of the centre's problems, the situation was graver than he had imagined. Still he said nothing. He recalled Hannah Wilde's words back in Calw.

We're fighting a war here, in that building behind me. Fighting a grim, backs-to-the-wall last stand: against nature, against the consequences of the Eleni outrages all those years ago. It's messy and it's horrific, and believe me if you stayed here a week and watched what we do you'd see how we suffer – and how we rejoice – with every inch of ground we advance or retreat. Do you think we don't grieve for each volunteer we lose? Do you think we don't live with their loss every day? Tell me a better way and I'll listen.

That was just it. There was no better way. He had pushed Hannah hard that day, had needed to hear for himself how she viewed their situation. And he had walked away from that meeting with his opinion cemented that what she was doing was the right thing; the only thing.

And now this.

Tóth came to a halt. 'We have a duty, do we not, to protect those who appoint us?'

'I couldn't agree more. And what greater obligation could we have than to avoid our own extinction?'

'Extinction? A rather dramatic choice of words, don't you think?'

'Would you deny that's what we face?'

'I certainly don't deny that if these reports of the programme's failings are true, then we're marching ourselves far closer to that kind of outcome.'

'Please. I know what your objections are, and they aren't that.'

'Perhaps not,' Tóth replied. 'It's difficult to form an objection to anything these days, when the truth is kept hidden like this. I remember a time when the *tanács* was empowered to debate issues openly, with all the facts in clear sight. I remember when the *Főnök* observed the tenets of the *Vének Könyve* and relied on her *tanács* for guidance, rather than shrouding herself in secrecy and ploughing her own course.'

'Ah. So that's what this is about.'

'We made a mistake with Catharina's appointment. You know that, I'm sure. In our grief over Éva's passing, we acted with our hearts instead of our heads. We appointed the daughter without questioning ourselves hard enough, and now we're witnessing the result. She takes her brother's counsel over our own, and she's far too invested in this Hannah Wilde to remain impartial. Catharina was the wrong choice, Anton. You can't refute it.'

'Of course I refute it. I'll grant you she made a few missteps in the early days, but—'

'*Missteps?*'

'But every *Főnök* needs time to carve out her role.'

'Yet time is exactly what you suggest we lack. And on that point, at least, I agree. Look, I know you're fond of her. We all are. But that must not cloud our judgement of what is required.'

'What exactly *is* required?'

'A change,' Tóth said, his eyes gleaming. 'Now's the time to force it. The *tanács* has been split for too long, and the *Főnök* has failed to bring unity. With new leadership . . .'

Anton's mouth dropped open. 'What are you saying?'

His colleague took a breath, drew himself together. 'I already speak for half the *tanács*. With one more vote we could end this disunity. Elect a new leader: someone with the strength to forge change, yet with the humility to listen to reason.'

Anton could not hide his anger just then. He felt his blood surging in his arteries. 'And who would you choose? You?'

The man's lower lip curled back. 'Despite what you might believe, I hold no thirst for power. Just a desire for the right leadership.'

'Who, then? Gabriel?'

Tóth snorted. 'He'd be my last choice. Gods, man, Gabriel would be his *own* last choice. No, if the *tanács* were to elect a new *Főnök*, my choice would be you.'

Anton flinched, shocked. 'Me?'

'I can think of no one better. We've had our differences over the years, but I'd be the first to vouch for your integrity, your strength of vision. Even though the *tanács* might be split on the issue of Hannah Wilde, you have friends on our side. Oláh, Saári, they'd both support your appointment. I've already sounded them out.'

Anton halted in the middle of path. He turned, studied Tóth's face. And then he laughed. 'You've been busy.'

His old adversary smiled, lizard-sly.

'You've been busy,' he continued, 'and traitorous. While Catharina concentrates her efforts on saving our people, you slink around in the shadows, trying to unseat her. And why? Because she won't share with you the finer details of a plan that might just save us all? Or because you're unhappy with some of the smaller parts you've heard? You come here talking of duty, when what you're really suggesting is a betrayal.'

'How dare you!'

'How dare *you*?' Anton exploded. 'There hasn't been an insurrection in the *tanács* for more than five hundred years, and you would plot one now? You, Ivan Tóth, and your poisonous cabal of whisperers? I'll mark this day, you'll see I will. Our *Főnök* has presided over the most difficult period we've ever faced, and she's done it with grace, strength and conviction.'

Such was the nimbus of fury surrounding the two men that their colleagues began to back away.

Tóth's eyes flared. 'Our *Főnök* is contravening the most fundamental laws that govern us. She's allowed herself to become the puppet of Hannah Wilde and Gabriel Szöllösi—'

'Hannah Wilde and Gabriel Szöllösi are doing something remarkable, you fool!'

'The woman's a *kirekesztett*.'

'She is *not kirekesztett*!'

'Look at her blood! For a thousand years or more the purity of the great families was sacrosanct. And now we're allowing Hannah Wilde's tainted blood to—'

'What about *your* blood?' Anton shouted. 'Is it pure? And what of your ethics, Ivan? Are they pure, too? You'll make no devil's pact with me. Nor with any I represent.'

Tóth's eyes, livid, bulged in his skull like a frog's. And yet somehow the man calmed himself. 'Don't be so sure of that,' he whispered. 'Just remember, when the time comes, that I gave you a choice. Clearly you've fallen under this Wilde woman's spell just as completely as the *Főnök*.'

Anton stabbed his finger towards the park's gates. 'Go on. Get out of here. *Crawl* out of here. Your plan will fail, I assure you.'

Tóth stared. His chest rose and fell. Straight-backed, he turned and marched towards the exit. Joó followed, lips pressed tightly together.

Anton watched the two *tanács* leaders pass through the gates and puffed out his cheeks.

'More coffee?' Oliver asked him lightly.

'I think I've had enough, don't you?'

'Perhaps. This changes things, I'd suggest.'

'Does it?'

'They only need one more name.'

'Like yours?'

'Of course not. But while we're on the topic, you should know I'm not entirely comfortable with the way Catharina has—'

'Enough, Oliver. Please. I don't want to hear it. Not today.' Anton raised his nose to the air. 'Do you smell that?'

'What?'

'I don't know. Something. I can't place it.'

'I can smell your coffee.'

He sighed. 'Yes, it's not good.' On their way out of the park, he threw the Styrofoam container into a rubbish bin and rubbed at the back of his neck. For some reason he could not dismiss, he felt as though he was being watched.

With barely a glance at his driver, Ivan Tóth slid onto the Range Rover's back seat. As soon as Joó was inside, the vehicle pulled out into traffic.

Removing a handkerchief from his pocket, Tóth blotted his face. He snapped out directions and sank back in his seat, loosening his shirt. 'Arrogant *sertés!*' he spat.

Joó glanced at him. 'He's stubborn, I'll grant you, but hardly arrogant. You offered him power and he rejected it. Politically, he still holds all the cards.'

'Not for much longer, he doesn't.'

'You have a plan?'

Already Tóth's anger was fading. Now he began to smile once more.

CHAPTER 23

Snowdonia, Wales

As Leah Wilde drew closer to the place where she had once experienced so much loss the light began to fade, as if the day read her memories and chose to slink away.

The mountains of Snowdonia slumbered beneath a granite sky that bled away their colour and left a landscape painted in ash. Leah did not recognise the road she drove upon, but she recognised the hill in front of her and knew what lay behind it. Her limbs felt heavy. A weight pressed her down in the seat.

She slowed the car as she approached the summit of the hill, and where the forest revealed a patchy clearing, she glimpsed – or thought she did – the old whitewashed building, waiting for her at the bottom of the valley.

Leah turned her eyes away. She would not look at it. Not yet.

Cresting the top of the rise, she took a turning and found herself negotiating a steep slope, its stones wet and slippery beneath the Mercedes' tyres.

Trees on either side formed a dense canopy, and inside it seemed as if the night had already come.

She gripped the steering wheel tight, knuckles whitening. Fifteen years of thinking about this place, attempting to exorcise its ghosts; and now, finally, she was here.

Leah had not wanted to return but she'd always known she

must. She needed to say goodbye, needed to wash off the years of grief that even now still clung to her.

Below, the track flattened out, breaking free of the trees and curving towards the crumbling stone bridge that crossed the river.

There, beyond it, pale in the leadening light, stood the old farmhouse itself.

Llyn Gwyr.

She had expected it, like many of the revisited places of childhood, to look smaller than she remembered. But the building defied her expectations. If anything, it appeared larger than before: more formidable; more unyielding. Although the ground-floor windows had been boarded up, the plywood slimy with mould, the upstairs windows remained untouched. They watched her like a row of dead eyes, and she felt an itch break out across her skin, as if she'd brushed through a stand of nettles.

You've come this far. Don't back out.

Leah brought the Mercedes to a halt. When she switched off the engine, the mountain silence flooded in. She opened the door and climbed out.

Immediately the wind dragged at her, its fingers damp and insistent. She pulled up the collar of her jacket, folded her arms and walked towards the bridge.

How long since anyone had been here? A decade? Longer? She knew her mother still held the freehold to the property and its land. Before their arrival here all those years ago, her grandfather's friend Sebastien had maintained a watch over the place. But the old man was dead and gone, and whether anyone still communed with Llyn Gwyr's ghosts, Leah did not know.

Although the house appeared firm, the bridge looked more decrepit than when she had last seen it. One side had collapsed entirely, as if some river creature had reared up and taken a bite. In the rushing waters beneath, the half-submerged stones were moss-slicked and cold.

She would not risk driving the car across what remained, but she thought it would bear her own weight without too much complaint. Leah crossed it hurriedly nonetheless, boots kicking up little storms of gravel.

A shriek shattered the stillness, and her feet nearly slid out from beneath her. But it was only a barn owl marking its territory. She would have laughed, had the landscape not oppressed her so heavily.

Safely across the bridge, she followed the track towards Llyn Gwyr, hugging herself tighter with every step. This close, the house seemed enormous, a colossal mass of abandoned stone. Vegetation grew in the guttering and a collection of bird's nests clung beneath the eaves. She noticed that a downpipe had cracked; water had poured down the wall, blackening the whitewash.

A memory surfaced, sudden and sharp: she stood inside Llyn Gwyr's dining room, nine years old, lining up a row of shotgun cartridges for her mother, and knowing that something was out there. Knowing that something was coming for them.

Shivering, she passed the front of the house, and now she recognised the outbuildings, and the patch of gravel beside the kitchen windows where Gabriel had arrived one morning with horses. The three of them had ridden up to Llyn Cau, where he had told her stories of lake-dwelling dragons and spectral hounds. Hannah had laughed and told Gabriel not to scare her, that such things could not exist. But worse things than those existed in the world, far worse.

Ahead, the lake was a steely depression in the land, wind-ruffed and bleak. Close to its shore, she saw the reason for her return: two graves, side by side: one belonging to her grandfather, the second to her father. Leah tucked her chin inside her jacket and walked towards them.

When she'd been here last, only her father's remains had lain beneath this hard-packed ground. Leah remembered Sebastien dragging Nate's body over the lip of the trench he had dug. She recalled the old man's voice as he read from the *Book of Common Prayer*, remembered the grains of earth falling on her father's face and the letter she had written him, clutched in his hands. Even now, she could recite the words it had contained: *Wherever you are, Daddy, one day I'll follow. I'll make you proud here first, and then I'll see you again. I promise.*

Where once a simple hammered cross had marked a mound of turned earth, now she saw a pair of neatly gravelled-in graves and two black headstones.

She had not expected to find this. Nor had she expected to see the pots of flowering plants, red petals trembling in the mountain wind.

At the nearest grave Leah stooped, reaching out to the slab of polished granite with its inlaid gold inscription. She hesitated there, no words coming to her lips, thinking of the times she had shared with Charles Meredith, his love and his warmth, his fierce intellect. She recalled their conversations and laughter, how her grandfather had taught her about the Romans, the Vikings, the Celts; how he'd inspired her love of books, of learning.

For twenty minutes or more she sat with Charles, and only after she had dredged every last memory of him could she turn, at last, to the gravestone belonging to her father.

This time she sank to her knees, heedless of the mud that soaked through her clothes. 'Oh, Dad,' she said, and her voice, out here in the wilderness, seemed bereft of strength. 'How have you been? Has Grandpa been entertaining you with his stories? You must have heard them a hundred times or more by now. I've a few of my own I could tell you.

'Can you hear me?' she asked, daring at last to reach out and touch his headstone. 'Have you been watching us?'

Nothing but the wind sighing in the trees and whispering through dead leaves.

'I went to meet the *kirekesztett*. I wasn't meant to, but I did.

A few of them want to be a part of this. And if others do, too, then we might still have a chance.

'I just . . . I don't know what will happen now. The *tanács* – I can't understand the way they think. Even the ones who support us, you could hardly describe as progressive. And the others . . .' She shook her head. 'Some of them, they'd rather see us fade away on the wind than contemplate any kind of dilution. *Poll*ution. It's been hard. Bloody hard.'

She heard the whine in her voice, and bottled it. She had not come here to do that. 'I miss you, Dad, but I'm OK. It's good to finally see you again. I don't even know, now I'm here, why I—'

The sound, when it came, was so slight that it was more a feeling, or a thought, than a pressure in her ears. It wasn't the crack of a twig snapping, or a scuff of gravel, or a rasp of breath.

Leah wasn't sure it had even been a sound; perhaps, simply, the absence of one. Had the birds been singing before? The air was silent now.

Ten yards to the left of the graves stood the edge of the forest, the ground inside it choked with bracken, rotten logs and leaf mulch. The trees grew in thick ranks all the way up the slope. Beyond the first few trunks, the darkness was absolute.

She heard it again. A vague, whispery, dragging sound: as if something large moved deep inside that impenetrable gloom, bending the branches of saplings and stripping their leaves as it passed.

The sound ceased, and the silence returned. Heart pounding now, each beat thudding like a fist against her chest, Leah rose to her feet.

Her first instinct was to run. But her feet were planted firm, and she knew enough to remain still. She felt the wind pressing at her legs.

Now, the papery crunch of twigs. A larger branch, snapping. And then the forest was alive with movement – a crashing, pounding crescendo of sound.

Leah leaped back from her father's grave, eyes scanning the forest's edge. She could see nothing moving beyond the nearest trees, could not tell from which direction the noises came.

Whatever made them was closing fast, racing towards her.

She had retreated another few steps when she saw an explosion of leaves twenty yards in front. From out of the forest crashed a stag. It lurched to a halt beside the lake, so close to the water's edge that its hooves sank into oozing black mud. The animal was huge: broad-chested and powerful, the largest she had ever seen. Its antlers swept out from its skull, a candelabra of bone, pale at the tips, dark and woody on the stems. When it dipped its head they pointed straight towards her, a lethal array of arrowheads.

Condensation blasted from the stag's snout. It tossed its head, flanks quivering. Leah took another step back, unable to control her feet, and then she forced herself to a halt.

Ahead, the stag sidestepped, hooves sucking clear of the mud. Gouts of steam rose from its flanks. It shivered, as if an effort of pure will kept it standing there, as if it was unsure whether to charge or bolt.

There was something wrong with the way it studied her, she thought; something not quite right about the way it rolled its head away one moment, unwilling to look at her, turning back a moment later to regard her with liquid-black eyes.

It lifted a foreleg. Planted it back down in the mud.

Leah heard another twig snap, echoing like a pistol shot across the valley floor. This sound came not from in front, where the stag stood, but from behind.

That was when fear almost paralysed her.

She didn't want to look back, convinced that if she turned from the stag for even a second it would charge, gouging her on that nest of spears. But turn she must, and when, finally, she gathered the courage, she saw, standing perhaps twenty yards away, in the centre of the gravel track, a man's dark shape.

Leah's breath froze in her throat. She heard the stag snort, and glanced over her shoulder. The animal had not moved.

She blinked, swallowed. Then she turned once again to confront the newcomer.

Tuomas.

That was what he had called himself when she'd met him at Etienne's mansion in London. She doubted it was his real name.

The light was dimming faster now. Tuomas stood silhouetted against a darkening sky.

He had followed her here, to Llyn Gwyr. All the way from London.

Behind her, the red stag roared.

CHAPTER 24

New York, USA

1929

Izsák was at work behind the counter of the Ready Eat Lunch Wagon, repairing the huge dome-topped Pavoni coffee machine, when he noticed Emil Otto in difficulty at the far end of the diner.

At nine a.m., the day's breakfast crowd had already stamp-eded in and out, leaving a wake of coffee rings, grease spots and tobacco smoke.

This was Izsák's favourite part of the morning. With no one else inside the Ready Eat except Otto and his daughter, the three of them could concentrate on readying the place for the lunchtime rush. Sometimes, while they worked, Otto would sing them old German hunting songs. Sometimes Izsák would turn up the wireless and, during a break from washing cups and plates, he would dance with Lucy. She had taught him the Black Bottom and the Charleston, and he had choreographed a polka that left them breathless with laughter.

Emil Otto had purchased the Ready Eat – a pre-fabricated steel box modelled on a railroad car – five years earlier, before cancer claimed Lucy's mother. The family had arrived from Hamburg in 'twenty-one, and when Otto saw the explosion of skyscrapers rising heavenwards on Manhattan Island he spotted the opportunity to make a living serving low-cost food to the army of riveters and catchers, carpenters and bricklayers, electricians and derrick men who made their homes in the Lower East Side. Tower-building was gruelling and intensive, and Otto's menu of ham, eggs, hamburger sandwiches and chilli, mixed with a few signature dishes from his homeland, scored an instant hit.

Despite that, over the last few years the Ready Eat had suffered an inexplicable decline in profits. Until Izsák had started to help out, Otto had been manning the diner's grill morning, day and night. He no longer had the money to pay staff, and the strain showed on his face. Always a heavyset man, with a physique thickened by grilled cheese and frankfurter rolls, his skin had recently developed an ashen cast, and he mopped constantly at his brow with a kitchen cloth.

Izsák had been working in the Ready Eat's kitchen for three months. He'd never had a particular love for cooking, but he had fallen in love with Lucy Otto. When she had brought him back to the diner one day to meet her father, and Izsák had grasped the seriousness of their situation, he'd taken off his coat, rolled up his sleeves, and by the end of the day had brewed somewhere in the region of two hundred cups of coffee, and had fried half that number of beef patties.

Otto called him his *Lebensretter*, and Lucy named him her *Liebling*. He worked like a dog: running the fryer and the grill, taking orders, fetching groceries, and battling daily with the steaming metal monster of a coffee machine that Otto had imported from Milan back when times were good. The only job Otto hadn't entrusted to him was the accounts, and Izsák suspected the old German's pride alone prevented him from sharing the stark misery lurking within the Ready Eat's ledger.

He hadn't noticed the man Otto was talking to come into the diner, but he noticed him now. The stranger reminded him of a pug dog; eyes wide-set, nose a squashed afterthought on a face that looked like it had been squeezed from wet clay. His dark hair was horribly over-oiled, so thick with grease that even his ears shone with it. He wore a tailored brown suit over a double-breasted vest and cap-toed shoes. His hat sat on the counter in front of him.

Izsák was too far away, and the Pavoni blasting out too much steam, to follow the conversation between the two men. Although Otto was talking animatedly, he was keeping his voice low.

The stranger glanced over at Lucy, who was mopping the floor at the opposite end of the diner, and made a comment. He grinned, revealing teeth stained yellow from too much tobacco.

For a moment, Otto's eyes went dead. Then his shoulders slumped. Reaching under his apron, he passed something across the counter. The pug in the suit pocketed it, and then shook his head. Otto opened his mouth but before he managed to speak, the pug turned and left. Outside the diner, the man slid onto the bench seat of an Oldsmobile idling against the kerb, which pulled away immediately into traffic.

Izsák put down his rag, moved to the entrance and locked the door. He went up to Otto. 'So,' he said quietly, keeping his back to Lucy. 'That's why you keep me out of the way on Monday mornings.' He'd only been at the Ready Eat at this hour because the Pavoni had broken down again. 'Suddenly a lot of things make sense.'

'I didn't want you to see that,' Otto replied, keeping his eyes on the counter.

Izsák glanced along it, checking that Lucy was still busy with the mop. 'There's no shame in it. How long has it been going on?'

'About a year.'

'How much do they ask?'

'More than I can afford. And the last two months . . . it's gone up.'

'How much did you give him, just then?'

'Half of what I owe.'

Izsák nodded. 'So he'll be back.'

'He's always back.'

'What's his name?'

'No, Izsák. I'm grateful, really. But you have no idea—'

'Emil, please. I'm going to marry your daughter. Who is he?'

The old German closed his eyes. When he opened them, Izsák realised just how tired his future father-in-law appeared. 'I know it's not even noon,' he said, 'but I have a bottle of whisky hidden out back. Let's close up properly. I'll send Lucy over to the apartment.'

'Sorrentino's his name,' Otto continued, once they'd shuttered the windows and retired to the diner's only booth. The whisky stood uncapped between them, two glasses filled. 'But it doesn't really matter what he's called. Sometimes it's him, sometimes it's another guy. Sorrentino's the worse of the two.'

'But they're just the collectors.'

'Yeah.'

'So where does the money go?'

'You ever heard of Frank Fischetti?'

'No. Should I?'

'Believe me, if you own any kind of business around here, Izsák, then you've heard of Fischetti. Some call him the Throat. Because that's what he does. He swallows everything up. Everyone. You'd think he'd be making too much money from his easies and his whores to bother folk like us. But he wants a hand in everything, and if you don't pay up . . .' Otto shrugged. 'That butcher's shop up the street? The one that's all burned out? Used to be owned by Marcus Septire. Nice guy. Well, one day Marcus didn't pay up.'

'Where does he live, this Fischetti?'

Otto shook his head. 'I said no. I've trusted you with this much. But you don't get involved. I'm not asking, I'm telling you. Do you understand?'

'You can't expect me to sit here and—'

'You want to marry Lucy?'

'Of course, but—'

'You want to be part of this family, you want to marry my daughter, then you obey me on this. My restaurant. My rules.'

'If this keeps up, there isn't going to be a restaurant.'

Otto bashed the tabletop with his fist. '*Izsák!*'

He flinched, shocked. Never before had he seen the man so agitated.

What do you think you're doing, anyway? Trying to impress your future father-in-law? You don't have the stomach for this. Nor the will. You know it and he knows it. Come on. Look for the easy way out, like you always do. Find the excuse. Grab it.

Angered by that voice, haunted by it, even as he held up his palms to placate the man, Izsák said, 'Emil, I understand. Your place, your rules. I didn't mean to upset you, truly. You know I care about you. About the diner. It's hard for me to sit here and do nothing.'

See? Wasn't difficult, was it? Congratulations.

'I know you want to help,' Otto said. 'You've a good heart. You'll make a good son. We'll work this out together, you and I. But for the moment, you leave things to me. Agreed?'

'Agreed.'

'I want your promise. Your word.'

He found the man's eyes. 'I give you my word, Emil. I'll leave things to you for now. But soon we'll talk. Will you agree to that in return?'

'I will. Now, let's shake on it, and then you can get back to fixing up that old metal monster. There's life in her yet. Just like me. Mind she doesn't scald you.'

Izsák smiled, but when he recalled that mocking voice inside his head, he found he could no longer meet Otto's eyes.

He was working in the Ready Eat's cramped kitchen, slicing cabbages for Otto's sauerkraut dish, when Sorrentino next paid a visit. The breakfast crowd had just cleared out, and Lucy had disappeared back to her father's apartment to collect some laundry.

Izsák heard the rattle of the blinds as someone came into the diner, but at first he paid it no attention. Only when he heard Otto's cry did he slam through the kitchen door into the restaurant. It took him a moment to understand what he was seeing.

Sorrentino stood in the middle of the Ready Eat, a savage smile on his face. He turned when he heard Izsák crash through the door, but he showed no fear, only surprise.

Otto was behind the counter, sweat coursing down his face. His right hand was palm-down on the countertop, pinned there by a knife. A line of blood, thicker than Izsák's finger and as dark as gravy, seeped from underneath and crept along the laminate. When it found the edge of the counter, it dripped onto the floor.

'Who the fuck is this, Emil?' Sorrentino asked, staring at Izsák. 'You told me you were broke.' The man's voice became a whining parody of the German's accent. '"I can't afford a cook, Mario. I don't have any money, Mario." If that's true, who's this monkey?'

'Mario, please,' Otto moaned. 'Take it out.'

'Gladly.'

Sorrentino lunged at the counter and yanked at the knife. It defied him, stuck firm; he had to lever it back and forward several times before he managed to pry it loose.

Otto screamed, collapsing against a rack of crockery. He dislodged cups and plates, sending them crashing to the floor.

The front door of the Ready Eat jangled and Lucy walked in. For a moment, nobody moved.

She saw Sorrentino standing in the middle of the diner, and Izsák hovering behind him. She saw her father slumped against the crockery rack. A moment later she noticed Otto's bloodied hand, and the blade held in Sorrentino's.

Izsák was utterly bewitched by how serene Lucy appeared at

that moment, how pure. She didn't scream; didn't panic; didn't run.

Instead, she walked up to Sorrentino, mouth set rigid, so invested with power that the man actually took a step backwards. 'You've done your work,' she whispered. 'Now get out of here.'

The pug laughed, eyes hard. But Izsák would never forget how the man had backed away as Lucy approached.

Sorrentino returned his attention to Otto. 'I'll come by tomorrow. With others, if that's what you want. You'll pay me what you owe, you Kraut fuck.'

When Izsák heard that, he felt something pop inside his head, a gasket blowing. For the first time in his life his rage ignited, so all-consuming that his legs shook from its effects. Images rushed at him, like cards dealt by a shark: the soles of his father's boots inside the Citadella; Katalin's hair as it burned; his uncle's body staked out on the floor of his study; his flight from Budapest; the years of wandering; the fear; the pain; the solitude. And, finally, this place in which he now stood; the sanctuary of simple love and humanity he'd found inside a German immigrant's catering business deep in the heart of one of New York's poorest districts.

His voice trembled when he spoke. 'You come back here tomorrow,' he told Sorrentino. 'And you'll get what you're owed. All of it. I give you my word.'

The thug stared. Raising his knife, he pointed the tip towards Izsák's face. 'See, Emil? This is what you lack. Business sense.' Cackling, he picked up his hat and swaggered out of the diner.

The moment he was gone, Lucy and Izsák scrambled behind the counter. Together, they helped Otto to the booth.

'I don't feel good,' he said.

'Get him some water, 'Sak,' Lucy told him. 'Bandages, too.'

'No,' Otto wheezed. 'Not yet. Don't go, Izsák. I think . . .'

His face was the wrong colour; in fact it lacked any colour at all. The sweat pouring off him was greasy and cold. He held out his good hand and Lucy gripped it.

Suddenly understanding what this was about – the knowledge hitting him with baseball-bat certainty – Izsák placed his hand over theirs, linking their fingers together. Otto panted for breath, once, a huge lungful. He clenched his teeth. The muscles in his jaw tensed, relaxed. And then he died, slumped in the booth between his daughter and the man who would marry her.

The Ready Eat was closed the next morning when Sorrentino came back. The shutters were down and most of the lamps were dark, throwing the diner's interior into deep shadow. The old Pavoni breathed no steam. The fryer remained unlit. The wireless was silent and the griddle was cold.

But the door was unlocked. Izsák sat alone in the single booth, his head bowed.

Sorrentino pushed open the door and walked in, noticing both the shadows and the silence. A moment later he noticed Izsák. 'What the fuck is this?'

'Take a seat.' Izsák said. He indicated a brown paper bag to his left. 'I have what you're owed.'

'Where's Emil?'

'You wanted to conduct business. So please; sit down, and let's work this out.'

'Business, yeah,' Sorrentino muttered, eying the bag. He slid into the booth. 'Who are you, anyway? I never seen you before.'

Izsák flicked a wall switch beside the booth. Above them, a bulb in a frosted shade winked on. He raised his head. 'I'm you, Mario. That's who I am. I'm you.'

The effect on the man was immediate and extreme. Blood drained from Sorrentino's face as if someone had pulled a plug. His eyes widened, so large they lent him an almost comic intensity. '*Che cazzo*,' he whispered, tongue flicking out to wet his lips.

'Do you believe in God, Mario?' Izsák asked.

'*No.*' The man stared. A pulse began to beat in his neck.

Violently, he shook his head. 'I didn't mean . . . I mean *yes*. I do. I do.'

'He's a long way from you right now. About as far away as He can get.'

Sorrentino's protuberant eyes moistened and then filled with tears. 'Are you . . . Do you mean you're . . . ?'

'That's right.'

'*Satana*.'

'In the flesh.' He held up his hands, noticing with some satisfaction how the other man cringed away. 'Well, in *your* flesh, I should say. What do you think? I'd say you're ugliness personified, wouldn't you? I'll bet you've never even considered just how far apart your eyes are set. It actually stings to wear your face for too long. Did you know that? That's how ugly you are, Mario. So ugly it hurts.'

'I . . . I'm sorry.'

'Don't be sorry. I'm not here because of your face.'

Izsák reached into the paper bag and removed one of the diner's filleting knives. Seizing the man's wrist, he drove the blade between the bones of his hand, pinning him to the table.

Sorrentino screamed.

'If you get a single spot of blood on those clothes, I'll cut off your face and feed it to you. Do you understand?'

The man nodded, eyes as round as moons.

Leaning over the table, Izsák patted Sorrentino down. 'Where is it?'

'Right pocket. I think . . . I think I'm going to be sick.'

Izsák pulled a Colt pistol from the man's jacket. He swung himself out of the booth, fetched a bowl from behind the Ready Eat's counter and set it down on the table. 'If you're going to be sick, be sick into that. Remember what I said: if you get blood on your cuff, on any part of your clothing, I'll make you eat your face. And if you're sick on yourself instead of in the bowl, I'll cut out your eyeballs and make you chew on them like gum. Do you understand me?'

Sorrentino was crying now. 'Yeah,' he whispered. 'I understand you. What you gonna do? What's gonna happen to me?'

'You're going to die, Mario. After that . . .' He shrugged. 'You'll see soon enough. But first I'm going to ask you some questions. The better the answers you give . . . well, I don't need to spell it out, I'm sure. Frank Fischetti. Where does he live?'

'What?'

Izsák clubbed the man's face with the gun, hard enough to split his cheek. 'Where does he live?'

'He . . . he's up in Riverdale.'

'Give me the address.'

Sorrentino told him.

'Describe him.'

'B . . . big guy, kind of obese. Early fifties. Double chin. Black hair, grey in places. Wears a lot of gold.'

'What's your connection?'

'I'm his nephew. Well, sort of nephew. Not directly, you know? I don't know what the word is. Hang on.' Noisily, he vomited into the bowl. He glanced down at himself, saw that he'd spilled nothing over his clothes. Sagged.

'Are you close? To Fischetti?'

'Yeah. We're close.'

'Who does he keep around him?'

'Why are you asking? Surely you—'

'You want to question me?'

'No, I—'

'Was that a question for me?'

'No.'

'Who does he keep around him?'

'Leo and Fabian. They're his sons. Then there's Bruno. Bruno's not related, but he's usually there. And sometimes Seve, too'

'Who's waiting for you in the car outside?'

'George.'

'Is that what you call him?'

'Yeah.'

'Who's in charge?'

'Huh?'

'Out of the two of you. Who's the boss?'

'Uh . . . I guess me.'

'Walk me through the house. Fischetti's house.'

'I . . .' Sorrentino stared at him, terrified and confused. He tried to stand.

'Not literally, you idiot. Your hand is attached to the table. Sit down. Now, walk me through it. Tell me where Fischetti will be.'

'It's a big place. Kind of . . . like a palace. Pillars out in front. This huge lobby. Frank's study is on the ground floor. You take the first left off the lobby, keep going. It's the big door at the end. What's this got to do with Frank?'

Izsák took a wad of napkins from the bag. He leaned forward and eased the knife out of Sorrentino's hand. Handed him the napkins. 'Stand up. Take off your clothes. Don't get blood on them.'

Eyelids flickering, looking as if he might pass out, the man shuffled from the booth, clutching the wad of napkins to his hand. Awkwardly, he shrugged out of his jacket. Then he removed the rest of his clothes, folding them neatly.

'Now back up. Over there in the corner.'

Quickly Izsák undressed. He threw on Sorrentino's trousers, shirt and jacket. Stepped into his shoes. Picked up the pistol from the table.

'I still don't get why you're asking me all—'

Izsák raised the gun and shot Sorrentino between the eyes. Then he walked to the door of the Ready Eat. On his way past the counter, he grabbed a leather satchel and a bag of pastries.

Outside, an Oldsmobile was parked against the kerb. Izsák opened the passenger door and slid onto the seat.

The man behind the wheel stared. 'You shot Otto?'

Opening the bag, Izsák took out a strudel and stuffed it into his mouth. 'Yeah. Take me to Frank's.'

The car pulled out into traffic. Izsák swallowed the pastry and took out another.

'You hungry or something?'

'Shut up and take me to Frank's.'

The Fischetti place was a Georgian-style mansion set back from the road on an impeccably manicured square of land. Izsák told George to stay in the car, and walked up the drive. A rake-thin man in a wide suit opened the front door, nodding when he recognised who was calling.

'Frank here?'

'Yep.'

'Anyone with him?'

'Nope. He's on the telephone. Guys are out back.'

Izsák strode across the parquet floor, took a left and kept going. At the end of the hall, between two ugly bronze statues, he saw a thickset oak door, just where Sorrentino had described. Without hesitating, he pushed it open and walked inside.

Frank Fischetti wasn't on the telephone. He was sitting at his desk, using a ramrod to insert a ball and patch down the barrel of what looked like an antique duelling pistol. Behind him, drapes were pulled across a pair of French windows. On the left, the door to a wall safe hung ajar.

Sorrentino had described Fischetti reasonably well, but he'd failed to explain the lizard-like quality of the man's eyes. Fischetti's face was pock-marked too, as if, in his past, he'd caught either a bad dose of acne or a round of birdshot. He glanced up as Izsák came in, and for the briefest of moments his eyes narrowed. Then he smiled. 'A pair of Mantons,' he said. 'You ever heard of Joseph Manton?'

'No.'

'One of the finest gunsmiths that ever lived. These were made in 1797. Just look at the engraving on the trigger guards.'

Izsák approached the desk, dropping his satchel onto the floor. A mahogany case in front of Fischetti contained the second pistol. It had already been primed. 'They sure are nice,' he said.

Fischetti nodded. Working with methodical slowness, he took a metal tube from his desk and tapped primer into the pistol's flash pan. Once he'd closed the frizzon, he lowered the weapon until the barrel pointed straight at Izsák's chest. 'Since when did you walk in here without knocking?'

Moving with the speed of a striking snake, Izsák snatched the Manton off him with one hand and punched him in the throat with the other.

Fischetti toppled back into his chair, hands darting to his neck. He gasped, choked. When he still couldn't get enough air, he panicked, tried to stand, and crashed instead to his knees.

'You're a scourge, Mr Fischetti. A parasite. Or you were,' Izsák told him. 'Not after today.' He opened his satchel, removing a bed sheet and several pieces of rope.

Working fast, he laid out the sheet on the floor. Then he picked up Fischetti's ankles and dragged him on to it. While the man clawed at his throat, Izsák stripped him of his clothes. He bound Fischetti's hands and feet, then dressed himself in the discarded garments.

Walking up to the safe, he peered inside. 'Are those what I think they are?'

Wheezing now, desperately trying to inhale through his crushed windpipe, Fischetti nodded.

The discovery of the safe's contents justified a revision to his plans. Five minutes later, after receiving a whispered explanation from Fischetti, Izsák knelt down and gagged him. He put his face mere inches from the man's own, studied the contours of his skull, his pocked skin, his eyes, his hair, took a deep breath, and *changed*.

Fischetti tried to scream, nearly suffocating himself on the gag. Grabbing him by the shoulders, Izsák rolled him up inside the sheet and secured him with the ropes. Then he opened the drapes covering the French windows.

Outside, four men were standing around a peppermint-green Lincoln, smoking. Two of them shared the same lizard-eyed stare as Fischetti.

Izsák opened the doors and shouted out to them. 'Get in here, all of you.' Once they'd assembled inside the room, and Izsák had locked the doors, he pointed at the body, wrapped in a bed sheet, writhing on the floor. 'This man,' he said, 'is a thief. He's stolen something from me no one can replace.'

One of the Fischetti brothers hawked and spat on the fabric. 'Well that was a fuckin' mistake. What did he do, Pa? What did he take?'

'I'll tell you once you've killed him.'

At that, Fischetti began to struggle more violently, like a newly formed moth trying to escape a chrysalis. The men raised their eyes to Izsák.

'Now? In here?' one of them asked.

'Yes, now. Yes, in here. But no guns. And keep him inside that sheet. I don't want him messing up the place.'

Grinning, the men removed their jackets.

As the blows began to fall, as the room filled with cries of animal excitement and hoots of laughter, as the white linen grew dark with blood, none of the four noticed the man who looked like Frank Fischetti pick up the two flintlock pistols from the desk and walk out of the room.

They continued to kick and howl and stamp, until finally the exertion got the better of them. Leo Fischetti was the first to stop. He rested his hands on his knees and bent over, panting, grimacing at the blood on his shoes. 'Boys, I'd say that's enough. Someone's gonna have to bury this shit sack. Any longer and it'll be like shovelling mincemeat.'

'Where's Pa?'

'Must have stepped out. Say, I want to see who this guy was. Don't you?'

A chorus of agreement.

Leo pulled out a switchblade and cut away the sheet from around the dead man's head. For a moment, everyone was still.

'Oh Jesus,' Leo said. 'Oh Jesus, oh *JESUS*.'

Balázs Izsák walked along the hall to the foyer and out of the front door, closing it behind him. He was halfway down the drive when the dynamite he'd found in Fischetti's safe detonated, vaporising the man's sons, blowing out every window on the ground floor and lighting up the building with flame. The air rained brick dust and plaster and glass.

George was waiting in the car parked at the kerb. When the house exploded he dived out, running up the drive towards Izsák.

Izsák lifted one of the duelling pistols and pulled the trigger. The flint struck the flash pan and the primer flared with a hiss. But the spark did not carry to the breach.

It sometimes happened with flintlocks.

George skidded to a halt, his mouth gaping. Izsák lifted the second pistol and fired. This gun worked perfectly, and the ejected lead ball took off a sizeable part of George's skull. The man collapsed to one side of the path.

Izsák climbed into the Oldsmobile, threw the pistols onto the seat and accelerated away from what remained of the Fischetti residence.

His ears were ringing from the explosion. But when, at last, the sound faded, all he heard was the Oldsmobile's engine and the hiss of its tyres on the road. For the first time in his life, the mocking voice inside his head spoke not a word of complaint.

CHAPTER 25

Snowdonia, Wales

In the dying light, the mountains were black humps against a bruised sky. Leah stood beside her father's grave, between the stag poised at the edge of the lake and the man called Tuomas on the gravel track.

Even the wind had faded. The only sound she heard in the valley stillness was the rasping breath of the animal behind her, so close it felt as if the stag blew gouts of steam against her neck.

She wanted to run, but where to? Not towards Tuomas, that was for sure. She could possibly make it into the trees before the stag reached her, but what then? The forest floor was choked with trailing vines and bracken. Further in, it was night-dark. Within seconds she would be disoriented, unable to see, even more vulnerable than she was in the open.

Leah could feel her legs trembling beneath her, a horrifying lightness to them, as if they'd been stripped of muscle and bone. And here was that feeling again, a spider-like prickling on her skin. Not simply another symptom of her fear, but the same strange sensation she had felt when she arrived outside Etienne's residence during her second visit.

Tuomas took a step towards her. He held something in his hands. It was too dark to see his eyes, or the expression on his face, but there was something grim and inevitable about his silhouette.

Behind her, the stag blew air from its snout. She heard it lift its hooves, the mud sucking at them.

A rifle. That was what Tuomas held. He raised it in a single fluid movement, until the barrel pointed at her face. He leaned his head into the scope.

Leah closed her eyes. Perhaps this was a fitting resting place, she thought. Her father lay here. Her grandfather too. She could think of worse places to die.

You're a Wilde. You don't close your eyes and wait for death. You fight. Until you have nothing left.

Taking a breath, she opened her eyes.

Tuomas said something to her, and it took a moment for her brain to process his words: *Get down.*

An explosion of movement behind her.

Hooves. First churning mud, then thumping across hard-packed ground.

She did not have time to run. Did not have time even to turn and confront the creature that charged her. Instead, she dived.

Tuomas chambered a round; the rifle's bolt snapped back, forward and down.

Leah hit the ground hands first, gravel chips slicing her hands like shards of glass. Beneath her she felt the vibrations of the charging stag.

The rifle blast, when it came, ruptured the air like two motor vehicles colliding. Still the animal came, hooves drumming against the earth.

Leah rolled onto her back. Saw it bearing down on her, a mountain of antlers and muscle. The front of its head was a mess of pulverised bone and flesh. Even as its forelegs dipped and its chest hit the ground, its momentum carried it onwards, antlers scouring the earth as it slid towards her. It came to a rest a yard from her feet.

Leah gasped, feeling the cold press of soil against her spine. Raising herself to her elbows, she stared at the animal's ruined skull.

She climbed to her feet and faced Tuomas. When he chambered another round, she raised her hands, backing away.

'Stop,' he said.

The smell of blood was rich on the air, mingling with the stag's musk. For some reason, her legs wouldn't obey her. She took another step backwards.

'Leah, I said stop. *Now.*'

She froze, registering the urgency in his voice. Her boots were a few inches from the tips of the stag's antlers.

'Listen to me,' he said. 'Whatever you do, don't touch it. Careful as you can, come towards me. Just a few feet. Until you're away from it.'

'You followed me here,' she said, and heard the fear in her voice.

'Yes.'

'Why?'

'You need to come away from there. It's not safe.'

'I asked you a question.'

Tuomas lifted his cheek from the rifle scope. Scanned the valley. 'You're being hunted.'

Leah swallowed. Looked back down at the carcass by her feet. Finally she complied, taking a step away, not towards Tuomas but to her right, towards the trees. 'What are you talking about?'

'How much detail do you need? You're being hunted, Leah.'

She felt her blood beginning to chill. 'By a stag?'

'By *lélek tolvajok*. Trust me. You really don't want to touch it.' Tuomas tilted his head towards the forest and paused, listening. 'There may be more of them. We need to go. Now.'

'Wait a minute. You're telling me that was one of them?'

'Yes, and I can't protect you in the dark. We've only a few minutes of light left.'

'If you think I'm going with you—'

'Is that your Mercedes by the gate?'

'Yes.'

'Then you don't need to go with me. But if you stay here and argue, you're going to be in serious trouble.'

She stared at him, wishing she could see his eyes in the failing light. But even though his sudden appearance had frightened her, he sounded sincere.

And how much value do you place on that? He's hosszú élet. *Of course he'll sound sincere. Look sincere. You know nothing about him. Who he is. Why he followed you.*

From somewhere beyond the ridge, she heard an animal wail, almost like a fox's scream. A moment later an answering cry rolled towards them from the other side of the lake.

Tuomas stiffened. 'They're coming. It's up to you, but we don't have time for debate.' He began to walk back up the track.

'Wait.' Leah broke into a run, reaching his side in moments. 'OK, so I don't know who you are. That's freaking me out. Or why you followed me. You just killed that thing, and I've no way of telling whether what you say is true.'

Another cry drifted across the water. Closer now.

'But you're right,' she continued. 'That's not a sound I've heard before. Something's out there.'

'Stay close,' he replied. 'In the dark, their vision will be better than ours. If we—' He raised a hand, and she stopped dead. Tuomas swept the night with his scope. Nodding, he said, 'Let's go.'

Her Mercedes came into sight a minute later, a black outline in the gloom. 'Don't unlock it,' he told her. 'Not until you're beside the door. The indicator lights will alert them.'

'What about you?'

'I'm parked at the top of the hill.'

'Then let me drive you there. If it's dangerous out here for me, that goes for you, too.'

He scanned the track in both directions. 'You're sure?'

Oddly, she found she was. As she unlocked the Mercedes its lights flashed orange.

Leah slid behind the wheel. Tuomas jumped into the passenger seat, clamping the rifle between his knees. He locked his door and she did the same.

'Drive,' he told her.

She didn't need any encouragement. Revving the engine, she threw the car into reverse and backed up, sliding it around as soon as she had the space.

She found first gear, floored the accelerator. The wheels spun, digging for traction before they bit on hard ground and the vehicle rocketed forward.

Leah switched on the headlights just as something crashed out of the bushes up ahead. She cried out. Instead of swerving to avoid it, she punched the car into second gear and accelerated. Tuomas braced his hand against the dash.

The impact bounced them out of their seats. The Mercedes' left headlight shattered and the vehicle sloughed around. Leah fought against the wheel, and for a moment she thought the car was going to spin. By sheer luck she managed to regain control, and then they were flying up the track, shredding vines and snapping tree branches.

'Did I kill it?' she shouted, throwing a glance at her mirror. Nothing was visible back there except darkness. Ahead, the track was lit only by her right headlight. She could see virtually nothing on her left but she couldn't afford to slow down.

Tuomas twisted in his seat. 'It's following.' He sucked in a breath. 'Two of them.'

Leah cursed, and then the car was barrelling over the lip of the track. Ripping the wheel to the right, she slid the Mercedes onto the main road and controlled the skid, tyres shrieking. With tarmac beneath her, she floored the accelerator once more. 'Where's your car?'

'Forget it,' Tuomas said, drawing the seatbelt across him. 'Drive.'

CHAPTER 26

Outskirts of Dawson City, Canada

1944

This close to spring, Izsák did not usually risk driving the fifteen miles from their cabin into town. The Yukon, frozen since October into a white slab of river ice, choppy with its crusts of snow, was finally beginning to thaw, and he did not like to test the truck's weight on its surface, preferring instead to hitch his dogs to the sled.

In two days' time it was Georgia's seventh birthday, and he had driven into Dawson to visit the post office and pick up the parcel that had arrived from Winnipeg. He and Lucy had pored over the Eaton's catalogue for three weeks before placing a mail order for the cherry-red bicycle with its bright silver bell.

They both knew there was nowhere near their cabin for Georgia to learn to ride. For more than half the year the area was covered with snow, and even after the thaw the ground was uneven and harsh. Izsák would worry about that later. The smile on Lucy's face when she'd seen the catalogue illustration had warmed him like a baker's oven. Buying Georgia the bike might not be practical, she had reasoned, but neither was raising their daughter in the frozen wilderness, with no electricity or running water. That hadn't stopped them from doing it, so why should a lack of roads prevent them from purchasing the bike?

Izsák agreed; rarely, he had discovered, was anything strictly practical particularly fun. Despite its challenges, he had grown to love the Yukon's savage wilderness almost as much as his wife and daughter. They'd built a perfect life here, full of wonder and peace; as free from the horrors of close-living humanity as they could possibly get. During the short Yukon summer they could sit out on the deck until midnight and still have enough light to read. Lucy's vegetable garden produced a steady crop of potatoes, carrots and turnips, and Izsák fished for grayling along the river.

But it was the wintertime he liked best. The world froze and grew still. The windows of their cabin thickened with ice and the wood stove burned day and night. Izsák shot caribou, elk and moose, hanging the meat from nearby trees to foil the attentions of scavengers. They clothed themselves in the heavy garments Lucy knitted from the wool Izsák picked up in town, and during the long nights they watched the ropey green ghosts of the aurora borealis and listened to the howling of the wolves.

They'd left New York fifteen years earlier. Izsák and Lucy's memories of the Ready Eat Lunch Wagon's last days grew dimmer each season, but they kept Emil Otto alive through stories, and sometimes Lucy would sing to Georgia the old German songs with which he had entertained her as a child. A framed photograph of Emil hung on the wall beside the stove.

A few miles due east of the cabin, Izsák guided the truck off the Overland Trail connecting Dawson to White Horse, and navigated along the track that skirted the black spruce forest close to their home. It was slow going, the old Chevy bouncing over ruts and frozen clods of earth. A raven circled above, the only movement in a sky so intensely blue it seemed encased in crystal.

Around a final bend and he saw it waiting in the distance, their cabin: a rough home of sawn logs with a covered porch, which Izsák had built the year before Georgia arrived. Beside the cabin stood the dog barn, attached to which was the lean-to that sheltered his sled.

He'd give his Malamutes a run later. In truth he should probably have run the dogs to Dawson – one of their last excursions before the weather grew too warm – but the Chevy's clutch had been playing up recently, and he hadn't wanted to leave the vehicle as Lucy's only means of transport should she need one. She was pregnant again, for the first time in seven years. He didn't know how that could be; he'd heard such a thing was impossible. But Georgia had arrived with barely a wrinkle in the fabric of their lives; Izsák had delivered her himself one evening as a white moon turned the snowy landscape into a field of diamonds.

Ahead, smoke was feathering from the stovepipe jutting from the cabin's roof. He frowned when he saw it. Even this close to the thaw, he could feel the crunch of ice crystals in his nose. Despite the effort he'd put into insulating the cabin the draughts still blew freely, and without a fierce steady heat from the stove the night ahead would see them shivering in their beds.

Nudging a little extra speed from the Chevy, he heard its snow chains crackle and pop. The cabin grew larger in his windshield and he noticed that its door was open, banging to and fro in the breeze.

If the sight of the thinning wood smoke had bothered him, the sight of the swinging door froze his blood. Now he spotted something else: a dark figure, sunk in a deep drift of snow, perhaps twenty yards from the door.

Izsák slammed on the truck's brakes and the vehicle canted sideways, slithering to a stop. Grabbing his hunting rifle from the gun rack, he killed the engine.

Immediately he heard the yapping of his dogs, and that was when he knew something dreadful had happened. The noise the pack was making was no Malamute greeting at his return;

they sounded crazy. Yet despite their agitation, none of them waited outside. Even Nero, his lead dog, had retreated to the darkness of the barn.

Throwing open the truck's door, Izsák dropped into snow up to his knees. He waded towards the stricken figure, his breath pluming, the frigid air like a cold brick pressed against his face.

Lucy. It could only be her.

She wasn't moving, and the thought of what that might mean nearly bent him double in despair. How long had he been gone? Four hours? Time enough for loved ones to die and life to change.

And where was Georgia? Unless Lucy had only just collapsed, surely his daughter would have noticed her mother's disappearance and gone to find her.

The whispery tendrils of smoke trailing from the chimney suggested his wife had been out here a while.

Don't panic. Panic and you lose them.

He reached Lucy's side and sank down beside her in crunching snow. She faced away from him, as still as a doll. Izsák pulled off his gloves, reached out a hand. Only then did he realise that the woman lying in the snow was not his wife.

The hair poking out from under her knit cap was grey instead of blond, that was the most obvious thing. Likewise, she was too small, too bent. He did not recognise her clothing. Relieved it wasn't Lucy, but heart knocking in his chest just as hard, Izsák pulled her onto her back and stared down into the ravaged face of an old woman.

The crone's eyes were milky with cataracts. Her skin, pouched and baggy, reminded him of dried fruit. Beneath a hooked nose, colourless lips were lined with wrinkles. Her mouth hung open. From between toothless gums seeped a thin mist of breath.

When he shook her, her chest heaved and her eyelids flickered. She whispered up at him, the word rattling in her throat. '. . . *Gonnne.*'

Releasing her, Izsák strained to his feet, trying to fend off the terrible memory that rushed at him. His breath came in shallow gasps. As he stumbled towards the cabin, he tripped, fell, and used the stock of his rifle to lever himself to his feet. He arrived at the front step, slipped on ice, sprawled onto his back.

Almost comical, he thought. How Lucy would laugh if she saw him.

With a jumble of half-formed prayers spilling from his lips he grasped the wooden rail, hauling himself up to the porch. Strange that his strength should leave him like this. Strange what terror could do to a man.

Izsák pushed open the door and staggered inside. When he saw the overturned table and the spilled soup, he sobbed.

The cabin had only two rooms, with a snug half-loft for Georgia. Right now he was in the big room where they lived during the day and cooked their meals. He crossed to the bedroom he shared with Lucy.

He found her inside, collapsed on the floor, hands cradling the swell of her belly. Blood mantled her.

Too shocked to cry out, Izsák dropped down beside her and took her hand.

Lucy opened her eyes. After a moment they focused, and she found his face. 'Oh, 'Sak. I'm sorry. I'm so sorry. It got inside me, eating me up. I tried, I really did. But it kept coming back into my head and I couldn't think. Couldn't do anything to stop it.'

'What happened?'

'It took her. It took Georgia.'

He stared at his wife. 'What took her? Where's Georgia, Lucy? What happened?'

'They . . . came. Two of them. The older woman and . . . the man with the strange clothes. Go, Izsák. Find her. Before it's too late.'

'Lucy, let me—'

She shook her head. 'No. Leave me. Find Georgia.' She

coughed, a dark clot of blood. Screwing up her face, she sucked in a breath and closed her seaweed-green eyes. 'Love you, 'Sak.'

'Don't say that to me!' he roared. He shook her arm, and when she didn't respond he grabbed her by the shoulders and shook her far harder than he ought. 'Don't you say that, Lucy! Don't you say that!'

It was pointless, and he knew it. The life had already left her.

Izsák screamed out his agony. The tears came, blinding him. He wanted to lay his head on Lucy's chest, to bury himself in her smell. Instead he dragged himself to his feet. Somehow he managed to turn his back on her. Bumping into furniture, bouncing off the rough-hewn walls, he navigated his way out of the cabin.

Izsák staggered down the steps, slipping and sliding on ice. He noticed that he clutched his rifle, that he must have grabbed it from the floor when he'd left Lucy.

It was useless until he loaded it. Hands shaking, he drew back the bolt and waded towards the old woman lying in the snow.

Her eyes were closed but breath still trickled from her mouth. Izsák dropped to one knee. He raised the gun and swept the area beyond the trees.

Nothing.

The landscape was frozen and still. Even the raven had vanished from the sky.

Izsák slung the rifle over one shoulder, slipped his hands under the old woman's armpits and dragged her back to the cabin. Her boots clattered against the steps as he pulled her up onto the porch.

Inside, Izsák rolled her onto the couch. He crammed three dry logs into the wood burner. From a jug he poured icy water into a tin mug.

At any other time he would have felt guilt for what he did next. He flung the water into her face.

The crone's eyes snapped open. Arching her back, fingers clawing at the couch, she let out a screech.

'Where have they gone?' Izsák shouted. '*Think*. Where will they go?'

'*Gone . . .*' the woman rasped.

'Gone where? Who are you? What's your name?'

'*Anke . . . my name . . . Anke . . .*'

'How old are you?'

Her eyes fluttered and closed. He slapped her, drawing blood from her mouth.

'I asked you a question! How *old* are you?'

She began to weep, an awful whimpering sound. '*I'm twelve,*' she said, voice like a child's. '*Please . . . d . . . don't hurt me, sir. I'm twelve, twelve years old. I'm Anke . . . Anke.*'

Izsák sat down hard, his heart a boulder in his chest. He stared at her, at the lines of her face, her milky white eyes.

And he knew: knew what had happened to Georgia.

Jumping to his feet, he went to the bureau beside the cabin door. He ripped open a drawer and pulled out boxes of ammunition, throwing them into a satchel he found on a hook. He picked up his rifle.

'I'm sorry. I have to leave you,' he said, knowing what that meant for her. Turning his back, he walked out of the cabin, down the steps and through snow towards his truck. He did not look back.

How much of a head start they had on him he did not know, nor what he would do when he found them. Inside the Chevy the first thing he saw, wrapped in brown packing paper and tape, was the cherry-red bicycle that had arrived from Winnipeg. He hauled it off the seat. Climbed behind the wheel.

Izsák started the truck. In the rear-view mirror his eyes looked dead.

Swallowing his grief, he tramped down on the accelerator and the truck lurched out onto the trail.

CHAPTER 27

Shropshire, England

On the outskirts of Shrewsbury they found a service station with a food court. Inside, at a quiet table beside the windows, Leah drank a coffee and listened as Tuomas told his story.

She could not rid herself of the chill that had enveloped her beside her father's grave. The memory of the stag – the way it stared at her, the way its skull opened like a flower when Tuomas's rifle round hit it – was too recent, too shocking.

Despite that, she found herself unable to look away from his solemn grey eyes as he told her the story of his life in the cabin outside Dawson City, so filled with laughter and love, and how it had ended. The more he talked, the less aware she became of the night pressing against the glass, and of the other patrons in the restaurant.

His tale was wrenchingly sad, and he told it so tonelessly, and with such resignation, that she wanted to reach across the table and touch his hand. But she was not used to contact like that – it would have felt awkward, wrong – and the table remained a gulf between them.

Tuomas paused, as if sensing that he'd lost her, and then he shrugged. Leah dropped her gaze to her coffee mug, glanced back up. 'You never found her.'

'Not yet, but I will. She's out there. I know that.'

'What will you do then?'

He closed his eyes for a moment, and when he opened them she saw flecks of azurite floating in the grey. 'I'll kill them both. There's never been a way to force a *tolvaj* to abandon a body against its will. Georgia was seven years old when she was taken. That thing's been riding inside her most of her life. Even if I could figure out a way to get rid of it, I doubt there's anything left of Georgia any more. She's been a prisoner too long. All I can do now is to try and end her suffering.'

'You could do that?' She flinched, dismayed at how accusatory her question had sounded. 'I'm sorry. I didn't mean it like that. I just . . . if the time comes, could you really carry it out?'

'I have to.'

Leah felt her shoulders dip with exhaustion. 'You've been looking all this time. Before the one at the lake, have you encountered others?'

'Several. For a while I was quite the expert at finding them. I've tracked maybe twenty, all told. Killed about a quarter of those. Not as much luck in recent years. They're dying out. Just like us.' Tuomas leaned forward in his seat. 'Those hunting you back at the farmhouse. That was no coincidence, them finding you there. They must have picked up your trail a while ago. You need to work out how long they've been following you, and where's safe for you to be from now on.'

'I can't just go to ground.'

'You have no choice.'

'You're right, I don't. I've made promises. To Etienne. Others.'

'If you don't take this seriously—'

'Of course I take it seriously. I'm hardly going to forget that thing. But at least you killed it.'

'No. I didn't. Not even close. We should have taken care of it permanently, but there wasn't time. It'll be back. I guarantee it.'

She saw he was telling the truth, and shivered. 'How do you kill them?'

'Burn the bodies until there's nothing left. Freeze them. Bury them in lime. There are ways.'

'My God.'

For a while, neither of them spoke. Leah finished her coffee, feeling his eyes on her. She looked up from her empty mug. 'What about your life before you moved to Dawson?' she asked. 'Before you met Lucy?'

'My life started when I met Lucy. There *is* no before.'

'You must have—'

Tuomas shook his head. 'No. I won't relive those memories. Not for you, not for anyone. I had a life in Canada, a wife and a daughter, and then I lost them. That's all there is to tell.'

'I'm sorry.'

'Don't be.'

'I must ask one thing, because it does affect what I'm doing. Your history with Etienne. That came before, didn't it?'

He hesitated, then nodded.

'I won't pry. I just needed to know.'

'Etienne and I . . . we knew each other a long time ago. And then one day our paths just crossed again. We keep in touch, very loosely. Sometimes she asks my advice. She's never had anyone else.' Tuomas pulled out a pocket watch and flicked open its hunter case. 'It's getting late,' he said. 'We should move.'

Leah hardly heard his words. The blood drained from her face. Transfixed, she stared at the timepiece. Reaching over, she trapped his arm under her hand. 'Show me that.'

Frowning, he pulled away, sliding the watch back into his pocket. 'What's wrong?'

With her eyes still on his, she lifted her hands to her neck and removed a chain from beneath her clothes. Swinging from it, a pocket watch of her own. Leah opened it and placed it down on the table. The gold case was dented and scratched. Inside, the numerals had burned away from its enamelled face.

It was the only thing they'd ever found in the smouldering

wreckage of Le Moulin Bellerose, the only evidence of their victory over Jakab. No bones. No teeth. The fire had been far too hot. Leah turned the watch over. She did not need to look at the back plate to know the inscription it bore.

Balázs Lukács
Végzet 1873

A pulse flickered in Tuomas's throat. 'Where . . .' he began. 'Where did you get this?'

'Show me,' she repeated.

His eyes pinioned her. After a moment's pause he took out his own watch, flipped it over and laid it beside the first. A replica. Almost.

Balázs Izsák
Végzet

Feeling as if a serpent coiled around her chest, Leah pointed at the name. She didn't want the answer, but she had to ask the question. 'Are you him?'

He nodded.

The serpent tightened its grip, squeezing the breath from her lungs. 'Jakab,' she said. 'Who was he to you?

Balázs Izsák's chin was trembling, now. 'I haven't heard that name in over a hundred years. I never expected to hear it again. He sent my father to his death. Killed Jani, too.' He bowed his head, stared at the watches lying side by side. 'Jakab was my brother.'

Leah wanted to run, but the strength had drained from her. Her legs wouldn't move. 'No,' she muttered. 'No.'

When he raised his head, his eyes looked haunted. 'Who was he to you?'

CHAPTER 28

I-15, south of Salt Lake City, Utah, USA

She had been driving for five hours without a break, the only sounds to accompany her the hiss of the van's tyres and the occasional muffled bang from the cargo hold. The interstate stretched out in front, two endless lines of grey separated by a wide patch of scrub.

Flanking her on both sides she saw the outlines of distant mountain ranges, their peaks dark, except for those already claimed by snow. In between the land was flat, bleached and barren, dotted here and there with squat round bushes.

On the passenger seat, her phone began to vibrate. She picked it up and held it to her ear.

'It's me,' said a voice.

Trapping the phone with her shoulder, she steered the van past two enormous Peterbilt cattle haulers. When she glanced over at one of the trailers she noticed, through its slotted metal side, the solemn eyes of its cargo staring out at the landscape. For a moment the sight nudged a memory in her – something she was meant to have done. And then the thought faded.

'I'm driving,' she said. 'But I won't be for long.'

'I'll be waiting,' he said, and hung up.

★ ★ ★

Off the interstate, a few miles south of Beaver, she spotted a brown-brick restaurant set back from the road. A row of American flags flew out front, and a sign invited diners with the promise: *HAPPY BITE GRILLE: THE BEST RIBS YOU EVER TASTED!*

Its parking lot was deserted. Swinging the van off the road, she pulled into a space furthest from the restaurant's doors.

Inside the Happy Bite, a TV set was tuned to a news channel. The voices of its anchors served only to amplify the restaurant's desolation. Empty booths lined two walls and empty tables studded the floor, each laid with cutlery and baskets of condiments. Along the far wall a glass-fronted chiller displayed glossy cheesecakes, pies and cakes. A wood-panelled service area held a stack of menus, a cash till, and a gap-toothed young man wearing a red *HAPPY BITE* polo shirt under a black apron. His name tag read *Sylvester*.

He jumped to his feet when he saw her and performed a curious double-take, eyes moving from the tips of her boots to her face, lingering for a moment on her breasts. Cheeks flushing crimson, glancing over his shoulder as if looking for guidance, he snatched up a couple of menus from the stack.

She ignored him, choosing a table by the window where she could watch the van. Nervously the youth approached, a novice matador edging towards a bull. 'Ma'am,' he said. 'Welcome to Happy Bite.'

She took the menu, scanned it and passed it back. 'Hickory ribs, coleslaw, fries, onion rings and a Coke.' She paused. 'A plate of nachos, too.'

The boy winced, shifting his weight to one foot. 'I'm really sorry, but we're not doing the ribs right now. How about a steak?'

She pointed at the sign out the front: *THE BEST RIBS YOU EVER TASTED!*

He nodded unhappily. 'I know. It pisses customers off no end. Ribs aren't on the lunch menu. We only start serving them from six.'

'Then I'll have a steak. Pan-fried. Rare.'

'That I can do.' He hesitated, glancing out of the window at her van. 'All this for you?'

'Yes.'

'You're pretty hungry, huh?'

'Yes.'

He grinned, displaying the large gap between his front teeth. 'Well, we do great steaks.'

She stared.

'Can I get you some coffee while you wait?'

'Yes.'

Sylvester scurried away and returned with a coffee mug, filling it to the brim. After placing cream and sugar down beside her, he disappeared through a door into the kitchen.

She pulled out her phone. Dialled. 'It's me,' she said. 'I'm off the road.'

'How are they?'

'Fading. But I have it in hand for now. Do you have any news?'

'Some. We lost the one we were following, but we're close.'

'They can't survive like this much longer.'

'They won't have to.'

She waited.

'*Kincsem*,' he added, his voice softening. 'You've sacrificed so much.'

'Can we come to you?'

'Not yet. We shouldn't move them until it's time. Not if they're as fragile as you say.'

'When?'

'Soon. I have to go.'

'*Szeretlek*,' she whispered. But already he had gone.

She put the phone back in her bag and stared out of the windows at the van. On the TV, the female anchor launched into a story about a local ice hockey team. The woman threw a comment at her male co-anchor, who rolled his eyes and shook his head.

Sylvester returned with her food, balancing the plates precariously. He laid them out before her, announcing each one with a flourish. When he saw her attention was on the TV, he flicked his head towards it. 'Pretty funny, huh?'

She raised an eyebrow.

'Those Grizzlies guys. Five of 'em, they say. Went out to a club two nights ago, then failed to show up for their game. Nobody's seen 'em since. Must have got pretty wasted, huh? One thing's for sure – they're in a world of trouble right now.'

'Grizzlies?'

He shook his head. 'You're not local. Grizzlies? Ice hockey team?' Sylvester's eyes began to roam again. 'Those boots. They real snakeskin?'

'Yes.'

'Cool.'

She waited until the silence grew too awkward and he wandered off. Immediately she tore into the steak, demolishing it in three bites. Cramming a fistful of onion rings into her mouth, she washed them down with a mouthful of Coke, then swallowed the rest. The coleslaw was next, followed by the fries. It took her less than a minute to consume them. Finally she turned her attention to the nachos.

Glancing down, she saw her blouse was blotched with ketchup and grease. She wiped the worst of the mess away, and called Sylvester over.

When he saw the empty plates his eyes bulged from his head. 'Goddamn, lady. You like to eat, don't you?'

'I need to order some take-out.'

'You're not done?'

'It's not for me.'

'What can I get you?'

'Five bacon cheeseburgers, with fries.' She paused. 'Root beers, too.'

'For five?'

She nodded.

He came back a few minutes later with two white bags, and she paid with cash.

'Got far to go?'

'Yes.'

He nodded at her van. 'What're you hauling?'

'Meat.'

'Uh huh.' He shuffled from foot to foot, licked his lips. 'You know, I get a discount here. Like, for staff. It's pretty generous.'

She stared.

'I mean, if you ever wanted to come back.'

She looked around the empty restaurant. 'Here?'

'If you ever wanted to try those ribs, I mean. Or, like, whatever.' He glanced down at his name badge. 'This job, it's only temporary. I'm saving for college.'

She stood, took the bags. Her sudden proximity seemed to unnerve him.

He moved backwards, nearly tripped. 'You know, if you liked, we could even—'

She stepped closer, closing the distance between them. 'Stop talking.'

His Adam's apple bobbed. 'Yes ma'am.'

He watched her go, his stomach flopping like an eel. Later, he would not sleep for thinking about her.

Twenty miles south of Beaver, she turned east onto State Route 20, a strip of road that led through a wilderness of gently sloping hills. She found an empty truck stop and pulled in, the van sending up a shower of gravel. Carrying the bags of take-out, she went around to the back and unlocked the doors.

It was dark inside, and it smelled bad. Urine and sweat.

The faces of five terrified young men stared out at her. Their wrists and their ankles were bound. Each had a rectangle of duct tape pressed across his mouth.

Leaning in, she studied them more closely. All wore black nylon jackets. For the first time she noticed the emblem they displayed: a grizzly bear with glowing red eyes, cradling a hockey stick and a sign that read: *Utah Grizzlies.*

When she moved to the nearest of her captives, he pressed his spine against the side of the van, eyes wide with horror. Reaching out, she ripped the tape from his mouth. Where it tore the skin from his lip it left a dribble of blood.

'You're hockey players,' she said.

He nodded.

'Time to eat, all of you. Take off the tape.' She handed the bags of food and drink to the young man whose gag she'd removed. When he opened his mouth to speak, she shut the door and climbed back behind the wheel.

She drove for another two hours, taking US-89 south before turning east towards Bryce Canyon. The rocks here had a reddish cast. Thousands of years of flash-flooding had carved channels and fissures.

Past the town of Cannonville, Garfield County, she took a left turn and twenty minutes later drove past the rusting metal sign welcoming her to the ranch.

As the van bounced along the track, she saw that the land was strewn with dark humps. It took her a while to realise they were the carcasses of dead cows – *her* cows – and now she understood why the sight of the cattle haulers on the interstate had pricked her memory. When she'd bought the farm a few weeks earlier she'd purchased its livestock, too. She recalled the realtor explaining about the irrigation ponds and the creek, along with the system of fences and gates.

Now the animals were dead, a hundred rotting hunks of beef. As she passed, a flurry of crows exploded from the nearest carcass. They'd stripped one side of its face down to the bone, and had dug into the soft flesh of its belly.

Another mile, and she saw the ranch house waiting ahead, a wide timber-built structure with dark windows and a gently sloping roof.

Pulling up, she switched off the engine, sitting quietly for a minute as she stared at the building. Then she took a knife from her bag, climbed out and went to unlock the van's rear doors. Inside, her captives had consumed their lunch of cheeseburgers and root beer. The stench had worsened considerably.

She leaned towards the youth she had addressed earlier and cut through the bonds tying his feet. Grabbing him by the ankles, she hauled his legs over the lip of the luggage bay.

'Get up.'

He nodded, eyes panicked, shifting his weight to his feet. Two days locked inside the van had driven the strength from his muscles, preventing him from standing fully, but he tried his best. He smelled like a sewer. 'I don't know what you want,' he said. 'But I'm not a bad guy. My name's—'

'Walk.'

'OK. I will. I'm doing it.' He shuffled forward, dragging his feet through stones. His hands, tied before him, began to shake. 'Why me? I mean, what about the others?'

When she declined to answer, his fear ratcheted up a notch. 'You don't need to hurt me, OK? Whatever it is you want, you don't need to do that.'

She unlocked the ranch's front door. It swung wide, revealing a wedge of darkness, and an odour that troubled her.

He caught it too. 'No, I don't want to go in there. Seriously. Let me stay out here, in the light, just for a while. Just for a while, OK? We'll work this out. If we talk. Come on. Please. I don't want to die.'

She turned to him. Stared. Lifted her mouth into a smile. 'What's your name?'

'J . . . Jason.'

'You're not going to die, Jason. Not here. Not today.'

'Then why—'

'I know this is distressing. But you don't have to be scared. I haven't brought you all the way out here just to kill you.'

His eyes moved to the shadows inside the ranch. 'Then what? What's in there?'

'Something incredible. Something that will change your life forever. Trust me, Jason. Now go inside.'

'I don't want to. I . . .'

She came towards him.

'No!' he shouted. 'Don't touch me again! I'll go in. I'll trust you.' He started crying as he shuffled across the threshold.

'Down the hall,' she instructed.

Inside, the air was thick with a rotten dead-poultry stench. Shadows gathered, pressing close. At the end of the hall they came to a door.

'Open it,' she told him. 'Go inside.'

Trembling, he obeyed, and she followed. Just enough light was seeping between the drapes to make out details: a large room, square in shape, lacking any furniture except five wingback chairs arranged in a semi-circle. The meagre light prevented her from seeing their occupants, but she heard a creaking of springs, and a whispery sound, like sheets of paper carried by the wind.

On the floor stood a Coleman lantern. She fired it up, the gas hissing as its light brightened the room.

Now she saw them more clearly, staring up at her. Their limbs were shrivelled and brittle, faces lined and pallid. Some had dried blood on their chins where they had spat out teeth. Cloudy eyes blinked.

'My darlings,' she told them softly. 'I'm here.'

'Oh, please God,' whispered the youth in the Grizzlies jacket. 'What the hell is this? What the *hell*?'

'All I ask,' she said, 'is that you do as I say.'

He raised his eyes from the chairs' occupants. 'Which is what?'

She led him to the nearest chair and instructed him to kneel.

The old woman sitting there had lost almost all her hair. Her hands, veined and liver-spotted, were clutched in her lap, aged before their time. Around her neck she wore an amber locket, its chain fashioned from interlinked beetles. She sighed, and with great effort she lifted a hand and draped it onto his head. Immediately the contact was made she slumped back in her seat, breath rattling out of her like an avalanche of stones.

The young man stared at the crone. The terror slid from his face, replaced by a reverential calm; he bowed his head. 'You honour me with your gift,' he said. Rising, he turned to the woman who had brought him and held out his hands. She cut through his bonds.

'Do you bring news?' he asked.

'He asks for patience.'

'We've *been* patient. It's killing us.'

'We won't abandon you.'

'You brought others?'

She nodded. 'Outside.'

'I'll fetch them.'

Once he'd left, she turned back to the old woman in the chair.

Her eyes were open. They scanned the room blindly, wide with confusion. '*What . . .*' she croaked, voice rasping and dry. '*Where is this? Where's it gone?*'

'Hush, Angel. It's over now. You did well.'

'*Where . . . Is it coming back? I can't see.*'

The woman with the seaweed eyes and sunlight hair moved towards her, holding out the knife.

CHAPTER 29

Villa del Osservatore, Italy

Tungsten clouds sailed the skies above Lake Como, darkening the water to an indigo hue. From her seat in the stern of the bow rider, Leah Wilde watched the lake's western shore as it slipped by. On its slopes she saw groves of olives, figs and pomegranates; solitary cypresses clinging to limestone crags. As their boat motored through the water, carving a wide white wash, the shoreline revealed inlets sheltering hidden villas and peeling *palazzi*. To the east rose the *Triangolo Lariano*, a mountainous wedge of land dominated by the snow-covered peak of Monte San Primo, which split the lower half of the lake in two.

Beside Leah stood one of the *Belső Őr*, closest of the *Örökös Főnök*'s personal retinue of guards. The man held himself as still as the statues that decorated the terraces of the villa they sought, staring north-east across the water with eyes that constantly shifted their focus. He had spoken little since welcoming her aboard at Cernobbio. Whether that was because he disapproved of her presence here, or it was simply his nature, she did not know.

Behind them, piloting the vessel, a second member of the *Belső Őr*, and in the bow, the five women Leah had brought along. Etienne and Soraya sat the furthest forward, eyes narrowed against the spray the boat kicked up as it knifed through the water. Behind them, on the second row of seats, sat the other *kirekesztett* volunteers she had recruited during her journey through Europe: from Budapest, Mária Wagner; from Milan, Alida Argento; from Paris, Delphine Binoche.

Clustered around a crag a few hundred metres above the western shore, she saw the collection of sixteenth-century chapels that formed the Sacro Monte di Ossucci. On the summit itself perched the even older sanctuary of the Madonna del Soccorso, its bell tower rising proud of the nearby trees.

It meant they were close. Leah heard their engine drop in pitch, and saw the bow dip down to meet the water. They motored towards a peninsula thrusting from the shore in a series of wooded humps.

On its rocky tip, dominating the scenery for miles around, stood the Villa del Osservatore. Breathtakingly beautiful, it comprised three individual buildings and a single watchtower, roofed in terracotta tile and connected by stone bridges and loggias. Its lush gardens and lawns encircled the peninsula in steadily descending terraces, and a wide stone-built staircase hugged the rock all the way down to the waterline, terminating at a landing stage edged with balustrades. Higher up the hillside she saw pergolas straining under the branches of ancient wisteria, and huge displays of azaleas and camellias. Ivy clung to the west-facing sides of the buildings and curled among its statues.

Built on the site of a former Benedictine monastery, the Villa del Osservatore had stood on the shores of Lake Como for nearly six hundred years. For half of those it had been owned by the *Örökös Fönök*, gifted by Clement XII in return for services rendered to the papacy. Although the villa was only one of a number of palatial European residences presented to the *hosszú életek* leader in times past, it was easily the most elegant.

Leah felt her stomach flutter when she saw it. Even now, the building raised a conflicting set of emotions in her: memories of pain and loss, but also of healing and discovery.

It was here she had come with her mother, immediately after the fire at Le Moulin Bellerose. Here, in its meditative gardens and graceful rooms, she had learned to live with her grief over her father's death. Here, too, her mother had begun the slow process of healing – not just from the physical injuries she had suffered during her encounter with Jakab, but from the psychological trauma the episode had inflicted.

Behind her, the *Belső Őr* skipper cut his engine and the boat arced towards the landing stage. Leah noticed Etienne and Soraya surveying Villa del Osservatore's landscaped terraces, and smiled.

In truth there had been no need to arrive via the lakeside entrance, but the *Főnök* had suggested it days earlier, and Leah understood why.

Although the *hosszú életek* leader acted unilaterally, without the consent, or even the knowledge, of her *tanács*, Catharina had realised this visit might just be perceived as a homecoming of sorts for the *kirekesztett* women inside the boat. Fitting, she had reasoned, that there should be an element of majesty to their arrival. The villa's lakeside vista arrested the senses in a way that could not be experienced as readily from the shore. The *Főnök* had desired to welcome these five women with a spectacle of beauty and serenity.

The craft bumped against the landing stage and its two crewmen jumped out, lashing it to the dock. Together they helped their passengers alight, remaining beside the boat as Leah led her party up the flight of steps. Above them, a gated entrance opened onto a manicured lawn shaded by cypress trees. On the final step, resplendent, waited the one hundred and thirty-third *Örökös Főnök* of the *hosszú életek*.

Catharina Maria-Magdalena Szöllösi wore a simple white dress, a gold torc encircling her throat. She smiled when she saw the approaching *kirekesztett*, her face radiating a warmth so all-encompassing that Leah felt her heart swell in her chest.

When Etienne and Soraya saw Catharina standing between the gates, they came to a halt a few steps below. The others paused behind.

For long seconds, nobody moved. A breeze feathered about them, carrying the distant chimes of church bells.

Finally the *Főnök* raised her hands, palms outward. 'Welcome to Villa del Osservatore. Welcome home.' She smiled. 'You know, I'd planned a quite lengthy speech. But sometimes speeches are a welcome of themselves, and sometimes they are not. Allow me simply to say this: I bow to your courage. I know coming here wasn't easy, and I'm sure you view me with a certain amount of distrust. You should know that the *tanács* is unaware of your presence. Through my own deficiencies I've failed to bring consensus in this task we face, which is why you – and what you attempt – must remain secret for now.

'Our society has fractured during your absence; its bonds have begun to unravel. I hope to save this once-proud family of ours and repair the ties that bound us, but I cannot promise you your safety, even as I welcome you home.

'I act not with the will of a unified *tanács*, but with the power I hold through the title of *Örökös Főnök*. I will not knowingly admit *kirekesztett* into these halls. I repeal, therefore, the sentence of banishment from all five of you. Enter as friends, and let us cast the past aside.'

She dropped her hands to her side and her smile returned, abashed. 'Forgive me. What was that if not a speech?'

Leah watched the reactions of her fellow travellers. Etienne's eyes, usually so flat and hinting at disdain, brimmed now with emotion. Trembling, she dropped to her knees. 'My thanks,' she said. One by one, the remaining women dropped to their knees too.

Her smile faltering, the *Főnök* hurried down the steps. She passed among them, touching shoulders, wiping away tears, urging them to their feet. Together, they ascended the remaining steps and passed through the gates into Villa del Osservatore's grounds.

A path led them across the first lawn. It curved up a steep slope bordered with boxwood and laurel. The second terrace was planted with magnolias and two enormous sycamores. A running balustrade with two crescent balconies overlooked the sheer face of the peninsula's western edge. Along it a row of statues, chiselled into the likenesses of past *hosszú életek* leaders, stared out across the water.

Catharina led them along a path bisecting a lawn outside the villa's main residence. The building rose three storeys in height, tall windows interrupting the creep of ivy across its façade.

Six huge doors on the ground floor opened onto a loggia adorned with stone benches and urns filled with star jasmine. Leah smelled their perfume as she followed Catharina into the house via the villa's music room.

Inside, pale walls were hung with gilt-framed artworks. A fifteenth-century Botticelli dominated the south end of the room, hanging above two concert grands. Elsewhere, pieces by Rubens, Titian and Holbein. Walnut-framed sofas on cabriole legs, upholstered in a rich cream velvet, surrounded a fireplace in the north wall.

Leah smiled as she looked at the people gathered inside the room. On one of the sofas, Kata Lendvai read a book to her children, Dávid and Lícia. On the floor nearby sat Ara Schulteisz and her daughter Tünde. In a corner, playing an intricate game involving metal soldiers, dominoes and dice, were some of the Calw programme's oldest children: seven-year-old Emánuel and his brother Levi; six-year-olds Carina and Philipp; eight-year-old Pia and her younger brother Alex. Even Flóra, a mother now only a few short weeks, was there with her son, Elias.

And, right beside the fireplace, Leah saw her mother. Hannah Wilde perched next to Gabriel on one of the sofas. Ibsen lay at their feet.

It did her heart good to see her family together like that, and for a moment she just watched them. After her father's murder all those years ago, Leah had thought the hole he had left in her mother's heart would never be filled. In the months and years that followed, Gabriel never sought to replace Nate in Hannah's affections, or Leah's; he'd simply offered them his love. The speed with which they had reciprocated it had surprised them all.

Gabriel raised his head and when he saw her he grinned and whispered something to Hannah. Leah picked her way through the children playing on the floor as her mother rose to greet her.

Do not cry, she told herself. But of course she did.

Hannah opened her arms and Leah folded herself into her embrace. For a while she felt so emotional that she struggled even to breathe. Her mother seemed smaller somehow, as if she had shrunk in stature since they'd been apart. But Leah knew it was an illusion. Her mother's physical presence, while by no means diminutive, could never adequately reflect the force of will it contained.

'How have you been?' Hannah asked.

'I'm fine. Good, in fact. Great to be here with everyone.'

It was true. Gathered in this room were all the people she cared most about in the world. Together they had worked towards a goal no one had thought possible, and even though the future had never seemed so bleak, they had already achieved something remarkable: the laughter of the children playing on the floor was testament to that.

'You can't fool me,' Hannah murmured. 'There's something. What?'

'Later. Not now, not in front of everyone.'

'We'll find somewhere quiet. I know Catharina wants to speak to you too.'

Leah released herself from her mother's embrace, and immediately found herself enveloped in Gabriel's.

'Little miss,' the Irishman said. 'You had us worried for a while. Glad you're back safe.'

'I blame you. All those stories of the *Cŵn Annwn* over the years must have given me itchy feet.'

He pulled back from her, grinning, and studied her closely. 'Did you meet any?'

'I met something,' she replied, the smile sliding from her face.

The *Főnök* crossed the room and slid her hand around Leah's arm. 'I'm intruding, I know I am,' she said. 'You should have some time alone. But we do need to talk, as soon as we can.'

Hannah's face grew serious. 'Thank you, Cat, but you're right. We all need to hear Leah's news, and I don't think we should wait. We'll have plenty of time to catch up later.'

Etienne watched Leah Wilde embrace her mother, her mind a whirl of emotions. She had not expected to be so overcome by her arrival at Villa del Osservatore. But the sight of the *Örökös Főnök*, waiting to greet her at the lakeside gate, had moved her to tears for reasons she could not explain. Perhaps it was the empathy she saw in the *hosszú életek* leader's eyes; perhaps it was her touch, or the words, whispered in her ear: *You're home, Etienne. I can't repair the past, but you have my love, my apology.*

Did the woman know Etienne had been cast out not for crimes she herself had committed, but for those committed by her family, *against* her? Etienne thought she must. Her words certainly seemed to indicate it.

An apology, even as sincere as the one she had just received, could repair not one hour of the suffering she had endured over the last one hundred years, but . . . her thoughts trailed away from her and her mouth fell open.

So you finally admit it, Etienne? You finally admit that you were hurt? That you can feel pain?

Yes, it seemed so. She stared around this grand old room, at the women playing with their children, at the nervous faces of her fellow volunteers, and suddenly felt shame. She was an impostor here, unfit to be around these innocent lives. For years she had locked away her feelings, selling her body to the highest bidder, fooling herself that she did good in the world, that she entertained the darkest fantasies of her clients so that others might not live them.

It had been more than a lie; it had been a betrayal. She had been damaged before she arrived at Tansik House, even more damaged by the time she left, and yet the longest years of suffering she'd endured had been delivered by her own hands. She had locked her feelings away so deep that now, as they flooded up to the surface, bitter and poisoned and so, so sad, she felt herself flailing, sinking beneath them.

Beside her, Soraya touched her arm. 'It's overwhelming, isn't it?'

Etienne stared, unable to speak. She thought of her Aviary back in London, of the rooms decorated to suit her visitors' tastes, and felt bile rising. It would go, all of it. For the first time in her life, she had an overpowering desire to be part of something: to be part of this; to be part of these people gathered here.

She watched Leah release herself from her mother's embrace.

Hannah Wilde. It was undoubtedly her. Until now, the woman had been little more than a face in a collection of old photographs, a role to play. Jakab had never revealed the reason behind his obsession with Hannah or the circumstances surrounding his loss of her, and Etienne had never asked, content to slip into the role he had cast for her and close her eyes to the rest.

Now, as she watched the woman disappear through a door with her daughter and others, she felt not violated, but violator. Even though they had been separated by hundreds of miles of space, she had assumed this woman's shape, had stolen her identity, had *supplanted* her.

Could there be a more intrusive crime than that? Could she ever hope to atone for what she had done?

Perhaps she could try; and perhaps the first step towards that atonement would be to admit what she had done. She closed her eyes.

Tell her? Are you crazy? Do you think they'll be grateful to hear the truth? How you've lived your life? Do you think, for one moment,

that they'll want you to be a part of this if you tell them your history?
No. Jakab is a memory. Just one more stain from your past. Erase him.
Forget him. That's all you have to do.

Decision made, she felt small hands reaching for her, and when she opened her eyes she found herself being drawn down towards to the floor, down into a game of metal soldiers and dominoes, down into smiling young faces and laughter and hope.

They reconvened inside Villa del Osservatore's library, a womblike space that smelled of wood varnish and old leather. Along one wall, mahogany bookcases, intricately carved and reaching almost to the ceiling, held thousands of titles. Heavily draped windows lined the opposite wall, offering views of the lake and the mountains beyond. A brass telescope stood nearby. At the far end was a mantelpiece of buttery Siena marble, and scattered around the room were occasional tables displaying antique scientific instruments: seismographs, ship's sextants, aneroid barometers, clockwork planetariums, galvanometers, Van de Graaff generators, hydrometers.

Leah sat in a chair beside her mother, opposite Gabriel and Catharina. With the library door closed, the noise of the children was muted. Her only accompaniment, as she told them of her *tolvajok* encounter at Llyn Gwyr, and the earlier incident in Interlaken, was the ticking of an ormolu portico clock above the fireplace.

Although her face remained calm, the *Főnök*'s eyes grew dark as she listened. When Leah finished her story, Catharina nodded. 'We'd thought a few of them might still linger,' she said, 'but this confirms it. And now they know about you. I don't know how many are left, but they'll be searching everywhere. It's not just you at risk, either. All the children here are potential prey, especially the older ones.'

Leah cringed at that.

'Don't,' Catharina said, sensing her distress. 'No one could have foreseen this, least of all you. The *lélek tolvajok* have preyed on *hosszú életek* youth for as long as we've both existed. They're part of the natural order of things.'

'But they've never had the opportunity to wipe us out before,' she replied. 'Which is exactly what could happen if they learn about what we're doing here.'

'True. Even so, it won't be their intention. They'd be signing their own death warrant.'

'If they do nothing, they'll be signing it anyway.'

Her expression grim, the *Főnök* said, 'That's also true.'

Hannah raised her head. 'So what do we do now? We have a responsibility to the mothers and children. We can't expect any of them to return to their homes once we tell them about this.'

'No,' Catharina replied. 'We can't. But Villa del Osservatore is large enough to house a number of them quite comfortably. With my *Belső Őr* in residence, it's defendable, too. We'll protect some of the families here, and the rest at other sites. In the meantime, we'll try to find out more about this nest of *tolvajok* Leah's stirred up, and work out how we can destroy them before they strike.'

'What about Etienne, Soraya, and the others?' Leah asked. 'Can we still use the centre in Calw?'

'There's no risk to them unless they fall pregnant,' Catharina replied. 'I think we're safe to continue running things there for now.'

Gabriel glanced across at Hannah. He reached out and touched her wrist. 'We'll need to tighten up our security.'

The *Főnök* nodded. 'I can help you supplement it.' Then she turned to Leah. 'I don't think you realise how lucky you were out there in Snowdonia. I want to hear more about this man who saved you too. I can't begin to work out who he could have been. In the meantime, until we have a better understanding of this *tolvajok* threat, I don't want you recruiting any more names from your list.'

'But—'

Hannah lifted her hand. 'No buts, Leah. Cat is right. Out of everyone here – out of all of us alive – you're their prime target. You can stay here or you can come back to Calw, but your recruitment of new volunteers is on hold until we sort this out.'

Leah opened her mouth to protest, and then she saw the fear in her mother's face and changed her mind. 'You're right.'

'I mean it, Leah.'

She gripped her mother's hand. 'I promise you,' she said. 'I won't take off again.'

Hannah squeezed her daughter's fingers. With her next words she addressed the room. 'This just got a whole lot more dangerous, didn't it?'

The ticking of the ormolu clock was her only response.

PART II

CHAPTER 30

Budapest, Hungary

Anton Golias strode across the open expanse of Heroes' Square, barely noticing the pigeons as they scattered from under his feet. He passed the square's centrepiece, a towering Corinthian column with its statue of the Archangel Gabriel, and glanced up. The angel gazed out across the city, pale green wings spread. In one hand he held the crown of St Stephen; in the other, a Patriarchal cross. Clustered around the base of his column, astride enormous mounts, sat representations of Árpád and his six chieftains, the warriors who had led the Hungarian race into the Carpathian basin back in the ninth century.

Anton could not remember the name of the sculptor who had cast those statues, but the man had been a genius. Every time he saw those terrible countenances staring out across the square his blood froze a little – yet he always felt a simultaneous prickling of awe.

Not today. Perhaps his blood was too frozen already. The sky seemed prescient: boiling grey clouds lit by a low sun that tinged their edges with copper. It felt to Anton almost as if a meteor had hit the earth or a volcano had exploded, pitching mountains of ash into the heavens. *The End Times*, he thought, half expecting, in this vaguely biblical light, the mounts of the statues to rear up and their riders to roar out a challenge.

Crossing the road that separated Heroes' Square from Budapest's Museum of Fine Arts, he saw Oliver Lebeau waiting for him at the top of its steps. His friend was pale-faced, barely murmuring a greeting. Together, they went inside.

'Where are we meeting them?'

'I'll take you,' Oliver said.

They passed through the Renaissance Hall and up a flight of steps to the first floor. Side by side, they arrived at the entrance to a bright gallery roofed in glass. Two *tanács* guards stood in the doorway, moving aside as Anton and Oliver approached.

At the far end of the room, hands clasped behind his back, Ivan Tóth stood beside Krištof Joó, his attention on a painting of the Madonna.

When Tóth noticed the new arrivals he came towards them, heels echoing on the wooden floor. 'Gentlemen, thank you.'

'I suggest you tell us what this is about,' Anton replied.

'New information, Tóth said. 'As a courtesy, I wanted to share it with you first, before we act.'

'Act?'

'Indeed. You'll remember how I've expressed my concerns about Catharina – not just her weaknesses of leadership, but her partisan approach. In particular, concerning this vile fertility programme.'

Anton opened his mouth to protest, but Tóth waved the objection away.

'No, no, I don't wish to revisit old ground. I realise you and I will never agree on the merits of that enterprise. You voted one way and I voted the other. Ancient history. But you'll remember, too, that the one area in which we found unity was the strict set of conditions that guided the project's operation.'

Anton did; he'd helped create many of those conditions himself, mainly in an attempt to alleviate the growing divisions he saw forming in the *tanács*, born from conflicting inter-pretations of *Vének Könyve* law.

Tóth said, 'I must ask: how would you react if you discovered every single one of those conditions had been breached?'

He frowned. 'Well, there'd be consequences, obviously. But I'm sure that—'

'And what would your counsel be, should you discover that not only had those conditions been breached, but they'd been breached with the specific approval of our *Főnök*?'

Anton felt the blood draining from his stomach. If there had been one thing he'd always sought to prevent, it was Tóth knowing something he didn't. He could feel himself being lured into trap here, from which escape might be impossible.

A year had passed since their meeting in Memento Park. Since then, his contact with Tóth had been infrequent. The *Főnök*, too, had become all but invisible. 'Perhaps you might share with us whatever information you have,' he said. 'And then we can discuss it.'

'Very well. It appears that a much wider group of volunteers has been receiving treatment courtesy of your beloved fertility programme. *Kirekesztett* women.'

Anton heard Oliver Lebeau's intake of breath. He glanced across at his friend and saw, in an instant, that if this were true, he might have lost him.

If this were true.

But he had become adept at reading Tóth's behaviour over the years, and now his old adversary was acting like a poker player revealing an unbeatable hand.

Sensing Oliver's shock, Tóth focused all his attention on the man. 'Not only have they been treating *kirekesztett*, the *Főnök* has been helping to *coordinate* it. She's even allowed some of the women to recuperate at Villa del Osservatore.'

Again Anton opened his mouth to speak, and again Tóth prevented him. 'The purpose of this grand scheme of yours, if I recall correctly, was to repopulate the *hosszú életek* race, not to bastardise it. What we've discovered is unforgivable. She's deceived us – her own *tanács*.'

'I've always maintained that fears of our imminent demise are unwarranted. Yes, we have far more to do. But don't tell me that our end is near. I simply won't accept it. We didn't agree on that sixteen years ago, and as a result this monstrous project was born. I hear that at least five of its volunteers have died as a result of its mistakes.' He shook his head. 'And for what: so we can bring a new generation into the world, conceived thanks to a woman who is half *kirekesztett* herself?'

'She is *not!*' Anton roared. 'Hannah Wilde is nothing of the sort, and I will not have you say otherwise! Yes, she's unfortunate enough to share a genetic link with the man of whom you speak, but it's five generations distant. We abandoned the law of *sorozat* a century ago.'

Tóth stared, eyes flat, a gladiator waiting to deliver the final blow. 'Hannah Wilde is the bastard offspring of Balázs Jakab, whether you like it or not. A *kirekesztett*. And now, that witch has somehow coerced our weakened *Főnök* into polluting the world with a mewling *litter* of the creatures, in a grotesque infringement of our oldest laws of purity. Will you stand aside and let that happen, Anton? Will *you*, Oliver? The *tanács* have a right to know your intentions.'

'He's right.' Oliver Lebeau had been silent throughout the exchange, but now he turned to his colleague. His face creased with conflicting emotions. 'If what Ivan says is true, then it's an abominable violation of our trust. I cannot, in good conscience, condone it.'

'Thank you,' Tóth said. 'Rest assured, I would not expect your support in this without proof. Know that in the meantime this information comes directly from sources inside the *Belső Őr* at Villa del Osservatore. The women sheltering there are *kirekesztett* volunteers. In fact, I understand that this very morning one of them left with her newborn and is, even as we speak, returning with the child to London. We have, I maintain, only one course of action available.'

'How do you know this woman is *kirekesztett*?' Anton interrupted.

'She's known to us.'

'What, may I ask, was her crime?'

'That's irrelevant.'

'I think it's extremely relevant.'

'Then you're a minority of one, Anton. You know what I intend to propose. I need to know how you stand.'

Three sets of eyes watched him, waiting for his answer.

You pledged yourself to Catharina. Look how she's treated you.

But regardless of what Tóth had unearthed at Villa del Osservatore, the man was wrong about one thing: they *were* facing extinction. Catharina might have misled him, but he knew that her intentions, however flawed, were pure.

What would you have done in her position?

As he pondered that question, another confronted him: *What will you do now?*

Could he stand by while Tóth took control of the council and forced a coup? They had not even talked of the details, but he cast a glance at Joó, standing beside Tóth, and saw the almost religious zeal in the man's eyes, sensed the hunger in him. If he remained silent while these two enacted their plans, the result, he knew, would be a bloodletting.

Tóth blinked. 'This isn't a game. You haven't lost and I haven't won. There's too much at stake here to allow our personal grievances to influence us. I want your support in this, but I won't beg for it.' His eyes grew hard. 'And I do need your answer.'

Anton looked around him. At the art on the walls. At the two *tanács* guards standing with their backs to the room. At the three men waiting for his answer.

It was probably futile, but he did it anyway. He wouldn't have been able to face himself if he hadn't. He ran.

Arms pumping, blood surging through muscles that hadn't been tested in years, Anton Golias tore through the galleries of Budapest's Museum of Fine Arts, leather-soled shoes cracking like rifle shots off the marble floor. He reached the first-floor staircase, slid around a banister, hurled himself down its steps. One flight, two.

Already, his lungs were on fire. Needles of pain whipped through his muscles. Too old for exertion like this. Too old and too soft.

He dared not look behind him, could not afford any delay to check whether he was followed. The *tanács* guards were younger, faster, more used to action. And ruthless.

Anton burst out of the museum's front entrance and tripped down the steps. He slipped, almost fell, recovered himself.

You have to warn them.

Yes, but first he had to get away. He saw a gap in the traffic and sprinted across the road to Heroes' Square.

Above, framed by swirling skies, the statue of the Archangel followed his progress with malachite eyes, wings outstretched, as if he waited for a gust of wind on which to soar.

Scattering pigeons and tourists alike, heart working like a piston in his chest, Anton dashed across the street at the square's north-eastern corner, overtaking pedestrians, weaving around cyclists, aiming for the road where he had parked his car. He was relieved to see so many people on the streets. It would make accosting him here far more challenging.

His car waited up ahead, parked in a single row of vehicles facing out into the street. Pulling the keys from his pocket, he activated the locks, saw its amber hazard lights flash.

He slid behind the wheel and slammed the door shut. From here, he could see the entire width of Heroes' Square. No one ran across it. No one crossed the road towards him.

Trembling as his heart recovered, sucking down painful lungfuls of air, he fished his phone from his pocket. He brought up the number he needed, dialled, and then blood erupted from his chest, spattering the steering wheel in a dark spray.

Anton bucked in his seat, teeth cracking. The phone skittered away from him, bouncing once on the passenger seat before tumbling into the footwell.

Looking down, he saw the serrated tip of a *Merénylő's déjnin* blade protruding from a tear in his shirt. He gasped, watching as the knife retreated back inside his chest.

The assassin was in the car, waiting. You never even checked.

The blade plunged into his back and out through his chest a second time, showering the windscreen with scarlet rain. This time the weapon's steel grated against bone, severing something in him. His fists beat down on the steering wheel. His feet danced, kicking at the pedals.

He tried to take a breath, couldn't. Tried to focus his eyes. Couldn't. Thought he saw, across Heroes' Square, through vision that jumped and hitched like film running through a broken projector, the Archangel spread his wings and soar up into the heavens.

It was a portent, perhaps. Or simply the product of his misfiring brain. But whatever that image was, it remained burned onto Anton Golias's retina long after death had claimed him.

CHAPTER 31

London, England

A gale tore through the royal parks of Central London, raising a ghost army from dead leaves and tattered newspapers and rain. Wind shrieked at the windows of Etienne's Mayfair residence, curled around its chimney stacks and rattled its iron gates.

Inside her bedroom, the paper shade of a child's night lamp rotated, casting a carousel of soft-hued animal shapes across the walls. Etienne stood at her window, looking down at the street below. The limbs of the trees lining the pavement whipped back and forth, occasionally relinquishing branches that would bounce across car roofs or skitter along the road.

She had returned only an hour ago, after almost a year away, and the building seemed an alien place: certainly not like a home. Although both Jackson and Bartoli were now resident downstairs, it had been deserted when she'd arrived. *Something*, however, lingered on in the empty rooms and halls; a sense of expectation, perhaps, as if the old house held its breath.

You're imagining it.

She walked to the crib beside her bed and stared down at Elijah's sleeping form. Her son's eyes were closed and he snored quietly. Hearing that sound made Etienne's chest swell with emotion. So fragile he was, so perfect. She knew every mother felt like this, that her feelings were hardly a revelation to the world. But they were a revelation to her. For years she had lived in a vacuum of emotion, and now emotions boiled in her: love, fear, hope, shame, self-pity, pride; each struggled for supremacy, ruling only briefly before surrendering to a contender that was sometimes darker and sometimes lighter, but always different.

She'd carried Elijah up the central staircase, unable to look along the hall where her old rooms of work waited: *Feroce, Chiuso, Bellicoso, Sostenuto, Duolo, Capriccioso*. The memories seeping from beneath those doors buffeted her. They made her skin itch and her neck prickle. Pressing Elijah's face to her shoulder, burying herself in the purity of his scent, she had hurried to the top of the house.

Tomorrow she would recruit an estate agent and rid herself of the place, and then – despite the pleas of her family back in Como (*family*, such a strange new thought, such a strange new concept) – she would take Elijah and they would disappear into obscurity.

Even considering that future served to calm her nerves: a feeling, if not of peace, then at least something approaching it. They could go anywhere, do anything, *be* anyone.

The phone beside her bed rang. Etienne raised her eyes from Elijah's face. She would begin all that tomorrow. But until then, there were still things to do here.

She sat on the bed and stared at the phone. Even though a handful of people had access to this line, she knew instinctively who the caller would be. Finally she plucked the handset from its cradle and lifted it to her ear. Etienne paused, and then she said, 'Jakab.'

'I trust you enjoyed your vacation,' he replied. His voice was quiet, his breathing measured, but she recognised the clipped tones that indicated he was upset.

'I've been back less than an hour. Have you been watching the house?'

'I need to see you.'

Elbows propped on her knees, Etienne supported her head

with her free hand, hair feathering across her face. 'That won't be possible.'

'I *need* to *see* you.'

'I told you, Jakab. No more.'

'I don't accept that.'

'Then I suggest you learn. This was never more than a business relationship, and you know it.'

He hissed. 'You can really be that cold?'

'After four conversations about this, yes, I can. My life is different now. That part is over.'

'What about my life, Etienne? You're making choices here that don't just affect you.'

'Your life is your responsibility. Not mine.'

'Don't do this.'

'It's done.'

Silence, followed by a click as he broke the connection.

Banshees of wind shrilled outside the window. Etienne crossed the room and closed the drapes. Returning to the bed, she dialled Jackson.

He answered on the first ring. 'It was him?'

'Yes. Is the alarm on?'

'A mosquito couldn't get in here without us knowing about it.'

'Everything's locked?'

'Like a vault.'

'Thank you. Call me if anything happens.'

Etienne undressed, put away her clothes and checked on Elijah. Her baby slept, back arched, tiny face pointed towards the top of the crib. His eyes moved behind their lids, chasing infant dreams.

After locking the door to her room, she slipped beneath the covers of her bed. The last thing she saw before she closed her eyes was the clock on the mantlepiece: five minutes to midnight.

★ ★ ★

Elijah's cries dragged Etienne from sleep an hour later. Fuddle-headed, her fingers found the light switch, and then she thought better of it. Sitting up in the darkness, she lifted Elijah into her lap. His cries grew more urgent, until she guided his mouth to her breast and he latched on. Etienne grimaced at the sudden nip of pain, and then she relaxed.

She thought, again, about everything she would do tomorrow. As well as recruiting someone to sell the house, she needed to buy a car. Perhaps she'd drive the two of them around Europe until they found a corner they'd be happy enough to call home: somewhere far away from cities and traffic and the sad press of crowds.

At her breast, Elijah turned his head away, a bead of milk on his lower lip. Etienne rubbed his back until he released his wind, and returned him to his crib. She was about to tunnel back into the residual warmth beneath her covers when she noticed the night lamp on the chest of drawers in one corner of the room. Earlier, the heat from its bulb had rotated the shade, projecting animal shapes around the walls. Now the bulb was dark, its shade still. Had she switched it off before going to sleep? Maybe, but she didn't think so.

She glanced over at the discreet security interface beside her bed. The unit's lights still glowed green, but the system relied on a separate supply. Even during a power cut it would continue to operate.

She lifted the phone's handset to her ear.

No dial tone.

Her heart knocked. Sweat prickled under her arms.

Etienne slipped from the bed and crossed to the window. Outside, the street was empty of life. Pulling on a silk robe, she went to the door and listened.

Silence from the hallway beyond. Inside the room, the papery rustle of Elijah's breathing and the thudding of her own heart in her ears.

He's here. Right now. Inside the house.

She shook her head, deriding herself. No. He couldn't be. No one could fool the building's alarm system and evade the attentions of both Jackson and Bartoli downstairs. It wasn't possible.

As soon as the phones stopped working, Jackson would have alerted you. Even if you were sleeping, he'd have come up here and knocked at your door.

And yet he hadn't.

Casting a glance back at Elijah's crib, she twisted her fingers together. Did she stay in the room? Tempting as it was, she was a prisoner here. The window offered no means of escape. The room's fixed telephone line was dead and she'd never owned a mobile phone, on which she could call for help.

The house boasted a panic room complete with its own air supply and a door that was virtually impenetrable. It was hidden away on the floor below her. She would need to take Elijah and hurry downstairs to the drawing room where the panic room's entrance was located. It was a journey that would take her perhaps twenty seconds.

She thought she heard a sound, deep inside the house.

Decision made, Etienne lifted Elijah out of his crib. She wrapped a blanket around him, holding him tight against her chest. Moving to the bedroom door, lips pressed tight to mute the sound of her breathing, she unlocked it. The handle was silent as it turned. The door whispered against the carpet as it swung open.

In the hallway, shadows gathered.

Etienne closed her eyes. Listened not just with her ears but with her skin, feeling for the touch of a draught that would indicate an opened window or door.

The air was still.

Supporting Elijah's head, she padded along the hall to the stairs and began to descend. The second floor came into view: a tunnel of empty space stretching into darkness.

Not empty, though. Not quite. Something slumped halfway along it. A human form.

She felt the skin on her scalp begin to crawl, fought the urge to turn and run. The panic room was still her best option.

The drawing room lay behind the first door on her left. Just in front of the crumpled shape in the hallway.

She edged closer. To her right loomed the grand staircase serving every floor of the house. She peered into its depths, trying to make sense of the darkness, searching for any threat that might lurk there.

Another few steps and she reached the drawing-room door, hanging ajar. Etienne paused there, listening. No sound issued from within. Before she slipped inside, she glanced down at the body on the floor. A lack of light prevented her from identifying it, but it could only be Jackson or Bartoli.

If she searched the corpse, perhaps she could retrieve a weapon. That would take time, though. She might wake Elijah. And Elijah might alert the intruder.

Instead, she edged into the drawing room. Paused again, ears straining. Closed the door behind her. Complete darkness now. A blindfold draped across her face.

The silence was a physical pressure in her ears.

Etienne knew this room intimately, knew the location of its chairs, its side tables, its statuary. One hand outstretched, she weaved a silent path. Her fingers touched a bookcase. She groped along it. Behind her, she heard the rasp of a match scratching into life.

Light flared; her shadow leaped towards the ceiling.

Etienne spun around, sickened, heart pumping so fiercely she could feel it in her throat.

From one of the chairs beside the fireplace, Jakab held out the match to the wick of a candle standing on a reading table. The tiny flame wobbled, grew brighter.

Shadows clothed most of his body, but his eyes were reflective pools in which two perfect miniatures of the candle burned. Etienne stared, and Jakab stared back.

Beside the bookcase stood a wicker Moses basket. After

lowering Elijah into it, she straightened to face her guest. 'What did you do?'

He raised an eyebrow.

'Outside. In the hall. Who was it?'

'He neglected to tell me his name.'

'You killed him.'

'And the world mourns. I'm sure you'll find new staff, Etienne. With the money I've paid you over the years, you should be able to afford a houseful.'

He stood, and she moved to her right. The candlelight was strong enough to brighten only a yard or so of space around the table. She shielded the Moses basket with her body.

Jakab approached, his shoes making no sound on the drawing-room rug. He lifted a finger to the lapel of her robe, eased it over her shoulder. When he withdrew his hand, the garment fluttered to the floor.

His eyes drank her in. 'You've put on weight,' he said. 'It suits you. Suits me.'

'I want you out of my house. I don't know how you got in, but the safest thing for both of us right now is that you turn around and—'

He slapped her. Hard across the face.

Jakab snatched back his hand, as if he'd burned himself on her skin. 'I'm sorry. I didn't mean . . . I should never have done that. It wasn't right. But I've missed you so much.'

He frowned, tapped himself on the chest. 'It's like a pain right here, an emptiness. There's nothing I can do to fill it. If you're telling me I can't have you, if you're really telling me that, I just don't know what I'll do.'

He reached for her and she cringed away, feeling her legs press against the Moses basket. Its wicker frame creaked.

Perhaps it was the movement that disturbed Elijah, or perhaps he sensed his mother's fear, but her son let out a cry of distress, and Jakab's eyes snapped away.

He stepped to her left. Spying the crib, he bent over it, and when he saw Elijah, his eyes widened. He drew in a breath.

'No,' she said. 'It's not—'

Already, tears were gathering in the corners of his eyes. 'I have a child?'

'You don't, Jakab.'

His attention drifted back to the crib, and his voice cracked. 'I have a child.'

'No.'

One of his tears spilled down his cheek. 'You concealed him from me?'

'He's not yours. Of course he's not yours.'

The wonder fled from Jakab's expression, replaced by rage. 'Then whose? You allowed someone to desecrate you? You *polluted* yourself like that?'

She'd always sensed his imbalance, always ignored it until now. His mind danced between extremes of emotion, unable to sustain any for long. Here, in this room, she realised there was likely no happy ending to this encounter, no peaceful resolution. 'Please, Jakab. Calm yourself.'

'I want to see Leah.'

'You're—'

'I want to see her *now*.'

There was only one thing she could do. One thing she could try. Etienne threw herself at him. Snarling with bestial savagery, she grabbed handfuls of his hair and yanked back his head. Teeth bared, she lunged towards his neck.

Staggering backwards, Jakab slammed his fist against her face. Blood burst from her lips. She felt something fracture in her jaw. He seized one of her wrists, ignoring the furrows she clawed into his flesh. Lifting her off her feet, he threw her across the room.

She fell, head smacking against the wall, so hard her eyes wouldn't focus. When she tried to stand, she found her legs wouldn't work either.

Jakab stalked towards her, shadow flowing up to the ceiling.

'I didn't want this,' he whispered. 'But we had agreement, you and I. You have an obligation to me.'

He knelt beside her. Wiped the blood from her mouth. 'You can be Leah again, I know you can.'

She shrank from his touch. The pain in her jaw was needle-sharp. Tilting her head, she saw the Moses basket rocking, saw Elijah's legs kicking and heard his cries.

If she did as he asked, she knew her life would end in this room. And what then for Elijah? Desire sated, Jakab would let her corpse grow cold on the floor, and he would walk away. She could not bear to think of what would happen after that. With the house locked up tight, with her guards dead, with no one to check on her son . . .

Etienne moaned. And then a monstrous idea jumped into her head, a thought so ruthless and dark she almost fled from the contemplation of it.

Hesitate, and you'll die. And Elijah will die with you.

She thought of Leah and her mother, of all the love they'd shown her. Of all their kindnesses and reassurances and warmth.

The Moses basket began to rock more violently. Elijah began to shriek. His cries steeled her, stripping away the humanity she'd learned, reducing her to the woman she had been before.

Jakab pressed a hand to her forehead. '*Be* her,' he hissed, and she felt a spike of pain, a blooming pressure behind her eyes.

'I know where she is, Jakab.'

'*Be her.*'

'Are you listening?' she asked, ignoring the pain. 'Leah Wilde. I know where she is. Her mother, too.'

His face was a depraved mask. Lips curled into a sneer. Eyes creased into slits. Pores greasy with sweat. 'You lie.'

'I swear to you. Leah Wilde. The girl in the photograph. And the woman, Hannah. Hannah Wilde. I've met them, Jakab. Both of them.'

'Hannah Wilde is *dead*.'

'Dead?' Etienne shook her head. 'She's not dead. Blind, yes. But not dead.'

'Liar! Filthy *kurva* liar!'

'No, I swear. I can prove it to you.'

His face was so close that even in the weak light spilling from the candle she could see the blood vessels swelling in his eyes. She could taste his breath on her tongue. An urgency to it.

'Prove it how?'

'There are cameras all over the house. Check the footage. I'll show you.'

Jakab removed his hand from her face and retreated, sitting with his back against the very bookcase that hid the panic room beyond. Inches away from safety. That was all she had been.

'If you're lying . . .' he said. 'Show me.'

'I will. And then—'

'No tricks. No delays. Show me.'

Etienne nodded. She rose to her feet.

In the building's ground-floor security office a television screen, quartered to show four separate images, provided a wash of blue light.

Etienne sat on a chair in front of the desk, Elijah held close. Beside her, Jakab stared at the screen. Most of the images showed static views inside the house. One of them focused on the street.

A silver Mercedes pulled up. The camera wasn't of a high enough resolution to capture the driver, but a few moments later the car door opened and Leah Wilde climbed out.

Jakab jerked in his chair. 'No,' he whispered. 'No.' Leaning forward, he watched Leah approach the gate. She pressed the buzzer, looked up at the house.

A camera inside the ground-floor hall captured Jackson opening the door. Ushering Leah inside, he began to search her. She endured, arms outstretched. A few words were exchanged.

'He *touched* her,' Jakab whispered. 'Did you see?'

Etienne watched in silence. She saw Jackson lead Leah deeper into the house. Another camera captured the girl as she climbed the staircase to the second floor. At the landing, she glanced directly into the lens.

'Pause it,' Jakab said. 'Just there.'

She complied, pressing a button on the keyboard.

'Full screen.'

Another button press, and Leah's magnified image stared out at them. Etienne closed her eyes, shame seeping into her like poison. Grainy security footage or not, she could not meet the girl's gaze.

Jakab reached out a hand to the screen, and his fingers brushed Leah's cheek. Tears rolled from his bloodshot eyes. A sob escaped him. 'She's beautiful. Perfect.' He wiped the tears from his cheeks. 'Yet so fragile, don't you think?'

'You never told me, and I never asked. But Leah and her mother: what were they to you? What links the three of you?'

He turned to her and his expression hardened. Moments later his attention returned to the screen. When he saw Leah's eyes watching him, he covered his mouth with his hands and began to shake. 'What did I do to you?' he whispered. 'Will you ever forgive me? *Can* you forgive me?' To Etienne, he asked, 'Can she?'

'Why do you need her forgiveness? What did you do?'

Again his expression changed. Reaching out, he switched off the screen that displayed Leah's face. 'Follow me,' he said.

CHAPTER 32

Utah, USA

In death, the sightless eyes of the *tolvaj* host seemed filled with reproach. Clawed fingers clutched the armchair in which he had died, body lost inside a dust-caked Grizzlies jacket. Blood coagulated on his chin in streaks and lumps.

He had lost all his teeth towards the end. They lay in his lap, a scarlet-spattered collection.

'I'm sorry,' she whispered. 'I'll carry your memory.'

'*As will we all,*' scratched a voice from the dark. '*Not for long, though. No, not for long, for long. Dying.*'

She turned, saw the hairless creature in the next chair, a more recent abductee but almost as badly ravaged. Its eyes, as they watched her, were hard pale stones. No blame resided there. Only fear.

'I won't let it happen,' she said. 'I won't.'

'*Too late, I think, soon. Too late.*'

Its breath was laced with decay. She stroked its hand, felt the ridges and valleys formed by the veins beneath its skin. 'I promise you.'

She stumbled through the house and found her way outside. The midday sun's dry heat was a sharp contrast to the room's cool shadows. Bending over, she vomited until her stomach was purged.

She took out her phone, dialled a number and heard a recorded message. 'Call me,' she muttered, and hung up.

She bowed her head and closed her eyes. Her phone rang.

'Talk,' he said, and she wondered how his voice could sound so close when she knew he was so far away.

'He died.' Her shoulders started shaking. She clutched her hair, pulled out a fistful. 'We can't wait any longer. We can't.'

His voice, when it returned, was wretched. 'The others?'

'Exactly the same.' She lifted her eyes to the sky. 'What are you doing over there? What are either of you doing to prevent this?

'We're close.'

'Close isn't enough! He's *dead*, do you understand? I had to look into his eyes and watch the life go out of them. Have you ever seen that? Do you know what that's like? I need to move them.'

'If we move them too early—'

'If we don't, they're going to die anyway. They can't survive on *simavér* any longer. While the pair of you saunter around Europe looking for meat, your children are *dying*.'

He hissed in a breath. 'That was tasteless.'

'I didn't mean it.' She collapsed into a crouch. 'I'm sorry. I'll do what you say, you know I will. But I think we have to come to you.'

'Arrange a flight,' he said, and his voice was cold.

'Where to?'

'I don't know yet.'

'Then how will I know where—'

'Charter a plane. Get to an airport. I'll phone you back and tell you where you're going.'

'When? I'm sorry, I don't mean to sound like this, but wh—'

The line went dead.

She stared at the phone. Blinked.

Gritting her teeth, she staggered back inside the ranch.

CHAPTER 33

London, England

Lit by flames flickering from a candelabra in Etienne's drawing room, Jakab bent over her baby's crib and traced his finger down Elijah's cheek.

'He's a miracle,' he whispered. 'Those eyes. You must love him more than life.'

She would have responded had she known what to say. But Jakab seemed so unstable as he stood there, so unknowable, that she feared the wrong comment might incite him to further violence. Already he had committed two murderous acts this evening, and she knew they could not have been his first; the deaths of Jackson and Bartoli seemed not to weigh on him at all.

He turned to her. 'I think,' he said softly, 'you'd better tell me everything.'

Etienne nodded. 'I will. I'll tell you. And then . . .' She closed her mouth, horrified that she'd been about to press him. He raised an eyebrow, daring her to continue. She cringed. 'I'll tell you.'

And she did. Everything she'd seen, every conversation she'd had, everything she'd managed to piece together. She knew she held the key to only a fraction of Hannah and Leah Wilde's history. The two had never mentioned this man, and throughout all the hours of Etienne's acquaintance with Jakab he'd never spoken of the reason for his obsession. She had no idea at all what thread linked the three together.

But *he* knew. And the longer she talked, the more animated he became. Jakab's face was a canvas of shifting emotions. He laughed, tears shining on his cheeks, and then his expression darkened and he clasped his shoulders, baring his teeth. Occasionally he would spring to his feet and she thought he was going to attack her. But then he'd retreat to Elijah's Moses basket, and the sight of her sleeping baby seemed to calm him.

Outside, the wind railed, pressing its face to the windows and howling its dismay. Ghost breath twined down the chimney, rocking the flames of the candles. The door to the drawing room swung gently.

'Where is Hannah now?' he asked.

Etienne didn't have a definite answer to that, but she had a good idea, and she told him, heart breaking at this latest betrayal, persuading herself there was time, should she survive, to put this right and warn the woman and her daughter of what was coming.

She was still talking when she noticed it: a vague note of putrescence in the air, an odour of bloated meat, sick-sweet. Casting her eyes past Jakab's head, staring into the slab of darkness revealed by the swinging door, she thought she caught sight of something. A glimmer of movement.

Jakab stiffened, and Etienne realised that he sensed it too. He turned just as a buzzing bluebottle looped out of that rectangular chasm. The fly arced around the room, heavy and slow, wings chattering as they strained to keep it aloft. Rising up, it flew over the candelabra, shadow flitting across the ceiling like a rat.

In the doorway a figure loomed: tall, almost seven feet in height. In its hand it gripped a walking cane, and between its fingers Etienne saw the scales of a silver python's head, the serpent's eyes picked out in gold.

Triggered by that graveyard stink, a memory surfaced: the night, all those years ago, that a nightmare had visited Tansik House, spiriting the boy János away. As the recollection grew clearer, she understood what stood before her. The knowledge pierced her heart.

The *lélek tolvaj* raised its head and sniffed. The stench of decay was now so ripe in the room – so thick – that Etienne felt her throat closing in protest, her bile rising.

It took a step towards them and the candlelight revealed more of its horror. Its eyes were recessed so deeply it seemed to regard them from scooped-out sockets. The flesh of its face was thick and glutinous, sagging from the skull to which it was attached. Its hat, a fedora with a single jay feather, covered a wormy straggle of dirty blond hair, matted with grease, that reached all the way down its back.

Without doubt, the creature was in desperate need of a new host.

In front of her, Jakab stared, his jaw slackening. She'd never seen fear on his face before but she saw it now, and felt it herself. A terrible, smothering terror, bowing her with its intensity and flushing her limbs of strength. 'Oh, what have you done, Jakab?' she moaned. 'What have you brought on us?'

The *tolvaj* tapped its cane against the floor, the hammer strikes like a punctuation to its thoughts. At the sound, two flies shook themselves loose from its clothing and spiralled towards the ceiling, where they buzzed and looped.

Their visitor swept the room with its gaze, face puckering. Spying the Moses basket, its mouth opened and it drew in a rattling breath.

Etienne tried to force herself forward. Tried to make her legs move and intercept it, even though she knew her attempt would be futile. She felt a pressure on her arm, discovered that Jakab had retreated to her side.

He gripped her, knuckles white. 'Don't,' he hissed. 'Be still.'

She tried to shrug him off, but it was a feeble protest; she didn't really want to intervene. It was what shocked her most of all. Even though Elijah lay alone in his crib, her terror consumed her so completely that she could only watch, paralysed, as the *tolvaj* approached.

When it looked down into the Moses basket it seemed to grow in stature, chest swelling, shoulders filling. It dropped its cane to the floor and its jaw hung open like a hound's. Saliva glistened on its teeth.

'*What we need,*' it whispered. '*Young, but what we need, we need.*'

It reached its hands into the crib and Etienne screamed.

CHAPTER 34

Budapest, Hungary

Ivan Tóth sat at the oval table in the debate chamber of the *tanács* town house, elbows resting on its surface, fingers steepled. A display of white lilies stood in the centre of the table. Their symbolism was not lost on him: white for remembrance, lilies to signify a passing. Their presence, he knew, was coincidental, but they bothered him nonetheless.

He felt watched; *was* watched. From the ceiling fresco above, the painted eyes of the gods seemed to regard him with looks no less disinterested than those around the table.

Although most of the chairs were filled, two remained vacant. One belonged to Anton Golias. The other, at the head of the table, belonged to the *Örökös Főnök*. Although he refused to look at it, he saw the eyes of those around him cast their eyes towards it every now and then. In the silence its emptiness seemed to scream.

Tóth stared at each *tanács* member in turn, refusing to move on until he had met their eyes. In some he saw anger; in others, fear.

Good. He would focus their anger. Manipulate their fear.

Satisfied that he had the room's attention, he placed his hands palms down in front of him and grimaced. 'I've lost count of the times I've sat at this table over the years, listening, debating, offering counsel. We've made decisions in this chamber affecting the lives of everyone we represent. Not all of those decisions have been the right ones, I'll admit. We've made mistakes, haven't we, in our time together? But at least we can say that our decisions have always been made for the good of our people, and with the intention of maintaining the purity of our race.'

In front of him, he saw Oliver Lebeau flinch at his choice of words.

'Yes, I'll say it again: the *purity* of our race. Since when did we begin to shrink from that word? Since when did we begin to shrink from that *task*?'

He waited, silent. The man did not reply.

'We've made difficult decisions, and while we haven't always been unified in our thinking, we've always been unified in our actions. We've never kept secrets around this table, never indulged in brinksmanship. None of us has ever acted unilaterally.

'When our forebears were murdered during the *Éjszakai Sikolyok*, we inherited an unenviable task. Our future looked bleak. To some, it looked as if we *had* no future. We inherited the leadership of a crippled society, a scattered and terrified people.

'But we didn't flinch from our commission. We worked hard. We spread our population far and wide. We rebuilt. And through it all we remained true to our laws and true to our history.

'I know some of you continue to worry about the future, but I tell you there is no need for fear. We continue to hold a *végzet*. And while for years, admittedly, the numbers were in decline, in our most recent season we saw the greatest attendance for eight years.'

Again, he glanced around the table. 'When you're part of a minority – even one which, on the surface at least, seems to enjoy such advantages as our own – the actions of a few can have far-reaching consequences. We only need to examine the legacy of the *kirekesztett* to see proof of that. You'll never hear me lay blame for the *Éjszakai Sikolyok* at anyone's door other than the Eleni's. But we can still ask ourselves whether the Crown would have sanctioned their actions if we'd punished more severely the crimes of our own kind. Only sixteen years ago we lost our *Örökös Főnök* Éva Maria-Magdalena Szöllösi due to the actions of our most infamous *kirekesztett* son. And let's not shy away from the reality: her replacement has been less than satisfactory.'

The silence was charged now, primed for the spark that would ignite it. 'But even through her missteps,' Tóth continued, 'even though she's divided us more than any *Főnök* who's gone before, we've remained loyal. She's made contentious decisions and we've supported her, even when we've disagreed.

'You all know of my personal opposition to some of those decisions. Still, like you, I recognised her ultimate authority, and I have always respected the right of our leader to cast the deciding vote in areas where we've failed to reach consensus. But I'll ask you this: it is the role of our *Főnök*, is it not, to *forge* consensus? And it is also our *Főnök*'s responsibility to keep her *tanács* informed in all areas of our governance. How else can we fulfil our role effectively?

'For over ten years I've held my tongue. I counselled against the founding of this fertility programme, counselled against the principle of introducing *kirekesztett* and *simavér* blood to the line. I was shouted down by some of you, ridiculed even. As a result, that programme has operated cloaked in a secrecy impenetrable even to those of us who sit around this table, *at the specific orders of our own leader.*'

Lajos Horváth, sitting opposite, cleared his throat. 'We all know the reasons for that. Besides, we imposed strict conditions—'

Tóth laughed. 'Ah, yes, the *conditions*. Let's examine those conditions, shall we? First, we would endanger no lives. Remember that one? Yet I hear that during the last year we've lost perhaps half a dozen of the very women we were elected to protect.

'As troubling as that discovery may be, over the last few days I've learned of something so reprehensible it's given me no choice but to summon you all here and demand that we act.

'It's always been clear to me that this scientific *meddling* is a heresy. While the success of our *végzet* continues to grow, the work of Hannah Wilde, and her supporters, has produced nothing except the deaths of those volunteers naive enough to support her, and the birth of a handful of children who are little more than *kirekesztett*-spawned bastards themselves.'

He saw bristling now, from all around the table. He wanted to rile them, wanted to inflame them. 'Whatever your view on that – and I know mine is not without controversy – at least we'd put controls in place. At least, one could argue, the influence of *kirekesztett* blood could be diluted over the coming generations: a distasteful but necessary evil.

'Over the last few days, however, I've learned that one of our most sacrosanct conditions has been breached. With the express approval of our *Főnök*, *kirekesztett* volunteers have been recruited into their ranks.'

Outraged gasps. Tóth was careful to keep his smile at bay.

Only Horváth now, and perhaps I can accomplish this without spilling too much blood.

'You've learned this how?' the man asked.

'The *kirekesztett* women are receiving treatment both at the original centre and also at Villa del Osservatore. I have eyes inside the *Belső Őr* who have confirmed it. Gentlemen, we've been duped, and history will judge us on the actions we take today. We have allowed ourselves, however unwittingly, to become accessories to the greatest threat facing us since the Night of Screams over a hundred years ago. Right now, even as I speak, Hannah Wilde's programme, in collusion with the *Főnök*, is impregnating *kirekesztett* women with *kirekesztett* life, in direct contravention of the laws laid down within the pages of our *Vének Könyve*. I spoke earlier of the purity of our race, and I tell you I am here to defend it. I already have the majority I need to force a change of leadership, but what I want is consensus.'

'What you *want*,' Horváth said, 'is a coup.'

'I'll tell you what I want,' he replied, straining to keep his voice calm. 'Let me lay it before you as clearly as I can. I want us to act before it's too late. I want us to disband this programme. I want us to end the senseless deaths of the very women we've sworn to protect. I want us to unite behind a leader who respects the counsel we offer. And I want us to prevent the inevitable decline into depravity that will result if we sanction the creation of an entirely new generation of *kirekesztett*.'

He looked around the room. 'Shall we vote?'

Only Horváth met his eye. 'What of Hannah Wilde? What are you proposing we do about her?'

'She's a Balázs, by inheritance if not by name. You know as well as I what needs to be done.'

'Then say it.'

'Hannah Wilde is a threat. We eliminate threats, or they eliminate us.'

'And her daughter? Do you intend to eliminate her too?'

'That's for us all to decide.'

'You think, if you kill her mother, you won't create an even stronger adversary in Leah Wilde?'

'Are you frightened of a young girl?'

The man stared. 'Why is Anton not present?'

'Anton made his choice.'

'Not what I asked. Where is he?'

Tóth didn't blink. 'He's dead.'

He waited for that news to sink in. Then, in a softer voice, he added, 'Anton died trying to warn the *Fönök* that we'd discovered her duplicity. I grieve his loss, and I hope his death won't be in vain – that it can avoid greater bloodshed.'

Horváth's mouth dropped open. 'This is how you build consensus, is it?'

Sitting back in his seat, Tóth glanced across at Joó. The man barked a command and the chamber's double doors banged open. Twelve black-clad *tanács* guards swept into the room, taking up positions behind the table's occupants.

'The *Főnök* can no longer be trusted,' Tóth said. 'I intend to remove her from office, and I offer to rule temporarily until a replacement is chosen. Do I hear objections?'

Horváth's face had drained of colour. He stared around the room at the assembled guards. 'You call this a choice?'

'Do you object?'

'God forgive me.' He paused. 'No.'

Tóth turned to Joó and nodded.

The man raised a phone to his ear. 'Do it,' he said.

CHAPTER 35

Villa del Osservatore, Italy

Leah Wilde was standing with Luca's sister Soraya by the tall windows of the villa's first-floor map room when she noticed the two vessels approaching the dock at the base of the peninsula.

For five months of the last twelve she had made Villa del Osservatore her home; but however long she stayed here, she knew she would never grow tired of this view.

The landscape seemed to evolve every hour, the sun, clouds and sky conspiring to mix an artist's palette of colours on the water's surface. This afternoon, a thick mist had unfurled across the lake and rolled up its shores, the moisture-laden air bleaching the shouldering mountains to grey. It seemed reluctant to release the two vessels that slipped from its clutches, chasing them with ghost-like tendrils as the craft approached the dock.

They came from different directions, as silent as basking sharks; the first appeared from the north, its twin emerging from the south.

Leah watched them drift closer. The moment they bumped against the landing stage, their crew leaped out and began to tie up.

Hands cradled around her swollen belly, Soraya moved to the window. 'Do you recognise them?'

Leah shook her head. 'Not from here.'

'Were we expecting anyone?'

She didn't know the answer to that. When the *Fönök* was in residence at the villa, as she was now, the woman received a steady stream of visitors, and while most of them arrived by road, many chose to enjoy the drama of the lakeside approach.

At the dock, the crewmen finished tying up. Now the two vessels disgorged further arrivals. Even from here, Leah could tell that they were, all of them, *hosszú életek*.

They seemed in no hurry to climb the staircase to the gates of the lower terrace. Instead, they gazed up at the villa.

She shrugged. 'I don't know. Maybe.'

'Strange for them to appear at once like that, from different directions.'

'Yeah.'

Leah moved closer to the window. Below, on the lawn outside the music room, she could see seven-year-old Emánuel and his brother Levi playing an improvised game of croquet with little Pia and her younger brother Alex.

Leah's heart began to beat a fraction faster. She glanced across at Soraya, saw the frown creasing the woman's forehead. Her friend had always been petite, but her pregnancy seemed to accentuate it tenfold. Face as pale as the mist that languished on Lake Como's waters, feet bound in her favourite Chinese slippers, she seemed as delicate as a lily petal. Leah didn't want to worry her unduly. Still . . .

'Not sure I like this,' she said.

Flecks of copper had appeared in Soraya's eyes. 'What shall we do?'

'Those boats won't have gone unnoticed. Stay here. I'll be back.'

The first-floor hall served rooms that for the past year had become living spaces for many of Calw's volunteers, partners and children. Leah darted along it, taking a left-hand fork to the building's west wing. Her blood was pumping faster now, and she felt her stomach shrinking away. Something about this felt wrong; badly wrong.

At the end of the hall she crossed the landing of a grand staircase, threw open a door and burst into the room beyond. Its only window faced west, offering a view back across the peninsula to Villa del Osservatore's roadside entrance.

A stone-built wall contained the grounds of the western border, culminating in a dramatic gatehouse. Usually, even during the day, its gates were closed. Now they gaped open. A dark-clad group stood on the roadside beside them.

With Jakab gone these last sixteen years, Leah's fear of being hunted had slowly faded. But the *memory* of it never had. Now it leaped at her, jubilant, clawing the air from her lungs and squeezing her chest tight.

Light-headed, she reached out a hand to steady herself. Who were they? Not *tolvajok*, surely. Too many of them for that.

Have you caused this? Is this happening because of you?

Nausea rolled in her. She thought of all the people in the villa to whom she owed a debt. The four children playing on the lawn. The others still inside the house; their mothers.

Go. Now. They're depending on you.

But the wrong decision, made in haste, might lead them further into danger. Did she go first to her room, to collect her gun? What about Soraya? Could she risk leaving the woman alone?

As clearly as if Hannah had been standing beside her, Leah heard her mother's voice. One word: *Act*.

Grimacing, teeth clenched against the return of that fear she'd thought she'd long since escaped, she bolted across the room and into the corridor outside.

Catharina Maria-Magdalena Szöllösi, *Örökös Főnök* to the *hosszú életek*, sat at the reading table inside Villa del Osservatore's library and listened as Ányos Szilágyi, most senior of her *Belső Őr*, gave his report. Ányos stood by the window, hands clasped behind his back, feet restless, looking like he wanted to pace the floor.

Except for Gabriel, she'd known him longer than anyone alive – knew, especially, how much he hated to be indoors, even during weather such as this. Despite his seniority he remained a cloistered man, presenting the latest intelligence succinctly, yet reluctant to offer his counsel unless asked.

Also around the table, Ferenc Werkner, Ányos's lieutenant, and his aide. Standing by the library's door, another of her *Belső Őr*.

A silver tray of crushed ice sat between them, upon which lay a spiral of oysters, their inner shells iridescent. Ányos knew they were her favourite delicacy, and he'd arrived back from England with a sack of them.

Unfortunately, the news he brought hardly whetted her appetite. 'So the trail is cold, then,' she said. 'We don't even know if the group hunting Leah is still in Wales.'

Ányos shook his head. 'I'm afraid not.'

Catharina turned to Ferenc Werkner. 'What's the latest from America?'

'Our biggest challenge,' the man replied, 'has been separating what might be incidents of *tolvajok* activity from the more regular – if you'll excuse the term – instances of abduction. Luckily for us, group abductions are relatively rare, which helps somewhat. We have the two families from Oregon that went missing last year, somewhere between Yosemite and Vegas. The mother's body was discovered a few months later, but none of the others was ever found; it certainly looks like the work of a *tolvaj*. Before that, we had the Swedish exchange students snatched from Lake Tahoe. Then there were those hockey players in Utah; again, never found. Two more groups disappeared not long after. First the ranchers in Colorado. And you've heard the Renata Hernandez story from Kansas: a young mother put her and her neighbours' kids in the car one morning for the school run and was never seen again. The police there are treating it as an abduction-suicide. We think differently.

'A few other things we can surmise. First, obviously, they're surviving on *simavér* hosts, which is why these disappearances are so frequent. Second, the frequency is increasing, which indicates they're not in the best shape. Third, the fact they're snatching whole groups rather than individuals suggests a certain amount of desperation.'

She nodded. 'And they've been heading east.'

'Over time, yes. It looks like this started on the West Coast. Those incidents follow a steady line through the centre of the country. Latest news is this: two days ago, an Atlanta parking attendant discovered five incredibly old men and women locked inside a van. Two of them died on the way to hospital, and the other three aren't communicating. The government agency there is holding it back, but they ran DNA tests and came up with matches to five teenagers snatched only a few days earlier.'

'A few *days*?' Ányos asked.

'That's what I heard.'

'If they're deteriorating that fast, they really will be desperate,' the man replied. 'Which makes them even more dangerous. Where exactly did they find this van?'

Werkner's face was grim. 'About seven miles south of the business district. Right outside Hartsfield-Jackson. It's one of the busiest international airports in the world.'

Quietly, Catherina said, 'They're coming.'

The room fell silent. And then, from somewhere, a soft trilling. She glanced up, irritated. 'I thought we had a rule about phones in here.'

Reddening, Werkner pulled a handset from his pocket and examined the screen. 'Not me,' he said.

'Sorry, Cat.' From the window, Ányos took out his phone and held it to his ear. He listened in silence, switched it off, and turned to face the room.

'Well?' she asked.

He nodded.

It happened so quickly. The *Belső Őr* by the door walked up behind Ferenc Werkner. Simultaneously, Werkner's aide rose to his feet. He was holding a knife. With the deftest of movements, he opened a wound in Werkner's throat so deep that the man had no hope of closing it on his own.

Werkner's eyes bulged and he tried to stand, but the two men grabbed his arms. Bright blood fountained from his neck. Droplets splashed into the oyster shells.

Catharina watched from her chair, rigid. She knew she was about to die in this room. Strange, how for a moment that image of Werkner's blood falling into the oyster shells mesmerised her with its terrible beauty.

She thought about all the things she'd failed to achieve, all the things she'd hoped to make right. When an image came to her of the children playing in the villa's ground-floor rooms, her throat grew tight.

A red tide cascaded down Werkner's chest. He kicked his legs, trying to throw off his assailants, but they held him firm. 'Don't fight it,' his aide whispered. 'There's nothing personal in this. Die well.'

Either the words themselves finished the man, or he had already lost too much blood. His struggles weakened and he slumped, head lolling forward, chest still.

Werkner's killers eased him out of the chair and laid him on the library floor.

Catharina glanced up at Ányos, and when she saw his expression she felt a hollowness in her chest. He moved towards her.

'Whose order?' she asked tonelessly.

'Tóth initiated it. But the *tanács* voted. It was unanimous in the end.'

She nodded. 'Then I join an exclusive club.'

In their entire history, only two previous *Örökös Főnöks* had been unseated.

He edged closer and she saw that he held a blade of his own.

'Let's do this gracefully,' he said, and when she caught the anguish in his voice it angered her.

'You'd presume to make the cut?' she asked, with ice in her tone. 'I think not, Ányos. There is a historical precedent for this, is there not?'

He hesitated. Then he retreated and his face relaxed. 'I had hoped you would remember that.'

'As if I could forget.'

When Csontváry Kisfaludi István had been usurped in Budapest, back in the fifteenth century, he had chosen to take his own life rather than die at the hands of his guards. Irinyi Gábor, a few hundred years later, had followed his predecessor's example.

Catharina went to a table beside the fireplace. On its surface rested an intricately carved box. Lifting the lid, she looked down at what it contained: an ancient *déjnin* blade. She removed it, feeling its cold weight, feeling the press of history in its metal. Drawing her thumb along its blade, she saw the scarlet line it scored. Still sharp, after all these years: the same knife Csontváry Kisfaludi István had used to take his life.

She turned back to face Ányos.

'I'm sorry, Cat,' he told her. 'I never wanted this. But what's happening here. It can't be allowed.'

'I take it you're not referring to my death.'

'You know what I mean. No one wishes you any malice. You made some mistakes, that's all. Everyone wants this to be as bloodless as possible. I wish we could include you in that. But you know it would complicate things. We need a fresh start.'

He dropped his eyes to the *déjnin* blade in her hand, and his chest swelled. 'I knew you'd choose the old-fashioned way. I'll make sure it's recorded. You have my word on that.'

Catharina turned her wrist upwards. Studied, with quiet contemplation, the raised blue veins just below her skin.

'Do you want to sit?' he asked.

'I prefer to stand.'

He nodded. 'Very well.'

Catharina lifted the blade. And then she threw it.

Realising how badly he'd misread her, Ányos began to move. But already it was too late. The *déjnin* knife, flashing like sun on water, whipped through the air and into Ányos's mouth, puncturing him with a sound like a bitten apple.

He staggered backwards. Biting down reflexively on the handle, his front teeth shattered. He dropped his own knife, lifting his hands to the one buried inside his mouth.

'I never liked the old-fashioned ways,' she said. 'And I can't abide traitors.'

Ányos fell to one knee. Sat down heavily.

Catharina dismissed him with her eyes, turning to his two conspirators. They closed on her, eyes wary, knives drawn.

No way she could defeat them both. At the other end of the room she saw a bust of her mother. Thankfully, the woman's eyes were cast towards the window. Bizarrely, it made the prospect of dying here a little easier to face.

She scowled at the two men edging towards her and opened her arms in invitation.

As Leah ran back along the first-floor hall to the map room where she'd left Soraya, she heard the bell in Villa del Osservatore's watchtower begin to toll. Someone else, at least, had realised they were under attack.

She burst into the room.

Soraya twisted towards her, face pale. Through the window Leah saw that the *hosszú életek* alighting from the two vessels at the dock had grown in number. An advance party was climbing the stone staircase to the lower terrace.

On the lawn outside the music room, the children dropped their bats and balls. They fled towards the house.

'It's a coup, isn't it?' Soraya asked. 'They've found out about us.'

Leah only nodded.

They ran into the hall, skidding and sliding along the marble floor until they reached a staircase. No time to check what lay at the bottom. Together they flew down it.

Perhaps they wouldn't kill everyone, she thought. Apart from Soraya, none of the mothers in the building was *kirekesztett*. But her friend's life, should she be captured, would almost certainly be forfeit. And what about the children?

Don't think. Act.

Down the last few stairs. Into a foyer with four huge doors, three of them closed. She saw Soraya hurrying to keep up, hands cradling her belly. Heard voices, growing closer.

Leah threw open the music-room door, waiting until Soraya rushed across the threshold before slamming it shut and locking it.

One of the mothers in the room, Ara Schulteisz, had shepherded the last of the children inside. Now she began to lock each of the six doors that opened onto the loggia.

It wouldn't help them. They were mostly constructed from glass.

Outside, Leah saw eight grim-faced *hosszú életek* crossing the lawn. She cast her eyes around the room. The children old enough to know that death approached stared at her, faces hollow. Even those too young to understand had sensed the growing panic. Two of them began to cry.

She took in their faces: the brothers, Emánuel and Levi; twins Carina and Philipp; Pia and her younger brother Alex; Dávid, Lícia and Tünde; cradled to Flóra's breast, tiny Elias.

Ten young lives. Not, by any stretch, all of the children from Calw. Catharina had set up a second residence on the shore of Lake Maggiore. Others, too. Leah did not want to think about what might be happening there. The possibility that the *tanács* remained ignorant of their existence was slight.

Along with herself and Soraya, she counted four other adults, mothers all: Kata Lendvai, Ara Schulteisz, Lidia Montigny and Flóra Glaus.

'What do we do?' Flóra asked. 'We can't stop them.'

'But we might be able to get the children out. Close the drapes. They know we're surrounded. I don't think they'll hurry.'

Leah went to a door behind one of the concert grands and yanked it open, revealing a servant's corridor, narrow and dark. From that lightless avenue, most of the villa's ground-floor rooms were served. To the children, she said, 'We're going to play a game. Who wants to do that? Yes? Then all of you, in here.'

The four mothers helped her coax the children through. 'That's it,' one of them called, her voice hitching. 'Quickly now. Do as Leah asks.'

In the far wall, the handle of the locked interior door began to turn. Leah heard voices behind it.

Six of the children had filed into the passage. Two stood on the threshold.

'We can't all go,' Flóra said. 'And I'll slow you down.' She held out her son to Soraya. 'Please. Take Elias for me.'

Soraya's face crumpled. She gathered the boy into her arms. Elias struggled away from her, reaching for his mother.

Flóra kissed his head. 'Go, *kicsikém*. Soraya will keep you safe.'

The handles on the loggia doors began to rattle.

Leah pushed the last two children into the passage. She picked up Tünde, one of the youngest, and turned to the mothers. 'Come on. Before it's too late.'

But they were shaking their heads. 'You've a better chance alone,' Kata Lendvai said. She smiled, tears on her cheeks. 'And I'm not leaving Flóra.'

'You can't just—'

'*Go*, Leah. Now.'

Heart aching at their bravery, she stepped into the passage

and flicked on a wall switch. Four dim bulbs winked on along the ceiling. The door slammed shut behind her. From the other side, she heard glass breaking.

Leah squeezed past Soraya and the children until she was at the front. 'Everyone stay close. Keep your eyes on me. Let's go.'

When the boats had arrived at the dock, the *Főnök* had been in the villa's library, in council with members of her *Belső Őr*. The *hosszú életek* leader might still be there.

The door that served the library was up ahead. Leah led the children towards it. Pressing a finger to her lips, she urged them to be as quiet as they could. She placed her ear to the wood, straining to hear anything from the room beyond.

Commotion behind them. The music-room door crashed open, filling the passage with light.

A man shouted.

Knowing they had no time left, Leah burst into the library. leading the children after her. As soon as everyone was through, she slammed the door and used a key to secure it.

'Lock the entrance!' she shouted to Soraya. She gazed around the room for something to brace the door from which they'd emerged, which was when she saw the carnage.

At the far end of the library, a table and three chairs had been overturned. On the floor nearby lay a man's corpse. His throat had been cut. Chips of crushed ice were melting into the blood pooled around him. A few yards away, Catharina Maria-Magdalena Szöllösi lay on her back. Her eyes were open.

In death, the woman wore an expression of savagery such that Leah had never seen. She was wreathed in blood, her body pierced and slashed. Another man lay dead beside her. Against the fireplace slumped one of her *Belső Őr*, his hands twitching as he tried to close the wounds puncturing his chest.

Catharina's adviser, Ányos Szilágyi, sat on the floor by the window, back resting against the drapes. His breath whistled in his mouth, around a *déjnin* blade buried up to its hilt.

Leah felt her scalp shrinking. So much death. She turned to the children, hopeful they had not seen what waited for them, but they stood in a circle, mouths hanging open. 'Eyes on the ceiling, all of you,' she ordered. Then, when they didn't respond, '*Do as I say!*'

To her left stood a mahogany coffer covered with antique navigation instruments. Sweeping them to the floor, she dragged the chest across the locked servants' entrance.

Soraya lowered Elias to the floor. The woman rushed to the library's main door, a thick slab of centuries-old hardwood, and twisted the key.

At the room's far end the two wounded men stared, and Leah saw, in their eyes, that they had been the cause, rather than the intended victims, of this slaughter.

Soraya seemed to see it, too.

'Don't let the children watch,' she said, bearing down on the *Belső Őr* guard by the fireplace. He kicked his legs, trying to worm away from her.

'Everyone's eyes back to the ceiling,' Leah urged. 'Now!'

Soraya reached the man and knocked him onto his side. Teeth bared, she grabbed his head and wrenched it around, snapping his neck. Turning, she stalked towards Ányos Szilágyi. His eyes widened as she approached, reaching up blood-soaked hands to fend her off.

Something slammed against the door to the servants' passage, rattling it in its frame. Leah heard voices outside the main library entrance. Its handle jinked back and forth.

By the curtains, Ányos Szilágyi crabbed backwards. Soraya planted a foot against his chest and pushed him onto his back. His head smacked down on the floorboards and he coughed, a dark mist of blood.

Bending, Soraya gripped the handle of the *déjnin* knife protruding from his mouth. Leah turned away, but she heard the sound that followed, and nearly gagged.

The library door shuddered as something heavy hit it from

the other side. In the far wall, the door to the servants' passage began to reverberate. The children backed into a tight group.

Soraya wiped her forehead, leaving a streak of blood. Her eyes, when she found Leah's, were flat. 'We're trapped,' she said. 'It's over.'

CHAPTER 36

Villa del Osservatore, Italy

As his Range Rover accelerated up the hill towards Villa del Osservatore, Ivan Tóth drummed his fingers on the rear seat's armrest. Beside him, Joó was shouting into his phone. Tóth could only hear one side of the conversation, but it didn't sound good.

Behind them a convoy of cars, containing the remaining five members of his *tanács*, followed them up the slope.

'Is it secure?' Joó snapped, fingers tight around his phone. 'That's all I'm asking.' He paused. 'Well, *find* them. Yes, we're almost here. He's beside me.'

When Joó hung up, Tóth said, 'Tell me.'

'Catharina's dead. Ányos, too.'

'Ányos? How the hell—'

'I don't know! Something went wrong. I told you I should have been there.'

'You had to stay away. Politically—'

'*Politically?* How do you think *this* is going to play out, politically?'

Tóth bit down on the retort he'd been about to deliver. Never before had Joó addressed him so abruptly. More disturbingly, he'd never seen his *tanács* colleague agitated like this.

'It's a disaster,' Joó muttered. 'That's what it is.'

The Range Rover pulled onto Villa del Osservatore's private drive, swept through the gatehouse and past two *Belső Őr*. The guardsmen's faces were grim, eyes dark. Even from inside the car's muted cabin, Tóth could hear the villa's watchtower bell pealing out its warning. 'What else?'

'Leah Wilde hasn't been found. Nor the children.'

'But they were *there*. They—'

'I know! But with Ányos dead, there's no one to lead.'

Their car slid to a stop in a rain of gravel. Tóth recognised Victor Makovecz, one of Ányos's lieutenants, waiting for them outside the villa.

Throwing open his door, he jumped out. 'I hear you lost them,' he said, striding towards the entrance.

Makovecz stiffened. 'I'm not sure you should go in there while—'

'You try and stop me,' Tóth hissed.

Inside the library, shocked by the two swift executions her friend had performed, Leah turned to Soraya and shook her head. 'No, there's a way. If we hurry.' She strode across the room. 'Children, I need you all to stand back.'

As her charges retreated, Leah crouched down in front of the blood-sodden rug covering the floor. She began to roll it up, grimacing at the fluids that oozed from its fibres. Quickly, she revealed a trapdoor cut into the polished floorboards. A recessed iron ring lay at its centre.

Catherina's mother had shown Leah the hidden exit years earlier, during a tour of the grounds. 'One of the benefits of inheriting a home from the papacy,' the old *Főnök* had told her. 'Historically, they've been quite adept at covering their backs.'

Leah grabbed the iron ring, braced her feet and pulled. The trapdoor yielded unwillingly, dragging with it a frayed matt of cobwebs as it swung upwards. Beneath, a flight of steps descended into darkness. The air smelled damp. Cold.

'I'll go first,' she told the children. 'Hold hands and follow me. Mind your feet. It gets slippery.' To Soraya, she added. 'Pull it closed behind you. There's a bolt on the underside.'

It would, she thought, grant them perhaps a minute's reprieve.

Leah activated her phone's tiny torch, took a breath and led them down the steps to the cave network beneath Villa del Osservatore.

Behind her she heard the boom of the trapdoor falling back into place, and a rattle as Soraya shot the bolt home.

From the other side, a crack like a pistol shot as the library door broke apart.

Tóth strode through the library's shattered entrance, and what he saw appalled him. The floor was a montage of bloody footprints. At its centre, an opening revealed a flight of steps descending into darkness. The splintered remains of a trapdoor lay to one side. Three *Belső Őr* stood beside it.

Behind them lay the blood-slicked corpse of Catharina Maria-Magdalena Szöllősi. Completing the grisly tableau, four more bodies, including that of Ányos Szilágyi.

Furious, Tóth marched up to the guards hovering beside the library's secret exit. Pointing to Catharina's corpse with one hand, he slapped the nearest man's head with the other. 'You're going to leave her lying there like that? Your own *Főnök*? Get a blanket, wrap her up, and get her out of here. *Now*. And show her some respect while you're doing it.' To Makovecz, the senior *Belső Őr* he'd met outside, he said, 'I'm putting you in charge. No one is to speak a word of this until I talk to them first.'

'Of course.'

'Do we have any more dead?'

'Four who remained loyal to her. We had no choice. And you'd already sanctioned it.'

'I didn't sanction this mess,' Tóth hissed. He took a breath, exhaled it explosively. 'It's not your fault. Get the rest of these bodies out of here. All of them. And somebody stop that goddamned bell from ringing.'

'I'll see to it myself.'

'Not you!' he shouted. 'It's a bell! Delegate it!' He took another breath, calmed himself. 'The rest of the household: where are they?'

'We're holding them in another part of the building. Do you want to see them?'

'Yes. But not yet. First let's—'

He broke off as he heard a commotion behind him, and saw the remaining five members of his *tanács* enter the room.

They stopped dead as they took in the scene.

'My God,' one of them whispered. 'What have we done?'

Tóth was glad the man had said *we*. He wondered how much time he had left before they started saying *you*.

In the darkness deep beneath Villa del Osservatore, Leah reached the bottom of the flight of steps. When she raised her phone, the bluish light of its torch beam revealed the entrance to a tunnel chiselled out of the surrounding rock. Its sides were lumpen and damp, the ceiling only a few inches above her head. Murmuring encouragement to the children behind her, Leah stepped into it. She glanced over her shoulder, counting the heads of those who followed. Dimly she saw Soraya's silhouette, bringing up the rear.

Ahead, the tunnel took an abrupt turn. They emerged into a natural cave. The walls opened out and a draught brushed her cheek. The rock ceiling dripped with moisture. Another few yards, and the torchlight reflected off water.

Leah heard a fluttering around her. Smelled the ammonia stink of guano. Lifting the phone higher, she saw hundreds of tiny eyes.

Bats.

They clustered together on the roof of the cave, a rippling skin of black wings and furred bodies. Behind her, one of the children cried out.

'It's OK, they won't harm you. You're safe, I promise.'

The torch picked out the dim grey shape of an open-topped

boat bobbing on the water, moored by a single rope attached to a bolt in the cave wall.

Leah pulled on the rope until the vessel nudged up against a rock jutting out into the water. 'Quickly now,' she whispered. 'Into the boat, and watch your step.' One by one, she helped the children aboard. The moment Soraya took her seat, Leah cast off the rope. She leaped into the stern, using her momentum to launch the boat forward.

Wanting to avoid starting the engine until the last possible moment, she reached out and used the walls of the cave to manoeuvre the boat along its course. They eased around a shallow bend. Ahead, she saw a glow of reflected daylight illuminating the last turn before the cave's mouth.

Behind her she heard voices. The tramp of boots on the steps. Above, the bats chittered, restless.

The boat bumped against the rock wall, and Leah shoved away from it, steering them around its curve. The cave mouth opened into daylight, and she narrowed her eyes against its brightness. Mist rolled and coiled on Lake Como's surface, so thick that they might have been emerging into the twilight domain of Hades.

A shout from behind. She glanced back, but the tunnel's curve now hid them from the secret dock. Her pursuers wouldn't be able to use their phones down here, wouldn't be able to notify the *Belső Őr* guarding the villa's main landing stage on the far side of the peninsula. Even so, she would have to be quick.

Bracing her foot on the back of the boat, she grabbed the outboard motor's ripcord and yanked as hard as she could. The engine fired into life on the first pull. Calling to the children to hold on, she dropped into her seat and twisted the throttle. The boat surged out of the cave and into the mist-wreathed waters of the lake.

One hand still on the tiller, Leah dialled a number on her phone.

Until now, her rush of adrenalin had caged her fear. But as the boat thumped along beneath her, as she saw the frightened faces of the children in front, as she considered what might be happening in Calw, in Lake Maggiore and elsewhere, it broke free to assault her, and she gritted her teeth against its power.

Please, she thought. *Please answer.*

And then she heard Hannah's voice.

For a moment her relief was so intense she nearly lost her grip on the throttle. 'Listen carefully,' she shouted. 'You don't have much time.'

CHAPTER 37

Calw, Germany

By the time Hannah Wilde let herself out of the complex and crossed the courtyard to the chalet she shared with Gabriel, the day was drawing to a close. She could feel the weak rays of the sun, low in the sky, as they struggled to warm her face. The last begonias wilting in the chalet's hanging baskets laced the air with a lemon and cinnamon fragrance.

Hannah opened the front door and went inside, and as it closed behind her she straightened, surprised that Ibsen hadn't padded into the hall to nose her hand in his traditional greeting. From the kitchenette she had expected the clatter of saucepans and the steamy aroma of cooking as Gabriel prepared dinner. But the chalet was silent, and all Hannah could smell, coiling towards her, was the hard odour of blood – so out of place in this gentle haven of theirs that it tossed her insides into free fall.

'Gabe?'

As soon as she called his name she regretted it. But the sound of the front door opening would have alerted any intruder to her presence. A multitude of dark scenarios flashed through her head. Despite them Hannah remained still, head cocked and mouth tightly closed, straining to detect anything other than her own accelerating heartbeat.

There.

Faint, oh-so-faint, from somewhere deeper inside the chalet;

a scratching, like the surreptitious investigations of mice inside the walls. Except that never in their time here had they suffered the incursions of rodents.

Gabriel had left her only ten minutes earlier. She'd stayed back at the complex, wanting to catch up with some of its volunteers. What had happened since? How much could her life have changed in that short interval?

Hannah reached out until her fingers touched the wall. Maintaining a light contact, even though she knew the layout of these rooms as well as the inside of her head, she moved along the hall towards the kitchenette at the chalet's rear.

The tang of blood grew richer.

Locked inside her sightless world, expecting at any moment to feel the touch of an assailant's hand or the prick of a blade, Hannah's fingers found the kitchenette's painted wooden doorway. Her feet moved from soft carpet to hard linoleum.

She could hear the rush of her breathing, the pulsing of her heart. From the living room behind her, the tick of a cheap plastic wall clock. And from somewhere else, perhaps from one of the two ground-floor bedrooms, that scratching sound.

She fought the urge to turn and run, to lunge back to the front door and slam through it, seeking help. Whatever had happened here – and *something* had happened while she'd been catching up with her friends – had happened because of her. If an intruder lurked inside the chalet, it was Hannah he sought. And if Gabriel were held captive somewhere in these rooms, she would not desert him. Even if she did attempt to flee, her chances of escaping from anyone who chose to pursue her were almost nil. Few of her potential aggressors would have any difficulty overpowering her. Not these days. Not now.

Considering anew what might have happened to Gabriel, Hannah began to shiver. Gabriel: endlessly patient and nurturing. Her friend of sixteen years; her laughter therapist; her cheerleader. With him she had found a different kind of love to that she'd experienced with her late husband Nate, but it was no less powerful. If Gabriel, too, had lost his life because of her—

Don't. Don't think about it.

It was the only defence she could muster. Laughable, really. Knowing that she made herself an easy target, doing it anyway, Hannah straightened her back and raised her head. She tried, and failed, to stop herself from shaking.

Another step further across the kitchenette floor and this time, when she lifted her left boot, the lino seemed unwilling to release it, parting with a sound like the smack of chewing gum. Her right boot landed in a pool of what could only be blood, and with her next step she nudged up against something large and soft.

Hannah closed her eyes in denial of what she felt just then. She crouched, reaching out her fingers, needing to know but desperate to delay the moment as long as she could.

Finally her hand touched smooth short hair. A curve of firm flank.

Ibsen.

She spread her fingers wide, feeling the warmth of him, waiting for what seemed like the passing of a season for the chest of her old companion to rise. But it remained still.

Hannah stroked him, moving her hand up towards his head. When she felt the wet tack of blood around his throat and a ragged, fur-clogged wound, she sobbed, choked.

Gone, just like that. A decade-long partnership of love and trust, torn from her in a instant.

She whispered a quick prayer for him, and even though she felt an aching guilt at her betrayal, her thoughts marched in front of her.

Ibsen was dead. Gabriel might still be alive.

Don't think. Act.

Her old adage. It had served tolerably in years past. Perhaps not so tolerably now, tethered in this prison of darkness.

Hannah rose to her feet. With slow, deliberate movements, hands outstretched, she stepped over the lifeless body of her dog and crossed the kitchenette to the countertop.

The drawer beneath the sink contained knives. She paused in front of it as a thought struck her, so obvious that only her seesawing emotions could have concealed it until now. Sliding her hand into the back pocket of her jeans, she withdrew her phone.

From the far side of the breakfast bar, a voice said, 'I'd been looking for that.'

Hannah's heart almost seized, and then it began to gallop. She flinched away.

It was a man's voice, but its timbre was high-pitched, the tone mocking and effeminate.

'Where is he?'

He laughed. 'You obviously haven't read the script, Hannah. That's not what you're meant to say at all. You're meant to say, *Please don't kill me.* Or, *What do you want?*'

'What do you want?'

'Ah, a little late, now. You've ruined the moment. What do I want? Well, I suppose I want to kill you, Hannah.' He paused. 'Actually, that isn't entirely true. I bear you no personal animosity. I rather admire you, if truth be told. Perhaps I should say instead, I wish to do my job.'

Even though she did not recognise this particular voice, she recognised, now, the soprano pitch of a castrated *Merénylő*.

It's over, then. You can't survive this.

'What's stopping you?' she asked, gritting her teeth.

'Unfortunately, not everyone in this splendidly dark world of ours is as efficient in their given tasks as I.'

'Have you killed him?'

'You ask a lot of questions,' he replied thoughtfully. 'I hadn't expected that. I'd expected a fight, actually. Perhaps even a chase. Although, considering your condition, a chase sorely lacking in any real sport.' Through his nose, he made a peculiar snuffling sound. 'Like hunting a stag whose hamstrings have been cut.'

'Please. Where's Gabe? What have you—'

'Ah, there it is. *Please*. I thought I'd hear it eventually. Was Gabe the Irishman with the soulful blue eyes?'

She nodded, knowing that he toyed with her, lengthening her anguish, but she had no power in this exchange. None at all. 'Have you . . .'

'Questions, questions. Let me ask a few of my own. Here's your first. It might be your last. Where's Leah Wilde, Hannah? Where's your daughter?'

Only the *Örökös Főnök* could instruct a *Merénylő*. Hannah knew that Catharina would never have sent this creature, which meant one of two things. Either the assassin was working on his own – unlikely – or the *tanács* had instructed him. If the latter were true, it meant Catharina had lost control of her council. Worse, it meant the *tanács* had discovered Calw's secrets, and this was their brutal response.

If the *tanács* had acted here, they would have acted in Italy too. Hannah knew they would have timed their attacks to occur simultaneously. If the *Merénylő* was asking questions about her daughter, it meant Leah must have evaded capture. It also meant that now, instead of receiving a quick death at the assassin's hands, Hannah was being recruited into the hunt. But if the creature in front of her thought she would become an accessory to that, he was deluding himself.

She felt the handle of the knife drawer pressing at her back. The *Merénylő* was still on the other side of the counter. She might just be able to yank the drawer open before he reached her. She could not hope to overcome him, but if she could find a blade quickly enough, if she could open her wrists . . .

And then Hannah realised something else: all he had to do was incapacitate her, and then he could pump his own vile blood inside her, reviving her for long enough to do as he pleased.

She shuddered. Remembered her urging from earlier: *Don't show your fear.*

With a clearer voice, she said, 'What you're asking, is a trade.'

He paused a moment, and when he spoke next, it was around a smirk. 'An unusual way of viewing it. Quite wrong, of course.'

'It's the only way you'll get what you want.'

'Again, quite wrong, Hannah. I know your story. I know what you've endured. But you've never endured *me*. Come, don't prolong this. Tell me what I need to know.'

'Is he dead? Gabe? Tell me that, at least.'

She heard him sigh. When she realised he was enjoying the cut-glass shrill of silence that followed, she felt a hatred for him so extreme that had it found physical release, he would have dropped to the floor with every bone in his body shattered.

'You know,' he continued, 'I can't quite remember what I did with poor Gabriel. Perhaps you could help me jog my memory. Perhaps we could start by talking about Leah.'

'Is he *dead*?'

Another sigh, followed by a flutter of air as he plucked the phone from her fingers. 'I'll indulge you, why not. Allow me to go and bring you what's left.'

Even though she heard nothing to mark his departure, she knew, from a subtle change in the silence, that she was now alone in the room. She heard one of the chalet doors unlocking. Heard a few muffled sounds, something heavy being dragged across the floor.

She sensed Gabriel then, caught his scent: the peculiar sharp maltiness that belonged only to him.

The tornado swirl of emotion nearly knocked her off her feet: elation, that her lover still lived; horror, at what might already have happened to him, and what she might be about to witness.

From the floor, Gabriel whispered her name. She sank to

her knees and embraced him. His flesh was cold, shockingly so. Hannah ran her hands over his face, across his cheeks. Finding his ear, she murmured into it. No words, just comforting sounds.

'You know, Hannah,' the *Merénylő* said, 'the *tanács* are terribly upset about this litter of *kirekesztett* bastards you've unleashed on the world. I've never studied the text of the *Vének Könyve,* so I couldn't comment on their justifications, but they do intend to wipe the slate clean of them.'

'They're crazy.'

'It does seem that way, doesn't it? But I want you to know that they gave me no instructions about what to with Gabriel, here. The discretion is mine. OK, here's the question, and before I ask it, let me remind you of this.' She heard two hard strikes: edged steel rapping against the formica countertop. 'You'd be surprised what a blade this sharp can do to a man. So tell me, Hannah Wilde. Where can I find Leah?'

She took a shuddering breath and thought of her daughter, out there somewhere in the world. Tightening her arms around Gabriel's body, she felt his shoulders tremble.

The two people she cared most about, and both of them beyond her protection. It was, even as she considered it, a ridiculous thought. What protection could she have hoped to offer either of them? She couldn't even protect herself any more.

Even in her grief, a thought formed. Her own life, she knew, had begun to wind down to its conclusion the moment she had entered this room.

She didn't really believe the *Merénylő*'s words about Gabriel. Despite what the assassin had said, she suspected he would take as much pleasure in ending her lover's life as he would in ending her own. But there was always a chance.

If Leah had managed to evade her pursuers, then perhaps Hannah could give this creature a snippet of information and secure Gabriel's safety without endangering her daughter's.

Decision made, she swallowed, lifted her head. 'Italy,' she

said. 'That's where she is. Villa del Osservatore, on Lake Como.'

The *Merénylő*'s fist struck her cheek, hard enough to fracture bone. Her head snapped backwards.

'I *know* she was at Villa del Osservatore, Hannah. But she's not there now, as I'm sure you've guessed. What I *want* to know is where she's going.'

He tapped the blade of his knife against the countertop, and when he spoke next, there was a hardness to his voice that had not been there before. 'Oh, this is growing tiresome. You have until the count of ten.'

Etienne stared out of the window at the passing scenery as the van rolled along the road, her body so weighted by helplessness that she felt as though she were sinking into the seat, as if the world's gravity had magnified, sucking her down.

For so many years she'd lived a life absent of emotion or companionship or love. She'd functioned as an automaton, acting out her part without feeling, lacking even the intro-spection to ask why she'd cast herself in this role, or where it all might end. It hadn't even been a lonely existence because she felt no loneliness; she felt nothing. Whereas now, she felt everything. Emotions festered in her; fear pecked like a carrion bird, guilt ripped and chewed. And, at her core, that crushing sense of hopelessness, threatening to consume everything that she'd started to become.

In the drawing room of her Mayfair town house, she'd been incapacitated by terror as the *tolvaj* approached: *crippled* by it. She'd watched, rigid, as the creature reached into her son's crib and spirited the boy away.

Etienne had never heard of a baby being taken. An infant, yes, but not a newborn: the *tolvaj* would be trapped inside its host for years until its physical body matured; the nest they'd stirred up must be desperate indeed. She wondered whether that offered Elijah any hope – whether, just possibly, he was for the *tolvajok* an insurance policy; a plan B.

Elijah.

The source of every single one of the myriad emotions that churned in her. In his few short weeks of life Elijah had swept out the lightless chambers of her heart, had filled her with a glow so intense she'd been surprised not to see it radiating from her skin – a sense of rightness with the world; a wholeness; an unbroken chain of candlelight encircling her; a crackling bonfire of red flames and heat.

And despite *all* that, she'd done nothing to save him. Jakab had held her back, admittedly, but she had not really wanted to intervene. She'd watched that abomination cradle her son to its chest, watched its eyes appraise her as its tongue flickered over its lips, triumphant. It had turned away and stalked from the room, and she had done nothing.

But what could you have done?

In the presence of a *tolvaj*, she was as powerless as any other. She had known that the instant she grasped the nature of what had walked into her house. But what clove her, what clawed and ripped and shredded and chewed, was the knowledge she had not even tried.

She found herself thinking of Hannah Wilde, the woman she had met in Italy. That was the difference, she realised, between the two of them. Hannah Wilde – even if she knew the odds of victory were precisely zero – would, at least, have tried.

Thinking of Hannah and her daughter opened a fresh wound. The two women had blessed her with a son, and she'd repaid them with treachery.

During the drive, with little else to distract him, Jakab had talked. He had told her the story of the mill fire in which he and Hannah had burned. Had told her how, as the flames of that inferno seared him, he had found a broken window and toppled into the waters of the Vézère. How he had floated, almost dead, until he'd been fished from its clutches by a group of Eleni who had not grasped the nature of their prize. And what had happened after that.

From the passenger seat, she glanced over at him. Hunched forward, hands tight on the steering wheel, eyes so red it looked as if tiny beads of blood were seeping from them, Jakab stared at the road, the expressions on his face twisting, cycling.

She had given up trying to work out his thoughts. His mind was a broken thing now, impenetrable to reason or inquiry. Her revelations back in London seemed to have tipped him over the edge. Emotions churned in him, too, just as fiercely. She saw rage compete with grief, hope compete with despair.

Outside, the wet black trunks of pine trees blurred past the window, the forest beyond as dark and threatening as those of any Grimm fairy tale.

They crested a hill, rolled down the other side. The road slung them around a curve, straightened. And there, to the left of the road, she saw it: a narrow scar in the press of trees.

Wide enough for a single vehicle to pass, the track was crowned by foliage so thick that the fading light fled from beneath it.

Etienne raised her finger. 'In there.'

Jakab nodded, pulling onto the trail. They bumped along in silence. A few minutes later he stopped the van and turned to face her. Staring with those bloodshot eyes, he said, 'I need to put you in the back.'

For one of the first times in her life – perhaps also for the last – Hannah had lost the ability to think. She could see no way out of this. No chance of redemption.

'Six,' the *Merénylő* said. His voice came from a different place each time he spoke, as if he danced back and forth inside that tiny space, restless for the violence she knew would follow. 'Seven.'

Damned either way. She accepted she was already dead. If she didn't cooperate, Gabriel would join her. Perhaps even precede her. The thought of witnessing his last moments made her so ill she thought her stomach might purge itself.

'Eight,' the *Merénylő* counted.

Even if she betrayed her daughter and gave the eunuch what he wanted, she knew he would renege on his promise; the idea that he would show Gabriel a sliver of mercy was farcical. At least it seemed Leah – either through resourcefulness or good fortune – had managed to escape.

She tried to conjure her daughter's face from times past. Images rushed at her: the night they fled to Llyn Gwyr all those years ago, Leah sleeping in the back of their 4x4; the day they rode up to Llyn Cau, Leah standing beside Gabriel and staring out across the lake; Leah, among the machinery at Le Moulin Bellerose, hollow-faced as she sent Jakab crashing to his knees.

For more than half her life, the girl had been at the core of everything Hannah thought, everything she did.

'Nine,' the *Merénylő* said.

She buried her face in the clean scent of Gabriel's hair. 'You know I love you,' she whispered.

'*Tell him nothing.*'

Speechless, she nodded.

'Ten,' the *Merénylő* said. 'Time's up. I need to know where Leah's gone, and I need to know now. One last time. Where is your daughter?'

How badly she had judged this. Only here, at the end, did she learn how little she understood the society of which she'd become a part.

Turning towards that voice, she jutted her chin, feeling the nerves in her face begin to twitch. 'Make it quick,' she said. Gritting her teeth, entombed in the darkness that had claimed her these sixteen years past, Hannah listened to the *Merénylő* hiss with excitement as he closed the gap between them.

Balázs Jakab moved through trees and ferns, over pine-needle mulch that oozed a brackish water as it sank beneath his weight. His breath plumed before him, a white smoke in the twilight.

The monstrous pain that had throbbed behind his eyes for

the last eight hours still pulsed, but in the shadows of these trees its power seemed diminished, offering him an opportunity to think with a somewhat clearer head.

He had not slept, had not eaten. His eyes were so grainy that even in the forest gloom it seemed as though insects crawled across their surfaces.

He had found them. And he did not know how to feel.

For sixteen years he had lived in a world where Hannah Wilde was dead and Leah Wilde was forever lost. Now that world had folded inwards on itself and collapsed into the cold earth, leaving him in a place that was as alien and frightening as it was wondrous.

He had found them. And he did not know how to feel. Did not know how to separate those two creatures in his mind.

Leah Wilde, as bright and as flawless as a diamond. Hannah Wilde, as cold-blooded and as poisonous as a gutter of snakes.

She had tried to kill him. He remembered it clearly. She had tried to kill them both. She had set a fire burning in their flesh, had roasted them until their skin crackled and crisped, sacrificing them to the wrath of those flames and that heat.

And for what? He wished he knew the answer.

Had she suffered as much as he? Did she remember that blistering inferno as vividly? Did she *relive* it the way he did?

All that pain. All that torment. All those years hungry for vengeance, knowing that vengeance could never be served. And now . . . *now* the world had changed and the old one was gone. In this new reality, Hannah Wilde survived – untroubled, no doubt, by any shred of remorse for how she had brutalised him.

If that alone were not enough, Leah Wilde, shining beacon of innocence and grace, thrived in a place he could almost reach out and touch. Leah had been nine years old when last he had seen her; how she must have changed in those intervening years. How she must have blossomed.

He wanted to smile – or curse – but the pain behind his eyes had renewed its attack: a glowing cattle brand pressed to his brain. He raised a hand to his face, found tears tracing wet lines down his cheeks, and stumbled from the forest into the day's dying light.

Ahead, in a clearing edged with gravel, stood the cluster of small chalets, just as Etienne had described. Jakab looked down at what he held. Tightened his grip.

What a reunion this would be.

The merest whisper of a draught as the *Merénylő* approached. Hannah could not tell from which direction he came. She felt nothing, smelled nothing, as if the room contained a vacuum that drifted steadily towards her. A faceless Death, silent and merciless.

She had promised herself she would hold onto Gabriel until the end. But she found, as another second ticked by, that she could not. Even if it was hopeless, even if all she did was prolong their pain, she could not stand here cowering and accept their fate without complaint.

Her father's voice, inside her head: *Keep fighting until you have nothing left.*

Unfurling her arms from Gabriel, transformed suddenly from the pitiable creature she had been, Hannah pressed him down towards the floor.

She spun around. Yanked open the knife drawer. Pulled out the first blade her fingers touched. Lucky choice. A heavy-handled carving knife. It wouldn't save them. But at least she'd die fighting.

Whirling back towards where she guessed the *Merénylő* lurked, she slashed out with the blade and met empty space, her arm swinging so violently it almost pulled free of its socket.

The *Merénylő* chuckled. The sound came from the right. She slashed again. Missed.

Another laugh. To her left this time? She bared her teeth, daring the darkness to attack. Angry now. Furious.

'If we're going to play that game,' the *Merénylő* said, 'then I believe it's my turn.'

A whisper of air as his blade carved a searing line across her face. It was a deep cut, opening her cheeks, parting the soft flesh beneath her nose. A muscle below her eye went crazy, grabbing and releasing, tearing the skin even deeper. Blood gushed from the wound. She felt a sickening pain, dizzying and brutal.

Hannah lunged forward and stabbed with the knife, heard the *Merénylő's* high-pitched cackle, felt the air part again, felt his knife gouge another channel across her face.

She cried out, screaming her anger, driving on her attack yet finding no target for her thrusts, and then – *then* – she heard, or thought she heard, a sound from far beyond her, outside the circle of space she knew the *Merénylő* must inhabit.

It came again, and she imagined he must hear it too, because the air moved once more, a breath of cold against the shuddering agony in her face. This time it was further away, as if her attacker had turned, and now she heard something strange, a wet sound, a *plummeting* sound, like an evisceration, an outpouring, and while she hadn't heard a second voice announce its arrival she heard the violence that it brought, a meat-like ripping. Someone fell against her. She probed with her spare hand, felt the *Merénylő*, knew it must be him from his lack, even this close, of any identifying scent.

Hannah plunged the knife into him. It entered his flesh with the softest of resistance, as if despite his calling his body comprised more of fat than muscle. She screamed again, cursing him, stabbing and cutting, driving the blade in and out, until he toppled away from her and she couldn't use her knife any more, couldn't use it in case she hit Gabriel by mistake.

Whatever had arrived to save her had not spoken, had not announced itself with anything except the silent killing it brought.

But now it did. And when it spoke, it opened a window in Hannah, opened a grave.

'Hannah,' it said, and its voice trembled with emotion.

Its voice.

Jakab's voice.

Her grip loosened on the knife. She heard it clatter to the floor.

She swayed, untethered. Felt the blood pouring from her butchered face.

Moaning, incredulous, she thrust her hands out in front of her, fingers splayed. She twisted left and right, felt the blood flying from her ruptured cheeks, heard it patter onto the linoleum floor like a sudden squall of rain.

It can't be. But it is.

He's dead. But he's here.

He's back.

CHAPTER 38

Lake Como, Italy

Enveloped in mist so thick she could barely see the surface of the lake, Leah ended the call with her mother and loosened her grip on the outboard's throttle. The boat's prow settled in the water and she canted her head to one side, listening intently for the sound of engines that would indicate either a pursuit or an approaching disaster in the form of another innocent vessel.

The faces of the children pointed towards her, searching her expression for signs that the danger was over. She wished she could offer them that.

At the front of the boat, Soraya still cradled one-year-old Elias. 'Call Luca,' she said. 'It's the only place we can go.'

Leah nodded. She dialled his number, and when it began to ring she twisted the throttle, planting her feet as the boat once again picked up speed.

He answered on the first ring. 'Leah.'

'I don't have much time. We need help.'

'Tell me.'

She swallowed, perilously close to crying. Refused to show her desperation to the young faces that studied her. 'The *tanács*. We were ambushed, Luca. The *Főnök* is dead. Others, too.'

'Where are you?'

'You don't need to know. But I have the children with me. They need protection.'

'Then bring them. Do you have transport?'

'Not yet,' she replied. 'I'm working on it.'

'How far away are you?'

'Not far. A few hours.'

'Leah—'

'It's OK. Soraya's with me.'

An expelled breath. 'Is she hurt?'

'No. She's fine.'

'You saved her.'

'We saved each other. I've got to go.'

Leah stuffed the phone into her pocket. Ahead, she saw a gap in the mist. She increased their speed and there, through a sliding curtain of grey, she recognised the stone-walled harbour of Menaggio.

The moment their boat bumped up against the dock, Leah jumped out and tied up.

On the lake, the mist seemed to be thinning. Not good news. Menaggio was one of the nearest towns to Villa del Osservatore; the *tanács* would almost certainly send one of their boats here.

'I'm going to find transport,' she told Soraya. 'If I'm not back in two minutes, get them out.'

Leah ran along the top of the harbour wall, eyes scanning the town's small square. Even this late in the season, tourists swarmed like bees: holidaying couples, families with pushchairs, coach parties following tour guides.

In the square itself, a car rally seemed to be in full flow. She saw polished rows of Volkswagen Beetles, Campers and Karmann Ghias. Leah slid into the crowd, allowing herself to be carried along towards the mass of enthusiasts chatting, laughing and drinking coffee as they hovered around their vehicles.

In a bay closest to this corner of the square, she saw an old split-screen VW bus. Wearing British plates, it sat low to the ground on polished chrome alloys. The driver's door was open.

A man in his fifties sat behind the wheel, nursing a Styrofoam cup of tea. His ears were pierced with rows of silver rings, and a cluster of feathered pendants hung from leather cords around his neck. Eyes closed, his lips moved in silent accompaniment to the music playing on the bus's stereo.

Leah studied his face as she drew closer, and then she crouched down beside the vehicle, head bowed.

A long time since she'd done this. And always, before, in privacy and with the luxury of time. She concentrated, drowned out the sounds of the square, and waited for the pain to hit.

A minute later, face smarting as if she'd been punched, she rose to her feet, leaned into the van and shook the driver by his shoulder.

His eyes snapped open, and when he saw her face his jaw dropped and he poured the cup of tea into his lap. Blanching, he groped for words, finding none to help him.

'I need your van,' she said, although it didn't sound like her voice.

He stared down into his lap at the spilled tea. When he found her eyes again he lurched upright, almost as if he were having a heart attack. He slid away from her onto the passenger seat. 'Which . . . which year?' he asked. When she didn't reply, he swallowed, adding, 'You don't look any older, so that's a clue. Aren't we meant to – I don't know – avoid each other?'

Leah stared at him, uncomprehending. And then she thought she understood. 'You're probably right,' she replied. 'I don't have time to explain, but you need to leave. Now.'

He scrambled out. 'Should I say the same thing? Next time?'

Leah slid behind the wheel of the bus, turned the key, heard its air-cooled engine splutter to life. 'Yeah, you definitely should.'

The man nodded. Something seemed to occur to him. 'Don't forget about the clutch,' he told her. 'It sticks, remember?'

Waving an acknowledgement, Leah edged the camper van out of the square and nosed through the throng of tourists to the harbour edge where she'd tied the boat.

When she saw Soraya, she sounded the horn and waved.

CHAPTER 39

Lake Como, Italy

Izsák tracked the white Porsche Cayenne as he followed, two cars behind, the winding street clinging to Lake Como's shore. He passed roadside trattorias squeezed between balconied apartment buildings, campaniles, high-sided walls with railed steps.

Ahead the road squeezed into a single lane, and Izsák resisted the temptation to sound his horn at the mopeds and delivery trucks cutting their way towards him.

The Cayenne began to climb as the route took them higher, curving up towards a wooded peninsula thrusting out into Como's waters.

Abruptly the road widened into two lanes, leaving the clustered buildings behind. Izsák wound through a grove of cypresses, and as he neared the hump of the peninsula he saw a tall stone-built wall begin to flank the roadside nearest the lake. Now three cars in front, the Cayenne slowed as it approached a crenellated gatehouse built into the wall. It turned in, sweeping between tall iron gates.

Izsák glanced through the gatehouse as he passed. A grand drive terminated at the entrance to a huge villa complex perched upon the rock, replete with covered walkways, arched bridges and terraces that stepped down all the way to the water's edge.

Villa del Osservatore.

He recognised it immediately, passing the entrance without

slowing. A hundred yards further on, the villa's twelve-foot perimeter wall receded from the road. Checking behind him, Izsák pulled his car over, scrubby plants snapping beneath the tyres. He stopped directly beside the wall and switched off the engine.

His vehicle wasn't hidden here, but he wasn't too concerned about that – if all went to plan, he'd be revealing himself soon enough. He grabbed a rifle case from the passenger seat and climbed out. Ducking down beside the car, he studied the top of the wall for cameras or motion-detecting equipment. He saw none.

Moving fast, he tossed the rifle case over, listening to it thump to the ground on the other side. After waiting for another pause in traffic, he clambered onto the roof of his car and leaped, grabbing the top of the wall and dragging himself over.

He landed in raked topsoil and threw himself flat. The rifle case lay a few yards away. Izsák crawled over to it and removed the weapon from inside. He snapped back its bolt and raised the scope to his eyes.

No one stood outside the villa. No guards patrolled its grounds. Outside the main entrance sat a cluster of three Range Rovers. Behind them, the Cayenne. Its engine was still running, but Izsák could not see its interior through the car's tinted windows.

Rising to a crouch, he crept towards the thin line of trees screening him from the villa's windows.

Off to his right, a flock of birds burst into the sky. Izsák turned in time to see another vehicle pass through the gates, this one a black van. It rolled along the drive, gravel popping from its tyres, and pulled up behind the Cayenne. Its engine died.

Izsák reached the tree nearest to the lawn and put his back against it. He took two breaths to calm himself, turned and dropped to one knee, lifting up the rifle scope.

The van's door opened and a figure stepped out. When he

saw who it was, the air punched from his lungs as if he had been struck. Izsák slid onto his backside, the rifle falling to the ground.

It was her.

It was Georgia.

Even though he hadn't seen his daughter since the day he'd driven into Dawson City to pick up her birthday present, even though scores of winters and summers had come and gone since, his heart told him what his eyes saw, and then it broke in two inside his chest.

Her eyes were the same seaweed green. Her hair, even in the misty half-light of Como's late afternoon, shone with captured sunlight. The baby fat had melted from her face in the intervening years, and in her fine bone structure and wide mouth he saw Lucy, his dead wife, and the sight brokered a pain in him that bent him double in the soft earth.

It isn't her, you fool. Even if Georgia is in there somewhere, she's been locked up alone for over eighty years. She's a memory, now. You know it.

He shook his head, gasping. Curled his lip and bared his teeth. Tensed himself against the pain that flickered, snake-like, through his guts.

Don't think about what you lost. Don't think about what's gone. You grieved for Lucy and Georgia both. Decades of grief. Do what you came here to do. Set her free.

Panting, he crawled back to his rifle. Its barrel was slick with moisture from the ground on which it lay. He picked it up, heard the breath rasping in his throat, saw it misting in front of him. He closed his mouth. Raised the scope to his eyes. Saw her again. Saw her blur in front of him.

Biting back his frustration, Izsák lowered the rifle. Scoured the tears from his eyes. Lifted the weapon a third time.

All those years, searching. All for this. He'd hunted *lélek tolvajok* across oceans and mountains, in locked warehouses and remote farmsteads.

He'd found a few. A nest, once, in the foothills of the Pyrenees. Another, deep in the uninhabited heart of the Białowieża Forest, on the border of Poland and Belarus. He'd destroyed them both, nearly lost his life on each occasion. But he'd never found the *right* nest, never found Georgia. And now, so close that he could be at her side in under a minute should he choose, here she was.

He squinted down the scope. Placed her head between its crosshairs.

While he'd spent all those years searching, only ever with the intention of ending her life, he hadn't expected that day to be this one.

Georgia gazed back along the drive to the gatehouse by the road. Sweeping it with her seaweed eyes, she turned and stared directly down the scope of his rifle, directly into his soul.

It was an illusion, of course; there was no way she could see him clearly from where she stood. But illusion or not, he felt his throat constricting in pride and in heartbreak at the beautiful shell his daughter had left behind.

His finger tightened on the trigger. He took a single breath. Emptied his lungs. Said goodbye.

A noise made him hesitate. A car door opening.

He lifted his eye from the scope, blinked, and saw the door of the Cayenne swing wide. A second *tolvaj* emerged from it, and Izsák could tell from its sunken eyes and hanging skin that the demise of this one's host was near.

The creature was dressed outlandishly, clad in three-piece tweed and polished Oxford shoes. A yellow cravat was tied at its throat. Its hair – wormy dreadlocks, matted with grease and trailing down its spine – was crowned by a fedora decorated with a single jay feather. In one hand it clutched a cane of smooth black wood, topped by a flared python head.

Its strange outfit, signature, perhaps, of just how long this specimen had stalked the earth, spooled from Izsák a horror so absolute he almost turned and fled. In all his years he had not seen one as ancient as this, so obviously belonging to a world far older than his own.

It swept the villa's grounds with eyes like focused swabs of darkness, and when Izsák felt its gaze pass over him he cringed away.

Holding its cane before it, the *tolvaj* limped towards Georgia, mouth open, crusted tongue poking from its lips like a segment of fire-blackened steak.

Izsák braced himself, hand slippery on the rifle's barrel, finger trembling against the trigger.

Don't let her down. Don't abandon her. Do it now. Pull the trigger. NOW.

His smell preceded him as he approached, that wet-rot stink of corruption that signalled the end was coming. Ignoring it, closing her nose to its foulness, she went to him. When she kissed his mouth, she tasted blood and swallowed it. 'Oh, my darling,' she said. 'Not you, too. We have to get you inside. Let me lead.'

He stiffened at her words, drawing himself taller. He did not like to be pitied.

'No need,' he replied, voice like birch twigs. '*No need . . . need.*' He caught the whispery repetition of his words, the slurring, and his expression darkened further, angered by that betrayal of his condition. His tongue whipped out, and when it licked his lips it left a dark smear. 'Are they here?'

She nodded. 'We don't have long. The journey's exhausted them. I need to go inside, make sure that—'

With a wave of his hand he dismissed her. She watched him move around to the rear of the van, his cane scraping on the gravel, and then she turned towards the villa, where salvation waited.

Ivan Tóth sat at the head of the table in the villa's banqueting room and surveyed the gathered *tanács* around him.

If only Joó, or someone else, had kept them out of the library, had spared them the sight of Catharina's blood-drenched corpse. They appeared visibly shaken by what they had seen.

No coup had ever been achieved without bloodshed, and no undertaking such as this ever went strictly to plan. But the scene that had greeted the *tanács* had been so visceral, so shocking, it had stained their consciences and destroyed their resolve.

Worse, the story that dreadful tableau had told was clear: the *Főnök* had faced unassailable odds and, instead of cringing away from her fate, she had faced it with bravery and stoicism, even managing to kill her attackers before succumbing to her wounds.

With so many witnesses, word would inevitably leak out. It was the kind of last stand from which legends were built. And Tóth knew that unless he walked a very careful path, history would judge his own part in this poorly.

On the far wall, a portrait of Catharina seemed to watch him. Tóth had sat at this end of the table deliberately; he had not wanted the less stalwart members of his council to labour under those reproachful eyes.

He might not have control of this situation, but the *illusion* of control was more pressing than its reality. 'Gentlemen, we have some decisions to make. And quickly. First we need to appoint a new head of the *Belső Őr*. I've placed Makovecz in temporary control. I'd like your thoughts.'

'It's an obvious solution,' Horváth replied, eyes cold. 'And one that hardly merits our time. What's the situation in Calw?'

'I expect an update from Calw shortly,' he replied, ignoring the man's tone.

'And Leah Wilde? Where is she?'

'We'll have her very soon. And then we can announce what we've achieved today, before—'

'What we've achieved?' Horváth shook his head. 'We haven't achieved anything. *You've* achieved chaos and slaughter. Little else.'

'We *voted* on this!' he shouted, furious at the man's accusations.

'With guns to our heads, we voted,' Horváth spat. 'Is that the kind of legitimacy we can expect from now on?'

Tóth's hands tightened into fists. With effort, he relaxed them. And then his phone started ringing. He cancelled the call. More bad news, he suspected. He wouldn't receive it in front of these increasingly hostile eyes.

The illusion of control.

Standing, he nodded at Joó to take command, marched to the banqueting room's doors and slammed through them.

The hallway was deserted. Ignoring the debris littering the library entrance, Tóth passed the staircase. He found the newly appointed head of his *Belső Őr* at the bottom.

Makovecz lay face down, mouth stretched into a silent scream, jaw hinged so wide that his teeth pressed against the marble. There was no blood. He appeared to have suffered no penetrating wound, no violence to his body.

'He's not dead,' said a woman's voice.

Tóth didn't need to look up. The warmth poured from his body as suddenly as if someone had pulled a plug.

When he raised his head, he saw staring back at him a set of green eyes that were as beautiful as they were terrifying.

Hosszú élet eyes, and yet not.

'He won't be quite the same, when he wakes,' she continued. 'But he'll live on, in his own way. You're Ivan Tóth.'

'I am.' His voice cracked as he confirmed it. He caught himself about to take a backwards step. It took every ounce of will to plant his feet. 'You're early. I wasn't expecting you until—'

'If anything, we're late. Where are the children?'

He swallowed.

It would have been such an elegant solution. All their crises resolved in a single act. But Leah Wilde had spirited the *kirekesztett* infants away, and the man he'd been relying upon to destroy this last nest of *tolvajok* was lying dead in the villa's library with a *déjnin* blade lodged inside his head.

The illusion of control.

He wanted to shield himself from her eyes, but such was their power that he floundered in front of them. 'We're rounding them up as I speak. I'll have—'

The woman cocked her head to one side. 'You're lying,' she said, as if his duplicity bothered her not at all; as if she made a simple observation, with no consequences. She strode over to him, extended a hand to his face and then, and *then* –

– *billowing wind in his head, a tearing, a stretching, a loosening, an opening. Doors slamming, shutters dropping. Monstrous, monstrous pain.*

He couldn't do it. Not here. Not like this.

Izsák lifted his cheek from the rifle. He wiped sweat from his eyes. Refocused. Outside the entrance to Villa del Osservatore, Georgia – or the thing riding Georgia's bones – kissed the *tolvaj* that had emerged from the Cayenne. Then she walked towards the house.

Eye pressed to the scope, Izsák tracked her. One shot, that was all he needed. From here he had no chance of missing. The back of Georgia's skull would erupt like a volcano, scattering blood and brain as if it were lava and ash, ending her suffering in a single, violent instant.

But to be this far away from her, to let her die like that without even seeing him . . . Izsák did not know if it were cowardice or genuine feeling, but he could not end her life that way.

I will. Just not like that. I will.

He watched his daughter disappear through the villa's front entrance, wondering if he told himself a lie. He felt the strength draining from him. The rifle seemed as heavy as lead, tugging his arms towards the ground.

He shook his head, tried to clear his thoughts. Switching his attention to the *tolvaj* that remained outside, he watched it limp towards the back of the black van in which Georgia had arrived. It paused outside the rear doors. One hand still gripping the cane, it opened them.

Izsák saw the vehicle rock on its springs, as if something moved within.

They climbed out – first one, then a second, then a third, until four ungodly horrors stood on the gravel, so decrepit and bleached of colour he could not tell whether they'd once been male or female. The creature with the wormy hair and the blood-stained lips kissed each of their foreheads in turn. Together, they shambled towards the house.

Izsák watched them go inside. He thought of Lucy, his wife, remembered how they'd danced in the Ready Eat as jazz played on the radio, remembered their lovemaking at the cabin he had built in the Yukon. He thought of her eyes the day she had glimpsed the illustration inside the Eaton catalogue of the bright red bicycle with its shining silver bell. He thought of how she had beseeched him, as she died on the cold floor of their bedroom: *Find her. Find Georgia.*

And Izsák *had* found her. He'd never given up.

Now, at the last, he could not back away from this. If his conscience refused to let him set Georgia free while he sheltered so far away, then he would do it up close instead.

Something else occurred to him, here, at the end. He found himself recalling the question that had troubled him so often as a boy: *What will happen to me?*

So many years since that poisonous thought had sprung into his mind. He knew he would never consider it again. Perhaps that was something for which he could be grateful.

Pulling himself to his feet, slinging his rifle over his shoulder, Izsák left the cover of the trees and walked towards the villa.

Horváth stared across the table at Krištof Joó, knowing that the man had damned himself, wondering if he had damned them all.

Joó's face was an oasis of calm: almost beatific, as if he had seen something wondrous in the violence visited upon the residents of Villa del Osservatore. It terrified him, that look.

'Have faith,' Joó said, and when Horváth realised the man addressed him he flinched in his seat.

'That's all we *can* have now.'

'You sanctioned this. Don't forget that.'

'I didn't sanction slaughter. None of us did.'

'You thought we'd achieve this without bloodshed?'

Horváth heard a sound in the hallway behind him. The remaining five members of the *tanács* turned their heads to the door. He heard them gasp, heard their chair legs scrape.

He swivelled in his chair. Saw, standing in the doorway, a young woman who was not really a woman at all. Her eyes were *hosszú élet* and yet not, pupils receding into a darkness so absolute they sucked the marrow from his bones. He saw death waiting in her face; both his own, and that of everyone who shared this table.

A bluebottle looped into the room, its body so swollen that its wings struggled to keep it aloft. It circled the table, dipping and rising, arcing towards the mullioned windows where it battered itself against the glass.

Now, a stench of rotting meat, so thick and sweet it adhered like glue to the back of Horváth's throat. Following on the heels of it, a creature from the earliest pages of *hosszú életek* history, something he had believed the world had lost forever.

He gagged.

Even hunched over its cane, the *tolvaj* reached almost to the height of the door. The flesh of its face, hanging from the bone in weeping folds, was bloated and ripe, eager to burst from the slightest of pressure. One patch, below its left cheek, had discoloured to the brown of rotting apples. Clotted blood clung to its chin.

It moved towards the table, cane clicking on the parquet floor, and Horváth saw that it led a larger group of shuffling *tolvajok* horrors. Their hosts appeared on the brink of death: baggy skin, toothless mouths, eyes like pouches of veined cheese.

Horváth closed his eyes, but he couldn't close his ears.

'Gentlemen,' the woman announced. 'We need you.'

Izsák sprinted to the black van and pressed his back against it. The villa's huge front door, into which Georgia and the rest of the *tolvajok* had disappeared, hung open and waiting. Perhaps forty windows looked onto the drive from this side of the building. Their panes were blank and dark.

Dropping to a crouch, he slid along the side of the van and paused beside a wheel arch. The Porsche Cayenne, parked ten yards closer to the building, offered him the next chance of cover. Beyond that, the line of black Range Rovers, and from there, the villa's entrance.

He checked the rifle's strap was tight against his shoulder. Surveying the grounds, he saw no movement to concern him.

In a running crouch, he closed the distance to the Cayenne and ducked down behind it. Sliding along its length, he paused when he heard the sound of a baby's cries.

They came from inside the 4x4.

Izsák frowned, tried to block them out. He crept to the front of the vehicle and glanced out at the windows of the villa. Nothing moved.

As if sensing his closeness, the baby's cries grew louder, more insistent. Izsák checked his weapon, tried to concentrate.

What was a baby doing in the car? He could think of only one reason, and it chilled his blood. Still he tried to ignore it, directing his thoughts to Georgia, to the creature that had taken her.

He was here for a single purpose. He didn't have time for distractions.

Lucy's face bloomed in his mind, and Izsák felt, for the first time in years, as if she watched him.

Clenching his jaw in frustration, he backtracked two paces

until he was beside the Cayenne's door. He swung it open just enough to allow him to lean inside.

Strapped into a car seat, face red with the exertion of crying, was a baby boy perhaps a few weeks old. Too young to serve as a *tolvaj* host, he'd been stolen even so. Izsák had never seen him before, but he recognised those eyes and knew who he must be.

Elijah, Etienne's child.

He closed his eyes. Shook his head.

No. He wasn't getting into this. He could come back later. Once he had found Georgia and ended her pain.

You might be dead later. And if you're dead, you know what this child's fate will be.

He did. It would be Georgia's fate.

Lucy's face appeared behind his eyes, silently pleading.

Izsák swore. He glanced through the Cayenne's windscreen at the villa. Swore again, louder this time. Turned back, examining the car seat.

It sat on a moulded plastic base, fixed to retaining bars recessed into the vehicle's back seat. He moved his hands over it, found a handle. Pulled. The baby seat popped free with a clunk, and Izsák lifted it out of the car. He shut the Cayenne's door. Checked the house again.

At his feet, Elijah watched him in silence, his cries forgotten.

At the dining table in Villa del Osservatore's conference room, Horváth had arrived at a place so beyond fear that its physical effects no longer seemed to trouble him.

He stared at Oliver Lebeau, opposite, the only other member of the *tanács* not to have been taken by a *tolvaj*.

Oliver had retreated somewhere deep. He stared, eyes unfocused, chest rising and falling in slow, measured breaths.

Joó remained at the top of the table, but it wasn't really Joó. Not any more. The light of fanaticism had faded from the man's eyes, replaced by a look of . . . what was that, exactly?

Around the table, the parquet floor resembled the aftermath

of a battle fought in hell. Four bodies lay in twisted heaps, fingers clawed, backs arched. At least they had stopped moaning. Three of them had died already, relinquishing their grip on life moments after the *tolvajok* discarded them. Only one held on. Eyes closed, limbs drawn up against its body, its jaw worked soundlessly, chin scraping across the floor.

He saw commotion by the door. The woman was back. She carried a leather-bound book, or perhaps it was a diary; her thumb held its pages open and, rather than printed text, Horváth thought he saw handwriting.

The *tolvaj* with the weeping face and the wormy strangle of hair stood by the window, hunched over its cane. Apart from the woman, it was the only one not to have taken a new host.

She moved to its side, and Horváth saw she was smiling. 'I think,' she said, 'I know where they've gone.'

CHAPTER 40

Calw, Germany

In the chalet's kitchenette, Jakab stood opposite Hannah Wilde and felt the floor beneath him shift, as if this tiny dwelling had cast off its mooring ropes and rose on a cresting wave of memories and pain.

It broke over him, a frothing, churning sea of images and sound, so vivid he had to close his eyes against it and hold his breath. Faces long dead; words spoken and heard; professions of love and regret and hate; episodes of intimacy as painful to recall as those characterised by violence.

And now, a final image: Hannah Wilde, inside the watermill at Le Moulin Bellerose, trapped in the machinery's teeth and crying out her daughter's name.

Even then she hadn't surrendered to him, striking a match and casting them into flames instead.

His body might have healed, but he had not survived that inferno untouched. When he recalled how once he'd had such conviction, such purpose, such *strength*, it made him weep. She had stolen all of that – had burned it from him as if she had cauterised a wound.

All this time she'd been alive. All this time he'd lived in ignorance of the reality that he shared this world with her still. And now here she was, and here he was, as if fate had conspired to pitch them together one last time.

It was difficult to look at her for long, but he forced himself, and saw, even through the mask of blood she wore, that he wasn't the only one changed by the events of that day. Etienne had told him how the fire had blinded Hannah, and in a way that was another thing she'd stolen from him: he would never even see in her eyes the awareness of his vengeance.

'Why?' he asked, listening to his voice, ensuring that it did not crack or hitch and reveal the emotions that boiled in him. 'Why did you submit us to that?'

Hannah wiped away the blood the *Merénylő* had unleashed from her face. Beneath, the flow had already stopped. The sides of her wounds were puckered and angry, but closed. She dropped to her knees, embracing the man slumped on the floor.

'You would have killed her,' she whispered.

Jakab's mouth dropped open. 'Leah?' he asked. 'I would have *loved* her.'

'It would have ended just the same.'

So far he had managed to hold his fury in check, but when he heard those words it *exploded* in him, and it took all his willpower not to lunge forward and rip the life from her right now, right here, before she could wound him with any more of her poison.

How *dare* she accuse him of that? How *dare* she tell *him* what might have been, if not for her interference that day?

He started to approach, saw that she tensed her shoulders in readiness for his wrath, trying to keep herself between him and the man she held.

The sight of her, so wretched like this, made him tremble not with the thrill of victory but with a tooth-cracking rage. This was not the Hannah Wilde of old. Killing this pitiable creature would be an act not just of vengeance but mercy.

From somewhere in the kitchenette a phone began to ring. He tried to ignore it, but when it continued to trill at him he looked away from her and noticed it lying on the countertop.

Jakab picked it up. He saw the name flashing on its screen and felt a lifting in his stomach, a lightness.

He glanced back at Hannah. Perhaps *this* was the reason fate had thrown them back together. Even though his memories of her, all these years later, were startlingly bright in his mind, he had forgotten the exact cadence of her voice, its weight. Now he would use it to his advantage.

Backing out into the hall, ready to cover the mouthpiece should she cry out a warning, he answered the call. In a perfect imitation of Hannah Wilde's tone, he spoke the name of the girl he thought he'd lost forever.

'Listen carefully,' Leah said, and when he heard her, heard her maturity and her strength, he felt as insubstantial as a feather. 'You don't have much time,' the girl continued. 'The *tanács* – they found out. I'm so sorry. They found out, and it's all my fault.'

Her voice broke, and Jakab found himself offering soothing sounds, a language without words. Just as well. In the space of seconds his world had fractured anew. He needed time to recover.

'I'm OK,' Leah said. 'I have the children and they're fine, I'm fine. But they'll be coming for you soon. You need to get out, right now. Find Gabe and run.'

'Where to?' he asked. 'Where are you going?'

'I'll give you the address,' she said. And she told him. 'I might be out of touch for a while, but I'll see you soon. Go. Don't wait. They might already be there.'

Jakab breathed, composed himself. 'I love you.'

'I love you too,' Leah replied, and then she was gone.

He pocketed the phone. Her words might have been meant for another, but they had the quality of sunlight nonetheless. He went back into the kitchenette, found Hannah. 'Get up.'

She rose to her feet, helping Gabriel to stand. 'Where are you taking us?'

'To a reunion,' he said. And, because he wanted to scare her, he pressed the tip of his knife to her neck.

The pain behind his eyes was back. Somewhere inside it, dark thoughts were beginning to flower.

★ ★ ★

The road led them from Menaggio to the town of Porlezza on the shore of neighbouring Lake Lugano, and from there Leah followed it to the border where they crossed into Switzerland.

The sun, as it began to set, was a glorious ball of fire in the heavens, as if it knew that tonight would bring an end for some, and wanted to mark their passing with a final display.

The old VW bus, its engine chugging steadily, lifted them over the first humps of the southern Alps, eating up a winding grey strip of road. They encountered the first snow, patchy at first, thickening until it lay unbroken across the landscape, a field of crystals blushed mauve by the sun's last rays.

Leah noticed her breath beginning to mist and turned on the van's heaters, grateful for the warm air that began to huff from their grilles. Behind her, the children sat in silence, squeezed on to the VW's bench seats and clustered on the floor.

Beside Leah, Soraya stared out of the window, clutching Elias on her lap. 'I can't stop thinking about her.'

'Flóra?'

The woman nodded. 'I don't know how she did that. I don't know how she handed over her child without any thought for herself.'

Leah thought of her mother, how time and again Hannah had placed herself in danger to protect her family, and thought she knew.

'Do you think she's alive?' Soraya asked. 'Do you think any of them are?'

The question had consumed Leah ever since she'd spoken to her mother to warn her of what was coming. What would the *tanács* do to those who remained? 'There's nothing to be gained from their deaths,' she said.

But it wasn't really an answer.

'What about Catharina?'

'It was a coup, Soraya.'

Leah intended to say more, intended to try and offer some

kind of reassurance, but the words were trapped in her throat. She knew enough *hosszú életek* history to understand that Catharina's future looked bleak.

To the west, the last red sliver of sun disappeared behind a mountain peak, and when the glitter sheen on the snow winked out, like a million tiny eyes closing at once, Leah felt a coldness steal over her that the van's heaters could not displace, as if the dying of the light augured horrors from which there could be no reprieve.

From the alcove beneath the dashboard, her phone began to trill. She scooped it up.

Odd, but even before she glanced down at the name that glowed on its screen, she knew who it would be. Returning her eyes to the road, she activated the phone and crooked it into her shoulder.

'It's me,' he said, and then he paused. 'You're driving.'

'Yes.'

'Good. Are you alone?'

'No.'

The line crackled and chirruped, and for a moment she thought she'd lost him. Twelve months had rolled by since Balázs Izsák had saved her life at Llyn Gwyr. Twelve months since she had discovered their connection: that not only was he the brother of the man who had brought her so much loss, but also her relative. An uncle, of sorts. Blood.

At first, it had been a revelation too overwhelming to process. She hadn't been able to tell anyone. Not the *Fönök*, and certainly not her mother. It wasn't that she wanted to keep Izsák a secret. She simply hadn't worked out how to talk about him in a way she thought anyone would understand.

Although Leah hadn't seen him since, they had spoken on the phone, each conversation stretching longer than the last. As much silence had filled those early calls as words, but gradually she had come to know him. And she could tell now, from the strain in his voice, that something momentous had happened.

Then it struck her. 'You found her,' she breathed. 'You found your daughter.'

'Yes.'

'Did you . . .'

'No. Not yet, but I will.' He paused. 'They had a baby with them, Leah. I think it's Etienne's son.'

'Elijah?' Leah's stomach plummeted away. 'Where is he now?'

'Right beside me.'

'And Etienne?'

'Just what I was about to ask you.'

CHAPTER 41

Interlaken, Switzerland

By the time they reached the private road serving A Kutya Herceg's home, the skies over the Alps had darkened to indigo and the moon was up, companion to a smattering of stars. Leah saw the jagged silhouettes of the Jungfrau, the Mönch and the Eiger. Where snow gathered on their gentler slopes it glowed in the lunar light, but their steeper faces were so dark they looked like shapes snipped from black felt.

Except for two channels of crushed ice where a few other vehicles had made the ascent, a foot of snow covered the tarmac. Pine forest pressed close on either side, so still it seemed to be holding its breath.

Leah flicked on the vehicle's full beams, illuminating a ribbon of snow curving up through the darkness. She didn't want to lose traction on the slippery surface, but if they were to have any chance of climbing the slope, they needed as much speed as they could get. 'Hold on, guys.' Dropping down a gear, she pressed her foot harder to the floor. The old bus surged forward, engine blatting. Soraya planted a hand on the dash, bracing herself in her seat. Leah coaxed more speed from the vehicle, feeling it seesaw as it bounced around inside the tracks carved into the snow.

A few more seconds and they broke free into open white space. The road arced up and to the right, and there in the distance she saw, clinging to the mountainside, A Kutya

Herceg's sprawling chalet home. The building blazed with light, as pretty as a Christmas village. Smoke chugged from its chimneys, feathering away into the sky.

Soraya looked behind her and for the first time, as she regarded their young passengers, she smiled. 'We're here,' she told them. 'You're safe.'

It was far too early to promise any such thing, but Leah kept her mouth closed, concentrating on the road. The engine was making a tortured rattling sound now, as if a bucketload of washers had been tipped inside.

Just as they came out of the turn, the rear wheels lost traction and the van began to slide. Leah compensated, turning into the skid, but the steering felt loose in her hands. Teeth clenched, she felt the wheels thump into a bank of frozen earth. The front end bounced up and then it crunched down. With a shudder, the engine died.

'Sorry folks.' Leah glanced behind her. 'Everyone OK?'

A series of startled nods.

She peered into her wing mirrors. Darkness behind her, as oppressive as a grave. A few hundred yards up ahead, the carnival of lights streaming from the chalet's windows.

With the engine dead, the silence around them was absolute. No breath of wind stirred the snow-laden trees. No animals hooted or cried.

Already the air inside the cab was beginning to cool. Leah turned the key in the ignition. She saw the headlights dim as the battery fed power to the starter motor, heard the pistons kick sluggishly. But the engine wouldn't turn over. She tried it a handful of times before conceding that the old bus had carried them as far as it could.

She forced a grin. 'Looks like we're walking.' Pulling off her fleece, she handed it to Emánuel, of all the children the most lightly dressed. 'Here. Put this on.' Beside her, Soraya unbuttoned her cardigan and swaddled Elias in it.

'It's going to be cold outside, but you'll be warm soon,'

Leah told them. 'I'll go first, and I want you to follow closely, holding hands, just like we did before.'

She cranked open the door and jumped down into snow up to her knees. The frozen air hit her like a slap in the face. Wading to the VW's side door, she rolled it open, feeling the vehicle's warmth spiral out into the night.

Already, her fingers were beginning to numb.

'Quickly,' she said, helping the children climb out. They'd been silent until now, but the frigid mountain darkness was an unsettling change from the snugness of the VW's interior. The two six-year-olds, Carina and Philipp, began to cry. 'I know it's cold,' she told them, 'but see that big bright house over there? That's where we're going, and I'm sure they'll have warm milk, all sorts of nice things. We do need to hurry, though. Come on, everyone walk in my footprints.'

Breath steaming from her mouth, Soraya appeared from the other side of the van, cradling Elias.

'OK?' Leah asked. The woman nodded, cheeks burning red.

Leah pushed through the snow, clearing a path for those who followed. Her teeth ached with cold. As her eyes began to water, the chalet fractured into a thousand twinkling lights.

Underbellies lit by the moon reflecting off the snow, moving like oceans liners on a dark sea, the first few wisps of cloud had appeared, emissaries of a much larger pack sailing in from the east.

Most of the children were crying softly now, an eerie sound in the stillness, like the distant baying of wolves. They'd covered perhaps a quarter of the distance to the chalet, and already Leah had lost the feeling in her hands and feet.

She saw, from up in front, the swabbing beam of a torch. It swung left and right, and then it picked her out. The light wobbled and stuttered, and Leah realised that whoever operated it was moving towards them. She narrowed her eyes against its glare; all she could see behind it was an impenetrable wall of darkness. But as the light closed on her she gradually distinguished a figure, large and cumbersome. Gouts of breath snaked from its mouth. She heard breathing, rattling and loose, from lungs unused to exertion.

Finally, a voice. 'I knew, from the moment I met you, that this would end in blood. You visit horrors on my home, Leah Wilde.'

A Kutya Herceg closed the last few yards to her, the torch beam's reflections picking out the shining points of his eyes.

'Hello, Ágoston,' she said.

He was dressed in furs so expansive that his body seemed lost within them. His eyes weren't kind as they appraised her, but when he trained his torch on the faces of the children she led, his mouth dropped open and his expression softened. 'Well, don't just stand there,' he barked. 'You'll freeze. Get up to the house. Now!' Playing the light over his daughter, he asked, 'Are you hurt?'

Shivering, Soraya shook her head.

'Gods, you don't even have a coat. Idiots, all of you.'

He clumped back towards the chalet, torch beam bobbing before him.

Despite his age, he was surprisingly spry. Leah struggled to keep up. 'Where's Luca?'

'Back at the house. A few things he had to do.'

'He sent you out here in this?'

A Kutya Herceg lurched to a stop and aimed his light at her face, blinding her. 'No one sends me anywhere,' he snapped. He moved away before she could respond, continuing his wheezing climb up the slope.

A few things he had to do.

Would her reunion with Luca Sultés be an awkward one? She hoped not. Neither of them had been able to hide the attraction they'd felt for each other when they'd first met, but Leah had never managed to reconcile her feelings with the knowledge of his father's deeds.

Perhaps that had been unfair, but she suspected that Luca

shared the same dark rage as his father when provoked. With a history like hers, she wanted none of that. He had contacted her a few times over the past year, had even offered to visit once or twice. Steadily, as she vacillated, his phone calls were replaced by silence.

Leah followed Ágoston across the driveway, shivering so uncontrollably now that she found it increasingly difficult to breathe. He unlatched the chalet's fortress-like entrance and a furnace heat rolled out to greet her. She led the children inside, greedy for its warmth.

Soraya was the last over the threshold. Ágoston closed the door behind her. Its mortices engaged with a clunk, and even though Leah was immeasurably grateful, she couldn't help thinking that it was the sound of a crypt slamming shut.

Stupid. She could not allow thoughts like that to infect her. Somewhere out there, a nest of *tolvajok* hunted them. They might already be on the mountain. She needed to think clearly, as her mother would – not surrender to the paralysis of fear. So far, her plan had been simple: get the children out of Italy, warn her family in Calw. That part of it was complete. Now she needed to focus on what came next.

Ágoston moved to the nearest wall and pressed a button on a security panel. The device scanned his iris, and then it chimed. He stamped his boots on the hardwood floor. 'This way.'

He led them along a short passage and into an industrial-sized kitchen. A bear-like man, with a rampant ginger beard and a huge belly restrained by a spotless white apron, was standing at a range, stirring a pot with a wooden spoon.

'This is Jérôme,' her host said. 'The best chef you'll meet this side of Le Maurice.'

She nodded a greeting. The aroma from whatever was cooking smelled so heavenly she felt her stomach mutter in response.

Jérôme smiled, and then he gasped in mock surprise as he saw the legion of children filing into his workspace. '. . . eight

. . . nine . . . ten,' he said, counting them off. 'Well, I guess we can handle that many. Who's hungry?' A forest of hands shot up, and his smile rose a notch. 'That's what I like to see. Hungry bellies! Why don't you all get settled over there?' He pointed to a long table by one wall, and Leah saw that ten place settings had already been laid. There was even a highchair for Elias.

With Soraya's assistance, she seated the children. Jérôme served up bowls of chicken stew and placed them on the table, along with baskets filled with buttered rolls. After the carnage at Villa del Osservatore, the sudden domesticity felt surreal.

She was about to pull out her phone and call her mother when Luca walked in. She straightened, found herself grinning awkwardly. Luca went to his sister, threw his arms around her and kissed her head. Then he turned to Leah. She'd expected him to greet her with more distance, if at all, but he wrapped her in his arms too, crushing her in his embrace.

'I'm glad you're safe.'

'I'm so sorry, Luca.' Horrified, she realised she was on the brink of tears.

'Why sorry?'

She closed her eyes, just briefly, a moment's respite. In the calming warmth of this kitchen, she suddenly felt exhausted. 'If I'd never come here,' she began, and then, because she knew her tears would flow after all, and because it wasn't right for the children to see that, she hid her face and ducked into the hall.

He followed her out. 'If you'd never come here,' he told her, 'then my sister wouldn't be pregnant. Nor any of the other women you've helped. And none of those children eating dinner would have a future.'

'Maybe they don't.'

He put his hands on her shoulders. 'Don't say that. Don't even think it.'

This close, his eyes were so intense that she couldn't look away. For a brief moment she thought he was going to kiss her, and even though it would have been wrong, she might have given in to it.

Instead, he pulled her into another tight embrace, rubbing her back. 'You're impossible.'

Leah laughed through her tears, surprised at how much better she felt at his closeness. 'Yeah, that's what I heard. But I am sorry. For involving you like this.'

'I'm already involved. And if there's one thing this family's good at, it's dealing with trouble. Come on, let's get you kitted out.'

He led her back to the entrance hall and into the cloakroom where, during her first visit a year earlier, he had relieved her of her pistol.

Lining the far wall stood the gun cabinets. At a keypad, Luca entered a code and the doors rolled open. Two cabinets held rows of handguns, hunting rifles and shotguns. The third contained boxes of ammunition and magazine clips.

She stared at the collected weaponry, eyes moving across the various pieces. Never had she been so relieved to see such an arsenal of destruction. She glanced back at Luca.

'Take your pick.'

Hesitating a moment, she plucked a Beretta from the rack.

'It's a nine-millimetre. Are you comfortable with that?'

Leah ejected the empty magazine, pulled back on the slide, checked the barrel was clear, released the slide stop, pointed the weapon at the floor and dry-fired it. From the ammo cabinet she helped herself to four pre-loaded magazines and snapped one into the gun.

'Point taken,' he said. 'Anything else?'

She selected a hunting rifle with a dark green stock and a Zeiss scope. 'What's this?'

'A Blaser R8.'

'What does it fire?'

'Here.' He picked up a clip from the ammo cabinet, took the rifle from her and loaded it before handing it back. 'Have 'you ever . . .' He stopped when he saw her expression. 'Forget it.'

Luca zipped himself into an ammunition vest, selected a weapon and loaded it, stuffing spare magazines into the vest's pockets.

The sight should have reassured her. It didn't. 'Tell me about Jérôme.'

'A good guy.'

'I'm sure. What else?'

'I've known him seventy years. He's *kirekesztett*. Wife and child killed during the cull.'

'What was his crime?'

'I killed a man,' said a voice behind her. She found the ginger chef standing in the doorway, arms folded over his gargantuan belly. 'OK, a couple of them. I was drunk, they were goading me.' He came over to the gun cabinet, picked out a Remington pump-action and began to load rounds into it. When it was full, he turned to her and shrugged. 'I used to drink. Now I don't.'

'Probably wise.'

He grinned. 'Those things hunting you, Leah? They'll have to get past me first. That's all you need to know.'

'Your other staff,' she said to Luca. 'Where are they?'

'We sent them away. There's no safety in numbers with *tolvajok*. The fewer of us, and the more spread out we are, the better.' He opened a drawer, removed three penlight torches. After checking their batteries, he pocketed one and handed out the others. 'Let's go up.'

'The children,' Leah said. 'Where's the best place to shelter them?'

'We'll put them in here for the night. There's enough space to lay out bedding. No windows, and that door is lined with an inch of steel. The lock is code-operated.'

'Can we change the code?'

'Of course.'

'Is there any way out, once they're locked in?'

'No. And phones don't work in there. No reception.'

'So we need to think about who gets that code. Too many of us and it's a risk, too few . . .' She didn't need to say it.

Luca nodded. 'Let's set it up.'

She followed him to the top of the house where she'd stayed a year earlier. A Kutya Herceg's collection of disturbing art works still hung from the walls along the hall. Tonight, the painting that had reminded her of Rubens's *Massacre of the Innocents* seemed horrifyingly prescient. She stared at it now, cringing at the gleeful expressions of the soldiers as they tore into defenceless civilians.

Luca moved to her side. 'Not the most uplifting artwork ever conceived,' he admitted.

His tone was light, reassuring. But his eyes darkened as he studied that picture. He might be trying to hide it but she understood, just then, that he too was frightened by what approached. Bizarrely, it made her feel slightly more at ease. She preferred fear to misplaced confidence.

He led them to a laundry room where they loaded up with blankets and pillows, carrying them to the lift that served every level of the house. They sent it down to the ground floor and took the stairs to meet it.

Back inside the gun room, Leah made up a row of beds. Luca returned with two Coleman gas lamps, along with a stack of children's books. Jérôme arrived with a trolley packed with bottled water, dry food and crockery.

By the time they were finished ten minutes later, the room boasted a couple of armchairs and a portable toilet, with a screen to offer a measure of privacy.

They had done their best to make it feel comforting, but it still looked like what it was: a rudimentary hideaway, claustrophobic and bleak.

Led by Soraya, the children filed in, faces solemn when they saw it. Behind came A Kutya Herceg, carrying Elias. Leah was surprised at the tenderness he showed the boy.

'Someone has to stay in here with them,' she said.

'I will,' Soraya replied, and Leah found herself relieved by her friend's offer. Of all of them, Soraya – stomach swollen with her pregnancy – was the least able to put up a fight. Even so, Leah could not imagine being locked in this vault, unable to see what dangers gathered outside and not knowing if the door would ever swing open.

A Kutya Herceg passed Elias to his daughter, kissed both her cheeks and stepped back.

Luca asked, 'You have everything you need?'

'Absolutely.'

In a voice loud enough to carry to everyone in the room, he added, 'Bit of an adventure, this. They won't know what hit them. Get a good night's sleep, everyone. We'll see you in the morning.'

He went to his sister, embracing her a final time. Nodding towards the gun cabinets, he added, in a far quieter voice, 'You remember how to use them?'

'I do.'

'If it comes to it . . .'

In their eyes lurked a scenario so dark that neither could give it voice. Soraya nodded once, almost imperceptibly, her eyes never leaving her brother's. 'We'll be fine,' she replied. 'You'd better go.'

Leah watched their exchange, teeth clenched. Once Luca had disentangled himself from his sister, she stepped forward and hugged her friend. And then, before the horror of those last words overcame her, she pulled away.

She didn't want to meet the eyes of the children who sheltered there, but she forced herself. Dávid and Lícia; Tünde and Elias; Emánuel and Levi; Carina and Philipp; Pia and Alex. Ten young lives. All of them born thanks to her mother's work in Calw.

And all their lives in jeopardy thanks to your own work since.

She bit down on that thought, angry that she should distract herself with a reproach like that now, however true it might be.

Rifle slung over her shoulder, one hand gripping her pistol, she stood between Ágoston and Jérôme as Luca swung the door shut. He keyed a code into the security panel and the door locks activated with a clunk.

His fingers continued to move across the keypad, until a single cursor flashed on the screen. 'Who gets the code?'

'Not just one of us,' she replied. 'Too risky.'

'Who here,' Jérôme asked, 'values their own life more than those ten kids in there? Not me. And I won't let a *lélek tolvaj* take me, no way. I'll take the code.'

Luca nodded. 'Leah, you know those children better than anyone. You should have it, too. Father?'

Ágoston barked a humourless laugh. 'I've lived a long life. I'm with Jérôme.'

'That's settled, then? We all take the code?'

A chorus of nods.

Luca keyed the pad. 'The number is eighteen eighty. Enter it in, press the green button, the door unlocks.'

Eighteen eighty.

An easy number to remember: the year of the *hosszú életek* cull. Even so, she wished he'd chosen something different. It felt like a bad omen.

'We're done here,' Luca said. 'Let's go take a look.'

Flanked by Ágoston and Jérôme, she followed him up the stairs to the first-floor living room.

Ceiling lights and wall lamps blazed inside. The central fireplace was bright with flaming logs. Reflections flickered in the glass eyes of A Kutya Herceg's animal-skin rugs.

The viewing window, curving the entire length of the room, was a black mirror to the night. To the left, Leah saw the dining table overlooked by the skeleton of *Ursus spelaeus*, and behind that the archway leading to the panoramic sun room.

'It's too bright in here,' she said. 'We can't see outside.'

Luca went to a wall panel and dimmed the lights. Instantly the room's reflection disappeared from the glass, replaced by a dark vista of rock and snow. The mountains were jagged silhouettes stitched into the night. The chalet's lawn, covered by a mantle of snow, receded into darkness.

To her right, Leah saw the private road bending down the slope, disappearing into the tree line below. To her left, the sheer drop which some parts of the building overlooked. At least, she thought, they could not be attacked from that direction.

A Kutya Herceg removed a bottle and four tulip-shaped glasses from a cabinet. He poured out four shots. 'I've been saving this,' he said. 'It's *békési szilvapálinka,* a plum pálinka from Békés. Bottled in 1848, the year of the Revolution. I don't know if it's still any good.'

He handed them out and Leah took one.

'*Vér és szabadság,*' the old man said, raising his pálinka.

They clinked glasses and repeated his words. *Blood and freedom.* Leah knocked back her shot. The spirit lit a fire in her throat, bringing tears to her eyes. 'My God, that's awful,' she said.

They laughed, all four of them, and she felt a kinship so powerful that for a moment it eclipsed the nauseous expectation growing in her stomach.

Each of these men, she knew, was custodian to a murderous history. And yet, while to some extent they acted, tonight, to protect the life of a daughter and a sister, they'd been under no obligation to take Leah and her charges into their home. Doing so put all their lives at risk, and even though their laughter still rang in her ears she saw the darkness gathering in their faces, sensed their fear. Over the years she had met all eight members of the *tanács* and many other *hosszú életek* besides. Few of them, she knew, would knowingly cast themselves into danger like this.

She saw Luca staring at her, a pensive smile on his lips. She didn't need to ask what he was thinking; she thought she felt it too: gratitude for their meeting, sadness for what could not be.

When his eyes moved to the window at her back, he straightened. 'Look,' he said.

CHAPTER 42

Interlaken, Switzerland

Beyond the windows a balcony served the entire length of the first floor, accessed by rolling glass doors at either end of the room, and by an exterior staircase winding up the side of the building furthest from the mountain edge. That entry point was secured by a locked gate of steel bars, eight feet in height.

Leah looked down at the snow-covered lawn. It receded steeply, terminating at a line of dense conifers. Even though Luca had dimmed the room's lights, they still blazed from the windows of the ground floor, illuminating an area of snow the size of two tennis courts.

Beyond that patch of light, darkness pressed. And, just on the threshold, where the snow's phosphorescence faded to night, black shapes flitted and danced.

Despite the heat thrown out by the fire, Leah felt a chill seep into her. 'What *is* that?' she whispered.

One of those cantering shapes slowed in its movements. A moment later it passed across that threshold of absolute darkness and coalesced into the form of what looked, to Leah, like some species of mountain goat.

Two sickle-shaped horns, at least a yard in length, swept up and around from its skull, describing an almost perfect circle. At their base they were thicker than her bicep, diminishing in a series of hard, gnarled ridges. Gouts of breath blasted from the animal's nostrils. Despite the thickness of its coat, it looked like it was shivering.

It took a hesitant half-step to its left. Tossed its head.

'Ibex,' Luca muttered. 'Or was.' Pulling the hunting rifle from his shoulder, he went to the nearest sliding glass pane.

'What are you doing?'

'I'm going to kill it.'

'You're going outside?'

'No,' he replied. 'You'll roll open that door for me. I'll take the shot and then you close it. The only way up to the balcony is from those stairs down there. Jérôme, keep watch. If anything gets over the gate, you shout, and Leah rolls the door shut.'

She felt adrenalin flooding her bloodstream now, quickening her heart. 'You're sure this is a good idea?'

'Nope.'

She tried to grin, grimaced instead. 'Me neither.'

'Can you think of a better one?'

She shook her head.

'Then let's do it.' He pointed at the door handle. 'Up to unlock, then you slide the panel back. Got it?'

'Yeah.' Heart thumping even faster now, mouth tasting rancid, she went to the glass pane and waited while Luca chambered a round.

'Jérôme?' he called.

'Clear.'

'Leah, *go*.'

She grabbed the door handle, yanked it up and hauled back. Despite its weight, the glass rolled back with startling ease. She staggered. Caught herself. Felt a wall of frozen air push inside the room.

Luca brought up the rifle's barrel, sighted down the scope. Emptied his lungs. Fired.

Such was the volume of glass around them that the air rang like a bell. Outside, the shot drew peals of thunder from the surrounding mountains.

A smoking hinge of blood-wet skull caromed off the ibex, the round's velocity punching the animal back on its feet. It rolled, legs kicking once, and landed in a patch of darkness just beyond the range of the chalet's lights.

'Door!' Luca shouted. Ears ringing from the rifle blast, Leah rolled the pane back into place and slammed down the lock.

Silence.

Outside, not a breath of movement. All that remained as evidence of the violence they'd wreaked was a dark stain in the snow; and, a few feet to the right, a piece of skull like a fragment of pottery, its concave surface black with the animal's blood.

Luca reloaded, ejecting the spent round. It pinged onto the floor and rolled towards Leah. She trapped it with her boot.

'Good shot!' Jérôme howled. 'Fucking thing is *toast*!'

'No,' Leah said. 'They're just testing us. Look.'

The patch of darkness into which the headshot ibex had been dispatched now spawned five more. The animals lined up on the snow and watched the house, silent and still, breath steaming like vapour from a sulphur lake.

'Then let's test them right back,' Luca replied. 'I can shoot ibex all night if I have to. Leah? Ready?'

But already the animals had retreated, wrapping themselves into the folds of the night's cloak.

Again, the land grew still.

And then – not one by one, or in banks of two or three at a time but together, in a single instant – every light in the chalet complex winked out.

CHAPTER 43

Interlaken, Switzerland

Where before the glass had been a window into the night, now it reverted to an obsidian mirror, in which Leah saw herself, her companions and the hungry flames of the hearth fire.

Beside her, Jérôme fumbled with his torch. 'No,' she said, putting out a hand. 'It'll bounce right back at us.'

Luca nodded. 'The backup generator should kick in any second.'

'How could they shut off the power?'

'There's a substation by the road. Maybe that's how.'

Leah waited, breath tight in her throat. Without light, their situation was immeasurably more bleak.

Wait for the generator, like Luca said. Just breathe, and wait.

She counted off the seconds in silence.

. . . five . . . six . . . seven . . .

Luca grabbed a poker by the fire and broke up the logs until their flames sputtered out. While it helped to dampen the mirror effect of the windows, the night remained impenetrable. Clouds had seeped across the sky in a tight mass, drawing a curtain across the moon and stars.

. . . eight . . . nine . . . ten . . .

'If we open that door,' Jérôme suggested, 'shine our torches out there . . .'

Luca shook his head. 'No point taking the risk. The generator—'

'Hasn't kicked in.'

. . . eleven . . . twelve . . . thirteen . . .

'You're right,' Luca muttered. 'It shouldn't take this long.'

Somewhere, out on the lawn, Leah thought she glimpsed a streak of movement, but it was so hopelessly dark that she couldn't be sure.

And then they heard it: a resounding bang from downstairs, reverberating up through the house.

Jérôme swore. 'What the hell was that?'

The lights came back on.

In an instant, their view of the lawn was restored. But the darkness seemed closer now, the illuminated patch of snow more fragile.

One of the ibex broke from cover and streaked across the snow towards the building. It disappeared from view, and they heard a second loud bang.

'The windows,' she said. 'They're trying to smash their way in.'

'It's toughened glass,' Luca told her.

'Yeah, but how tough? Come on. We should take a look.'

Another ibex raced out of the darkness. It disappeared below the balcony and they heard a boom from downstairs as its skull slammed against the window.

Holding her pistol tightly, Leah ran into the hall. Luca followed. She hurtled down the stairs to the ground floor, two at a time. 'Which way?'

'Left, by the lift.'

She paused beside a closed door. 'Here?'

He nodded.

Leah threw it open.

The room beyond was half the size of the one they'd left, and bathed in light: four sets of wall lamps; rows of halogen ceiling bulbs. A snooker table stood at its centre, the green baize lit by a canopy containing a pair of fluorescent units. In one corner was a wet bar and a scattering of leather club chairs around an oak table.

Unlike the room directly above, with its uninterrupted glass wall, this space held only two of the floor-to-ceiling window panels. Both could be rolled back on metal runners.

The pane nearest the bar was black and smooth, but the one nearest the door bore clear signs of attack: three enormous white starburst patterns, centres frosty with chips of broken glass. It looked bad, but only the outer layer had been breached. Even so, she wasn't confident of how much more punishment it could take.

Something trotted past the windows, a blur of brown and grey. It vanished before Leah had a chance to seize upon it, but she thought she glimpsed curved horns, a single amber eye.

She turned back to Luca. 'Can we turn out the lights?'

He reached past her and flicked off a bank of switches. The room plunged into darkness, but enough light streamed from the windows of the adjacent room to illuminate the scene outside.

Protected by the balcony above, the deck immediately beyond the windows was clear of snow. Crushed glass lay heaped beneath the pane the ibex had attacked.

Beyond the deck, the snow on the lawn was criss-crossed with hoof prints. The closest patch, hidden from the first-floor living space, was thick with them. Clearly the *tolvajok* had been busier than she'd thought.

From upstairs, a second rifle shot fractured the silence. Leah jerked back, so quickly that she sat down hard on her rear. Through the glass she saw an ibex charging across the lawn towards her. Behind it, snow rained down from where the errant rifle round had impacted. The animal jinked left, accelerated towards the window. Put its head down. Leaped.

At floor level, the impact was even more horrifying, a sound like a car hitting a wall. The window bowed in, webbed by another starburst of cracks. Rebounding, the animal fell onto its back. It rolled to its feet, shook its head and cantered back towards the line of darkness.

Another rifle blast from upstairs, the report crashing like an orchestra of cymbals. This time the round struck the escaping ibex in its flank, knocking it off its feet in a red spray. It tumbled, a blur of thrashing hooves. Finally it came to a rest, forelegs twitching, hind legs bicycling, gouts of condensation pluming from its mouth.

The next shot drilled through its torso just behind its left shoulder, destroying heart and lungs. The animal kicked for a handful of seconds. Then it lay still.

Leah crabbed backwards until she felt confident enough to push herself to her feet. 'How much more can these windows take?'

'Honestly?' Luca shook his head. 'I don't know. A while yet. Not all night.'

'We need to seal off the rooms on this side of the house. How many are there?'

'This one, and the library next door.'

She pointed to a set of doors in the left-hand wall. 'Library's through there?'

'Yeah.'

'Let's do it.'

Luca crossed the room and locked the connecting doors. 'If they get into the library, these won't hold them for long.'

'What about that?' she asked, pointing to the snooker table. 'Can we move it?'

'Too heavy. We'd need to take it apart.' He went to the low table near the bar. 'Let's use this.'

Between them they dragged it in front of the doors, stacking the club chairs on top.

'Is there another entrance?'

He was about to reply when the rifle fired again from upstairs. Leah twisted around in time to see another ibex – a monster, this one – leap at the window, striking it with such force that one of its horns snapped off just above its skull. The animal collapsed, senseless. Arterial blood fountained from the stub of its horn, steaming like a geyser in the frozen air.

Leah struggled to turn her eyes away. 'Is there another entrance? To the library?'

'Out in the hall.'

'You go. I'll stay here.'

He pointed at the doorway through which they'd entered. 'Any problems, get out and lock it. It's solid. Much stronger than those two.'

Leah nodded, watched him leave. Heard her teeth grinding together.

Was this going to be their strategy? Concede the various parts of the building, room by room? Where would that end?

She thought of the children sheltering inside the windowless gun room and wondered how they'd felt as they heard the gunfire, knowing nothing of what occurred outside.

When she turned back to the damaged window, all that remained of the stricken ibex was a curving spear of broken horn, and a dark slick of blood.

Standing in its place, Leah saw, was something far, far worse.

CHAPTER 44

Interlaken, Switzerland

It was Flóra.

Naked, the woman stood on the other side of the ruined glass, hands pressed against its surface. Her skin was milk-white, lips blue. Convulsing with cold, she stared at Leah with eyes that were dark and terrified and pleading. 'Let me in,' she mouthed, glancing over her shoulder at the waiting darkness. 'Please, Leah. Let me in.'

Heart kicking in her chest, Leah took a step closer to the glass. Her throat constricted, as if unseen hands strangled her.

You left her. You left Flóra at the villa.

And they took her.

When the woman saw Leah make no attempt to let her in, she banged her fists on the glass, screaming, and although the window was thick enough to dampen sound, Leah still heard her words.

'Let me *in*!' Again, Flóra glanced over her shoulder. She seemed to see something move out there, beyond the range of the lights. Her assault on the window intensified, and where she pounded on the splinters of outer glass, they sliced into her skin. The pads of her balled fists stamped vivid red blotches.

'I'm sorry,' Leah whispered. She wanted to close her eyes, wanted to excise the woman's image from her mind, but she couldn't. Neither could she do anything to help.

Behind her, Luca returned from the hall. He hissed when he saw Flóra. 'Do you know her?'

Outside, Flóra's hammering grew more frenzied. She smeared half-moons of blood across the glass. '*LET ME IN! PLEASE, LEAH! LET ME IN! LET ME IN!*'

'Her name's Flóra,' Leah whispered, hand covering her mouth, tears sliding down her cheeks. 'She's Elias's mother. I left her.'

'You saved her son.'

'What about her?'

Luca grimaced. 'There's nothing we can do. It's a test, Leah. That's all this is. They're probing you for a weakness.'

Sensing, perhaps, that her efforts were in vain, Flóra closed her eyes and rested her forehead against the fractured glass. When she looked up a few moments later, all traces of humanity had bled from her expression.

Her mouth, still ringed with blue, hung slack. Her body stopped shivering. Her chest ceased its heaving.

Flóra raised a hand, spread her fingers wide, and when she opened her mouth to speak, Leah read on her lips the words she spoke, and thought she heard them in her head.

We want five. That's all. Five . . .

'Come on,' Luca said. He slipped his hand around her arm. 'You don't need to see this.'

But she was unable to look away. She *had* to see this – a price she must pay for abandoning the woman at Villa del Osservatore.

Five. You choose. Choose, choose . . .

Leah shrugged off Luca's arm, her grief igniting into fury. The mere suggestion that she would barter the lives of the children she'd pledged to protect outraged her in ways she hadn't imagined. 'I'll die before giving you a single one of them!' she screamed. 'And I'll take you with me! *All* of you!'

Flóra stared. And then she tilted back her head and slammed it against the glass. Blood ran down her face, dripped from her chin. She turned, and walked out into the night.

Head suddenly light, Leah slumped over, supporting herself with her hands on her knees. Luca approached her, but she waved him away. 'No. Give me a second. I'll be all right.' She took a breath, clenched her teeth. Stood. 'Let's go.'

After locking the games room door behind them, they rejoined Ágoston and Jérôme back on the first floor. The pair was standing by the windows. Empty brass shell casings littered the floor.

'How is it?' asked Ágoston.

'Secure,' Luca replied. 'We locked up the rooms, just in case. They're going to—'

When he hesitated, Leah heard it too: outside, the revving of a diesel engine.

Just enough light leaked around the side of the house to illuminate the heated patch of driveway in front of the garage.

A black Range Rover, engine roaring, erupted from the darkness, wheels squealing as they bounced off snow and chewed into tarmac. Lunging forward, two tonnes of steel powered by a thundering five-litre heart, the vehicle accelerated towards the chalet's front entrance.

'Door!' Jérôme yelled, snatching up his shotgun. Ágoston reacted instantly, sliding back the glass pane.

Chambering a round into his Remington, Jérôme swung the barrel to track the 4x4. He fired.

A plate-sized section of glass exploded in the Range Rover's windscreen. But the vehicle kept coming. Kept coming.

Jérôme reloaded, fired. Reloaded, fired. The air burst around them. Hard, angry sounds.

So many things happened at once, after that, that Leah struggled to comprehend any of them, or slot them into a meaningful order.

A tyre exploded on the Range Rover's nearside, its wheel rim striking up a trail of sparks while, much closer, a human form dropped onto the balcony from the floor above, landing on all fours directly in front of Jérôme.

Leah opened her mouth to shout out a warning, wheeling her hands as if she back-pedalled through water. She saw Ágoston's eyes widen as he registered the ambush and pushed his weight against the door, saw it begin to roll forward along its runners, incredibly slow, inch by inch by inch, saw whatever had landed on the balcony rise to its feet in a single fluid movement and lunge towards Jérôme, saw Jérôme stagger backwards but late, far too late, face contorted in panic as the dark shape touched his cheek before the sliding wall of glass intervened, knocking the creature away and sealing it outside. She saw Jérôme turn as the door rolled shut, saw his eyes change as if a pair of shutters had slammed down, saw him lift the barrel of the Remington towards Ágoston and pull the trigger, saw the shotgun's muzzle flash and A Kutya Herceg's face dissolve in blood, saw the *kirekesztett* leader fall back as Jérôme – what had *been* Jérôme – twisted towards Luca, mouth stretched wide as he racked another round into the gun, saw a spent cartridge tumbling end over end through the air, balletic almost, a smoking tube of plastic and brass, saw Luca's handgun loom into view, saw the Remington's barrel jump as it unleashed another red tongue of fire, saw a fusillade of buckshot burst open Luca's chest even as he squeezed the trigger of his own weapon, saw the shotgun swing towards her now, another empty shell jumping into the air, heard Jérôme reload, saw Luca's pistol pump round after round into the man's skull, saw the shotgun kick a third time, saw her jeans shred in a spray of blood, felt the impact punch her off her feet, felt herself falling back, falling, falling, felt pain exploding in her like a thousand stabbing knives, felt the floor slam against her back, felt the breath whoosh from her lungs, felt her head smacking against wood, saw her world darken, consumed by pain and shock and disbelief.

Blink.

Ágoston crashed to the floor, arms outstretched. Jérôme, faceless, fell like a tree, the Remington flying from his hands. Luca sailed backwards, legs lifting up to reveal the soles of his shoes. He landed on his back and slid, leaving a trail of bright blood.

It wasn't over, not yet.

Outside, engine screaming, the 4x4 slammed into the chalet's front entrance in an explosion of buckling steel, wood splinters and glass.

A final empty shotgun cartridge bounced to the floor and spun, around and around and around.

Then, finally, shocking silence.

Leah lay still, listening to the sound of her breathing, trying to make sense of what she'd seen and heard.

Ágoston was dead. She knew that. *Hosszú élet* or not, no one could sustain a head injury like that and live. And while whatever lurked inside Jérôme's corpse might still cling to life, the same could not be said for its host. The man's skull had revealed its secrets like a gristly Pandora's box.

The pain in her leg was monstrous. She squeezed her eyes shut against it.

Don't move. Not yet.

Think.

She was losing blood. Fast. Opening her eyes, she propped herself up on her elbow. From just above the knee, her right leg was a mulch of pulverised flesh. Blood spurted from the wound in rhythmic pulses.

Femoral artery. You have minutes left. Unless you concentrate.

She was beginning to hyperventilate. She needed to slow her breathing, her heart.

Leah lay back down on the floor. Emptied her lungs.

Outside, the Range Rover stuttered back into life. Its engine revved. In a cacophony of shearing metal and popping wood, it extricated itself, reversing back onto the drive.

Forget about the car. Put it out of your head. You're dying here.

She tried to concentrate on the flow of blood through her leg, the sensations from her nerves. But the agony intensified and a convulsion seized her. As if a cord had been pulled taut, every muscle in her body contracted as one. Her head slammed against the floor and her eyes shot open.

A warmth soaked into the back of her jeans. Her blood, she realised. Pouring out of her.

You're the only one left. If you die here, then they win, and the children are lost.

Leah screamed. Angry now, furious. And there, *there*. With sudden clarity, she sensed the edges of the artery's tear. She'd never had to do this before, but she remembered Gabriel's words, saw his face floating above her: *Pinch and sew, Leah. Pinch and sew.*

She tried to do as he urged, grimacing at the effort, thought she had it – *pinch and sew* – felt the repair she'd worked split apart like an overripe pea pod.

Again.

This time, incredibly, the seam held. She glanced down, sickened by what she saw. A lake of blood had spread underneath her. The flesh she glimpsed through her tattered jeans was puckered and raw. But blood no longer fountained.

She glanced over at Luca, lying on his back. Shook her head. He had taken the full brunt of the Remington's round in his chest. Feeling the tendons of her neck straining, she forced herself back onto an elbow, closing her eyes as the room swayed away from her.

The dizziness passed and she opened her eyes again, staring around the room at the three bodies that littered the floor, staggered by the enormity of what had just happened.

One *tolvaj* did this. Just one. And now all three of her companions lay dead or dying.

Her head pulsed, ears deafened from the gunfire that had ripped the air apart. She sat up, saw her pistol lying close. Wormed over to it, dragging her injured leg. Shoving the weapon into a pocket, she pulled herself to Luca's side.

His eyes were open but unfocused, breath coming in shallow gasps. Alive, barely. She wanted to help him, but she had no blood to give. No time, either.

From somewhere above them she heard a hollow-sounding boom. A moment later, another one followed.

Tolvajok.

Up on the second floor, trying to break the windows. They were everywhere now, swarming all over the house, confident that only Leah remained to thwart them.

A third echoing boom, followed by a fourth.

Outside, she heard the Range Rover's gearbox rasp, its three remaining tyres squeal. A few seconds later the car punched into the front entrance again, unleashing a hailstorm of metal and wood.

Had the building been breached? She had to find out. Dragging herself to the dining table, she used a chair to lever herself to her feet.

Don't touch Jérôme. Don't go near him.

Tentatively, she put weight on her injured leg. A flash of agony ripped through her, a forge-heated needle melting the marrow of her bones. She concentrated, emptied her mind. Tried to build a wall around the pain.

Again, she put her weight on the leg. Took a tentative step. Better.

She hobbled to the door and out into the hall. Leaving a bloody trail behind her, she edged towards the stairs. From here, the angle was too steep to see the main entrance.

The booming above her intensified.

Down the first few stairs. Pause for breath. Down a few more.

Stop. Breathe. A few more stairs, and now she was close enough to the bottom of the flight to see the entrance hall before her.

Dust hung thick in the air. Chunks of rubble and plaster lay strewn across the floor. The door was still inside its frame, but the brickwork surrounding it had been punched inwards. Two large cracks, wide enough to accept a hand, had appeared on either side. Frozen air leached through.

Leah made it to the bottom of the flight. The Range Rover revved its engine, ear-shatteringly loud, as if its exhaust had torn loose. Now a squeal from its tyres, and through the narrow panes of glass in the door's transom she saw an onrushing shape.

The vehicle crunched into the entrance and this time it punched through. Bricks shattered. Mortar burst into wicked grey shards. The entire bottom half of the door snapped off and skittered across the floor.

As the dust settled, she saw the mangled front end of the 4x4 wedged tight inside the breach. Steam and smoke boiled from its grille.

Leah's leg gave way beneath her. She sat down hard, staring at the wreckage. If the Range Rover managed to reverse out of the destruction it had wreaked, it would leave a gaping hole open to the night.

She heard the engine, stalled after the impact, turn over. It rattled, and then a darker cloud of smoke, greasy and toxic, erupted into the hallway.

Leah gagged when it touched her throat. Her vision blurred from its sting. And then she saw the first yellow licks of flame. They spread quickly, curling from beneath the broken door, crackling as they consumed the first sharp splinters. Outside, a car door slammed.

Most of the building was constructed from wood; it would feed the fire with unrelenting passion. Already, the panelling either side of the entrance was beginning to smoulder. Soon the air would be too clotted with smoke to breathe.

To her left stood the locked door to the games room, where earlier she'd watched the ibex hurling themselves at the glass. To her right, the sealed door to the gun room, behind which sheltered Soraya and the ten children she'd hoped to protect.

From inside the games room, Leah heard a crash of breaking glass, knew that the window had finally been breached. A few seconds later, something hit the back of the games room door with such force that a crack raced down it from top to bottom.

The *lélek tolvajok* were inside the house.

CHAPTER 45

Interlaken, Switzerland

Sitting on the plywood floor of the van's cargo hold as it bumped and swayed beneath her, Etienne prayed. She did not close her eyes, did not clasp her hands together in supplication. No sound emerged from her throat, but her mouth formed the words nonetheless.

Please, God, if you're listening. Help me make amends. I'm sorry for all the bad things I've done, sorry for all the good things I've failed to do.

I know this prayer comes too late, that I don't have the right to ask You for anything at all, but please, God, for Elijah's sake, just hear me now. I'll give my life, I'll give anything. Just don't let it be too late for Elijah. Please. Show me what to do. Don't abandon us.

Inside this barren, windowless space, the only illumination came from a tiny rectangular fixture attached to the ceiling. It shed a murky yellow light. Hannah Wilde sat opposite, legs stretched out before her, back resting against the tall metal side of the van. Gabriel lay curled on the floor, head in her lap. Pale-faced, his eyes flickered behind their lids. Etienne did not know what the *Merénylő* had done to him, but since Gabriel had lapsed into unconsciousness an hour earlier they hadn't been able to rouse him. Hannah had wrapped an oily tarpaulin around his torso, warming him as best she could.

The woman held her head erect, defiant. Dried blood

had stiffened on her clothes; and there was so much of it. The gashes carved into her face by the *Merénylő* had closed, but two ugly red lines remained, and it would take time for them to fade.

Who knew whether they had any of that?

Etienne was grateful, at least, that she did not have to meet Hannah's eyes and see the woman's contempt. So different, the two of them: the paths their lives had taken, the people they had become. Etienne had allowed herself to be washed along life's drain, never swimming against the current, mixing with the effluent until her spirit was sodden with it. Hannah Wilde, in contrast – despite all the horrors she had faced – had stood firm against the tide, had refused to be swept away. Never once had she turned her face from danger, or considered her own safety before the wellbeing of her family.

With the road rolling beneath them, the two women had nothing to do except talk. It seemed to Etienne that she had told Hannah everything in the hours that had passed since leaving Calw: her life before Tansik House; the years of abuse at the hands of both her own family and those whose task had been to protect her; her later years; her dealings with Jakab; finally, the encounter with the *tolvaj* that had spirited away her child.

While she knew Hannah must *feel* contempt for the story she heard, Etienne couldn't see any evidence of it on the woman's face. If anything, Hannah looked stricken, sympathetic; visibly upset.

But after living so many years bereft of the most fundamental human experiences of love or compassion or friendship, Etienne was no authority on emotion, or the interpretation of its expression. Whatever she thought she saw in Hannah's face, that contempt, she knew, must exist. How could it not?

Once she had finished her story, Hannah herself began to talk, and the woman's revelations were so compelling, and of such magnitude, that for a while Etienne forgot they sat inside the van as prisoners, ferried to a destination where more violence doubtless lay in wait.

She didn't think she would she see Elijah again in this life, and she had been careful not to ask for it in her prayer. That was not a request Hannah Wilde would have made, and Etienne was determined to follow her example. All she had asked was that Elijah be saved.

Praying to a God she had never before considered might be as foolish as all her previous choices, but right now, in this half-frozen cell, it seemed like the only option left.

Please, God, he's so young. Elijah deserves a life. Do what you want with me. Please just give my baby a chance.

For the last few hours, the hiss of the van's tyres on the road had been a constant companion. But now the vehicle slowed, and abruptly she heard that hiss become a muted crunch of wheels rolling through snow

The van seesawed. It slipped and climbed. Hannah's head bounced on the side wall.

'Smoke,' she said, bracing Gabriel against her as the floor rocked beneath them. 'Something's burning out there.' Her face grew taut, as if dark memories spooled inside her mind. 'Remember what I said. Together, we can do this. But I need your help.'

'I'm not sure I—'

'Yes. You can. You have to.'

'We don't really know what he's thinking,' Etienne said, cringing at the pitiful tone in her voice, remembering the words of her prayer from moments earlier: *I'll give my life, I'll give anything.*

'He's a monster, Etienne. You know that as well as I do.'

The van lurched to a halt and the engine died. She heard movement from the driver's compartment. The floor tilted and the suspension creaked.

Footsteps along the side of the vehicle, through collapsing snow.

'Whatever happens, keep your thoughts on Elijah,' Hannah whispered. 'It'll give you strength.'

The back doors opened, revealing Jakab. If Etienne had been cold before, now her blood froze in her veins. The moment she glimpsed him, she knew that she would be unable to do what Hannah asked, would fail to become an instrument of her own redemption. A feeling of hopelessness and sorrow enveloped her, turning her limbs to lead.

Death rode in Jakab's eyes. Red-rimmed, they swept over the van's occupants. He muttered to himself, crooning, the words too indistinct to decipher. In one hand he held a gun.

Beyond the doors Etienne saw a vast night vista: silhouetted mountain peaks and sky. At first she thought it was raining, until a flurry of snowflakes blew inside, settling on the scarred plywood floor.

'Out,' Jakab said, gesturing at the two women. 'Not him. He stays here.'

Hannah turned her face towards his voice. 'It's too cold. He'll freeze.' On her lap, Gabriel stirred, curling himself into a tighter ball. She placed her hand on his forehead and stroked it back through his hair.

In response Jakab racked the slide on his pistol. It was a brutal sound, unforgiving. 'He stays.'

Hannah closed her mouth and Etienne saw her considering her options. A moment later, with aching tenderness, she lifted Gabriel's head from her lap and lowered it onto the tarp. She bent over him, kissed his face, whispered something into his ear. Then she slid herself towards the rear of the van until her legs dangled over the edge, and hopped down into snow.

Jakab turned to Etienne. 'Out.'

She climbed to her feet, trembling as much from fear as from cold. Moving to the doors, she asked, as gently as she could, 'What are you doing, Jakab?'

He ignored the question, and she could tell from his expression that he could not have given her an answer. Madness and confusion swirled in his eyes; she guessed that only a fraction of what he saw belonged to this particular time and place.

Etienne jumped down into the snow. Frozen air sluiced into her bones.

In the distance, at the summit of a steep incline, a huge chalet complex clung to the mountainside, one corner hanging over a sheer precipice. Lights blazed from the upper levels.

A fire was taking hold on the ground floor. Someone had driven a 4x4 straight through the building's entrance.

Jakab locked the van's doors. 'Start walking,' he said, and when the words left his lips Hannah sprang at him, fingers curled into claws. They pitched over into snow and rolled, her hands scrabbling at his chest, Jakab's gun spinning away from him. Somehow she ended up on top.

Grasping handfuls of his hair, she smashed his head against the frozen ground. He bellowed, trying to knock her loose, but she wrestled out of reach. 'Help me!' she screamed. '*Help* me!'

But Etienne could only watch.

Hannah yanked Jakab's head forward and slammed it down again. This time, instead of trying to throw her off, he enfolded her in a hug, trapping her arms to her sides.

She struggled to get loose, and when she realised that wouldn't work she went limp, falling against him. Her mouth pressed against his face, teeth bared.

Jakab thrashed, and then he screamed. Hannah lifted her head, chin dark with blood. She spat a lump of his face into the snow. Her thumbs found his eyes. '*ETIENNE!*'

The gun was so close. Just a few yards from her. And yet it might as well have been a continent away.

Jakab's fist swung around and met Hannah's head just above her ear. It was a monstrous blow, connecting with a crack like a snapping tree branch, and sent her sprawling onto her back.

For the space of a single breath she lay stunned. In the time it took her to recover and roll to her feet, Jakab had scrabbled away, leaving a deep trench in the snow.

His fingers found the fallen pistol. Closed around it.

Silent, blood running from his cheek in a black torrent, he rose, eyes blank holes of fury and hate.

CHAPTER 46

Interlaken, Switzerland

One moment he was closing the doors to the back of the van, frustrated by the cold stiffening his fingers and cursing himself for not bringing any gloves, and the next the world had tipped and he was on his back, the breath knocked from his lungs, and Hannah Wilde was on top of him, scratching and clawing like a wildcat.

She grabbed his hair and slammed his head into the earth – once, twice – and with each impact her face dissolved in two. He tried to shove her away but she twisted, serpent-quick. When he wrapped his arms around her and pulled her close, she loosened and he felt her jaw working against his face, and then a pain burst over him like boiling oil.

He screamed, outraged. Saw her spit a chunk of his face into the snow. Heard her calling Etienne's name, beseeching the woman for help.

Jakab closed his hand into a fist and swung. The blow cracked against Hannah's skull and sent her sprawling. He rolled in the snow, leaving gobs of black from his damaged face.

He saw the gun and snatched it up, felt its weight and its contours in his fingers, as if it had been moulded just for him.

With one hand pressed to the fleshy crater she had bitten out of him, Jakab climbed to his feet. Blood flowed between his fingers. He raised his weapon and pointed it at her, this woman who had caused him so much misery, so much loss.

Even now, after he'd saved her from a *Merénylő*'s execution, she tried to destroy him. Even now.

He had not known what he was going to do when he arrived here; the future had been an unscalable wall inside his head. For a short while during the drive, he had considered sparing Hannah's life. Perhaps, by showing mercy, he would ingratiate himself with the young woman he had come to find. Now, as if that wall had crumbled to dust, he saw the foolishness of the thought for what it was.

A single future beckoned him. A clear path.

Decades of sorrow and loss, he had suffered. And all of them caused by this woman crouching in front of him with his blood on her lips.

Jakab raised the gun, watched Hannah reach out her hands. Wretched, as blind to her destiny as abattoir fodder led by a slaughterman's rope, she wandered into his sight line and presented herself for his vengeance.

He didn't even have to aim; all he needed to do was pull the trigger. And so, with inexpressible relief, Jakab did exactly that.

Around him, the mountains roared. Perhaps they scorned him – perhaps that cymbal clash rolling amongst their peaks was mocking laughter – for in that hair-thin instant before he pulled the trigger, intent on expunging forever the trauma this broken creature had wrought, Etienne launched herself at him and knocked his hand away, the pistol round blasting harmlessly into the night.

'Jakab, *no!*' she shrieked. And now, as if those mocking mountain peaks desired to throw yet another obstacle across his path, the snowflakes whirled about them, a thickening vortex of white.

'Out of my way!' he roared, furious that Etienne should involve herself in this. He sidestepped her but she matched him, keeping her body between Hannah and his gun.

'You don't know what you do, Jakab!' she cried. 'Please! You don't know what you do!'

'*Get out of my way!*'

If she wouldn't move, if she wanted to sacrifice herself like this, then he wouldn't stop her. His finger tightened on the trigger.

'She's your *blood*, Jakab!' Etienne shouted. 'Don't you *understand*? She's part of you! *Család!* Hannah is family!'

He stumbled.

The words were like a whisk inside his brain.

No sense. They made no sense. He grimaced, shook his head, tried to clear it. In front of him, Hannah's face shimmered, as if glimpsed through water. 'No,' he muttered. 'That's not right.'

It wasn't Hannah now, though, was it? It was someone else, or the vaguest hint of someone else. Someone he had loved, once.

He heard something pop inside his head, like a seal breaking, and a rushing sound like a vacuum being filled, as if his ears were equalising from an imbalance of pressure.

It dizzied him.

'Yes,' Etienne said, her voice insistent. '*Think*, Jakab. Look at her, look at Hannah and think. You know it's true. You must.'

He did look at her. But was it Hannah Wilde he saw in front of him? Or was it the other one? The girl he'd loved all those years ago.

He couldn't even remember her name any more. When, he caught himself wondering, had he started to forget?

'It can't be,' he whispered. That inrushing draught carried nightmare images, scenes of slaughter. He heard screams. Tasted blood. 'It can't *BE*!'

He wanted that voice to stop, needed to silence it, needed to slow this down before it all spun away from him. His thoughts were too fractured to put in any kind of order.

'But it can,' Etienne said. 'It is. And you have a chance, now, Jakab. You have a chance to—'

He closed his eyes, or thought he did, and then the mountains were roaring at him once more, their laughter or their accusations rolling like thunder, and when he opened his eyes Etienne, instead of standing in front him, was lying prone in the snow, and Hannah was screaming and he was sinking to his knees, fingers throbbing from the recoil of his gun.

'What have I done?' he murmured, lifting his face to the night. 'What have I done?'

Jakab watched Hannah drop to all fours. She crawled, fingers feeling blindly, until she came across Etienne's legs. Moaning, she worked her way up the woman's body, until she found the solitary chest wound that steamed in the frigid air.

'Animal,' she hissed. Then, with a vitriol that stung him more than he could have imagined, she said it again, louder. 'You *animal*.'

Jakab stared. He didn't even remember shooting Etienne, but he was the only one holding a weapon. The fingers of his right hand tingled.

'I just wanted her to stop,' he moaned. 'I just . . .'

And then another thought occurred to him, a question. It was too terrible to voice at first, but he must. He had to understand.

Staring at Hannah, trying to hold back those images of violence and pain lest they sweep him away entirely, he asked, 'Is it true?'

Ignoring him, she moved her fingers to Etienne's wrist, feeling for a pulse.

'Is it *true*?' he screamed.

Hannah lifted her head towards him. Her breath frosted on the air. 'Yes,' she replied. 'It's true.'

Etienne spasmed. Her leg kicked and she coughed, staining the snow beside her.

Jakab turned away. He could not look at Hannah; could not look, either, at the evidence of what he'd wrought. The gun was heavy in his hand.

He couldn't breathe, couldn't accept any air into his lungs.

Up ahead, the chalet, where he'd come to find Leah, twinkled like a Christmas bauble. Something bad had happened there, and something bad was probably still happening inside. Footprints, or hoof prints, marked the snow all over the lawn. He saw the shapes of dead animals scattered everywhere about. Broken windows . . . and flames.

Fire crackled around the silhouette of a large 4x4 lodged in the building's main entrance. Despite the altitude and the cold mountain air, it would not take long to spread.

The flames captivated him, at once both beautiful and terrifying. They seemed fitting, in a way. He had lost Hannah Wilde to fire. Now, at the end, it reunited them.

So many questions unanswered. But perhaps that was for the best. The memories pressed at him, wrapping him in shackles and strangling him with their chains. He turned back to Hannah, raised the gun. 'Get up,' he told her.

CHAPTER 47

Interlaken, Switzerland

Whatever was behind the games room door slammed against it a second time. Another crack appeared in the wood, branching out from the first. Through it, Leah saw a slice of perfect darkness.

Smoke rolled from the grille of the vehicle lodged in the wreckage of the chalet's main entrance. Flames licked up towards the ceiling.

Death, coming from both directions at once. If Soraya and the children remained inside the gun room, they would suffocate on smoke even before the fire claimed them.

Again, the games room door shuddered.

Eyes stinging, throat burning, Leah pulled herself to her feet, leaving a macabre blot on the stairs where her blood had soaked into the carpet. She had mere seconds now: seconds until the air grew too thick to breathe, seconds until whatever attacked the door managed to smash its way through.

She put weight on her injured leg. Felt something tear. Gasped. Felt blood begin to spurt once more from her damaged artery.

Limping to the security panel, shadows swimming at the edges of her vision, Leah typed in the code: *1 8 8 0*. She heard the mortices disengage with a clunk. The door swung open.

Soraya stood behind it, aiming a pistol-grip shotgun. Behind her, the children stood in a line.

'We need to go,' Leah said.

Soraya's eyes swept over the devastation in the hall, and then they returned to Leah, taking in her shredded jeans, the blood. She raised the barrel of her weapon. 'How do I know?'

Leah frowned, and then she understood: Soraya had no way of knowing whether she was friend or enemy. The woman stared, eyes black. A wrong move would see her finger tighten on the shotgun's trigger.

The games room door splintered and Soraya cried out.

Leah spun around. Saw the door, hanging open now, the jamb smashed to pieces. In the doorway stood a creature so ungodly she wondered if loss of blood had incited her brain to weave hallucinations from the shadows.

But no hallucination could reek as badly as the thing that loomed before her. Waves of corruption rolled off it, a sweet-sour stench that mixed with the steam and the smoke and clung to Leah's throat, her tongue.

The flesh of its face had sagged down its skull like the semi-liquid folds of a guttering candle, and where the skin had split it leaked a milky sap. Only when she saw the hair trailing down its spine, matted into greasy ropes and speckled with the carcasses of dead ticks and lice, did she finally recognise it: the *tolvaj* that had appeared in the restaurant that day back in Mürren. How visibly it had deteriorated since then. When its eyes found her, it grunted in triumph.

Soraya pushed Leah to one side. Ramming the barrels of her shotgun into the *tolvaj*'s mouth, she pulled the trigger. The muzzle flash lit up its eye sockets like a Halloween pumpkin, and the back of its head exploded in a dark and bloody gout. It pitched backwards into the darkness.

Choking on smoke, Soraya reloaded. 'Watch that door!' she shouted, darting back inside the gun room. When she reappeared she had Elias tucked under one arm. To the children, she urged, 'Quick now, all of you. Follow me.'

Leah leaned against the wall, feeling like she might faint,

trying not to breathe in a lungful of smoke. Shapes were moving inside the games room. It wouldn't be long before they ventured out.

She tried to raise her pistol, but her strength had abandoned her. Instead, she whispered the names of the children as they passed, determined not to leave anyone behind. '*Dávid, Lícia, Tünde, Emánuel, Levi, Carina, Philipp, Pia, Alex.*'

One more child. She tried to think, tried to empty her head of pain and smoke. Soraya had reached the top of the stairs; she turned and shouted Leah's name.

One more.

And then she realised: Soraya was holding Elias. There was no one left.

Leah lurched after them, limping in an awkward backwards gait, keeping her eyes on the door from which the *tolvaj* had emerged. But it was impossible to see anything now. The smoke was blinding. Asphyxiating.

Coughing, dragging in a breath of air that pricked her lungs like hot needles, her heel knocked against the first stair. She struggled up.

Something emerged from the smoke. A face that once had belonged to Ivan Tóth. Its eyes lit on her and, when it saw the children climbing the stairs, it revealed a set of blood-wet teeth.

The last of her energy was ebbing now, like rainwater draining through topsoil. Her right leg felt like a lump of wood strapped to her hip. She dragged it up the stairs behind her, leaving a bloody trail in her wake.

Soraya reached the first floor and hurried past the living-room doors. At the end of the hall she disappeared around the corner, towards the stairs leading up to the floor above. A moment later she reappeared.

The instant Leah saw Soraya's face, she knew what had happened.

Tolvajok. Somehow they'd broken in at the top of the house, and were working their way down.

Left hand holding Elias, Soraya had no way of using the shotgun grasped in her right. Instead she retreated, leading her charges back down the hall towards Leah. When she arrived outside the living room where her father and brother had died, she ushered the children through.

Leah tried to call out, tried to warn the woman of what she was about to see, but she had no voice left. Behind her, a shadow rose up on the wall. It was an effort even to find the energy to look over her shoulder but she managed it, turning in time to see the thing that had once been Ivan Tóth lurch up the final stair. As she backed along the hall, she saw a second shape loom out of the darkness from the opposite direction.

Another of the *tanács*: Krištof Joó. She had never liked the man. What she saw now, she liked even less.

Tolvajok: behind her and in front. Leah struggled into the living room, blinking tears from her eyes, coughing smoke. To her right, she saw the children follow Soraya through the arch into the sun room.

You failed them. You failed them all.

But she wouldn't. Not in this last task.

Her pistol was loaded. She knew what she had to do.

The brass caps of spent rounds twinkled on the floor. She saw Luca, lying on his back. The shattered corpses of A Kutya Herceg and the man she'd known as Jérôme.

At the dining table Leah paused for breath, using one of the chairs to hold herself upright.

Faces appeared in the doorway leading from the hall. Ivan Tóth came first. Krištof Joó followed. They were in an appalling state, faces hanging loose, mouths bloody, but the sight of her, so close, seemed to renew their energy.

Leah hauled herself along the dining table, chair by chair by chair, towards the sun room's entrance.

Hisses of excitement. Horribly close.

She staggered to the arch, and when she passed through it into the chamber beyond, she felt something give in her leg.

Crashing across the floor, Leah slammed against one of the viewing windows, cracking her skull against the glass. The blow loosened an avalanche of sparks inside her head. She spun away from the pane. Glimpsed the first of the *tolvajok* step into the room, followed by a second.

At the far end of the chamber, Soraya had opened the only door, revealing a cramped storage space and a narrow flight of stairs leading up. Ashen-faced, she pushed the children through.

A third *tolvaj* slouched into the room, following Tóth and Joó.

Soraya screamed out Leah's name, beseeching her to hurry. But Leah had no movement in her right leg at all now, and no strength in her left.

The door where her friend waited was five yards away, but it might as well have been five miles. She would never make it.

She gestured to Soraya, used her pistol to demonstrate what she intended to do.

The woman stared back, grimacing. She nodded, mouthed, *I'm sorry.*

Leah smiled, watching as her friend closed the door and locked it behind her. 'Me too,' she said.

Outside the windows, snowflakes spiralled and danced. The snow on the lawn glowed orange with reflected firelight.

The final *tolvaj* stepped onto the viewing chamber's floor. They came at her, all four, an inexorable mass of clutching, groping fingers.

Keep fighting till you have nothing left.

Her grandfather's favourite phrase. Leah watched the horde shambling towards her, and realised that she *had* nothing left.

Chapter 48

Interlaken, Switzerland

Using the barrel of his gun to push Hannah Wilde along, Jakab crunched through snow towards the bright lights of the chalet.

A mountain wind gusted around them, fanning the flames at the front of the building and stirring the falling snowflakes into a blizzard of white.

Tattered threads of smoke coiled from a broken window on the ground floor, nearest to where the fire burned. It offered the only route inside. How long they would be able to breathe in there, he did not know. But it didn't really matter. He didn't think he'd be coming out.

How could he have lived so long without knowing the connection they shared? Without even suspecting? When he thought of what he had sacrificed while chasing a dream that could never be, he wanted to weep. But he was past tears; past caring. He just wanted this to end.

He pressed the gun into Hannah's back with greater force. He knew that she heard the flames. Smelled the smoke. But she did not cry out, did not try to plead with him; she was far too stubborn for that. It was, he realised, a trait they shared. How strange, to suddenly consider it.

Her boots crunched on glass shards and she came to a halt, coughing out smoke.

'There's a broken window in front of you,' he told her. 'It

reaches all the way to the ground. You won't cut yourself if you walk straight.'

She tilted her head, listening to his voice: listening, perhaps, for other sounds, too. But he knew she wouldn't try to attack him a second time – not now that he was expecting it.

Hannah folded her arms across her chest and stepped through the wreckage into the room beyond. Jakab followed, pulling a penlight torch from his pocket.

He switched it on, swabbing the beam left and right. A dark shape loomed in the smoke. He saw it was a snooker table, the balls on its surface glinting. On the far side of the room, a smashed door, hanging ajar. Smoke billowed through.

Clamping the penlight in his teeth, grabbing Hannah by her collar, he pushed her through the shattered doorway, holding his breath and narrowing his eyes at the stinking grey cloud.

She stumbled forward and he yanked her to the right. In the hazy light cast by the torch, dark shapes flittered like bats.

The heat drew beads of sweat from his brow. He felt his heart begin to thump in his chest. Even now, fifteen years since his burning, fire still terrified him; he was gratified by his newfound ability to challenge it. Perhaps he had healed from that experience more fully than he'd known.

Into a hallway, and he saw eyes peering down at him through the smoke. Jakab removed his hand from Hannah's collar. Taking the penlight from his teeth, he played its beam over the walls.

Masks. Hundreds of them. So many different kinds, from so many different places in the world.

Even though he knew it must be a trick of the light, he thought he recognised, among them, the faces of the dead. And, as he stared at them, he began to remember names too.

Nathaniel Wilde's was the first face he saw. He'd killed Nate, hadn't he? Had shot him with that old Luger pistol. But he hadn't been himself at the time, he'd been someone else, someone called . . . Charles Meredith, that was it: the professor.

Hanging beside Nate, Charles watched him with blank eyes through which nightmares curled. Jakab had killed him, too, hadn't he? It disturbed him to realise he didn't even remember how.

He'd been Charles for a maddening short chapter in his life, but his memories of that time, although as hazy as the smoke thickening around him, were good. Until the end, of course, when the man's wife had attacked him. Nicole Dubois had died as a result of their encounter. She stared down at him from the wall, eyes haemorrhaged, blood glittering on her cheeks.

How he'd loved her. How difficult it was to see her again after so long.

Earlier, he'd believed he was beyond tears. Now he found that wasn't true.

Next, he saw Nicole's father, Eric Dubois, the big-hearted Frenchman from Carcassonne who had been his friend, had given him a job and had taught him a trade. Something had happened, something. He remembered cutting off Eric's face, burying him in the woods. For what, though?

There was his reason. Alice Dubois. A woman he had loved. A woman who'd plied him with drink and tried to kill him. Another episode of fire.

But Alice hadn't just been Eric's wife. She'd been, Jakab now knew, something far more important than that. She'd been his own daughter. He couldn't have known it at the time. Even so, when he thought of the intimacy they'd shared, he felt his stomach heave with nausea and shame.

On the hallway wall, his history stretched out before him.

Past Alice, he saw Helene Richter, Carl Richter and Hans. Their dead eyes stared; their punctured faces gaped like broken jigsaws of skin and muscle and flesh.

'You should have told me,' he moaned. 'You should have told me where she went.'

He had not known that his child was growing in Anna Richter's belly, had not known that he spilled the blood of his own child's grandparents that night in Sopron. There had been so *much* blood; by the time he had finished with them, his hands were crimson with it.

Past those three sightless faces, and now a brother loomed: Jani. All he remembered of Jani was a single image: the young man's head breaking apart as Jakab shot him on the balcony in Pozsony. On the wall, Jani's forehead smoked, the edges of the wound blackened and crisp.

Jakab moaned again; he had not wanted to see that. And then he saw something even worse, and finally remembered the name that had eluded him.

Erna.

Why did he have to meet her like this? The bright young face she'd once possessed had gone. He saw instead how she'd appeared at the end: her cheek sunken, her eye destroyed, the wooden flights of a crossbow bolt emerging from its ruins.

Erna Novak.

He had bought her a ring. Had asked her to marry him.

And then the *tanács* had sent out its hunters, and he'd lost her.

All those faces watching him, tormenting him. He thought he saw a question lurking in their eyes. When he considered what it might be, he had to look away.

Ahead, Jakab saw the outline of a staircase rising into darkness. He nudged Hannah on, warning her of its presence. She moved hesitantly, sweeping each foot in an arc before her, until she made contact with the bottom stair.

Steadily, she began to climb. After fourteen steps they reached the first-floor hallway. Double doors to their right, hanging open. Jakab was about to push her past them when he saw a body lying on the floor. Shell casings. A pool of blood.

Here. This was where he needed to go. This was where she would be. He shoved Hannah into the room, saw two more corpses on the floor. Both had lost their faces to gunfire. He wondered if they hung in the hall he'd left behind.

Beyond the dead bodies, a huge window curved the length of the room. Snow and ash eddied outside. He saw the silhouette of a dining table. Against the far wall, a bizarre skeleton hanging from an iron rod. Next to it, a dark arch.

And through that arch, Jakab saw something else.

Something amazing.

CHAPTER 49

Interlaken, Switzerland

In the last moments before the *tolvajok* reached her, even though her head felt light from lack of blood, even though her heart pumped what little remained so fiercely she thought it might tear itself apart, Leah sent her mind somewhere else.

It tumbled through days and weeks and years, gifting her not with visions of horror or pain, but with memories of joy and love. She saw her father's smile, his twinkling eyes. She heard his laughter. So long since Leah had seen him, but time had not abraded her memories. She wondered if he watched her now. She wondered if he waited for her.

She thought of her grandfather, of Gabriel, of all the others she'd met and loved. And finally, she thought of her mother.

If there remained in this world one person to whom Leah owed so much, it was Hannah Wilde. Her mother shone in her thoughts, glorious: warrior, teacher, friend. Even after everything Hannah had lost, she'd always retained her ability to look into her daughter's soul and know the words Leah needed to hear.

If her mother had taught her one lesson above all others, it was to *believe*.

Believe in your strength. Believe in your power. Believe you can face the impossible. Believe that your spirit can endure.

She knew what she had to do. And she was scared. Terrified.

But she couldn't let her mother down, not after everything Hannah had sacrificed.

Leah took a step back. Her spine pressed against the drapes hanging beside one of the windows. In front of her, the creature wearing the body of Krištof Joó hissed. Its eyes were globes of darkness.

Her legs trembled, the last threads of her energy dissolving away. She wrapped her arm around the curtain, determined to maintain her dignity, determined not to fall to her knees.

Her heart was beating even faster now. Surely close to breaking. A yard of empty space separated her from the clutching hands of the *tolvajok*. She wanted to close her eyes. Instead, she tried to raise the gun.

Couldn't.

But she didn't need to. Not for this.

The first time she'd been in this room with Luca, she'd nearly fainted away. Perhaps it was a tacit acknowledgement of her tendency to find danger, to gravitate towards self-destruction, but she'd been terrified of heights all her life.

She stared at the glass floor of the sun room – a polished black face, like the entrance to another world.

No time left, Leah.

She aimed her gun and pulled the trigger. Seven shots, rupturing the air like cannon fire.

Beneath her feet, the floor became a sea of ice. It cracked, splintering and popping, like the calving of an iceberg.

For a single frozen moment, the floor held, and then the glass slab she'd imagined as the entrance to another world *became* another world, one that was infinitely more dark than this.

Shrieking with rage, the *tolvajok* plunged down into it. Leah felt the floor beneath her own feet disintegrate. Pistol tumbling from her fingers, she fell.

Weightless, her stomach lifted into her throat. A brutal wind blasted her.

The drape tightened around her arm like a tourniquet and

suddenly she was dangling over the brink. A flurry of snowflakes erupted out of the darkness, stinging her cheeks.

Below her, the five black shapes of the *tolvajok* tumbled into the abyss, flailing like broken marionettes. With a dull whump they hit the first rocks jutting from the cliff face and ricocheted off into darkness. Awaiting them, a fall of three hundred feet before they met the jagged snow-covered landscape below.

Leah managed to grasp the curtain with her other hand. Its fabric was attached to the rail by circlets of steel stitched into the cloth. But while the curtain would hold her weight, the rail itself would not. Already, she saw one of its fixtures pulling loose.

Where the glass floor had met the wall, only a single horizontal retaining strut remained. Leah swung onto it, but because the viewing window remained intact she couldn't balance there and, even if that had been possible, her legs would no longer support her weight.

Clinging to the curtain, she saw, above her, the first of the railing's fixtures pop loose. She dipped a few inches. Held her breath.

A foot to her right, a vertical strut divided two of the window panels. On the other side of that, another curtain, flapping like a shackled wraith. If only she could get to it, it could support half her weight.

And then what? Even if she managed that, the only way out of this chamber was either via the archway at her back or the door in the far wall. Both meant crossing yards of empty space. It would have been a daunting leap even without her injuries. With her wounded leg, it was impossible.

She rappelled sideways, bloodied jeans smearing the window glass. Reached for the second curtain. Missed. Felt her grip loosen. Dropped another foot towards death before she managed to anchor herself. Snowflakes lashed her face like nipping teeth.

Above, another railing fixture began to work loose.

This time, Leah used every last shred of energy to grip the

curtain with her left hand before rappelling across and reaching out with her right. She grabbed the second drape just in time.

The last two retaining bolts popped loose from the wall and the first rail crashed onto her head. It bounced away and the curtain tightened around her arm.

Leah clung to the second drape with both hands. It held. But now there was nowhere else to go. Glancing down, she saw the rail swinging loose below her, connected by the strip of curtain wound around her arm. She sank her teeth into the fabric, biting down with all her strength as she shrugged herself out of its folds. Slowly, she began to reel it up.

The curtain still supporting her trembled. Looking up, she saw the first of its three fixtures beginning to buckle. Plaster rained down on her face. She felt her hands numbing. Wondered whether they would give out before the brackets.

If she bridged the gap across the floor with the broken rail, maybe she could drag herself across it. But to avoid the risk of it plunging into the abyss while she placed it, she would have to slide down the curtain until she hung at floor height.

A fixture above her popped loose. The second bracket began to bend. Leah loosened her grip and dropped another foot closer towards death.

Blood ran down her forehead and into her eyes. The world swam.

Teeth clenched, she rested one end of the rail on the lip of the support encasing the window at floor height. She eased the rest of it out across the gap. It wasn't going to be long enough. The metal was greasy in her fingers. She was going to drop it.

But somehow, she didn't. The far end clanged down on the living-room floor. It reached, just. A hand's span of grace.

Above, the second bracket popped loose from the wall. The bar began to bend outwards, dangling her further over the void.

She had seconds now. Gripping the curtain in both hands, she lowered herself down it until she felt the cold pressure of the lifeline between her legs. It bowed a few inches, the ends lifting in a grin.

The final wall bracket surrendered with a pop and the remaining curtain rail tore loose. She screamed as it plummeted past her. Letting go of the drape just in time, she grabbed onto the bar in front. Both hands now. Beneath her, empty space and glittering rocks. A long fall to a violent death.

The mountain wind shrieked, tried to tear her loose. Her wounded leg swayed useless under her. Blood poured off the toe of her boot like a waterfall, whipped into spray by the wind. The pain was brutal.

Breath coming in staccato rasps, Leah leaned forward until her chest pressed tight against the bar. With excruciating slowness, she began to drag herself, hand over hand, along it. Beneath, she felt that hungry mouth opening wide in anticipation.

She heard words tumbling from her lips, a repeated prayer – *please don't let me fall, please don't let me fall.*

If she moved too quickly, she risked dislodging the support. If she moved too slowly, her weight would likely buckle it. Either outcome would see her spiralling down after the *tolvajok* into the waiting darkness.

Halfway across now, and no way back. She could drag herself along, but she couldn't turn around, couldn't retreat. The metal support bowed beneath her. She could see the tip resting on the living-room floor lifting up. Grimacing, she pulled herself forward. Two yards to safety. One yard.

She screamed again. Frustration and rage. Her hands were shaking so badly she hardly dared to raise them. Clenching her teeth, she willed her muscles to obey. Inches now.

Leah reached out, felt the living room's smooth wooden floor. She flung out her other arm. The curtain rail vibrated beneath her. And then it fell away.

The world turned white.

The brightness dazzled her, and for a moment she thought

she had slipped, and in falling towards the rocks below her mind had acted to extinguish those final seconds of terror.

But she wasn't falling, not yet, and this was not a brightness from within her head. It came from without.

She lifted her head to its source. There, through the archway, she saw two figures she had not expected to meet again in this life.

The first, standing further back, arms crossed against her chest, was her mother.

The second lingered a few feet away, in the archway itself. And while she did not recognise his face, she recognised his eyes.

It could not be, but it was.

It was Jakab.

CHAPTER 50

Interlaken, Switzerland

He watched her through flat grey eyes, his expression impossible to read. In one hand he held a pistol.

Leah moaned. Her mother had killed him, had burned him to a cinder at Le Moulin Bellerose. Yet somehow that couldn't be true, because he was here, staring at her. Complete.

She saw Jakab blink, and then something strange happened to his eyes. They seemed to shine. Specks of amethyst appeared, bright chips of jade. Moments later a shadow crossed his face, and those eyes grew lifeless once more.

She wanted to call out to her mother, wanted to tell her that she didn't face Jakab alone. But if Hannah heard her daughter's voice she would doubtless run to it and, with no knowledge of the chasm in front of her, she would fall to her death.

Leah's grip slipped on the floor and she slid backwards, fingers squealing on the wood.

Jakab moved closer, and now he knelt, placing the gun down beside him and reaching out. Breath spiralled from his mouth like smoke. 'Take my hand.'

How can this be? How can this be?

She stared, tried to read his eyes, but they were as unknowable now as the time, all those years distant, he'd stolen her father's face. Was he pretending to offer salvation only to pitch her to her death moments later? Did she even consider accepting help from this creature who had robbed her of so much?

She slipped another few inches. Felt the void sucking at her. The wind shrieked, victorious.

'Take my hand,' he repeated. 'I won't let you fall.'

Pointless to question the sanity of it. Leah reached out, and a moment later Jakab grabbed her.

CHAPTER 51

Interlaken, Switzerland

Jakab seized her hand, and Leah clenched her teeth against a scream. Pain rushed up her arm. Exploded in her shoulder.

She dangled there, staring into Jakab's eyes, so close that she could see the pores of his skin, the spittle on his teeth, the beads of sweat like moon-kissed jewels studding his brow.

He grinned, panting with the exertion of holding her, and she saw those glints of colour in his eyes rise to the surface once more, a panoply of twinkling minerals and precious stones.

Was this why he had rescued her? So that he could suspend her over the brink, savouring the moment, forcing her to acknowledge the power he held over her before opening his fingers and watching her plummet to her death on the rocks below? His eyes, rich with vengeance, would be the last thing she saw before the void swallowed her.

Jakab opened his mouth and she realised he was talking, even as he dangled her above that hungry darkness. 'I *know*,' he said, the lights in his eyes rising. Louder, now: 'I know what you are.'

She saw her own breath, a ragged cloud of white. Felt the sting of snowflakes boiling up from beneath, the sweat from her hand beginning to lubricate their grip. She heard the rush of mountain wind. Sensed the clamour of the darkness below.

The tendons bulged in Jakab's neck. And then he began to lift her. Leah rose an inch. Two, three. She managed to swing her free arm over the floor's lip. Jakab pulled harder, and then her torso was over and she was writhing, eel-like, until she lay on her back, stunned, listening to her heart as it crashed in her ears.

Jakab crouched on his haunches. Already he had retrieved his gun. He climbed to his feet, and then he held out a hand to her.

Leah ignored it, rolling onto her front. She managed to raise herself on to all fours. Through sheer will, she dragged herself upright. Jakab withdrew his hand, mouth tightening.

Waiting at the far end of the dining table stood Hannah. Earlier Leah had not dared to call out, fearful that her mother might rush towards her voice and topple out into the night. Now, she cried her name.

'Leah?' Hannah's shoulders slumped.

'There's a drop. Stay where you are. I'm OK.'

You're bleeding from a wound that's going to kill you. That's if this monster from your past doesn't do it first.

Hardly OK.

'Is he still here?'

Leah opened her mouth, but Jakab interrupted. 'Quite the reunion, don't you think?'

Hannah stiffened. It was a while before she spoke. Finally she said, 'What now? What do you want from us?'

Jakab glanced down at the gun he held. He laughed. 'What do I want?' His eyes moved back to Leah. She could feel them scuttling across her skin, like the legs of inquisitive locusts. 'What do I want?'

From the confusion in his expression, she sensed it was a hopeless question. He did not know. Years of hate and obsession had twisted and poisoned him, had wrung from him every surviving drop of humanity.

And then, with a gasp, Leah realised something else: that this was no longer a reunion of three, not at all, but a gathering of four.

Because the prickling sensation on her skin was not the crawl of Jakab's eyes, but a warning transmitted by some half-grasped *hosszú élet* sense. It scoured her, shrinking her scalp, itching behind her eyes. Finally, she understood what it meant.

In the doorway leading out into the hall, a stranger had appeared.

The woman moved with a slow and terrible grace. She stepped around the fallen bodies and empty shell casings, careful not to dip the soles of her snakeskin boots into the blood pooling on the floor.

Her beauty was matchless, face so elegantly crafted that she appeared ethereal; unreal. But while nature had clearly bestowed the gift of physical perfection, it had not breathed the warmth of humanity into its creation.

Before her, Leah acknowledged, stood the immaculate nightmarish marriage of *lélek tolvaj* and *hosszú élet*.

The woman's eyes glimmered, only a few errant striations of green lacing that ebony stare. Her cheeks were flushed red, her wheat-blond hair dusted with melting snowflakes. In her hands she held her instruments of death: two enormous pistols, so highly polished they looked as though they'd been forged from silver.

Leah cast her eyes over to Jakab, and saw that he, likewise, was entranced – similarly gripped by that strange prickling sensation. His fingers twitched.

Only one person this woman could be.

'Where are they?' Izsák's daughter asked, and her voice was like syrup flowing over ice. She raised her silver pistols, revealing the midnight circles of their barrels. One of them pointed at the back of Hannah's head. The other aimed at Jakab. 'Where are they?' she repeated, and this time Leah thought she heard a note of desperation in her words. 'I won't hesitate. I'll kill all three of you right here, right now. Where are my babies? Where are my darlings?'

So this was how it ended. To Leah's left, the man who had

killed her father. In front, the thing that would kill her mother. And, at her back, the waiting chasm of darkness that had consumed this creature's brood.

It was over. All her mother's years of work and sacrifice. The *tanács* had destroyed any chance of a future, and now this last *lélek tolvaj* would steal what remained.

'They're dead,' Leah said, and when she realised how softly she had spoken, she raised her voice and said it again. 'All of them. They're dead. I killed them.'

A flicker of fear crossed the woman's face, followed by disbelief. 'Liar.'

'If you don't believe me, take a look.' With a flick of her head, she indicated the destroyed floor of the sun room behind her. 'There won't be much left of them. It's quite a fall.'

The woman's eyes narrowed to slits. The barrels of her pistols trembled. 'That's not right,' she said. 'That's not right.'

Senseless to prolong what little time remained. Leah smiled, matching the woman's arctic stare with one of her own. Goading her. 'But it *is* right. They're gone. All of your babies. All of your cursed darlings. Smashed on the rocks. Dead in the snow.'

'If you killed them—'

'Pulverised. Destroyed. Lost.'

– 'then I'll kill you.'

'No. You won't.'

Not Leah's voice, that one. And when her eyes moved back to the doorway that had produced the *tolvaj*, she saw that they were no longer a reunion of three, nor a gathering of four, but a pitiable *family* reunion of five.

Balázs Izsák stood in the doorway. He held a gun of his own, and he pointed it at what once had been his daughter.

CHAPTER 52

Interlaken, Switzerland

Leah felt her throat tighten with emotion as she saw him standing there alone. He wore his years heavy tonight: eyes shadowed, skin as grey as the ash settling on the windows from the fires burning downstairs.

Izsák stared at his daughter, so captured by her presence, so enthralled by her, that he seemed blind to the rest of them standing like islands in a sea of broken flesh.

The woman turned her eyes towards him but her arms remained locked, guns still pointing at Jakab and Hannah. Her hair, lifted by the wind that blew through the broken floor, feathered around her face like spun gold. 'I know you,' she said. 'I *know* you.'

Izsák shook his head. He held his gun at arm's length, its barrel pointed at her heart. 'No,' he whispered. 'You don't. But the little girl you stole knew me. Once.'

Her eyes, as dark as polished meteorites, lost their focus for a moment, and then they cleared. 'Georgia,' she said, and when that name crossed her lips, Leah saw Izsák flinch as if he had been stung.

'Her name was Georgia,' the woman continued. 'A long time ago now, but I remember. Dawson City. The cabin beside the forest. You . . . were her father.'

A tear trembling on Izsák's eyelashes broke free and cascaded down his cheek. It clung to his jaw for a moment before falling, jewel-bright. His voice cracked. 'I *am* her father.'

Downstairs, something exploded deep inside the fire's raging heat, and the snow on the lawn became a lake of reflected flames, as if the house stood not on the edge of a mountain but on the slope of a volcano, and a river of lava flowed around them.

Above, the lights flickered.

The woman who once had been Georgia laughed. A hard, scornful sound. 'Do you really think,' she asked, 'that after all this time, anything of your daughter remains?'

Izsák's hand was trembling so badly that Leah thought he might drop the gun. 'Let me speak to her. Just once.'

The woman swung the pistol she'd been aiming at Hannah until it pointed at his chest. 'I'm not yours to command,' she replied. 'You know how this ends. I'm faster than you. All of you.'

'Then you've won,' he said. 'So why not be gracious in victory? Let me hear her voice. Just once. It's all I ask.'

'It's all you *ask*? She flicked the pistol towards Leah and Jakab. 'Go and stand over there with the others.'

'Let me talk to her.'

'I won't ask you again.'

He stared, eyes unreadable, and she stared back. Neither of them moved.

Beside her, Leah heard Jakab muttering. Eyes wide, face drained of colour, his mouth moved gently as he repeated his brother's name, over and over. '*Izsák . . . it's Izsák . . . Izsák . . .*'

Another explosion shook the house, far louder than the first. A fraction of a second later, every light in A Kutya Herceg's chalet winked out.

For a moment, they were plunged into darkness as impenetrable as an ocean trench. And then Leah witnessed a blossoming of furious light.

Silvery flashes of fire from the woman's pistols. Answering

gouts of crimson flame, like dragon's breath, as Izsák returned fire.

The exchange burned phosphorus-bright images on Leah's retina, so dazzling, so disorienting, it seemed to her as if two gods of the mountains clashed inside the room.

Guns flashed. Shadows hopped. Sparks danced.

Beads of blood defied gravity, hanging in the air like drops of dew caught in a web.

Holes appeared in cloth. Flesh burst. Barrels smoked.

And then, finally, the thunder receded, capering out into the night as if fleeing from the carnage it had wrought.

In the aftermath of that killing light, Leah's eyes refused to register anything except the carnival of flashing colours that marked its departure. Her ears rang. The tang of gunpowder was sharp in her nose.

Slowly, those deftly weaving hues faded, and the room became a room once more.

Waiting for her, at its heart, was the most awful sight Leah had ever seen.

CHAPTER 53

Interlaken, Switzerland

Worse than seeing her father shot dead at Le Moulin Bellerose when she was nine years old; worse than seeing her grandfather's corpse beside the track at Llyn Gwyr; worse than seeing Flóra – or what had once been Flóra – pounding her head against the window as she shrieked to be let in from the cold.

In the doorway, where the firelight grew steadily brighter, Izsák lay on his back, torso ripped open by the eviscerating volley from Georgia's guns.

Georgia lay by the window. Bullets had torn through her chest and neck.

Harrowing as those images were, Leah saw it all in a blink.

Because in the very centre of the room, thrashing and convulsing like a wounded spider, curling in on itself one moment only to extend its limbs and flail about the next, was her mother.

And yet not.

Hannah Wilde writhed, a jagged shape of wheeling arms and coiling muscles. Her jaw worked savagely, teeth snapping together, face a knot of panic and confusion.

She went left, crashed into the table. Grabbed onto chairs, feet splashing in blood. Rearing upright she spun in a half-circle, raised her hands to protect her face, lunged around again.

And then she stiffened, head canted to one side, chest heaving, nostrils flaring.

Leah felt the breath go out of her as she realised what had happened.

Somehow, even as Izsák's guns consumed her, Georgia had cannoned into Hannah. That fleeting contact had allowed the *tolvaj* to abandon its dying host and transition across. And what had once been her mother was now something else entirely, something impossible to evict.

Leah glanced across at Jakab.

He still held his gun. Whatever reason he might have had for killing her mother, he had ten times the reason now. Yet his weapon remained pointed at the floor. His eyes brimmed with a curious mixture of pity and fascination.

After all that her mother had achieved, after all the battles Hannah had fought, to be taken like this at the end – to have her own body stolen from her – seemed a betrayal of everything she had given to the world.

With the remaining *tolvajok* dwindling inside the corpses of their frozen *tanács* hosts, there had been a chance – a slim chance – that all was not lost. The children had been saved. And with Hannah still alive, the work, feasibly, could have continued.

But now, with her mother taken by this abomination that fed on the lives of others, that journey would end in failure. The power to save the *hosszú életek* resided in Hannah Wilde alone. Years earlier, when the programme they'd established in Calw had begun to falter – when they'd started to realise that despite all they were doing, it might not be enough – Leah had asked to be tested. What she'd discovered had devastated her.

She was barren. Unable, not only to conceive, but to offer even a source of viable eggs to their family of *hosszú élet* surrogates.

You know what you have to do.

She did. But it was hard, even so.

She would never be a mother; she would only ever be a daughter.

Leah stared at the thrashing silhouette. Backlit by the glow of flames rising in the hall, it presented a hellish sight.

You know.

She tried to focus, tried to think of a memory that would sustain her: a perfect snapshot of her mother's love. She had a million from which to choose, a lifetime's worth. But the one that rose in her mind, and, even now, brought a devastated smile to her lips, was the night on her grandfather's farm when the calf had been born.

They'd walked together to the barn, Leah holding her mother's hand, Hannah lighting their way with a torch. They found the Ayrshire lying on her side, in obvious distress. Her water sac had ruptured and was hanging outside her vulva, steaming on the cold night air. But they could see no sign of the calf.

Hannah stripped down to her vest, and at a sink in the corner of the barn she washed her right arm all the way up to the shoulder. After pushing her hand deep inside the Ayrshire, she explained that one of the calf's forelegs was turned back on itself.

By now, the agony of the pregnant cow had reduced Leah to tears. Sitting on the straw, she watched Hannah grasp around inside it, sweating and straining, until she managed to pull out both the calf's forelegs and attach a set of birthing chains. Steadily she began to pull, until the steaming, mucus-slick newborn erupted onto the cowshed floor.

It lay unmoving. Working quickly, with the Ayrshire twisting her head back to watch, Hannah cleaned the calf's face of fluid and tickled its nose to stimulate breathing. But its chest remained still.

Leah knew what that meant and began to sob, but her mother bent her face to the creature's own, covered one of its nostrils and blew air into the other.

And then, suddenly, it kicked out and breathed.

Hannah scooted backwards. She crawled over to Leah and they sat there, laughing and crying, watching the exhausted mother greet the shaky newborn they would later name Henrietta.

Even then, Hannah had been a bringer of life. Even then.

You know what you have to do.

What was the value of one life, against the future of a race?

Hannah had given life not just to Leah, but to all the children who sheltered here tonight, and countless others, far and wide.

Now it was Leah's turn.

Grimacing against the pain in her wounded leg, determined not to let it fail her here at the end, feeling her heart begin to race in anticipation of the fate she went to embrace, Leah limped towards the creature that had taken refuge in her mother's form, and offered herself instead.

CHAPTER 54

Interlaken, Switzerland

In a room that seemed to exude darkness and death, it was the most beautiful sight he had ever witnessed. His life had been so empty of moments like this, and now, despite the swirling smoke and the ash and the blood, it seemed to brim with them.

Leah Wilde struggled towards her mother and she seemed to *shine*: purity personified, leaving Jakab an awestruck observer of the girl's sacrifice.

So many unusual things he had encountered in these last few minutes; he struggled to make much sense of them. He'd seen Izsák, for a start. The arrival of his younger brother had opened a door in Jakab's heart that offered him glimpses of memories blissfully free of pain.

And then he'd looked at the woman his brother had come here to kill, and the curtain of revelation lifted higher, and he realised that a *family* gathered here in the arms of these mountains. A broken family, but a family nonetheless. *His* family.

Then the lightning came, and the thunder, and that family of five became three, and now it became two.

For years he'd pursued Hannah Wilde; at first because of love – misplaced love, admittedly, rotten love – and later because of hate. But he hadn't known the truth, of course, hadn't known. He'd pursued Leah Wilde as well, although that search had borne no fruit until now.

When Jakab thought of the lives he had ruined in pursuit of

these two fierce and perfect women, his legs nearly buckled beneath him.

Earlier, he had passed through that hall of masks, had seen the faces of those he'd killed, and had forced himself to meet their eyes, every one: *Balázs Jani*; *Hans Richter*; *Carl Richter*; *Helene Richter*; *Eric Dubois*; *Charles Meredith*; *Nicole Meredith*; *Nathaniel Wilde*; *Etienne*.

And then, of course, there was the last name. Or, in many ways, the first. The girl who had died not by his hand, but had died because of him all the same.

Erna Novak.

Little more than a wisp of memory now, a dream cast into the sky. As ephemeral as rising steam. A fading face. A name.

Earlier, before the *tolvaj* had taken her, Hannah Wilde had asked him a single question: *What do you want?*

He had imagined he wanted a hundred things; a thousand. But really, even though he had not spoken his answer aloud, he found he only wanted one.

I want this to end.

Now, as Jakab watched Leah limp towards her mother, as he marvelled at the young woman to whom he was related by an unravelling trail of string, which wound through generations and geography and the ceaseless marching boots of time, he realised that he wanted something else, too.

I want to atone.

He couldn't, of course. Nothing he did now could atone fully for what he had done. But he could do one thing. Just one.

He had to be quick. Not only because Leah was a handful of steps from her mother, but because if he delayed too long he might lose his nerve, and if he allowed that to happen, if he allowed Leah to sacrifice herself while he was saved, he would be twice damned. Eternally so.

Silent, he moved to Leah's side. Reached out and gripped her arm.

She turned, face as white as freshly poured milk.

Jakab shook his head. And then he offered her the gun.

In her eyes, he saw his own face reflected.

Leah blinked, her mouth dropping open, and he yearned to hold her and say goodbye. But of course he didn't deserve that. And he knew she would never grant it.

Leah took the pistol off him and turned it over in her hands, studying it as if it were a piece of alien machinery beamed here from another world.

She looked back up.

'Don't mourn me,' he said. Because it was a joke, a sick joke, and because – at the end – he needed a little dark humour to sustain him.

'I won't.'

'Don't miss, either.'

'No chance of that.'

Jakab grinned. Perhaps she was not quite purity personified, after all. He would have liked to get to know her, this strange relative of his.

He turned towards Hannah Wilde and closed his mind to what coiled inside her. She was Hannah. Just Hannah.

His Hannah.

Jakab opened his arms and went to meet her.

CHAPTER 55

Interlaken, Switzerland

When Jakab snagged her arm and held her back, Leah nearly shrugged him away, furious that he should choose to interfere, to mock her like this, so close to the end. And then she saw his eyes and she nearly cried out.

They blazed with a wild beauty.

On two velvet circlets of grey, gemstones twinkled; ferocious sparks of emerald, glinting sapphires, prismatic opals reflecting colours of every possible hue.

During the years he had pursued them, they had comforted themselves with the knowledge that while Jakab could control the contours of his face, he could not control his eyes.

Perhaps, she realised, he still couldn't; perhaps he wasn't even aware of the fireworks that danced there.

He handed her the gun, and she accepted it.

'Don't miss,' he said, and she almost laughed. Perhaps it was what he wanted. But she couldn't. Not at that.

Jakab looked into her eyes a moment longer, and then he turned away. Lifting his head, he walked towards her mother, arms outstretched.

Leah raised the gun.

Jakab closed in on Hannah, and then he enfolded her into his embrace.

Hannah stiffened as she felt him against her and they stood

motionless, as if by some night magic his touch had turned them both to stone.

And then Jakab opened his arms and she slumped to the floor, and when he whipped around to face Leah he was Jakab no more, was something immeasurably more wicked.

His lips skinned back from his teeth when he saw her pistol, and he sprang across the floor, so fast it seemed as if some mythical beast charged towards her, one of Gabriel's *Cŵn Annwn*, perhaps.

Leah pulled the trigger. Felt the gun punch back in her hands. Saw its greedy lick of fire. Saw a bullet take Jakab in the heart. She shot him again. Again. Again. Again.

Bullets ripped though him. Chewed him open. Still he came, a half-dead monster with a blown-out chest and shattered head, and Leah almost stood her ground and let him come, until, with a jolt of horror, she realised what that would mean. Pushing off with her good leg, she dived to one side as Jakab – dead now, irrevocably so, even if the creature behind his eyes was not – sailed past her, out into that vault of darkness and down, down into its throat.

Leah sat up, and found that she was crying. She wiped her eyes with the backs of her hands.

A few yards away Hannah lay on her back, gasping. Leah dragged herself over. For a moment she had to press her forehead to her mother's, and just be close like that.

'You're safe,' she whispered. 'You're safe.'

Hannah's face contorted.

'Don't speak. Don't move. Not an inch, OK? There's something I've got to do.'

She hoped there was still time.

CHAPTER 56

Interlaken, Switzerland

He could do little else, but Izsák could still see. Flame-spawned shadows capered on the ceiling above him and he watched them, transfixed. He felt no pain. And even as his lungs filled with blood and his heart began to labour, even though he felt a curious wetness in the places where many of his organs should have been, the fear he had imagined might grip him at the end felt strangely absent.

He managed to move his head. Saw Leah Wilde bending over her mother. Angled his head a little further. Saw Georgia.

His daughter lay on her back, eyes closed. And it *was* Georgia now, he noticed, although exactly how he knew that he could not say.

The firelight dimmed, and now a larger shadow became a shadow not at all, but a face. Leah's.

'How do I look?' he asked, and when he spoke he couldn't contain a cough, and when it came it was followed by a gush of blood.

'You look like shit,' she told him. She tried to smile. Tears rolled down her cheeks.

His eyes swung over to the part of the room where Georgia lay. 'I want to be with her.'

He saw that Leah was about to protest, was about to tell him that he was too weak, that he needed to conserve his strength.

And then he saw her change her mind, and somehow, moments later, he was lying beside his daughter.

Izsák coughed again. However much blood he swallowed, there was always more. Georgia's eyes were closed, but she was breathing, barely. Her face was contorted, a childlike expression of fear. It shattered him, to see that. But at least he was close. At least he was by her side.

Izsák snaked out his arm, amazed at the effort it caused him. His fingers found hers.

At his touch, her breath quickened.

'You're not alone,' he whispered. 'Georgia, you're not alone.'

She took another breath, and then her chest stilled.

He wished he could have said more, could have told her he loved her, could have explained to her what had happened, where she'd gone, and where she went now. But perhaps – just perhaps – the few words he had managed were the ones she'd needed to hear most.

Izsák closed his eyes, felt his lungs deflating. How long he had travelled to get to this place.

Nineteen forty-four: that had been the year his wife had died on the floor of their cabin outside Dawson City; the year the *tolvaj* had visited and spirited away his child.

What year was it now? He couldn't even say. But finally, the task to which he'd dedicated himself was done.

Peace.

That was what he felt. And then—

Opening his eyes, he saw Leah leaning over him. She had snaked her hands inside his shirt, and where her skin touched his, it burned.

Pale-faced, eyes wide and brimming with compassion, yet lacking any of the teaching that would give her the means to succeed, she attempted to heal him.

He coughed, another thick gout of blood, and shook his head. 'No.'

She ignored him, and he saw her teeth clench, her chin tremble.

'Leah, you don't have the strength.'

'Then hold on. I'll get Soraya. My mother. Just hold on, OK? I'm not letting you go. I'm not.'

He reached up, encircling her wrists with his hands, and gently pulled them free. 'I want this,' he said.

'But—'

'I want this.'

A sob escaped her. She entwined her fingers in his. 'Are you sure?'

Izsák smiled up at her. He closed his eyes. And died.

EPILOGUE

Interlaken, Switzerland

They made a strange procession down the mountain: an old Volkswagen bus, following the six-wheeled behemoth that was Luca's Ford pick-up. A black sky above them released a billion white angels to mark their passage.

They'd used the winch on the truck to tow the camper out of the snowbank, and after a rolling start the VW's engine had fired, surprising them all. If Leah ever managed to trace the man in Menaggio who'd donated it, she would thank him profusely before returning it to his care.

While Izsák had chosen to follow his daughter to that place where souls rest, Luca Sultés, as Leah had known he would, chose to fight. Hardly any life had remained inside him, but what was left stubbornly held on. It took the combined strength of all three of them to bring him back. Soraya shouted worried commands, which Leah and her mother followed as best they could. They nearly lost him twice before his heart regained enough strength to beat under its own rhythm.

They found Gabriel – half-dead – still locked in the back of Jakab's van. Parked further down the slope they discovered an abandoned Lexus; inside, a driver's licence containing Izsak's photograph, and a childseat containing Elijah, Etienne's son.

In the snow on the lawn below the chalet they found Etienne, still bleeding from the bullet she'd taken from Jakab's gun, but alive. When Leah saw her renuited with her boy, she failed to hold back her tears. It took them five minutes before they could prise Elijah from Etienne's arms so that they could begin to treat her wounds.

Wearing gloves, they pitched into the flames the carcasses of the dead ibex that lay on the chalet's lawn. The likelihood that any of those remains hosted a *tolvaj* was remote, but they wouldn't take the chance.

They found Flóra's body in deep snow. With infinitely more care, they offered it, too, to the fire.

Leah drove the pick-up down the hill, her mother beside her. Gabriel slumped in the back, next to Etienne and her son. Behind them Soraya piloted the old VW bus, Luca hunched over on the passenger seat and the children crowded behind.

They could have stopped in Interlaken. But it seemed, to all of them, far too close. With snowflakes dancing in the headlights and chasing the wipers across the glass, they drove and they drove.

Leah did not know what the future held. Its mysteries were wound too tightly to unravel. But she wasn't alone. And that was good.

Behind them, halfway up the mountain, flames leaped, fires burned and sparks, like the twinkling miracle of *hosszú életek* eyes, rose up into the heavens and, winking, disappeared into the night.

GLOSSARY OF TERMS

állj   **wait** (*Lit*. Hungarian)

balfácán   **idiot** (*Lit*. Hungarian)

Belső Őr   **inner guard** (*Lit*. Hungarian)
The *Örökös Főnök*'s personal guards.

capsich   **blood–cuff** (*hosszú életek*)
A metal instrument used during public executions, in which a *hosszú élet's* arteries were severed and held open, preventing the victim from healing and causing death by blood loss.

család   **family** (*Lit*. Hungarian)

déjnin   **déjnin** (*hosszú életek*)
A ceremonial edged weapon. No direct translation.

elég   **enough** (*Lit*. Hungarian)

Eleni   **Eleni** (*Lit*. Hungarian)
The organization, commissioned by the Hungarian Crown, responsible for the *hosszú életek* genocide of 1880.

Éjszakai Sikolyok   **Night of Screams** (*Lit*. Hungarian)
hosszú életek term for the Crown-sponsored genocide that occurred in nineteenth-century Hungary.

fiú   **boy** (*Lit*. Hungarian)

Főnök/Örökös Főnök   **leader/eternal leader** (*Lit*. Hungarian)
Hosszú életek head of state. A lifetime position, although not always hereditary. With the exception of formal occasions, usually shortened to *Főnök*.

gyermekrablók	**child snatchers** (*Lit*. Hungarian) Little-used alternative name for the *lélek tolvajok*.
hosszú élet/életek	**long life/lives** (*Lit*. Hungarian) A mythical race, mentioned in *Gesta Hungarorum*, one of Hungary's oldest historical texts. Known for shape-shifting, extreme longevity and the ability to heal themselves and others.
jövendőmondás	**fortune** (*Lit*. Hungarian) Hungarian tarot cards.
kedves	**darling** (*Lit*. Hungarian) Term of endearment.
kicsikém	**my little one** (*Lit*. Hungarian) Term of endearment.
kincsem	**my love/sweet one** (*Lit*. Hungarian) Term of endearment.
kirekesztett	**outcasts** (*Lit*. Hungarian) 1. Those banished from *hosszú életek* society as punishment for criminal acts. 2. Sentence of banishment passed down by the *tanács*.
kurva	**slut** (*Lit*. Hungarian) Vulgar.
lélekfeltárás	**soul-sharing** (*hosszú életek*) 1. A means of mutual identification through voluntary stimulation of the iris. 2. The most intimate act of *hosszú életek* lovers, performed by far more intense and prolonged stimulation.
Merénylő	**assassin** (*Lit*. Hungarian) A formal position, in the exclusive service of the *Örökös Főnök*.
Örökös Főnök	See *Főnök*.
sertés	**pig** (*Lit*. Hungarian)

simavér/simavérek	**flat blood/flat bloods** (*hosszú életek*)
	Pejorative. A person of non-*hosszú életek* descent.
sorozat	**inheritance** (*Lit.* Hungarian)
	Old *hosszú életek* law, extending the sentence of *kirekesztett* to an offender's descendants. Abandoned early in the twentieth century.
szar	**shit** (*Lit.* Hungarian)
	Vulgar.
Szeretlek	**I love you** (*Lit.* Hungarian)
tanács	**council** (*Lit.* Hungarian)
	The eight elected governors of *hosszú élet* society. Advisors to the *Örökös Főnök*.
te jó ég	**my goodness** (*Lit.* Hungarian)
végzet	**fate/fate night** (*Lit.* Hungarian)
	A series of four formal masked balls (*kezdet, második, harmadik* and *negyedik*) that mark the entrance of *hosszú életek* youth into adulthood and provide a venue for ritualised (and compulsory) courtship.
Vének Könyve	**Book of Elders** (*hosszú életek*)
	The oldest *hosszú életek* text in existence, dating to AD 748. Sets out the laws of governance strictly enforced by the *Örökös Főnök* until the events of the *Aséjszakai Sikolyokor*. Viewed as outdated by some, its doctrines are the cause of a growing ideological split.

Food and Drink

halászlé	A river fish soup spiced with paprika.
kürtőskalács	A sweet chimney-shaped pastry, made by winding a sugared dough around a

	tapered spit and hanging above a fire.
paprikás krumpli	A simple potato and sausage stew, usually cooked with green peppers, onions and tomatoes.
pálinka	A brandy made from orchard fruits.
békési szilvapálinka	A plum pálinka from Békés.

Acknowledgements

It's been a memorable journey these last four years, following the exploits of Hannah and Leah Wilde, but it hasn't been one I've walked alone. Fitting, then, that I should mention some of the people who came along.

Thanks first to my fantastic editors, John Wordsworth, Josh Kendall and Claire Baldwin. Thanks also to the rest of the team at Headline and Mulholland, past and present: Anna Alexander, Jason Bartholomew, Marlena Bittner, Pamela Brown, Catherine Cullen, Nicole Dewey, Siobhan Hooper, Keith Hayes, Joanna Kaliszewska, Elizabeth Masters, Garrett McGrath, Wes Miller, Michael Noon, Caitlin Raynor and Lynsey Sutherland. Thanks too to my agent, Sam Copeland, and all the others who offered guidance along the way.

Éva Pallaghy did a fantastic job educating me in the Hungarian language – all mistakes are, of course, my own. *Köszönöm, tanárnő.*

Special thanks to my family for tolerating me throughout: my endlessly patient wife, Julie, and our three boys. In order of age, Obi-Wan Kenobi Skywalker, Hulk Smash and Hulk Smash Baby. Their names, not mine.

Finally, to you, the reader, for getting this far: my heartfelt gratitude. Books without readers are like roads without travellers. Thanks for taking the trip.

Author Q&A

What made you become a writer?

Quite simply, I've always needed to tell stories. I wrote obsessively during childhood, college and university. After graduation, I fell into an advertising career. Working in a busy London agency offered little free time for writing, but it did teach valuable lessons: the importance of grabbing an audience's attention and holding it; the discipline required to meet tight deadlines. A few years ago, with my wife expecting our second child, I told myself that however little free time I thought I had, I would find some. I bought a laptop and started work. *The String Diaries* was written late at night, during snatched lunch breaks and days off. I took just under two years, start to finish.

What was it that led you to write in this genre?

It's one I've always loved. Growing up, my heroes were Dean Koontz and Stephen King. I love writers that show you something wonderful and unexplained, and then explore its darker possibilities.

Are locations important to your writing?

Sometimes a location can feel like a character in its own right. And while certain stories can exist independently of their chosen setting, I think some are inextricably linked. If I'd picked somewhere other than Hungary as the birthplace for the *hosszú életek*, for example, *The String Diaries* and *Written In The Blood* would have ended up as very different books. In fact, one of the most enjoyable aspects of writing them was the opportunity to spend time in some truly inspirational settings.

Who are the writers you read to relax?

More and more, I find that I'm reading individual books rather than following particular writers – there is such a lot of great stuff out there and so little time. Most of the authors I still read regularly are those I discovered in childhood.

Who are your favourite villains in books and film?

Hannibal Lecter, Gollum, Annie Wilkes and Darth Vader. That would be some dinner party, wouldn't it?

What do you think hooks a reader into a story?

When I read, I want to feel that I'm being thrown headfirst into a story. I want to feel like the party's alrady started and I'm racing to catch up, that I've entered a place that's both magical and frightening, where bad things can happen to good people and all my emotions will be tested. The faster I feel any of that, the faster I'm hooked.

What next?

I'm currently writing a standalone novel. A few readers have asked if I'll return to the world of the *hosszú életek* in the future. It's definitely a possibility, although I do have a number of other stories I want to tell first.

The String Diaries

Stephen Lloyd Jones

He has a face you love. A voice you trust. To survive you must kill him.

The rules of survival are handed from mother to daughter. Inherited, like the curse that has stalked Hannah and her family across centuries.

He changes his appearance at will, speaks with a stolen voice and hides behind the face of a beloved, waiting to strike.

Generation after generation, he has destroyed them. And all they could do was to run.

Until now.

Now, it is time for Hannah to turn and fight.

Praise for *The String Diaries*:

'So gripping, you'll want to read late into the night; so terrifying you shouldn't' Simon Mayo, the Radio 2 Book Club

'Original, richly imagined and powerfully told' *Guardian*

'Will keep you awake late into the night' *SFX* magazine

978 1 4722 0468 4

headline

THRILLINGLY GOOD B
FROM CRIMINALLY
GOOD WRITERS

CRIMEFILES

CRIME FILES BRINGS YOU THE LATEST RELEASES FROM HEADLINE'S TOP CRIME AND THRILLER AUTHORS.

SIGN UP ONLINE FOR OUR MONTHLY NEWSLETTER AND BE THE FIRST TO KNOW ABOUT OUR COMPETITIONS, NEW BOOKS AND MORE.